Translation and the Languages of Modernism

Translation and the Languages of Modernism

Gender, Politics, Language

Steven G. Yao

palgrave
macmillan

TRANSLATION AND THE LANGUAGES OF MODERNISM
© Steven G. Yao, 2002

All rights reserved. No part of this book may be used or reproduced in any manner whatsoever without written permission except in the case of brief quotations embodied in critical articles or reviews.

First published 2002 by
PALGRAVE MACMILLAN™
175 Fifth Avenue, New York, N.Y.10010 and
Houndmills, Basingstoke, Hampshire, England RG21 6XS
Companies and representatives throughout the world

PALGRAVE MACMILLAN is the global academic imprint of the Palgrave Macmillan division of St. Martin's Press, LLC and of Palgrave Macmillan Ltd. Macmillan® is a registered trademark in the United States, United Kingdom and other country. Palgrave is a registered trademark in the European Union and other countries.

ISBN 0–312–29519–7

Library of Congress Cataloging-in-Publication Data

Yao, Steven G., 1965–
   Translation and the languages of modernism: gender, politics, language/by Steven G. Yao.
     p. cm.
   Includes bibliographical references and index.
   ISBN 0–312–29519–7
    1. Translating and interpreting. I. Title.

PN241 .Y36 2002
418'.02–dc21
                                                                                                            2002070395

A catalogue record for this book is available from the British Library.

Design by Newgen Imaging Systems (P) Ltd., Chennai, India.

First edition: December 2002
10 9 8 7 6 5 4 3 2 1

Printed in the United States of America.

Grateful acknowledgement is given for the permission to reprint selections from the following works:
By Ezra Pound,
from CONFUCIUS, copyright © 1947, 1950 by Ezra Pound. Reprinted by permission of **New Directions Publishing Corp.**
from PERSONAE, copyright © 1926 by Ezra Pound. Reprinted by permission of **New Directions Publishing Corp.**
from SELECTED LETTERS OF EZRA POUND, copyright © 1950 by Ezra Pound. Reprinted by permission of **New Directions Publishing Corp.**
from SELECTED PROSE 1909–1965, copyright © 1973 by The Estate of Ezra Pound. Reprinted by permission of **New Directions Publishing Corp.**
from THE LITERARY ESSAYS OF EZRA POUND, COPYRIGHT ©1935 by Ezra Pound. Reprinted by permission of **New Directions Publishing Corp.**
from "Translator's Postscript" from Remy de Gourmont, Translated by Ezra Pound, from THE NATURAL PHILOSOPHY OF LOVE, COPYRIGHT © 1935 by Ezra Pound. Reprinted by permission of New Directions Publishing Corp.

By H.D.
from COLLECTED POEMS, 1912–1944, copyright © 1982 by The Estate of Hilda Doolittle. Reprinted by permission of New Directions Publishing Corp.

By Louis Zukofsky
from COMPLETE SHORT POETRY, pp. 243, 245, 247–248, 256–257, 310, 311, 313, 319. © 1991. Paul Zukofsky. Reprinted by permission of the Johns Hopkins University Press.
LETTERS FROM LOUIS AND CELIA ZUKOFSKY, copyright Paul Zukofsky; may not be used without permission.

I would also like to thank the journals *Paideuma: A Journal Devoted to Ezra Pound Scholarship* and the *Canadian Journal of Comparative Literature* for permission to reprint earlier versions of Chapters 1 and 5 in the current volume.

It can't be all in one language.
>—Ezra Pound, Canto LXXXVI

Translation is a mode.
>—Walter Benjamin, "The Task of the Translator"

To my parents: Marjorie ManJu Yao (余曼如) and Steve Sin Ping Yao (姚心平), whose courage, hard work, sacrifice, and love afforded me the gift of the freedom to pursue my own dreams.

Contents

Acknowledgments		x
Introduction	"every allegedly great age": Modernism and the Practice of Literary Translation	1

Part I Translation and Gender

Chapter One	"to-day's men are not the men of the old days": Ezra Pound's *Cathay* and the Invention of Modernist Literary Translation	25
Chapter Two	"My genius is no more than a girl": Exploring the Erotic in Pound's *Homage to Sextus Propertius*	52
Chapter Three	"from Greece into Egypt": Translation and the Engendering of H. D.'s Poetry	79

Part II Translation and Politics

Chapter Four	"Uplift Our State": Yeats, Oedipus, and the Translation of a National Dramatic Form	117
Chapter Five	"better gift can no man make to a nation": Pound, Confucius, and the Translation of Politics in *The Cantos*	153

Part III Translation and Language

Chapter Six	"transluding from the Otherman": Translation and the Language of *Finnegans Wake*	191
Chapter Seven	"dent those reprobates, Romulus and Remus!": Lowell, Zukofsky, and the Legacies of Modernist Translation	209
Conclusion		234
Appendix	Transcription of Notes for "Ballad of the Mulberry Road" from the Fenollosa Notebooks	239
Notes		248
Index		286

Acknowledgments

My work on this book has spanned both many years and great distances, and I would like to take this opportunity to thank all those who have helped me along the way in translating my intuitions and obsessions into the comprehensible language of an argument.

To begin, I would like to express my gratitude to the various organizations and institutions that have given me their support and enabled me to devote so much time to this project: to the Woodrow Wilson Foundation for a Mellon Fellowship in the Humanities; to the University of California, Berkeley, and its English department for supporting my ambitions in numerous ways, including a dissertation fellowship, and for offering an intellectual environment unmatched in its diversity and intensity; to the College of Humanities at the Ohio State University for a Humanities Research Fellowship; to the Harry Hunt Ransom Humanities Research Center at the University of Texas at Austin for a Dorot Foundation Fellowship that provided a crucial period of residency in a remarkable environment during which I completed the final revisions of the manuscript; to the Ohio State University Research Foundation for a Seed Grant that, among other things, covered costs relating to publication; and finally to Hamilton College for its ongoing support of my efforts as a teacher and a scholar. I would also like to thank the staff and librarians at both the Humanities Research Center at U.T. Austin and the Beinecke Library at Yale University for making my visits to these archives at once pleasant and productive.

I would also like to thank my advisors at Berkeley, Robert Hass and especially John Bishop, for serving as models of professional and personal accomplishment. I owe them a debt I can never repay. In addition, Cyril Birch, Edward Schafer, and Kwong-loi Shun each helped in his own way to spark and to focus an interest in translation that lay the foundations for this project. Also important to me during my time at Berkeley and in the years since, have been Andrea Solomon, Alyson Bardsley, Jeff Ewing, and Marc DaRosa. Among my colleagues in the English department at the Ohio State University, I would like to acknowledge Murray Beja and

Sebastian Knowles for their efforts on my behalf, and John King for serving as an example of intellectual integrity. I would also like to extend my thanks to Jeredith Merrin for her generosity of spirit, friendship, and keen intellect, and for always reminding me of why I came to poetry in the first place. George Hartley was especially helpful in showing me a way to rethink my project at a crucial early stage, as well as in demonstrating that kindred spirits can be found anywhere. Similarly, Yvonne Paschal has remained a source of professional counsel that has always proven remarkably insightful, even if I did not always recognize its wisdom. Appreciation is also due to Elizabeth Renker for her interest in my work from the beginning and for the exemplary critical acumen that she brought to reading it. Also very important to me among my departmental colleagues have been Jared Gardner and Elizabeth Hewitt. They have shown me a way to live and love in a complicated world. I would also like to thank the following people who provided guidance and inspiration, oftentimes in ways and for reasons they could never know: Clifford Vaida, Mary Pat Martin, Ric Livingston, and Georgina Dodge.

Among other colleagues at Ohio State, I would also like to thank Xiaomei Chen and Kirk Denton of the Department of East Asian Languages and Literatures and Julia Andrews of the Department of Art History for helping to create a supportive and vibrant intellectual community that transcended departmental lines. I hope to continue enjoying, as well as deserving, their friendship. In this regard, Patricia Sieber, also of DEALL, merits special recognition for her generosity, humor, and intelligence in exchanging ideas about living as well as writing. I consider it a tremendous gift that she has been and will continue to be my friend. Thanks are also due to Dick Davis of Near Eastern Languages and Cultures for making suggestions on an early version of the manuscript, and for his sustained encouragement. Colleagues at other institutions to whom I would like to extend my thanks include Elizabeth Richmond-Garza, Tom Garza, and Kurt Heinzelman at the University of Texas for their generous hospitality during my stay in Austin. Particular thanks go to José Benkí at the University of Michigan for exemplifying the spirit of intellectual curiosity, and for showing me that intensity and a devotion to learning must apply to all phases of life. I would also like to thank Mark Morrison for making numerous helpful suggestions on the manuscript. Likewise, I appreciate the incisive suggestions made by Lawrence Venuti, which helped me to improve the overall argument of this work. I hope someday to be able to return the enormous favor they have done me. In this regard, I would also like to thank the anonymous readers for Palgrave for their endorsement and, most especially, for their numerous helpful suggestions. Similarly, I would like to thank my editor, Kristi Long, for her interest and faith in my project, and for her expert guidance in the process of publication. I would also like to express my appreciation to Rick Delaney for his invaluable assistance in the preparation of the manuscript. Needless to say, all shortcomings and errors that remain in this book are my sole responsibility. Thanks also go to the following people with whom I have had enlivening and ongoing conversations about translation and the larger issues of cross-cultural poetics: Haun Saussy, Eric Hayot, Timothy Billings, Chris Bush, Laura Chrisman, and Kyoko Omori.

I would like to thank all the people outside the academy, in a number of different places, who have sustained me in my work, making it both bearable and worthwhile. In Ohio, I would like to thank Paul Heimann for his enduring curiosity, generosity, and life advice. Thanks are also due to Debra Little Heimann for her willingness to endure my company for the sake of her husband. In Texas, I would like to thank John Wing and Beth Grana Wing for always making trips home an adventure as well as a pleasure. Deep love and gratitude are also due to my family, my mother, father, grandmother, and brother Spencer, for supporting me in my decision to become an academic even when the demands seemed to everyone to outstrip the rewards. Among those in California to whom thanks are due include Diana Naylor Chiang for her compassion and emotional wisdom; John Hoffman for his kindness, generosity, and interest in exploration; and the Berkeley Tuesday Night Wake Group for a lively community of Joyceans and for showing me how learning can be a lifelong activity, one not merely confined to the narrow halls of a university. I would also like to acknowledge Alice Xiajun Lin: she was with me at the beginning of this project, and she will always have a special place among those I count as loved ones.

Finally, I would like to express my gratitude and love for Kyoko Omori, who has made my life immeasurably richer and more fun than I had come ever to expect. I hope to live up to the standard of emotional fortitude, dedication, and strength that she continues to set every day, in work and in life. Her meaning in my life defies translation into words.

Introduction

"every allegedly great age"
Modernism and the Practice of Literary Translation

In 1923, the philosopher and critic Walter Benjamin published his translation into German of Baudelaire's *Tableaux parisiens*. As an introduction to this volume, he included a probing and deeply felt essay, entitled "Die Aufgabe des Übersetzers," or "The Task of the Translator," in which he attempts to define the proper approach toward the rendering of a literary work from one language into another. In the course of his discussion, he makes the rather startling and, in the end, metaphysical claim that,

> Translation...ultimately serves the purpose of expressing the central reciprocal relationship between languages. It cannot possibly reveal or establish this hidden relationship itself; but it can represent it by realizing it in an embryonic or intensive form. This representation of hidden significance through an embryonic attempt at making it visible is of so singular a nature that it is rarely met with in the sphere of nonlinguistic life.[1]

Over the years that followed, of course, Benjamin's evocative and metaphorically dense meditation has prompted a vast array of commentary debating both the practical utility and the theoretical implications of his views on translation as a mode of literary production.[2] In fact, the essay has emerged as one of the key documents for the relatively new discipline of Translation Studies, which began to establish itself in its current form in the 1970s. Within this still evolving field, numerous critics have gone on to explore the significance, as well as the history, of translation as an instrument of both personal and ideological expression in a range of different languages and cultural contexts, further demonstrating its fundamental imbrication with such basic conceptual categories as gender, nation, and language itself.

Among his contemporaries, however, Benjamin was by no means the only, or even the first, writer to consider that the scope of translation reaches far beyond just "the sterile equation of two dead languages" (73). Rather, he is merely one of a number of Modernist writers, in both Europe and the United States, who confronted the significance of translation as a literary mode, either as critics, as translators themselves, or, in certain rare circumstances like Benjamin's, as both critics and translators. Seven years earlier, in 1916, the poet, critic, and translator Ezra Pound was reflecting upon the role that the practice of translation plays in the development of a major literary culture. In the second of a series of short essays eventually published in *The Egoist* as "Elizabethan Classicists," Pound hypothesizes that "A great age of literature is perhaps always a great age of translations; or follows it."[3] By 1929, any lingering doubts he might have harbored about the generative importance of the practice of translation in the rise of English literature had completely disappeared and, in "How to Read," his first attempt at a primer for Modernism, he summarily declared that, after the period of purely indigenous Anglo-Saxon works such as "The Seafarer" and *Beowulf*, "English literature lives on translation, it is fed by translation; every new exuberance, every new heave is stimulated by translation, every allegedly great age is an age of translations" (*LE*, 34–35).

Benjamin's quietly mystical claim that translation "serves the purpose of expressing the central reciprocal relationship between languages" participates in a long and rich history of reflection in Germany upon the meaning, the linguistic, literary, metaphysical, religious, and historical significance, of the act of translation that stretches unbroken from Luther in the sixteenth century all the way through Hölderlin and Nietzsche in the nineteenth to Benjamin himself in the twentieth. In this tradition, as Antoine Berman has shown, translation has always occupied a place of central and formative importance within the cultural field known as *Bildung*, or culture and education.[4] Within the culture of English, by contrast, where translation has always been relegated to a position of distinctly ancillary significance as a mode of literary production, Pound represents something of an anomaly, being arguably the first broadly influential writer since at least the seventeenth century to bestow upon translation, over and above merely so-called original composition, an explicitly primary and generative, rather than a derivative and supplementary, role in the process of literary culture formation. Dante Gabriel Rossetti summarized the predominant attitude in English up to Pound concerning the significance of translation as a literary mode when, in 1861, he called it "the tributary art."[5] Even John Dryden, undoubtedly the most important figure in the history of English translation before Pound, did not consider translation a driving force either in the development of a distinct national literature or the growth of a language, and his approach to the practice reflects such a theoretical bias. In the preface to his translations from Virgil, issued in 1697, Dryden explains of his rendering, "I have endeavored to make Virgil speak such English as he would himself have spoken, if he had been in England, and in this present age."[6] Far from letting Virgil's Latin change the idiom of the day, Dryden proceeds from the conviction that he should domesticate the foreign language to a contemporary vernacular, to smooth over any "heaves" caused by the contact between English and another language. Dryden's method as a translator, as well as his ongoing canonization within the domain of English literature, together reflect the dominance of "fluency" that Lawrence Venuti has described as the prevailing ideology for translation in Anglo-American culture.[7] At the same time, such an approach also casts translation as a formally derivative mode of literary production, one that merely domesticates or assimilates foreign texts to established conventions and norms of stylistic expression in English. Accordingly, then, the truth of Pound's typically bold and sweeping assertion that "every new exuberance, every new heave [in English literature] is stimulated by translation" remains to be proven, much less, after the fashion of an Austenite narrator, universally acknowledged. Thus, it succeeds less in revealing an undiscovered dimension of English literary history (though it certainly contains some degree of accuracy) than in underscoring the crucial importance of translation as a literary mode within Pound's own critical framework and the trajectory of his individual career, as well as, indeed, that of the "allegedly great age" of Modernism as a whole.

Beginning at least as early as the summer of 1901, with Joyce's youthful renderings of two plays by Gerhart Hauptmann, *Before Sunrise* and *Michael Kramer*, and continuing all the way through to the publication in 1956 of Pound's deeply personal and idiosyncratic version of Sophocles' *Women of Trachis*, feats of translation not only accompanied and helped to give rise to, but sometimes even themselves constituted, some of the most significant Modernist literary achievements in English. In addition to these examples at either end of the temporal bounds of the Modernist period, several other major Modernist writers engaged in translation, either as a sustained practice or at various, and sometimes crucial, points in their careers. Working on them between 1926 and 1927, at the very height of his powers as a poet, William Butler Yeats concluded his investigation into Greek tragedy as a model for the formation of a national, Irish dramatic culture by translating and producing on the stage both *King Oedipus* (1928) and *Oedipus at Colonus* (1934). Similarly, H. D. devoted considerable time and energy throughout her career to translating Greek poetry and drama, culminating in her 1938 translation of another classical Greek play, Euripides' *Ion*, and, as I shall elaborate in a subsequent chapter, this lifelong practice profoundly affected her development as one of the most important women poets of her time.

4   Translation and the Languages of Modernism

Another, H. D.'s contemporary and one-time classmate at Bryn Mawr, Marianne Moore, published her translations of the moral fables of La Fontaine in 1954, and when asked if the act of translation had helped her as a writer, she replied, "Indeed, it did. It was the best help I've ever had."[8] H. D.'s husband, Richard Aldington, produced four volumes of poems by various Greek and Latin poets in *The Poets' Translation Series* published by the Egoist Press. Extending to two sets of volumes with numbers in each by such other figures as H. D. herself, Edward Storer, F. S. Flint, and A. W. G. Randall, this series, as its very title suggests, bespeaks the fundamental interconnection between translation and other modes of literary production within the writing practices of the Modernists.[9] Comparably, William Carlos Williams translated poems by numerous French and Spanish writers, including Nicanor Parra, Silvina Ocampo, Pablo Neruda, Octavio Paz, Miguel Hernandez, Rafael Beltran Logroños, Mariano del Alcazar, Nicholas Calas, and even one poem, "The Cassia Tree," by the Chinese poet Li Bai.[10] And in addition to rendering numerous critical articles from French for publication in *The Criterion*, T. S. Eliot produced an English translation of St. John Perse's poem *Anabase*, which he considered "a piece of writing of the same importance as the later work of Mr. James Joyce, as valuable as *Anna Livia Plurabelle*."[11]

Nor was the practice of translation limited during this time to poets rendering poems or dramas, or focused primarily on the classics. Virginia Woolf produced versions of Dostoyevsky's *Stavrogin's Confession* and *The Plan of the Life of a Great Sinner* in 1922 in collaboration with S. S. Kosteliansky, as well as rendering under similar circumstances A. G. Goldenveizer's *Talks with Tolstoi* in 1923. And even though he took pains to hide the fact because he thought it wouldn't "do for [him] to appear to dabble in too many things,"[12] D. H. Lawrence also expended considerable effort as a translator. By himself he translated three novels by the Italian writer Giovanni Verga,[13] and in collaboration with Kosteliansky and Leonard Woolf, he also translated a work by the Russian writer I. A. Bunin, *The Gentleman from San Francisco and other Stories*. Finally, Ford Maddox Ford, who exerted a profound influence on the generation of Modernists that followed him, rendered at least one novel from the French, Pierre Loti's *L'Outrage des Barbares*, or *The Trail of the Barbarians*.

Ezra Pound, of course, stands as the preeminent example of an Anglo-American Modernist for whom translating constituted not just a sustained, but more important, a generative writing practice. Both the sheer amount and the enormous scope of his efforts as a translator make his achievement, quite simply, staggering. By the time he declared the importance of translation to the evolution of English literature in "How to Read," he could have made a respectable case based virtually on his individual output alone, having produced by 1929 an extensive version of the poems of the fourteenth-century Italian poet Guido Cavalcanti in *Sonnets and Ballate of Guido Cavalcanti* (1912), an exquisitely rendered set of medieval Chinese lyrics based on the notes of Ernest Fenollosa in *Cathay* (1915), as well as a highly unconventional, and so critically reviled, treatment of the odes of the Latin poet Sextus Propertius in *Homage to Sextus Propertius* (1919). Over and above these major works of translation, he produced a version of the *Dialogues of Fontenelle* (1917), one of Rémy de Gourmont's *The Natural Philosophy of Love* (1922) and another of his *Dust for Sparrows* (1922), as well as one of *The Call of the Road* (1923) by the French writer Edouard Estounié, and a rendering through an intermediary French source of the Confucian governmental classic, the *Ta Hio* (1928), or, as he later came to call it when he translated it again in 1945, *The Great Digest*. In addition to these volumes specifically dedicated to his work as a translator, other significant translations Pound produced before 1929 include versions of some twenty poems by the Troubadour poet Arnaut Daniel published in *Umbra* (1920), and a rendering of the Anglo-Saxon poem "The Seafarer," first published in *Ripostes* (1912). After 1929, the list becomes even more impressive in its diversity, both of languages and subjects. Such feats range from complete and fascinatingly incorrect versions of two more books in the Confucian canon of political and social thought, *The Unwobbling Pivot* (1947) and *The Analects* (1951), together with the *Shi Jing* (詩 經), to which he gave the rather verbose title, *The Classic Anthology Defined by Confucius* (1954), to a collection of *Love Poems of Ancient Egypt* (1962), as well as his rendering of the *Women of Trachis* mentioned earlier. The list could go on considerably. From its very inception to even beyond what are normally considered its closing years, then, the age of Modernism was, quite literally, an age of translations.

The sheer abundance of translations produced during the period gives concrete, textual expression to the interest on the part of Modernist writers, both in England and the United States, in foreign cultures and, most especially, languages as sources of both instruction and inspiration for renewing their own culture and expanding the possibilities of expression in English, an interest that also manifests in the explicitly multi-linguistic dimensions of so many major Modernist texts. Pound titled poems in various languages, and in *Hugh Selwyn Mauberley* (1919) he rhymes words in French and Greek with ones in English. In *The Cantos*, he incorporates passages of Greek, Latin, Provençal, and Italian, as well as Chinese characters and Egyptian hieroglyphics as vital strands in the textual fabric of his "poem including history" (*LE*, 86).[14] Similarly, Eliot employs passages from various foreign works in their original languages as epigraphs for many of his most important poems, and *The Waste Land* (1922) includes lines in German, French, Italian,

Latin, and Hindi as crucial elements. Like Pound, Wallace Stevens titled many of his poems in French, and he once remarked, somewhat cryptically, that for him French and English were the same language. *Ulysses* contains numerous languages, which the characters in the novel vary in their ability to comprehend, and in *Finnegans Wake*, Joyce redefines the limits of English itself by investing it with the capacities of some sixty different languages, including such exotic specimens as Beche-la-Mar (a Melanesian pidgin), Samoan, Shelta, Gipsy, Norwegian, Kiswahili, and Bearlagair Na Saer. Even as avowedly American and nativist a poet as William Carlos Williams gave one of his volumes of poetry the Spanish title *Al Que Quiere!* (1917). In their efforts at cultural renewal, the Modernists employed languages other than English with such frequency that Pound's famous injunction to "Make it New" seems in large measure to have meant "Make it Foreign."

The Modernist concern with and use of foreign cultures and, most especially, languages bespeak a general attitude to which Pound gave explicit articulation when he declared in "How to Read" that, "Different languages—I mean the actual vocabularies, the idioms—have worked out certain mechanisms of communication and registration. No one language is complete" (*LE*, 36). Twenty-six years later, with the publication of the "Rock-Drill" section of *The Cantos*, Pound reiterated this concern and made it a subject of his own *poetic* expression, declaring in Canto LXXXVI, "It can't be all in one language."[15] Indeed, much of the formal innovation in Modernist poetry embodies an attempt to infuse English with the energies of other languages and their "mechanisms of communication and registration." Thus, in "The Return," Pound not only announces the reappearance of Greek gods in the modern world, but he seeks to enact a recovery in English of the rhythmical possibilities embedded in the poetic meters of the Greek language itself. Comparably, in the second section of his own meditation on the poet's craft, "Little Gidding," Eliot invokes the "familiar compound ghost"[16] of two earlier masters, Swift and Yeats, in a section of fabricated English terza rima as a strategy for investing his own language with the possibilities and cultural authority of Dante's medieval Italian. And in this light, Marianne Moore's predilection for syllabic poetry can be seen as an attempt to shape English according to the rhythmic dimensions of French.

Within the context of these efforts and concerns, translation represented for the Modernists much more than either just a minor mode of literary production or an exercise of apprenticeship, though for some writers it continued to fulfill such a traditional function. Rather, it constituted an integral part of the Modernist program of cultural renewal, a crucially important mode of writing distinct from, yet fundamentally interconnected with, the more traditionally esteemed modes of poetry and prose fiction. As I will show over the course of this study, during the Modernist period translation served as a specific compositional practice by which different writers sought solutions to the various problems and issues that have come to be understood as the primary thematic concerns of Modernism, concerns about the disappearance of any stable religious or moral values by which to ground a viable society, the staggering realities of world conflict and economic collapse, the perceived radical inability of established artistic forms and genres to confront and accurately represent the new realities of the world as it existed, and, consequently, the need to develop new formal and representational possibilities more in tune with the demands of the expressly modern world.

Throughout the period, translation as a literary mode functioned, and was recognized, as a kind of dynamic procedural lens through which the Modernists could at once view both the past as well as other cultures and, perhaps even more importantly, focus their images of these traditions in their own times and in ways that could serve their individual ideological and aesthetic purposes. As a mode of literary production, translation helped Modernist writers to expand the range of cultural, linguistic, and generic fields in which they could actively participate; it helped them to determine and establish the defining boundaries of their own cultures; it provided a means by which to broaden their sources for material and inspiration, thereby enabling them to begin moving beyond the limits of a strictly English-language literary practice and history to explore territories other than those already mapped by their literary antecedents as a way of expanding the very linguistic dimensions of English literature as a whole. Through the practice of translation, Modernist writers undertook to extend the limits of English itself, which in turn led them to discover new possibilities for their own expression.

For beyond simply producing a great many renderings of documents from various cultures and traditions, Modernist writers also engaged in translation as a technique in the composition of their own "original" works. Fragments and even extended passages from a vast array of texts in a wide range of languages comprise constitutive elements in a number of Modernist poems and novels, which themselves oftentimes take the process of translation as one of their subjects. Here again, Pound serves as the prime example. *The Cantos* opens with a translation of a Renaissance Latin version of the Nekuia episode in Homer's *Odyssey* and, in the inimitable words of Hugh Kenner, Canto I "is not simply, as was Divus' Homer or Chapman's Homer or Pope's, a passing through the knot of a newer rope. It is *about* the fact that self-interfering patterns persist while new ways of shaping breath flow through them. It illustrates that fact, and its subject is in part that fact"[17] (emphasis in the original). Indeed, translation figures so largely as both technique and subject in the remainder of Pound's poem, most notably in the "Malatesta" and "Chinese History" Cantos, that another critic has gone so far as to call *The Cantos* an "epic of translation."[18]

On a smaller scale, H. D., as we shall see, incorporates translations of such classical Greek poets as Sappho, Meleager, and even Plato into poems in which she explores the relationship between gender and the process of poetic production. Similarly, Yeats blurred the distinction between original poetic composition and translation when he concluded both "A Man Young and Old" and "A Woman Young and Old," the two final sequences in arguably his two finest collections of verse, *The Tower* (1928) and *The Winding Stair and Other Poems* (1933), with poetic renderings of choral odes from *Oedipus at Colonus* and *Antigone* respectively. And in a lyric written in 1949, entitled, logically enough, "Translation," William Carlos Williams integrates the act of translation with his theory about writing as a form of sexuality, saying in the opening stanza of the poem,

> There is no distinction in the encounter, Sweet
>   there is no grace of perfume
> to the rose but from us, which we give it
>   by our loving performance.[19]

At a more conceptual level, many Modernist texts encode translation into the very act of reading itself. The multi-linguistic fabric, allusiveness, and formal structure of such works as *The Cantos* and *The Waste Land* require readers to engage, often quite literally, in translation to derive any sort of meaning from the text. Analogously, readers of *Ulysses* must render the distinctive language of each chapter into a common idiom in order to reconstruct the narrative contained in what one critic has termed the "odyssey of style" in the novel.[20] In *Finnegans Wake*, this demand reaches down to the level of the most basic unit of the text, the level of the word. What Fritz Senn has said about Joyce's fiction could be applied with equal validity to a number of Modernist texts: "Joyce's works consist of translation and glorify all cognate processes."[21] As both a compositional procedure and a conceptual structure, then, translation informs the entire range of Modernist literary production, most especially poetry, but likewise some of the more extreme achievements in the novel.

Moreover, as the poem by Williams cited above suggests, translation constituted a subject of considerable critical reflection throughout the Modernist period. Modernist writers and translators repeatedly, if never systematically, theorized about both the larger cultural meaning and the proper methods of translation as a literary mode. They afforded it a place within the Modernist critical framework equal in significance to that occupied by the more traditionally esteemed modes of poetry and prose fiction, as a well as a role of constitutive importance in the process of culture formation. This helps to explain the frequency with which the Modernists both engaged in translation and employed it as at once a compositional and a conceptual strategy. Thus, when Pound declares in "How to Read" that "some of the best books in English are translations" (*LE*, 34), later specifying this assessment in the *ABC of Reading* by calling Arthur Golding's sixteenth-century version of Ovid's *Metamorphoses* "the most beautiful book in the language,"[22] he implicitly endorses the capacity of translation to function as an avenue of genuine aesthetic expression and as a source of enduring literary value.[23] Similarly, the lavish praise he offers to Lady Gregory's rendering of Irish folktales in *Cuchulain of Muirthemne* makes it clear that Yeats considered translation a means by which Ireland could establish its own particular identity amid the crowd of world contemporary, and even historical, cultures: "I think this book is the best book that has come out of Ireland in my time. Perhaps I should say that it is the best book that has ever come out of Ireland; for the stories it tells are a chief part of Ireland's gift to the imagination of the world—and it tells them perfectly for the first time."[24] And in laying out the plans for the stock company of the proposed Irish Literary Theatre in the *Samhain* of 1901, Yeats tacitly presents translation as a crucial instrument in the formation of a robust national cultural identity. By "making it a point of performing Spanish, and Scandinavian, and French, and perhaps Greek masterpieces rather more than Shakespeare," the Irish Literary Theatre, he proposes, "would do its best to give Ireland a hardy and shapely national character by opening its doors to the fours winds of the world, instead of leaving the door that is towards the east wind open alone."[25] Operating from a different set of ambitions and concerns entirely, H. D. gives in her novel *Bid Me to Live (A Madrigal)* a fictionalized account of her own approach in translating Greek. With a series of metaphors that moves from a decidedly masculinist "attack on those Greek words" to a method of productive exchange in "bargaining with each word," and finally to an explicitly reproductive and feminine image as her thinly veiled fictional self-representation "brooded over each word, as if to hatch it," she adumbrates a theory in which translation serves as a method for critiquing and engendering alternatives to masculinist constructions of both knowledge and literary production. William Carlos Williams summarized this aspect of Modernist thought on translation when he said in a letter to the French Surrealist poet and art critic Nicholas Calas, a small number of whose poems he translated, "You know, all this fits well into my scheme. I don't care how I say what I must say. If I do original work all well and good. But if I can say it (the matter of form I mean) by translating the work of others that is also valuable. What difference does it make?"[26] No longer the bastard child in the family of literary genres, translation came over the course of the Modernist period to function and be recognized as a distinctly vital and generative writing practice.

Together with legitimizing its cultural pedigree as a mode of writing, the Modernists also reconfigured the parameters for the very practice of translation itself, cleanly decoupling its linguistic from its more expressly literary dimensions, and thereby making possible such subsequent achievements as the radical versions of the odes of Catullus by Louis and Celia Zukofsky, as well as the diverse efforts of contemporary poetic translators like Stephen Mitchell, W. S. Merwin, Kenneth Rexroth, and Robert Hass. During the course of Modernism, translation as a literary mode rose to a level within the generic hierarchy fundamentally different from that which it occupied during other periods of English literary history, and this difference manifests in both the scope and the methods of the Modernists as they engaged in the practice of translation itself.

Before Modernism, literary translation functioned primarily as a means for renewing and strategically deploying the authority of the classics, which explains why the most renowned translators in English of earlier eras— Golding and Chapman in the Elizabethan, Dryden and Pope in the Enlightenment, and Browning, Rossetti, and Swinburne in the Victorian—all derive their reputations specifically as translators from their renderings of various Latin and Greek writers and other figures explicitly connected with the classical tradition.[27] While the Modernists certainly coveted the monumental authority of classical writers, especially Homer, they also explored alternative sources for such enabling models, employing translation as a strategy by which to underwrite their own cultural ambitions and advance their own aesthetic and ideological ends. In doing so, they expanded the geographical and temporal domain of literary translation to include works outside the Western tradition entirely, as well as more recent figures by no means assured of their place in the canon. Thus, long before he gave a conceptual rendering of Homer in *Ulysses*, Joyce sought to promote in Ireland his taste for nineteenth-century Continental drama when he translated Gerhart Hauptmann, a relative contemporary, in his youthful version of *Vor Sonnenaufgang*. If Yeats and H. D. directed their efforts as translators exclusively to classical Greek drama and poetry, William Carlos Williams translated exactly contemporary poets writing in Spanish and French. Pound translated not only Sextus Propertius, but also Li Bai, and while *The Cantos* opens with a rendering of the Nekuia episode in *The Odyssey*, the poem also includes long passages culled from a Qing dynasty historical treatise. Indeed, as will become clear in a subsequent chapter, some of his most important translations include his deeply unorthodox, yet fascinating treatments of books from the Confucian tradition of political and social thought.

Without a doubt, however, the most dramatic indication of the change that took place during the Modernist period in the dimensions of translation as a literary mode lies in the extent to which formal knowledge of the source language no longer constituted a requirement for its practice. Before the Modernists, translators in English simply proceeded under the assumption that full comprehension of the source language represented a necessary condition for translation.[28] Indeed, theorists of translation before the Modernist period made such knowledge a formal requirement for the practice itself. Thus, in 1711, Dryden asserts that "The qualification of a translator worth reading must be mastery of the language he translates out of, and that he translates into," though he concedes that "if a deficience be to be allowed in either, it is in the original, since if he be but master enough of the tongue of his author as to be master of his sense, it is possible for him to express that sense with eloquence in his own, if he have a thorough command of that."[29] Exactly 150 years later, Matthew Arnold, the most influential theorist of translation during the Victorian period, took this requirement one step further, asserting that proper translation must include scholarship as a major component. In his famous essay "On Translating Homer," which began as a series of lectures at Oxford University in 1860, he argues:

> [The translator] is to try to satisfy *scholars*, because scholars alone have the means of really judging him. A scholar may be a pedant, it is true, and then his judgment will be worthless; but a scholar may also have poetical feeling, and then he can judge him truly; whereas all the poetical feeling in the world will not enable a man who is not a scholar to judge him truly. For the translator is to reproduce Homer, and the scholar alone has the means of knowing what Homer is to be reproduced. He knows him but imperfectly, for he is separated from him by time, race, and language; but he alone knows him at all.[30] (emphasis in the original)

Ideally, for Arnold, translation unites the sensitivity and skills of a poet with the knowledge and learning of a literary scholar.

By contrast, Modernist writers repeatedly engaged in translation, and sometimes achieved remarkable results, with partial, imprecise, faulty, and sometimes even no formal understanding of the languages in which the texts they translated were originally written. Moreover, as the case of Pound alone most clearly illustrates, Modernist translators' knowledge of the source language had little to do either with their willingness to translate a given text or, indeed, the success of their translations. Joyce had at best a tenuous grasp of German when he undertook *Vor Sonnenaufgang*. After considering his translation of Hauptmann for performance at the Irish Literary Theatre and showing it to a friend versed in German, Yeats wrote to Joyce, chiding him lightly "that you are not a very good German scholar."[31] Yeats himself knew absolutely no Greek when he translated *Oedipus Rex* and *Oedipus at Colonus* in 1928, piecing together his versions from a number of preexisting renderings. H. D.'s knowledge of Greek remains a subject of considerable scholarly debate. And while Pound's formal training as a graduate student in comparative literature, as well as his individual gifts for languages underlie his translations of Cavalcanti, Arnaut Daniel, and other Romance poets, by the time he began work on *Cathay* in 1914, he had absolutely no knowledge of Chinese. Indeed, as he continued over the course of his career to translate works from the Confucian tradition, he came to believe that his lack of knowledge, far from being a hindrance, actually represented a decided advantage in his attempt to reproduce even the mode of signification encoded within the very characters of the texts themselves. His adherence to the evocative, but vastly oversimplified theories of Ernest Fenollosa about the nature of the Chinese language merely allowed him to justify his own ignorance and, indeed, see it as a positive trait, one that made it possible for him to penetrate the layers of scholarship that had accumulated over time to arrive at a genuine, poetic understanding of Confucian political wisdom. Likewise, as we shall see, H. D. and Yeats explicitly rejected classical training as a barrier to authentic translation. And even though many of the translators themselves knew the languages from which they made their renderings, the editors of *The Poets' Translation Series* expressed the pervasive Modernist distrust of scholarship when they described their intentions in the following terms:

> The object of the editors of this series is to present a number of translations of Greek and Latin poetry and prose, especially of those authors who are less frequently given in English.
> This literature has too long been the property of pedagogues, philologists, and professors. Its human qualities have been obscured by the wranglings of grammarians, who love it principally because to them it is so safe and so dead. ... The translators will take no concern with glosses, notes, or any of the apparatus with which learning smothers beauty. ... The first six pamphlets, when bound together, will form a small collection of unhackneyed poetry, too long buried under the dust of pedantic scholarship.[32]

Understandably, perhaps, such unorthodox beliefs and practices continue to raise objections, either as expressions of an imperialist arrogance or, at best, as convenient rationalizations that serve to mitigate personal failings. Nevertheless, this valorization of their own ignorance and the consequent willingness (and even insistence) to undertake renderings of texts for which they lacked command of the source language together fundamentally differentiate the Modernist practice of translation from that of previous eras in Anglo-American literary history. Thus, during the Modernist period, translation came into its own, serving as an expressly generative and literary mode of writing, rather than a principally linguistic operation limited in scope simply to reproducing the "meaning" of a foreign text. No longer governed by traditional conceptions of semantic fidelity and the constraints of linguistic knowledge, it functioned, and should be viewed, as a mode of literary production fundamentally comparable to and, indeed, deeply constitutive of the other major Modernist forms of poetry and prose fiction.

Up to this point, critics have generally failed either to recognize the central role of literary, and especially poetic, translation within the development of Anglo-American Modernism as a whole or to consider the ongoing significance of the changes wrought over the course of the period in the operative parameters of the actual practice itself. For many years, criticism of Modernist translation proceeded along two basic, yet distinct, lines of thought, each with its own particular, and very real, limitations. More recently, in addition, the establishment of Translation Studies as an autonomous field of intellectual inquiry has brought renewed, though markedly different, attention to select Modernist renderings in a theoretically sophisticated effort to map the history, as well as the very conceptual dimensions, of translation as a manifold cultural activity. Yet even here, despite (or perhaps precisely because of) their broad historical concerns and the considerable insights they have provided into the philosophical intricacies of the practice as such, critics in this vein have neglected fully to trace out the complex and fundamentally generative relationship between translation and the more widely renowned achievements of Anglo-American Modernism in other modes of expressly literary production.

The first and certainly most common approach has been to evaluate specific feats of translation performed during the Modernist period according to an uneasy mixture of philological and aesthetic criteria, and to offer praise or condemnation to the translators themselves for the perceived quality of their efforts. As by far the most dedicated, ambitious, and expressly innovative of the Modernist translators, Ezra Pound has undergone the vast majority of this sort of critical attention, and the reception of his various translations illustrates the range of opinions stemming from this approach in all its limited diversity. And, with the possible exception of *Cathay*, no single work in the large body of Pound's translations, or indeed that of Modernist translations generally, has elicited more, or more divergent, critical assessment than the *Homage to Sextus Propertius*.

Almost from the moment of its earliest partial publication in the March 1919 edition of *Poetry*, the *Homage* has inspired a long line of both bilious attacks and spirited defenses based on its status as a translation. In a now famous letter published in the very next edition of *Poetry*, the University of Chicago classicist William Gardner Hale lambasted Pound's abilities as a translator, enumerating various grammatical errors and other linguistic "howlers." He concluded his review by asserting: "If Mr. Pound were a Professor of Latin, there would be nothing left but suicide. I do not counsel this. But I beg him to lay aside the mask of erudition. And if he must deal with Latin, I suggest he paraphrase some accurate translation, and then employ some respectable student of the language to save him from blunders which might still be possible."[33] Such a sense of moral outrage at Pound's methods has continued through the ensuing decades since the appearance of Hale's screed. As recently as 1961, another academic, Gilbert Highet, fumed about Pound:

> His *Homage to Sextus Propertius* is an insult both to poetry and to scholarship, and to common sense. ... On every page Pound displays his ignorance, as though confident that, for scholars, his verse will be too subtle, and, for amateurs, his knowledge of foreign languages will be overpowering. But he can grasp neither the important little details nor the large essentials; and the suave and delicate rhythms of Propertius' poetry are quite beyond his grasp ... The misinterpretation of Propertius' words is disgusting but explicable and even, from some points of view, amusing. What is more disgusting is that Pound, himself a poet, should have degraded the sensitive thoughts of another poet. ... This is not a mistake in language. It is a fundamental failure in taste.[34]

The directly personal character of these criticisms and many others like them not only reflect the long-standing dominance of a narrow, semantically construed conception of "fidelity" in the assessment of Modernist translation; perhaps even more important, they indicate the extent to which Pound, together with Modernist translators more generally, openly departs from such a notion in his manifestly unorthodox practice as a translator.

At the opposite end of the spectrum of opinion, operating from a considerably broadened view of "accuracy" that includes pragmatic, tonal, and other criteria, J. P. Sullivan has coined the term "creative translation" in an attempt to recuperate the *Homage* as "a Model for Verse translation of Classical Authors."[35] The same dichotomy marks the treatment of Pound's rendering of Chinese poetry, as well as his versions of books from the Confucian tradition. Countless articles and monographs have traced the various grammatical errors, simplifications, and missteps Pound committed in translating, for example, Li Bai, while others, taking into account the influence of Fenollosa, have sought to justify his decisions in aesthetic terms in light of his fundamental misconceptions about the Chinese language. Wai-lim Yip's celebrated study does for *Cathay* what Sullivan's did for the *Homage*.[36] A similar, if at once less crowded and less volatile situation exists in the critical treatment of both Yeats's and H. D.'s translations of Sophocles, as well as the more recent efforts of Robert Lowell and Louis and Celia Zukofsky.

Yet, for all the insights they provide into the linguistic particularities of the various Modernist translators' individual practices, critics who principally attempt to evaluate the "accuracy" or "fidelity" of the translations undertaken during the Modernist period fail to recognize the deeply contingent nature of the works themselves and reproduce that contingency within an ostensibly objective critical framework. For just as the translations themselves are products of a specific historical period, arising out of a certain set of aesthetic preferences and standards (preferences and standards to which we still largely subscribe), so qualitative judgments, both positive and negative, simply apply a new (or sometimes the same) set of no less contingent criteria and an equally limited sense of the "original" in all its linguistic uniqueness and individuality. They fail to recognize what the Modernists themselves understood about the historicity of languages and of their relationships to one another, a matter that Pound himself articulated in "How to Read" when he said, "A master may be continually expanding his own tongue, rendering it fit to bear some charge hitherto borne only by some other alien tongue, but the process does not stop with any one man. While Proust is learning Henry James, preparatory to breaking through certain French paste-board partitions, the whole American speech is churning and chugging, and every other tongue is doing likewise" (*LE*, 36). Moreover, the implicitly normative dimension of such studies of specific feats of Modernist translation precludes a consideration of the importance of translation as a literary mode, the various types of cultural work that it performs, within the development of Modernism as a whole. As Andre Lefevere has written in another context:

> An approach to translation which rests content with decreeing which translations ought to exist and which ought not is very limited indeed. Rather, it should analyze texts which refer to themselves as translations and other rewritings and try to ascertain the part they play in a culture. The sheer number of rewritings should alert writers on translation of this ilk to the fact that they may not be dealing adequately with the matter at hand, just as the repeated and regular incidence of what they refer to as "mistakes" ought to alert them to the fact that an isolated mistake is, probably, just that, whereas a recurrent series of "mistakes" most likely points to a pattern that is the expression of a strategy.[37]

The second approach in the study of Modernist translation recognizes the fundamental importance of translation within the overall trajectory of Modernism, but only as a *theme* and not as a concrete means of textual production. Espousing translation as a guiding conceptual motif in the works of Pound and Joyce respectively, Hugh Kenner and Fritz Senn have each fruitfully pursued this line of thought, showing how the *idea* of translation illuminates the complexities of these writers' most involved and demanding achievements.

Yet both critics neglect to examine any specific details of the actual renderings of works in other languages undertaken by these renowned Modernists figures, and so fail to recognize the precise ways in which translation as a compositional procedure helped to give rise to their radical innovations in the forms of both poetry and the novel.

In addition to their specific individual limitations, these established methodologies for examining Modernist translation assume an absolute, qualitative distinction between translation and "original" composition, a distinction that the Modernists themselves, in their efforts as writers and translators, that is, as producers of texts, tended to blur. As will become evident throughout this study, I regard both these more established approaches to Modernist translation as fundamentally inadequate because they each in their turn fail to recognize the crucial importance of translation as *at once* a compositional procedure and a conceptual structure that informs virtually the entire range of Modernist literary production. For, as Antoine Berman has written:

> It is impossible to separate the history of translation from the history of languages, of cultures, and of literatures—even of religions and of nations. To be sure, this is not a question of mixing every thing up, but of showing how in each period or in each given historical setting the practice of translation *is articulated* in relation to the practice of literature, of languages, of the several intercultural and interlinguistic exchanges. (emphasis in the original)[38]

Indeed, grounded in such critical (in all senses of the word) observations, the field of Translation Studies has grown considerably in recent years and featured various efforts at tracing the history and theorizing different aspects of translation as a complex cultural activity.[39] These have included projects ranging from attempts to establish a practical ethics that allows for the preservation, rather than the erasure, of cultural difference, to considerations of the function of translation in colonial and post-colonial settings.[40] Most relevant to the concerns of this study, various critics have gone beyond more traditional approaches by examining the relationship between the activity of translation and other basic categories of cultural identity, as well as carefully delineating its conceptual articulation and ideological function in a number of different linguistic traditions and historical contexts. So, for example, Lori Chamberlain has pointed out the remarkable continuity in Western culture, since at least St. Jerome, of expressly gendered theorizing about translation, tracing a persistent association between metaphorical thought about the literary practice and figures of femininity and (hetero)sexual conquest.[41] To be sure, such an association finds its most obvious expression in the very time-worn concept of "fidelity" that continues to mark even contemporary assessments of translation generally and of different individual renderings.[42] Somewhat more recently, synthesizing a considerable body of scholarship in feminist Translation Studies, Sherry Simon has examined the play of gender issues in such diverse cultural contexts as the history of Anglo-American women translators of fictional and religious texts, the rendering into English of noted works of French feminism, and contemporary Bible translation.[43]

In a related vein, other critics have examined the role of translation in establishing, maintaining, and challenging the boundaries of the nation as a cultural entity. Here, Lawrence Venuti has discussed, among other things, how debates over the propriety of "foreignizing" versus "domesticating" translation conducted in Romantic Germany and Victorian England respectively each reflect different strategies for constituting a national cultural identity.[44] Similarly, Michael Cronin has traced the importance of translation in the establishment and continuing redefinition of Irish culture from the Middle Ages to the contemporary moment.[45] These and other critics have convincingly demonstrated the extent to which translation has served in various ways and in different historical contexts as an instrument for negotiating larger issues of culture and identity.

Alongside such culturally situated analyses, another group of thinkers has followed in the wake of Benjamin to probe the philosophical significance of translation and its consequences for the matter of language itself. Among these include, most famously perhaps, George Steiner, whose magisterial *After Babel: Aspects of Language and Translation* not only helped to establish a foundation for the contemporary rise of Translation Studies as a distinct discipline, but also continues to exert a recognizable influence over the entire field by connecting the phenomenon of translation to fundamental questions of language. In addition, such important figures in literary theory as Paul de Man and Jacques Derrida have each written on the conceptual dimensions of translation, emphasizing, perhaps not unexpectedly, its paradoxical status as a task both "necessary and impossible" (Derrida 170). Such theoretically minded critics and those following them have gone a long way in exploring the philosophical depth that underlies the deceptively obvious connection between translation as a mode of literary production and the question of language itself.[46]

Despite all the valuable insights they have provided into the different histories, meanings, and politics of translation as a distinct cultural activity, however, critics operating from within a Translation Studies perspective have addressed only a small portion of the numerous renderings of works from various linguistic traditions undertaken during the period of Anglo-American Modernism. So, for example, in his generally impressive history of translation in English from the seventeenth century to the present, Lawrence Venuti limits his analysis of Modernist translations in *The Translator's Invisibility: A History of Translation* to the work of Ezra Pound, and only to the poet's treatment of texts originally written in Italian and Provençal at that. While this strategy represents an eminently understandable, and in some ways even admirable, methodological modesty, it nevertheless has the effect of obscuring an important change that took place in the practice of translation as a literary mode during the Modernist period. For, as we shall see, one of Pound's most significant, as well as consequential, achievements as a translator lay in expanding the scope of expressly literary translation in English to include works from languages entirely outside the European cultural tradition, most notably Chinese poetic, socio-political, and historical texts.

It remains, therefore, to give a more comprehensive and detailed account than has been offered up to this point of both the development of Modernist translation as a mode of literary production and its fundamental importance for the development of Anglo-American Modernism as a whole. Accordingly, then, over the course of this study I will at once examine how various Modernist writers conceived of translation as a literary mode, in both cultural and practical terms, and, in turn, demonstrate the ways in which their specific practice as translators contributed to the development of Modernism throughout its lyric, epic, and novelistic dimensions; how it helped to generate both the internationalist content of Modernism, as well as the intensely linguistic focus of its formal innovations; how it functioned as a strategy for negotiating issues of gender, politics, and language that various recent studies have addressed as shaping concerns of the period; and how it provided a means of reconciling the contradictory aesthetic imperatives to "Make it New" and to gather "from the air a live tradition" (LXXXI, 522).

The first three chapters comprise part I, "Translation and Gender." Chapter one addresses the best-received example of Modernist translation, Ezra Pound's *Cathay*. The chapter discusses how *Cathay* consecrated the most fundamental change in the practice of literary translation in English wrought by the Modernist period. Radically reconfiguring the operative parameters of translation as a literary mode, Pound's achievement obviated intimate knowledge of the source language as a pre-condition for translation by demonstrating that successful (i.e., aesthetically pleasing and culturally influential) results could be attained without thorough understanding of the original language of the text one translated. At the same time, through both his choice of which poems to translate and many of the specific details of his renderings of the Chinese lyrics contained and glossed in the Fenollosa notebooks, Pound offered in *Cathay* an extended meditation on the place of women and women's voices in his own developing conception of poetry. This complicates the long-established picture of Pound as a misogynistic writer and demonstrates the importance of translation in the process by which he arrived at his overtly masculinist conception of poetic production.

Chapter two takes up the other most (in)famous feat of Modernist translation, Pound's much maligned *Homage to Sextus Propertius*. Instead of revisiting the tired question of whether Pound's achievement merits the designation of "translation," this chapter argues that the *Homage* represents the first Modernist work in which translation serves as a constitutive method of textual construction. In this light, the *Homage* emerges as much more than just a selective and frequently poorly executed version of the Roman poet's odes. Rather, the sequence embodies Pound's personal inquiry into the Modernist viability of erotic verse as it offers an enabling configuration of masculine and feminine poetic roles, his individual test of the poetic proposition: "My genius is no more than a girl." Thus, I argue, the *Homage* carries forward through the practice of translation the inquiry that Pound began in *Cathay* into the relationship between gender and poetic production. In the end, he discovers the terms for his own explicitly masculine expression by arriving at a conception of the erotic as a logical precursor to epic achievement.

By contrast, translation functioned for H. D. as a way of challenging the masculinist sexual poetics advanced by so many male Modernist writers. In a literary culture that conceived of "Modern" poetry, indeed all truly original writing, as "the expression of virile thought,"[47] translation represented an ambiguously gendered mode of literary (re)production that insistently raised the question of the relationship between gender and writing. Chapter three delineates the ways translation as a mode of writing helped H. D. to establish her own Modernist, feminine poetic practice by both providing a concrete textual means for recovering the feminine energies she perceived in various classical Greek texts and serving as a strategy for negotiating between the equally problematic examples of her nineteenth-century female literary predecessors and her male contemporaries. From functioning as the conceptual impetus for the writing of her very first "Imagist" poems to furnishing the guiding metaphorical structure for the visionary dimensions of her major late sequence *Helen in Egypt*, translation played a crucial role throughout H. D.'s entire development as a poet.

Part II, "Translation and Politics," begins with a discussion of how for Yeats translation served both a pedagogical and a constitutive function within his attempts to establish an Irish national theater. Chapter four examines the importance of translation as a means of assimilating foreign dramas in Yeats's efforts to create an Irish national culture through the cultivation of an authentic dramatic form. In doing so it traces the evolution of Yeats's conception of translation from a necessary task of negotiating the rift between the Gaelic roots and English realities of modern Ireland to a vital instrument, in the form of his 1928 renderings of *King Oedipus* and *Oedipus at Colonus*, for critiquing the idea of national culture as promulgated after the establishment of the Irish Free State. By providing a way to confront and absorb foreign dramatic masterpieces, translation contributes to the development and definition of Irish culture. Thus, translation becomes for Yeats a mode of writing essentially equivalent to original composition, which explains why he came to serve as a translator long after he had already established himself as a playwright, as well as why he employed translation as a technique in the writing of the concluding poems of both *The Tower* (1928) and *The Winding Stair and Other Poems* (1933).

Chapter five returns to the work of Ezra Pound, by far the most important theorist and prolific practitioner of Modernist translation, and considers the relationship between his efforts as a translator and his most ambitious, and problematic, achievement as a poet, *The Cantos*. In this chapter, I elucidate the explicitly political content and radical formal armature of the middle and late *Cantos* as functions of Pound's attempt both to incorporate into his own poem the social wisdom of several classical Confucian texts and to reproduce the very representational modes, as he understood them, of the Chinese language itself. By examining the role that such texts play in his "poem including history," as well as his independent translations of such Confucian documents as *The Great Learning*, *The Unwobbling Pivot*, and *The Analects*, I maintain that translation offered Pound a strategy for achieving the contradictory demands of his own aesthetic (as well as political) program, a specific, textual means to "Make it New" even as he "gathered from the air a live tradition." This explains why, after the fiasco of Pisa and his temporary abandonment of *The Cantos*, Pound remained committed to producing his Confucian translations, which became his principle avenue of literary production in the years immediately following World War II.

Beginning part III, "Translation and Language," chapter six confronts the towering, though by no means capricious, obscurity of *Finnegans Wake*. Drawing inspiration from his early effort as a translator of the German dramatist Gerhart Hauptmann, I discuss Joyce's career as the result of a lifelong fascination with the aesthetic possibilities arising from the manifold intersection of different human languages. From the boy narrator's meditation on such words as "paralysis," "gnomon," and "simony" in the first story of *Dubliners* to Shaun the Post's practice of "transluding from the Otherman or off the Toptic" in *Finnegans Wake*, I trace Joyce's concern with the limits of English itself. After exhausting both the discursive and syntactic resources of English in *Ulysses*, I argue, Joyce in effect turns to translating English itself into a different language as a way of rejuvenating the possibilities of the novel. His achievement represents the most rigorously pursued, but obverse, expression of the Modernist interest in translation as a literary mode. From such a perspective, *Finnegans Wake* appears as a logical outgrowth of Modernist concerns, rather than as simply perhaps the period's most singular, and inexplicable, exception.

Concluding part III, chapter seven traces the legacy of Modernist translation practice through its two principal inheritors: Robert Lowell and Louis Zukofsky. Focusing primary attention on Louis and Celia Zukofsky's remarkable, sound-based treatment of the odes of Catullus, chapter seven discusses their achievement as the logical culmination of the Modernist revolution in translation as a literary mode. For they not only engage in translation as an expressly collaborative enterprise, thereby absolutely decoupling the linguistic and literary dimensions of the practice. Perhaps even more radically, they also redefine the very principles of translation itself as a mode of literary production by expressly adopting sound rather than semantic meaning as the basis for their rendering. Through their efforts, they at once push translation to its very conceptual limits and definitively establish the terms of linguistic knowledge by which such contemporary translators as Stephen Mitchell, Gary Snyder, W. S. Merwin, Robert Hass, Robert Pinsky, Ursula LeGuin, Jane Hirschfield, Seamus Heaney, and others practice translation not as an exercise in apprenticeship but rather as a privilege and expression of established reputation. Lastly, the conclusion summarizes the larger points made throughout the book, and suggests possible avenues for further research by pointing out the importance of translation as a literary mode for various other twentieth-century literary movements in a number of different linguistic and cultural contexts.

From its earliest beginnings, Anglo-American Modernism always sought to negotiate between a variety of conflicting impulses. Even as they sought to break away from the established modes and stances of their Victorian predecessors, Modernist writers like Yeats, Pound, H. D., and Joyce turned to the ancient past for sources of inspiration and models of literary creativity. And even as they sought to bring literature to the forefront of culture, they produced texts expressing at best indifference, and sometimes outright hostility, to even the most attentive and devoted readers. And even as they sought to make English into a world language by producing works with expressly epic ambitions, they used a wide range of foreign languages and texts to extend the possibilities of both the literary forms they inherited and even the English language itself. As a strategy for negotiating these demands, translation became an immensely important literary practice, gaining over the course of Modernism a significance in the realm of English literary culture that it had not possessed since the time of Dryden.

Throughout the Modernist period, then, translation occupied a manifold conceptual space: it constituted an autonomous literary activity that inspired sustained and varied critical reflection; it functioned as a specific technique in the construction of texts in a variety of different modes, ranging from "original" works to so-called adaptations to "translations" proper, as that term has been traditionally understood, texts by which various writers both expanded the scope of Modernism and explored issues of gender, politics, and language itself; and it embodied a comprehensive textual strategy for negotiating between the demands of transmission and transformation, between the authority of tradition and the demands of innovation, between the endowments of the past and the imperatives of the present. In their drive to develop and renew different formal and social possibilities, the Modernists writing in (and into) English turned to translation and, in turn, reinvented it as a uniquely important mode of literary composition.

Part I

Translation and Gender

Chapter One

"to-day's men are not the men of the old days"[1]
Ezra Pound's *Cathay* and the Invention of Modernist
Literary Translation

I

First published in 1915 as a modest volume presenting fourteen freshly rendered classical Chinese poems, Ezra Pound's *Cathay* fundamentally altered the dimensions of several fields of literary culture within English.[2] Most obviously and immediately, the collection redefined the place of Chinese poetry in the West, not only virtually establishing its significance as a literary tradition for England and America, but also permanently transforming the way in which it was henceforth to be presented to general audiences through translation by poets and even scholars.[3] Creating both the predominant idiom and image of Chinese poetry in English for Anglo-American Modernism, *Cathay* continues to exert an enormous influence on the transmission, and hence popular apprehension, of the Chinese poetic tradition in the West.[4] Ask non-specialists about their impressions of Chinese poetry and you are overwhelmingly likely to receive answers indelibly stamped with Pound's influence. Even relatively seasoned readers with broad exposure to different translators of various poets will probably speak of intense imagery, verbal concentration, and a mystical harmony with nature rather than of "rhyme and strict form," the two characteristics that Arthur Waley, Pound's contemporary and closest rival as the chief interpreter and transmitter of Chinese poetry to the West, considers the most salient aspects of Chinese verse.[5] So, for example, the contemporary poet Hayden Carruth offers in his 1989 lyric, "Of Distress Being Humiliated by the Classical Chinese Poets," a vision of Chinese poetry as a cultural tradition wherein "everything happens at once, no conflicts can occur." As Robert Kern rightly notes, the salient characteristics of "Chinese" poetry for Carruth, as well as for Western readers generally, remain "its imagism, its focus on natural events and things themselves" (Kern, ix). Thus, T. S. Eliot's (in)famous remark that "Pound is the inventor of Chinese poetry for our time" remains as true today for the Anglophone world as when he first made it in 1928.[6]

Less immediately, perhaps, but certainly no less significantly, *Cathay* also helped to underwrite a change in the course of poetry in English. For in the densely evocative Chinese poems contained and glossed in the notebooks of Ernest Fenollosa, Pound felt he had discovered a preexisting, historically authoritative validation of the principles he had been seeking to bring to Modernist poetry in English for some time. Four of the six lyrics that comprised Pound's contribution to the first Imagist anthology, *Des Imagistes* (1914), were explicitly modeled on Chinese poems that had been previously rendered by the famous nineteenth-century sinologist Herbert Giles: "After Ch'u Yuan," "Liu Ch'e," "Fan Piece for her Imperial Lord," and "Ts'ai Chi'h."[7] The weightier, more extended accomplishment of *Cathay* definitively proved the viability of an approach to poetry, namely Imagism, that Albert Gelpi has called one of the two "generative strains of poetic Modernism" in English.[8] In the words of George Steiner, Pound's translations of Chinese poetry into English "altered the feel of the language and set the pattern of cadence for modern verse."[9]

Finally, and most important for the purposes of this study, *Cathay* consecrated the most fundamental change in the practical dimensions of literary translation in English wrought by the Modernist period, a change virtually without precedent in the history of translation as a literary mode in English. Radically reconfiguring the operative parameters of translation as a mode of literary production, Pound's achievement obviated intimate knowledge of the source language as a precondition for translation by demonstrating in an irrefutable way that successful (that is, both aesthetically pleasing and culturally influential) results could be attained without thorough (or indeed, as in this case, even any) understanding of the original language of the text one translated. For when he began working from the notebooks of Ernest Fenollosa to produce his versions of the (mostly) medieval Chinese lyrics presented in *Cathay*, Pound had absolutely no knowledge of the Chinese language. At that time he had yet to assimilate Fenollosa's deeply problematic theory of the Chinese written character, so he did not even have the benefit of an *incorrect* understanding of Chinese. Indeed, the Fenollosa notebooks themselves oftentimes did not include Chinese characters, frequently giving instead only the Japanese pronunciation of the lines in the Chinese poems, together with meticulous word-for-word glosses in English and stilted interlinear renderings. Consequently, in many cases Pound would not have had access to the Chinese poems themselves even had he been able to "read" them in whatever fashion in their original language. As we shall see in a subsequent chapter, much later he would come to insist upon the necessity of actually *seeing* the original Chinese characters in order to achieve a "proper" understanding (as well as, therefore, an "accurate" rendering) of classic Confucian texts such as the *Da Xue* (大學), the *Zhong Yong* (中庸), and the *Lun Yu* (論語), or *The Analects*. But at the time of *Cathay*, he proceeded as a translator of Chinese poetry without any apparent compunction over his almost complete lack of familiarity with the Chinese language, the most basic of the traditional "requirements" for translation. Accordingly, then, the significance of Pound's achievement in *Cathay* has at least as much to do with the history of translation in English as a mode of literary production, as with the long tradition of Western thought about the Chinese language and its capacities as a medium for poetic expression, a tradition that includes such Continental thinkers as Descartes, Leibniz, Jean Pierre Abel-Rémusat, Friedrich Schlegel, Wilhelm von Humboldt, Otto Jesperson, Julia Kristeva, Roland Barthes, and Jacques Derrida, among others.[10]

Yet, for all these seemingly considerable "problems" with his approach to translating Chinese poetry in *Cathay*, practically no one at the time, except for a few scholars, challenged the authority of his versions.[11] In contrast to the situation of Latin and the furor over the *Homage of Sextus Propertius*, Chinese then remained exotic enough to afford Pound the protection of a broad cultural ignorance among his audience.[12] Even more important, still fewer, either then or since, have denied the felicity of his renderings as works in English. Thus radically (and perhaps irretrievably) decoupling literary translation from an operative requirement of semantic comprehension, *Cathay* successfully reformulated the terms of translation practice in English to emphasize poetic creation and expressivity over linguistically grounded semantic conversion. In doing so, it set the stage for numerous later feats of Modernist "translation" such as Pound's own *Homage to Sextus Propertius* (1919), Yeats's versions of both *Oedipus Rex* (1928) and *Oedipus at Colonus* (1933), H. D.'s rendering of *Euripides Ion, Translated with Notes* (1937), as well as such ostensibly "Post-Modernist" works as Robert Lowell's *Imitations* (1961) and Louis and Celia Zukofsky's remarkable sound-based treatment of the odes of Catullus (1969). Indeed, Pound's achievement in *Cathay* underlies such important contemporary work in translation as Stephen Mitchell's versions of Rilke and the *Dao De Jing* (道德經), as well as the efforts of such American translator/poets as Jane Hirschfield, W. S. Merwin, Robert Hass, Kenneth Rexroth, and even Ursula LeGuin, among others who translate works into English from (typically, though not exclusively, Asian) languages of which they have little or no formal knowledge.[13]

Precisely because Pound so cavalierly violates an ancient and entrenched theoretical orthodoxy about the requirements for translation (also known as "common sense"), and because he furthermore defies the considerable weight of a long practical tradition, critics since Eliot have been slow to recognize the significance of *Cathay* as an unprecedented, liberatory moment in the history of literary translation in English. Instead, adhering to a narrowly linguistic, and even philological approach, they have tended to evaluate Pound's achievement strictly within the terms of the traditional binary opposition between "fidelity" to and "freedom" from the original, and, as I mentioned in the introduction, extended praise or condemnation for the perceived "quality" of his renderings. Countless monographs and articles have enumerated various grammatical errors, simplifications, and missteps Pound committed in translating, for example, Li Bai (李白). Others, taking into account the influence of Fenollosa and the limitations of the notebooks themselves, have sought to justify or rationalize in aesthetic terms his deviations from the semantic content of the originals in light of the imposed constraints of his source. Even more than thirty years after its publication, Wai-lim Yip's celebrated and largely sympathetic study, *Ezra Pound's* Cathay (1969),[14] remains the best of this sort of treatment, offering a discussion of Pound's efforts in light of a thorough and native familiarity with the Chinese language and poetic tradition, though due to the ban on access to the Fenollosa notebooks in place at the time, the work suffers somewhat from its methodological reliance on speculative reconstruction, rather than direct analysis, of the source material.

Yet, for all the insights they provide into the particular linguistic details of Pound's versions of different Chinese poems, such assessments generally neglect to consider either the specific thematic concerns or the broader cultural significance of *Cathay* as a carefully orchestrated volume of radically unorthodox translations. They consistently fail to address the fundamental importance of the collection within not only Pound's own poetic career, but also the overall framework of Anglo-American Modernism, as well as the ongoing history of translation as a literary mode in English. Accordingly, then, I want in this chapter not merely to point out yet again Pound's various "failures" and "triumphs" as a translator of Chinese poetry. Rather, I want to discuss the way in which the collection both redefines the practical terms of translation as a literary mode and reflects Pound's concerns with the relationship between gender and poetry at practically every level of its construction. Thus, in addition to its monumental significance within the history of literary translation in English, *Cathay* also marks a crucial early stage in the development of Pound's deeply sexualized, overtly masculinist conception of literary production, a matter that continues to raise concerns among various, and especially feminist, critics of Modernism.

For in so clearly extending the procedural boundaries of translation, as well as the horizon of its significance as a literary mode, beyond merely the "accurate" or "felicitous" reproduction of semantic meaning, *Cathay* lay the foundation for Pound's own subsequent procedures as both a translator and, indeed, an "original" poet. Moreover, in doing so, it enabled other of his contemporaries like William Butler Yeats and H. D. to regard and employ translation as a vital strategy for addressing their own particular concerns of establishing an authentic national Irish dramatic culture and reconfiguring the conceptual relationship between gender and writing respectively. As one of the principal goals of this entire study, I will show in subsequent chapters how the collective efforts of these and other writers of the period to rethink both the meaning and the practice of translation made it an integral part of the entire Anglo-American Modernist cultural and aesthetic program. And this, in turn, solidified a change in the conception of the operative parameters of translation itself as a mode of literary production that continues to hold sway up to the present day.

With regard to the issue of gender, Pound, of course, has long been a favorite target of (largely first-wave) feminist critics intent on exposing the sexist assumptions and masculinist biases of canonical (male) Modernism and its subsequent promoters in the academy. Most notably, perhaps, Sandra Gilbert and Susan Gubar have attacked Pound as an "openly misogynistic" writer who sought to promulgate an expressly masculine conception of literary production for Anglo-American Modernism.[15] In recent years, however, the tenor and focus of feminist criticism has shifted from defensive denunciations of the misogyny expressed by male Modernists to attempts at contextualizing such misogyny and masculinism as a response to specific social and historical forces, in particular, turn-of-the-century feminism. Thus, Marianne DeKoven argues that these forces "produced in modernist writing an unprecedented preoccupation with gender, both thematically and formally," which in turn expresses "an irresolvable ambivalence toward powerful femininity that itself forged many of Modernism's most characteristic formal innovations."[16] Still, she chooses Pound to illustrate "male Modernism's self-imagination as a mode of masculine domination."[17] To be sure, the views of particular women figures and of the feminine generally that he voiced especially in his later poetry, together with his attempts in various essays to link artistic creativity to male sexuality and masculine experience, attest to Pound's clear sexism during the majority of his long career. And both the virulence and the variety of such statements undoubtedly reflect an anxiety about the power of the feminine. To select only one from a vast series of possible examples, in Canto VII, Pound casts the historical figure Eleanor of Aquitaine as an example of the archetypal destructive power of femininity by connecting her with Helen of Troy through invoking traditional punning epithets on the latter's name in Greek. Reaching back to such classical sources as Stesichorus, Sappho, and Euripides, Pound calls her "Ἑλανδρος" ("destroyer of men") and "Ἑλέπτολις" ("destroyer of cities") (VII, 24).

I will take up the matter of the masculinist sexual poetics of Modernism, as well as Pound's participation in its establishment, at greater length at the beginning of chapter three. At this point, I want merely to say that Pound's practice as a translator in *Cathay* directly contradicts his later overtly misogynistic statements, thereby complicating even the current, theoretically and historically nuanced views of his expressed attitudes regarding the fundamental masculinity of poetry and his equally problematic views of the feminine. For both in the poems he chose to include in the collection and in the way he translated them, that is to say, both thematically and technically, Pound displays an abiding concern for, as well as a sensitivity to, the position of women in the medieval Chinese poems and, by extension into his own contemporary circumstances, in the increasingly martial world of 1914–15 England. Such concern can perhaps be best understood as one of Pound's earliest sustained meditations on the place of women and of women's voices in his own developing conception of poetry. Thus, as a carefully selected anthology of idiosyncratically rendered Chinese poems, *Cathay* introduces a temporal aspect to DeKoven's otherwise powerful framework for understanding the sexism of so many male Modernists. For Pound's overtly misogynist attitudes toward the feminine and its place within the process of literary production did not simply appear, Athena-like, fully formed as a response either to the efforts of women writers of the preceding generation or to the "revolutionary horizon"[18] of feminism. Rather, it too evolved, had to be earned as it were, and Pound arrived at such a conception in significant measure, as we shall see, specifically through the practice of translation.

Moreover, given his later declarations about the essential masculinity of poetry, as well as the extent to which they successfully permeated both the poetic and critical discourse at the time and afterwards, *Cathay*, as a collection of deeply mediated renderings of the work of other poets, arguably confronted Pound early on with questions about the gender inflection of his own work as a translator and of translation itself as a literary mode. Indeed, the widespread acclaim of *Cathay* notwithstanding, critics have persisted in viewing the translations of Pound and other Modernists as suffering from a kind of "diminished creative potency" in comparison to their "original" works. Even today, *Hugh Selwyn Mauberley* routinely (and uncritically) receives attention over *Homage to Sextus Propertius* as the more "significant" work. Such ongoing tendencies give contemporary expression to the long-standing association in Western thought between translation as a literary mode and the category of the feminine, a matter that Lori Chamberlain and others working in the field of feminist Translation Studies have explored in considerable detail and breadth.[19] At every level, then, from the technical to the thematic and even to the generic, *Cathay* negotiates issues of the relationship between gender and poetry.

II

From its initial publication in 1915, Pound called attention to the way in which *Cathay* both draws upon and deviates from a traditional conception of the practice of translation as a literary mode. Provocatively gesturing in two directions simultaneously, the descriptive note on the title page explicitly identifies the poems to follow as "translations," while at the same time placing Pound himself in a distinctly international chain of transmission that already indicates both his great debt and his decidedly unorthodox method as a translator. With centered, progressively shorter lines, the page reads:

> CATHAY
>
> TRANSLATIONS BY
> EZRA POUND
>
> FOR THE MOST PART FROM THE CHINESE
> OF RIHAKU, FROM THE NOTES OF THE
> LATE ERNEST FENOLLOSA, AND
> THE DECIPHERINGS OF THE
> PROFESSORS MORI
> AND ARIGA.[20]

An informed reader instantly recognizes the mediation of Japanese in Pound's practice of translation through his use of the name Rihaku (the Japanese name for Li Bai) as well as the mention of Mori and Ariga.[21] Yet even for those (undoubtedly vast majority of readers in 1915 England) without an awareness of the differences between Asian languages and their systems of naming, the note announces a significant departure from the process of translation conventionally understood as the transfer of semantic meaning directly from a source to a target language by an individual versed in both. Up to this point in the history of literary translation in English, it had simply been assumed that translators must know both the languages between which they worked.[22] Indeed, in all his own previous efforts as a translator, Pound had worked only with languages of which he had at least some formal knowledge, however shaky: Italian for his *Sonnets and Ballate of Guido Cavalcanti*; Provençal for the Arnaut Daniel poems in *Umbra* and *Instigations*; and Anglo-Saxon for "The Seafarer."[23] By contrast, in explicitly mentioning the Fenollosa "notes" and the "decipherings" of two Japanese professors on its very title page, *Cathay* implicitly declares Pound's ignorance of the Chinese language, acknowledging an intermediate source for his renderings of the poems in the volume.

More important, perhaps, it also adumbrates a theory of translation itself as a collaborative mode of textual production by presenting his effort as merely the latest (though not necessarily final) in a series of engagements with the original Chinese. Far from seeking to diminish or even elide the importance of the translator in the process of the dissemination of Chinese poetry, *Cathay* openly recognizes the several participants contributing to the creation of what Walter Benjamin has called a form of "afterlife" for literary works.[24] By explicitly distinguishing between the "semantic" and the "poetic" dimensions of translation as a literary mode, Pound not only set a precedent for the work of such contemporaries as Yeats and H. D., but he thereby also helped to inaugurate the common contemporary practice in English of producing translations (especially of poetry) through the collaboration of two or more people, one (or more) who possesses an actual understanding of the original language, and the other who boasts an ostensibly more supple English literary sensibility.

Interestingly, within the perhaps less broadly familiar tradition of English translations of Chinese poetry, a number of writers anticipated Pound in his collaborative method of rendering in *Cathay*. As Kern points out, summarizing Teele, around the turn of the twentieth century, Lancelot Cranmer-Byng produced a book of "translations" of Chinese poetry that were based not on any sort of first-hand, scholarly examination of original works, but on the preceding efforts of Herbert Giles. As I mentioned earlier, Pound had done the same thing for his early Chinese-inspired poems that he submitted for publication in *Des Imagistes*. Similarly, in 1910, the poet Clifford Bax and a Japanese Buddhist monk, Tsutomi Inouye, together produced a slim volume entitled *Twenty Chinese Poems*, though Bax only really laid claim to having "paraphrased" rather than more strictly "translated" the Chinese works.[25] It remains beyond the scope of this study to consider in detail why Pound's *Cathay* achieved greater recognition than these other efforts, which remain little more than obscure footnotes to Sino-English literary history. Undoubtedly, much of it has to do with the quality of Pound's versification in English, rather than with any greater degree of "accuracy" or "fidelity" in representing Chinese poetry. And this, in turn, merely underscores the historical contingency of translation itself as a mode of literary production, the variability of its standards according to different social, political, cultural, and linguistic circumstances. But for whatever reason, precisely because of its greater renown, Pound's *Cathay* stands as the formative event not only for such roughly contemporaneous feats of collaborative translation specifically of Chinese poetry as *Fir Flower Tablets* (1921) by Amy Lowell and Florence Ayscough and *The Jade Mountain* (1929) by Witter Bynner and Kiang Kang-hu, but also more generally for the current approach to the rendering of other languages into English, as seen, to choose only one example, in the collaboration between Robert Hass and the Polish writer Czeslaw Milosz.[26]

To be sure, if the title page did not give sufficiently forceful indication of Pound's largely unprecedented method as a translator in *Cathay*, then a somewhat polemical note included at the end of the 1915 first edition vigorously underscores his break with the constraints of traditional translation theory and practice. Repeatedly (indeed, insistently) characterizing the work as "translation," Pound nevertheless stipulates to both the partiality and the linguistic uncertainty of his achievement. Even so, he justifies the enterprise with a characteristic mix of bravado and paranoia:

> I have not come to the end of Ernest Fenollosa's notes by a long way, nor is it *entirely* perplexity that causes me to cease from translation. ... There are also other poems, notably the "Five color Screen," in which Professor Fenollosa was, as an art critic, especially interested, and Rihaku's sort of Ars Poetica, which might be given with diffidence to an audience of good will. But if I give them with the necessary breaks for explanation, and a tedium of notes, it is quite certain that the personal hatred in which I am held by many, and the *invidia* which is directed against me because I have dared openly to declare my belief in certain young artists, will be brought to bear first on the flaws in such translation, and will then be merged into depreciation of the whole book of translations. Therefore I give only these unquestionable poems.[27] [except for *invidia*, emphasis mine]

By indicating that both a definite selectivity and a degree of grammatical surmise underlie his work as a translator in *Cathay*, this note underscores the necessity of considering the larger textual environment, as well as the specific details, of Pound's initial engagement with Chinese poetry as presented in the Fenollosa notebooks. For if part of the significance of the collection lies in its implicit retheorization and practical reconfiguration of translation as a literary mode, it also necessarily presents a complex of meanings as a text with its own individual dynamic of expression, over and above its particular qualities as a group of renderings of various Chinese poems.

Over the years, several different interpretations regarding the overriding thematics of *Cathay* have been put forth. Kenner's long-standing assertion that "*Cathay*, April 1915...is largely a war book,"[28] has been modified and sharpened, but never completely overturned. More recently, though, other critics like Sanehide Kodama and Ron Bush have considered the development of and modifications to *Cathay* 1915, and argued that the collection "may reflect Pound's own state of mind at the time" of his being a newly important poet, and the loneliness associated with that situation.[29] Comparably, basing her assertions on a thorough examination of the notebooks themselves, Ann Chapple argues that "Pound's selection methods may be traced to personal tastes which stemmed from his 'Imagist' doctrine and earlier related interest."[30]

Yet such accounts fail to recognize the fundamental importance of gender issues within both the construction and the expressive logic of the collection.

For from the very beginning of his engagement with the Chinese poetry contained in the Fenollosa notebooks, Pound chose to incorporate women and their situations as an integral part of the whole of *Cathay*. Pound received the manuscripts of the late Ernest Fenollosa from his widow, Mary, near the end of 1913, and he took them with him to work on at Stone Cottage over the first of his three winters acting as Yeats's secretary there.[31] He did not begin seriously to address the notes on Chinese poetry, however, until the autumn of 1914. Once starting, he worked quickly, and the first edition of *Cathay* was published on April 6, 1915. The notebooks contain, according to Pound's count, some 150 poems that Fenollosa had cribbed and roughly translated with the help of various Japanese scholars of Chinese poetry whom he met and studied with during his second stay in Japan.[32] Of these 150 poems, 48 were by Li Bai, known in Japanese, and therefore to Fenollosa and to Pound at the time, as Rihaku. As a number of commentators have shown, Pound experimented with the contents of *Cathay*.[33] After an initial survey of the notebooks, he marked seventeen Li Bai/Rihaku poems for additional attention. Upon further examination, he delineated six for inclusion in the collection.[34] Eventually, he decided to include a total of eleven Li Bai poems in *Cathay*.

Importantly, however, out of the forty-eight poems of Li Bai in the notebooks, only three had women either as subjects or as speakers. Pound selected two of these three in the original group of six poems that comprise the heart of the volume: "The Jewel Stairs' Grievance" and "The River Merchant's Wife: A Letter." Moreover, Pound's own notes within the notebooks further demonstrate that the issue of women and women's voices occupied his mind in compiling *Cathay*. Indeed, of the fourteen Chinese poems in the first 1915 edition, three concern women directly, either as speakers or as subject matter. In the end, he included "The Beautiful Toilet" by Mei Sheng together with the Li Bai poems about women.[35] This quantity of poems matches that given to the other great concerns of the collection: war, about which there are three poems; loneliness, about which there are also three; and separation, a theme taken up by the suite of "Four poems of Departure."

Clearly all of the poems in *Cathay* give expression to feelings of isolation, loneliness, and distance against the backdrop of a world scarred by martial conflict and shifting political terrain. Inasmuch as they do, they lend weight to Kenner's claim that they reflect "a sensibility responsive to torn Belgium and disrupted London."[36] Yet these emotions arise through distinctively gendered conduits. Indeed, the fact that it is populated with such stereotypical figures of both genders—soldiers and government officials/poets on the one hand, and abandoned wives and courtesans on the other—helps to indicate the extent to which concerns about the very category of gender inform the poetics of the collection at every level. Arguably, then, in *Cathay* Pound sought through translation as much to test a variety of gender-coded activities and subject positions for their expressive potential as to offer an oblique commentary on the emotional ramifications of his own contemporary situation, which, in 1914–15 England, meant the context of "the Great War."[37]

Moreover, even as the work grew, anthologized first in *Lustra* (1916) and later in *Personae* (1926), the volume retained its substantial focus on women. Of the four poems that were added to *Cathay* in these and later collections ("Sennin Poem by Kakuhaku," "A Ballad of the Mulberry Road," "To-Em-Mei's 'The Unmoving Cloud,'" and "Old Idea of Choan by Roshoriu"), one directly concerns the social position of women: "A Ballad of the Mulberry Road." Thus, Pound's choice of which poems from the Fenollosa notebooks to translate in *Cathay*, both in its early and later, more extended versions, betokens a sustained concern with the category of the feminine and, more particularly, its relationship to the act of poetic production. As we shall see, such a perspective not only clarifies the particular expressive dynamics of *Cathay*, but it also helps to explain how the practice of translation itself came to function with the larger framework of Anglo-American Modernism as a strategy for exploring and even (re)configuring the conceptual relationship between gender and writing.

III

Pound addresses the place of the feminine within the domain of poetry not only through his selection of poems that focus upon women and feature women speakers, but also in the details of his renderings. In each of his translations, Pound systematically elevates the position of the female subjects in the lyrics of *Cathay*, giving them a stronger voice and greater presence in the arena of poetry than either the originals or, more important, Fenollosa's notes imply. The brevity and concentration of Li Bai's "Jade Stair's Complaint" (玉階怨) make it easy to see just how Pound negotiates issues of gender through his practice of translation in *Cathay*. In his notebooks, Fenollosa did not provide the Chinese characters of this poem, but rather only the transliterated Japanese pronunciation. To facilitate an understanding of Pound's efforts against the larger background of the Chinese poetic tradition and its dissemination in the West, I include the original poem here along with Fenollosa's notes, which read as follows:

玉	階	怨
Gioku	Kai	Yen
Jewel	stairs, ladder	grievance grief, slightly tinged with hatred, resent.

玉	階	生	白	露
Gioku	kai	sei	baku	ro
Jewel	steps	grow	white	dew

The jewel stairs have already become white with dew
(dew was thought to grow on things)

夜	久	侵	羅	襪
Ya	kiu	shin	ra	betsu
night	long	permeate attack	transparent gauze	stocking

Far gone in the night, the dew has come up to my sock.

却	下	水	精	簾
Kiaku	ka	sui	shō	ren
let	down	water	crystal	curtain
		crystal		

So I let down the crystal curtain

玲	瓏	望	秋	月
Rei	rō	bo	shū	getsu
adj. transparent	adj. clear	look at	autumn	moon

And still look on the bright moon shining beyond.

Working only with Fenollosa's glosses and without any additional knowledge of Chinese poetry, Pound rendered the above poems as "The Jewel Stairs' Grievance":

> The jewel stairs are already quite white with dew,
> It is so late that the dew soaks my gauze stockings,
> And I let down the crystal curtain
> And watch the moon through the clear autumn.

In addition, he added a now famous "Note" explicating the logic of the poem:

> Note: Jewel stairs, therefore a palace. Grievance, therefore there is something to complain of. Gauze stockings, therefore a court lady, not a servant who complains. Clear autumn, therefore there is no excuse on account of weather. Also, she has come early, for the dew has not merely whitened the stairs, but has soaked through her stockings. The poem is especially prized because she utters no direct reproach.

Adapted from Fenollosa's explanation in the notebooks, this syllogistic "Note" not only explicates the Imagist aesthetic of obliquity and verbal concentration that Pound had been seeking to bring to Modernism for some time, but it also underwrites that aesthetic by grounding it in the putative bedrock of a long-standing foreign literary tradition with its own supposedly authoritative and clearly articulated system of value. In doing so, it presents a case of two separate cultural traditions coinciding with (or perhaps more accurately, reinforcing) one another with regard to some basic assumptions about both the "proper" aesthetic criteria for poetry, as well as certain "prized" traits of femininity, namely those of reticence, emotional intensity, and expressive subtlety. Thus, rather than simply giving an "accurate" report about the aesthetics of Chinese poetic expression, Pound's "Note" *enacts* or *asserts* a convergence between the cultural values of China and the West for the purpose of advancing his own poetic agenda. Needless to say, perhaps, this reveals less about Chinese poetry itself than it does about Pound's own interests and needs at the time of *Cathay*. But if this smacks of the pervasive "Orientalism" that Edward Said has so influentially documented in Western representations of the "East," it also illustrates the changing terms of translation itself as a mode of literary production within the execution of that process during the Modernist period.

The original poem belongs to the category of "abbreviated-form poems" (絕句), a genre that obeys specific metrical and thematic rules of composition.[38] As is well known, classical Chinese poetry often specifies referents and subjects without using pronouns, the conventions of "regulated verse" being so strong as to render them superfluous. Instead, verbs imply the relationship between the action and the actor or acted upon. Li Bai's poem contains no pronouns. Nevertheless, it remains clear that the voice of the poem belongs to a third-person narrator who observes the actions of the woman subject. The adversative/resumptive particle *que*, or *Kiaku* in Japanese (却), which can mean "but," "still," or "and then," is normally used in narration by a third-person observer. Hence it implies an exterior standard of judgment, or expectation against which the subject's actions contrast. The woman's actions, then, surprise the speaker in the original poem insofar as they differ from what he expects as a response to having waited alone long enough to have been soaked by the dew. Moreover, within the larger semiotic framework of Chinese poetry during the Tang period, women often stood in as figures for neglected government officials. So, by convention, readers would have understood this poem as the poet speaking about himself or some other male official in the guise of a woman.

Given that he studied such poetry with distinguished Japanese scholars of Chinese literature, Fenollosa probably at least had exposure to the form and its conventions, including those of voice. Interestingly, however, in his gloss he consolidates the speaker with the subject, injecting a possessive and a personal pronoun where a more literal rendering in English calls for third-person pronouns, as translations by others demonstrate.[39] In voicing the poem through its female subject, Fenollosa opens up an avenue of sympathy not explicitly available in the structure of the Chinese original. Where Li Bai's speaker may deign to pity the woman (or the male civil servant she represents) from his detached, implicitly superior perspective, Fenollosa's "personalized" narrator eliminates the distance between speaker and subject. This at once reflects and elicits a sense of compassion for her as an individual of equal status. Moreover, the consolidation of voice and subject underscores the righteousness of her grievance, a sense further emphasized by both his gloss on the word *yen* (怨) in the title as "grief, slightly tinged with hatred, resent [sic]" and the longer note included on the facing page in the notebook explaining the poem as a whole.

Pound, of course, knew nothing of either the textual or cultural conventions of Chinese poetry and the ways in which they differ from Western reading practices. Having access only to the glosses of each character (or more precisely, each transliterated Japanese word), rough translations, and Fenollosa's other, thoroughly unsystematic discussion of Chinese poetry throughout the notebooks, Pound had no way of recognizing the allegorical, quasi-political dimension of the original Chinese poem. Consequently, in arriving at his version of, as he first saw it, "Gioku Kai Yen," he adopts Fenollosa's slightly imprecise reading, and its consolidation of speaker and subject, without an awareness of the way in which it already elides various aspects of the original. Even so, in his presentation of "The Jewel Stairs' Grievance" in *Cathay*, Pound further amplifies the note of sympathy for the woman in the poem. This indicates his own concern at the time with the place of women both in the world at large and, more specifically, in the domain of poetry. Tightening and sharpening Fenollosa's somewhat flabby locutions, he introduces the adverbial intensifiers "already" and "so" in the first two lines of his translation. Drawing out the implicit logic of the poem as he understood it through Fenollosa, such words imply that the woman speaker knows exactly how long she has been waiting alone and is therefore justified in her complaint. And even if by replacing Fenollosa's causative "So" at the beginning of the third line with a merely resumptive "And" he gently mutes the idea of waiting and resenting somewhat by obscuring the logical connection between the female speaker's situation and her reaction, Pound still maintains the movement of images from an exterior surface to a physical action that implies an emotional state. Moreover, his "Note" appended to the poem in *Cathay* provides an interpretation that underscores the validity of the woman's complaint. Not only does he specify that the man she awaits "has no excuse on account of weather," but he asserts the value of the poem because "she utters no direct reproach," which implicitly accepts the justice of that reproach. Contrary to the general view of his tendencies toward indirectness in *Cathay*, Pound makes his poem less oblique and more judgmental even than Fenollosa's notes require. In "The Jewel Stairs' Grievance," the female speaker sits at the moral center of the poem, which implicitly asks readers to identify with her emotional situation as one both just and worthy of compassionate identification.

Even such a brief, relatively simple example as "The Jewel Stairs' Grievance," then, illustrates the way in which Pound engages through the practice of translation in *Cathay* in an examination of the place of women and women's voices in his own conception of poetry. This becomes even more clear in a poem like "The Beautiful Toilet," which lacks an explicitly acknowledged female speaker. In his notes for this poem, Fenollosa included the original Chinese characters, and this adds another dimension to consider in examining Pound's effort at translation:

[NO NAME]

青	青	河	畔	草	鬱	鬱	園	中	柳
Sei	sei	ka	han	sō,	utsu	utsu	en	chū	riū
blue	blue	river	bank side	grass	luxuriantly	spread	garden	in	willow

盈	盈	樓	上	女	皎	皎	當	窗	牖
Yei	yei	sō	jō	jo,	Kō	kō	tō	sō	yō
full in full bloom of youth	full	storied house	on	girl	white brilliant luminous	" "	just, face	window	door

娥	娥	紅	粉	妝	纖	纖	出	素	手
Gu	gu	kō	fan	so,	Sen	sen	shutsu	so	shu
beauty of face	" "	red of berry	powder	toilet	slender	" "	put forth	white, not dyed	hand

昔	爲	倡	家	女	今	爲	蕩	子	婦
Seki	i	shō	ka	jo,	Kon	i	tō	shi	fu
In former times	was	courtesan	house	girl	now	is	dissipated	son's	wife

蕩	子	行	不	歸	空	床	難	獨	守
Tō	shi	kō	fu	ki,	Kū	shō	nan	doku	shu
dissipated	son	go away	not	return	empty	bed	hard	only one alone	keep

In producing "The Beautiful Toilet," Pound displayed consummate skill in matching the reduplication of characters in the first three couplets of the original poem, while maintaining readability in English. This has been well demonstrated by both Yip (128–38) and Kenner (192–95) and I will not duplicate their efforts here. More important for the present purposes, I want to discuss the way in which Pound generates a speaking voice much more sympathetic to the woman subject of the poem, and more judgmental of her drunken husband, who "leaves her too much alone."

The original poem from which Pound produced "The Beautiful Toilet" is known in Chinese as "Song Number Three of the Nineteen Ancient Songs," and it follows the conventions of "ancient verse" (古詩).[40] Though a mark of colloquialism in its original context, the reduplication of characters in the opening three couplets signals, at least to an untrained reader like Pound who could only view it through a Western conception of poetic diction, a formality of tone that suggests a detached voice simply reporting the conditions of the woman's life and ending with an almost proverbial declaration of sympathetic understanding. This last line has been translated by Yip as "Empty bed! Alone! How hard it is to keep"; by Waley as "it is hard to keep an empty bed"; and by Giles, whose version Pound had read, as "Ah, if he does not mind his own/He'll find someday the bird has flown."[41] The first two of these translations preserve the declarative, impersonal quality of the Chinese original. The third deviates markedly from the original semantic content of the final line and in so doing overstresses an extreme interpretation of the potential for erotic transgression inscribed within it. All of them, however, maintain a detached, almost formal tone throughout.

Each of these translations differ in significant ways from Pound's version, at which he must have purposefully arrived, since Fenollosa's notes for this poem, though somewhat sparse, are quite clear and relatively semantically accurate. Indeed, Pound completely alters the tenor of the second part of the poem, and his modifications signal his effort to discover a vehicle for expressing sympathy for the woman subject of the poem. His translation reads as follows:

> Blue, blue is the grass about the river
> And the willows have overfilled the close garden.

> And within, the mistress, in the midmost of her youth,
> White, white of face, hesitates, passing the door.
> Slender, she puts forth a slender hand;
>
> And she was a courtesan in the old days,
> And she has married a sot,
> Who now goes drunkenly out
> And leaves her too much alone.

In his version, Pound eases the apparent formality and detachment of the original and clearly establishes the lamentability of the woman's position through a voice that issues a harsh judgment on her drunken husband. The speaker of "The Beautiful Toilet" occupies a position outside the woman subject's mind, yet familiar with her emotional and physical circumstances. The word "mistress" inserted in the third line suggests the voice of a serving girl or other such subordinate. This explains both the colloquialism of the second half of the poem, as well as the close sympathy for the woman. At least in Fenollosa's rough gloss of the original Chinese poem, the perceived voice belongs to a detached observer, one familiar with the woman's situation, but emotionally undemonstrative and unevaluative until at least the penultimate line. Pound's speaker, by contrast, enjoys a familiarity that allows her to reveal that the woman was a courtesan "in the old days," a phrase that suggests both a particular social status and a long-standing acquaintance with the woman in the poem. Moreover, his rendering of the binome 蕩子 as "sot" rather than the more stiffly formal "dissipated son" reinforces the colloquial, judgmental aspect of the speaker. Indeed, it reflects a purposeful intensification of the associations with alcohol only latent in the original and Fenollosa's gloss.[42] Pound then expressly generates an image of danger out of Fenollosa's simpler statement of fact. From "dissipated son go away not return," Pound reemphasizes the associations he began with "sot," and describes the man as one "Who now goes drunkenly out." Both the original Chinese and Fenollosa's notes for it lack specific tense indicators, which could have suggested a past completed action, that is, that the "dissipated son" or 蕩子 has long since gone away and not returned.[43] In his rendering, Pound casts such actions as ongoing habitual neglect.

Finally, as I mentioned earlier, Pound ends his poem with an explicitly moral judgment upon the behavior of the "sot" husband, eliding, or simply missing, the erotic, transgressive possibilities so overstressed by Giles. Though he eliminates the potential for infidelity by the woman, Pound nevertheless asserts her superior moral position, and hence the sadness of her situation. Given the circumstances of so many women left "too much alone" in England because of the departure of male family members and mates due to World War I, Pound manages through translation to explore and comment upon a pervasive emotional toll exacted upon women around the time of *Cathay*. He shows that the war affected everyone: those men at the front lines, and those women who suffered at home. Here Pound employs translation to present an obviously inequitable moral situation as a commentary upon one of the less obvious costs of the Great War. Such surprising sympathy not only betokens Pound's particular interest at this time in feminine subjectivity as an avenue for poetic expression, but it also adumbrates the general connection between translation as a literary mode and the exploration of the relationship between gender and writing during the Modernist period.

"The River Merchant's Wife: A Letter," one of the two undisputed masterpieces of *Cathay* (the other being "Exile's Letter"), also reflects Pound's attempt to explore for himself the poetic potential of feminine subjectivity by transforming the woman subject of the original poem into a figure more applicable to the situations of women in England, and Europe in general, during World War I. Pound's female speaker is more assertive both intellectually and emotionally than the woman speaker of Li Bai's original poem. Fenollosa's notes again omit the original Chinese characters, but they include semantically accurate glosses, as well as explanations of various allusions. Thus the changes in content and tone Pound made through the practice of translation reflect a definite pattern of intention. Unlike the two poems already discussed, Li Bai's 長干行 clearly features a woman speaker, as the first character in the poem, the first-person particle *qie* (妾), shows. Moreover, the poem's genre, the 行, or song, differs from the more regulated *shi* (時) genres of the other two poems already discussed in that it allows for a range of different speakers, and for a more relaxed tone and diction, which conceivably, via Fenollosa's notes and his own ear, suggested to Pound that this poem was a letter in verse form.

In his glosses for this poem, Fenollosa describes the work as a "narrative song," but he neglects to explain the connotations of self-reference in Chinese poetry. The *qie* (妾) character that Li Bai's female speaker uses is a humilific particle. During Tang times it was used as a first-person pronoun to demonstrate respect toward the addressee.[44] Fenollosa, however, only gives the Japanese pronunciation for the character and glosses it as "Chinese lady's I or my." This contributes to Pound's revisioning through translation of the woman speaker of the poem. Roughly the same, though inverse, situation obtains with the second-person pronoun *jun* (君) also employed early in the poem. Overall, because Fenollosa did not provide the connotations of respect inscribed within these Chinese pronouns, Pound produces a speaker more intimately familiar with her husband, who can, therefore, give voice to her own emotional investment and needs in their relationship.

More to the point in assessing the larger thematic significance of Pound's work as a translator in *Cathay*, the speaker of "The River Merchant's Wife: A Letter" displays a sense of loss and disappointment in the first line of the poem, when she relates that, "While my hair was still cut straight across my forehead/ I played about the front gate, pulling flowers." Fenollosa's notes here give the opening line simply as, "My hair was at first covering my brow," with the additional clarification of the image as "(Child's method of wearing hair)." The Poundian invention of the word "still" implies a nostalgia for the past and for her own innocence since lost through the maturing experience of marriage. It thus anticipates the note of regret in the recollection at the end of the first stanza of "The River Merchant's Wife: A Letter" that she and her husband were once "Two small people without dislike or suspicion"—a line that, in Ron Bush's words, "unmistakably announces that those feelings have arrived."[45]

Another deliberate, and perhaps even more telling, change that Pound works on the Fenollosa notes comes in the sixth and seventh lines of the original poem, which contain allusions to two famous Chinese stories. Fenollosa explains these references on the facing page of the transcriptions with two notes written in pencil:

> referring to the story of a youngster Bisei who once promised his love to be waiting for her below a bridge—she was late in coming, and the water gradually rose in tide, yet faithful to promise he clung onto the pillar and was drowned.
>
> Reference to a story where a wife, looking out for her husband, who was late in returning, she died in that position and was petrified. The rock still pointed out and was called Bofutai.

Several commentators have already explained the legends that Li Bai alludes to here, and Pound's changes are well known. Kodama even makes the case that by rejecting these allusions, Pound "sliced off the 'educated' side of the speaker's character."[46] However, if we recall that Pound himself had no idea that Li Bai alludes here to a story in the *Shi Ji* (史記), and that Fenollosa's notes merely recount the stories as if they were ubiquitous legends, the above assertion fails to be convincing. Instead, it seems likely that Pound considered these stories part of what every Chinese person, educated or not, would know. Thus, these changes must, I think, be attributed to his attempt to "translate" the poem into a vital idiom that could apply to the West and to the lives of women involved in World War I, that is, to his attempt to "make it new." Conceivably, Pound rejected the story of Bisei because no comparably renowned Western analog exists, and any allusion here would either have to remain enigmatic, or be explained with a footnote. Either of these options would mark the poem as unmistakably foreign, and hence lessen its potential applicability to World War I England, but also make for dull reading.[47] Pound's translation of the passage runs:

> At fifteen I stopped scowling,
> I desired my dust to be mingled with yours

> Forever and forever and forever
> Why should I climb the look out tower?

Pound transforms the allusion to Bisei into three "forever"'s, the simple repetition of which reinforces the idea that the speaker now looks back on her own earlier views of her relationship as somewhat naive in their aspirations to eternity. Pound decided, however, to keep the allusion to "the husband looking out terrace," possible because Widows' Watches on the East coast in America, where sailor's wives searched the horizons for the ships of their husbands coming into port, constituted a viable Occidental analog to the "husband looking out terrace" in the Chinese story. In addition, he also might have considered that such feelings as led to the construction of these towers were prevalent in England at the time due to the separation of couples that had been imposed by the war. Thus, Pound's rendering transforms both the nature of the speaker and the sentiment that she expresses into an analogous Western situation. Pound not only translates the semantic meaning of the poem, but he "carries over" the feelings that might have given rise to such words in the first place. The question that ends the stanza, then, remains ambiguous. Pound's speaker recalls her previous feelings for her husband, and also demonstrates an ongoing evaluation of her current emotional obligation to him. Her question indicates that she has begun to consider her own needs and what kind of life she wants for herself.

The next stanza concerns the husband's departure, and the Fenollosa notes give a literally accurate transcription of Li Bai's original:

十	六	君	遠	行	瞿	塘	灔	澦	堆
Jū	roku	kun	en	kō,	ku	tō	yen	yo	tai
16		you	far	go	name of locality		yen yo-rock eddy?		

At 16, however, you had to go far away, towards Shoku passing through the difficult place of Yentotai at Kuto
both yen and yo are adj. expressing form of water passing over hidden rocks

五	月	不	可	觸	猿	聲	天	上	哀
go	getsu	fu	ka	shoku,	en	sei	ten	jō	ai
5	month	not	must	touch	monkeys	voices	heaven	above	sorrowful

In May not to be touched
The ship must be careful of them in May   Monkeys cry sorrowful above heaven

In Li Bai's poem the wife warns her husband that the place through which he must travel is dangerous during the flood season during the fifth month of the year, and that the rocks "cannot be touched" (不可觸). Li Bai's speaker remains completely devoted to her husband's well-being, aware of the dangers he has already faced, and empathetic enough to be able to imagine the sorrowful cries of the monkeys over his head as he traverses the Three Gorges.[48] Significantly altering the literal sense of the passage in order to deepen the ambivalence he created in the immediately preceding stanza, Pound changes the above glosses into:

> At sixteen you departed
> You went into far Ku-to-en by the river of the swirling eddies,
> And you have been gone five months.
> The monkeys make sorrowful noise overhead.

Pound adds the personal address "you" in three of the four lines of the stanza, something not required, but easily allowed, by the absence of pronouns in the original and in Fenollosa's notes. These direct addresses distance the speaker from her husband, taking on an almost accusatory tone in the line "And you have been gone five months," a line that Pound obviously changed on purpose, since Fenollosa's glosses clearly translate the 五月 here in the original as "May." Pound's speaker, then, exhibits much more ambivalence toward her relationship with her husband than does Li Bai's dutiful wife. Sanehide Kodama has claimed that Pound's changes here, and his coinage of "Ku-to-en" out of "Yenyotai at Kuto," cast the speaker into "an innocent, modest, helpless and lonely woman."[49] But Pound could hardly have expected his audience to realize the mistake of the contraction, a surmise upon which this reading depends. Indeed, Pound himself could easily have mistaken the first three words of the sixteenth line in Fenollosa's glosses as a place name, and hence "mistranslated" it. Whatever the actual cause, it must be remembered that the poems of *Cathay* were presented, and largely accepted, as "straight" or conventional, semantically accurate translations. With the benefits of hindsight and deeper linguistic and cultural knowledge, critics have since recognized, and often enumerated, Pound's various errors and simplifications. But the significance of these "mistakes" must be evaluated in light of Pound's own ignorance of Chinese poetry and the general lack of knowledge about Chinese cultural traditions on the part of Western readers even today. Thus, the vast majority of readers of "The River Merchant's Wife: A Letter" would not have been in any position to realize the speaker's mistake and therewith consider her innocent, as Kodama suggests.

Moreover, Pound changes the speaker's warning to her husband from Fenollosa's "The ship must be careful of [the hidden rocks] in May" to the potentially accusatory "And you have been gone five months." In addition, the woman in Pound's poem then makes an observation that resembles an embryonic version of what would become one of the principles of Modernist poetics in the form of Eliot's notion of "objective correlative."[50] She notes that the monkeys over her head cry out sorrowfully, as if to match her mood.

Fenollosa's notes leave the exact location of the monkeys ambiguous, so Pound's decision here reflects a choice to focus upon the emotional experiences of the woman, rather than on the physical ones of her husband. The speaker here not only asserts her own hardships, but she implicitly admonishes her husband for having been gone too long.

Through the remainder of the poem Pound continues to trace the female speaker's complex emotions of love and disappointment; and the changes he makes to Fenollosa's notes reinforce the speaker's transformation into a woman who subtly, but irrevocably, demands emotional equality. For the most part, Pound adheres, though somewhat loosely, to the semantic content of the next three couplets in his translation, which demonstrate the woman's genuine love for her husband. She notices the mosses that have overgrown his footprints, which she has been reluctant to clear away because they remind her of him; and she sees the onset of autumn and the aging of paired butterflies, both of which highlight her own solitary experience of maturation. Pound then emphasizes the woman's understanding of her own feelings with the simple, declarative line, "They hurt me. I grow older." Fenollosa's notes for the line read thus:

感　　　此　　　傷　　　妾　　　心
kan　　shi　　shō　　shō　　shin,
affected (by) this　　hurt　　my　　mind
　　　　　　　　　normal
Affected at this (absence) my heart pains

坐　　　愁　　　紅　　　顏　　　老
za　　shū　　kō　　gan　　rō
gradually　lament　crimson　face　decay-older
　　　　　　　　　　　　　　become old
The longer the absence lasts, the deeper I mourn, my fine pink face, will pass to oldness to my great regret.

Pound eliminates the abstract references to the woman's pain and the line about her aging face. By stripping the embellishments off the original line, Pound creates a moment where the woman realizes how much she misses her absent husband, but also how much she is willing to do to keep their marriage alive.

The final lines of both poems are worth comparing in detail:

早　　　晚　　　下　　　三　　　巴　　　濉　　　將　　　書　　　報　　　家
Sō　　ban　　ka　　sam　　pa,　　yo　　shō　　sho　　hō　　ka
sooner (or)　later　descend　three　whirls　beforehand　with　letter　report　family-home
　　　　　　　　Name of spot of Yangtse Kiang, where waters whirl

If you be coming down as far as the Three Narrows sooner or later,   Please let me know by writing

相	迎	不	道	遠	直	至	長	風	沙
Shō	gei	fu	dō	yen,	choku	chi	chō	fu	sa
mutually meeting	not	say	far	directly	arrive	long	wind	sand

a port on the Yangtse
(the port just this side of Sampa)

For I will go out to meet you, not saying the way be far   And will directly come to Cho-fu-sa

Pound gives these lines as

> If you are coming down through the narrows of the river Kiang
> Please let me know beforehand,
> And I will come out to meet you
>   As far as Cho-fu-Sa.

Each of the changes Pound makes in his translation contribute to creating a woman speaker who, unlike the one suggested by the notes on the original, asserts her own needs and sets a limit on the emotional difficulties that she will bear willingly for the sake of her distant husband.

In Fenollosa's rough translation, the woman speaker addresses her husband, requesting that if he travels "*down as far as* the Three Narrows," would he let her know. The comparative preposition shows that his speaker knows and accepts her husband's continued travel, and therefore her own perpetual loneliness. She merely asks that if he should happen to travel to a place near enough for her to visit, would he please inform her so that she could traverse the distance. By contrast, the woman in Pound's poem fully expects her husband to return home. The only question that remains is the route he will take. Pound eliminates the "sooner or later" and changes "down as far as" into "through," thereby modifying the woman's chronic separation and loneliness into a temporary hardship, a distinction that arguably better characterizes the way women in World War I England viewed their imposed separations from their husbands. Moreover, where Fenollosa's woman says that she "will go out to meet, not saying the way be far./And will directly come to Cho-fu-Sa," Pound's river-merchant's wife quietly asserts the limits of her subservience: "I will come out to meet you/*As far as* Cho-fu-Sa" (emphasis mine), the implication being, "no farther." Pound's speaker does not love her husband any less than Li Bai's or Fenollosa's. She merely recognizes the legitimacy of her own emotional needs, and in turn, demands that her husband assume some responsibility toward them. In this poem, Pound acknowledges the legitimacy and necessity of including women's experiences in his subtle critique of the emotional impact of the Great War.

IV

In *Cathay* 1915, then, Pound not only carefully selected poems from the Fenollosa notebooks that focused on women, but he systematically amplifies their presence in his renderings of these poems. One convenient, though perhaps somewhat overly neat, explanation for Pound's interest in and sympathy with women in *Cathay* lies in his social and emotional circumstances around the period he worked on the collection. From the tine he received the notebooks in late 1913 to the time of the book's initial publication, Pound was involved with at first proposing and arranging his marriage to Dorothy Shakespear, which took place on April 20, 1914, and later with adjusting to the realities of married life. Moreover, one of Pound's early biographers, Noel Stock, indicates that the couple planned to continue their honeymoon in Spain the winter following their marriage, but that the war intervened.[51] Britain became involved in the war in July of 1914, only three months after the marriage. The proximity of all these events arguably made Pound sharply aware of the gendered emotional impact of the war, of the ways in which the same event affected men and women differently according to their sociosexual roles. From this perspective, Pound's marriage arguably played as large a role in creating the cognitive and emotional environment in which he compiled and translated *Cathay* as did World War I. Indeed, the translations of Chinese poetry in *Cathay* 1915 can be seen in part as exploring the divergent impact of the Great War along the axis of gender.[52]

Yet the matter of the social position of women (and by extension their place in the realm of poetry) constituted for Pound an even more lasting concern than did the emotional ramifications of war. As I mentioned earlier, of the four translations that he appended to *Cathay* in later collections of his work like *Personae* (1926), one poem, "A Ballad of the Mulberry Road," deals directly with a woman and the effect her beauty has on men, thereby exploring one of the traditional roles for the feminine within the domain of poetry.[53] The original version of this poem in Fenollosa's notes runs for fifty-three five-character lines, slightly more than three times the length of Pound's translation.[54] Elsewhere in the notebooks, Fenollosa gives a summary of the complete poem:

> A young girl named Rafu is in the field to pluck mulberry leaves. Her appearance—dress and face—are minutely described. end of 1st part. Then a noble passes by, riding in a carriage. She refuses. end of 2nd part. (This is minutely narrated, tho [sic] not very long.) Then she goes on to speak to the noble of her own husband—so he can't take her now.—this is 3rd part.

Through its narrative of a beautiful woman who steadfastly resists the advances of a gentry official, the original poem casts Rafu as the embodiment of the traditional patriarchal value of feminine fidelity. In translating this poem as "A Ballad of the Mulberry Road," Pound significantly alters the overall tenor of the original by rendering only the first fourteen lines, which comprise roughly the first part of the poem in Fenollosa's schema:

> The sun rises in the south east corner of things
> To look on the tall house of the Shin
> For they have a daughter named Rafu
>   (pretty girl)
> She made the name for herself: 'Gauze Veil',
> For she feeds mulberries to silkworms.
> She gets them by the south wall of the town.
> With green strings she makes the warp of her
>   basket,
> She makes the shoulder-straps of her basket
>   from the boughs of Katsura,
> And she piles her hair up on the left side of her
>   head-piece.
> Her earrings are made of pearl,
> Her underskirt is of green pattern-silk,
> Her overskirt is the same silk dyed in purple,
> And when men going by look on Rafu
>   They set down their burdens,
> They stand and twirl their moustaches.
>
>   (*Fenollosa MSS., very early*)
>   (*Personae* 1926, 140)

This translation exhibits several details characteristic of Pound's practice as a translator in *Cathay*. Most obviously, it demonstrates yet again his virtually total ignorance of the Chinese language and Chinese cultural practices at this point in his career, as well as his resulting complete dependence on Fenollosa's notes (and the mediation of Japanese) for understanding the semantic content of the original. First, he employs the Japanese pronunciation for the name of the woman in the poem.[55] Second, the silkworm diet consists of mulberry leaves, not mulberries.[56] And third, he employs the Japanese pronunciation, "Katsura," for the character 桂 in line eight of the original instead of its literal English meaning of "cassia" or "cinnamon," presumably for the sake of exoticism since in his notes Fenollosa renders this character as the decidedly mundane "ivy."

Much more important than these cavils regarding Pound's well-known limitations as a sinologist, however, "A Ballad of the Mulberry Road" confirms the persistently central importance of the feminine within the overall thematic ambitions of *Cathay*. In doing so, the poem underscores the extent to which Pound seeks in the collection through the practice of translation to explore and ultimately configure for himself the relationship between gender and poetry. For in his radically shortened rendering of the poem he not only elides any mention of his own considerable editing of the original as presented in the Fenollosa notebooks, thereby expressly employing translation as a means for producing a structurally and thematically distinct text, rather than merely a subordinate or derivative "version" of some "original" in another language. Equally significantly, he recasts the Chinese heroine from her role as the linchpin of a patriarchal moral order to one more akin to and common for the traditional Western muse, a role that Pound himself repeatedly came to assign to the feminine throughout his own later "original" verse: namely, that of an object of overt male sexual desire who, through the dangerously subversive potential of her physical beauty, threatens the establishment of culture by disrupting the regular flow of commerce. Throughout its development as a collection of translations of Chinese poetry, then, from the earliest stages of selection from the notebooks of Ernest Fenollosa to its initial publication in 1915 to the final organization it now displays, *Cathay* revolves around issues of gender and, in particular, the question of the place that women have both in society and in the world of poetry.

Over the course of his long and notoriously varied career as a translator and poet, Ezra Pound kept returning to the Chinese poetic tradition and confronting the relationship between poetry and gender. During later stages of his life, this trend found perhaps its clearest expression in an explicitly masculine sexualization of poetry. In 1958, several years after having published complete and thoroughly unorthodox versions of four works from the classical Confucian canon, *The Great Digest* (1946), *The Unwobbling Pivot* (1948), and *The Analects* (1951), as well as one of, as he called it, *The Classic Anthology Defined by Confucius* (1954), Pound reviewed Professor Mori's lectures on Chinese poetry in the Fenollosa notebooks at his castle residence in Brunnenburg and produced the following:

> Poetry speaks phallic direction
> Song keeps the word forever
> Sound is molded to mean this
> And the measure molds sound.[57]

While this quatrain, understandably, can be taken to buttress claims about Pound's essential misogyny, it more importantly demonstrates the remarkable persistence with which issues of gender, sexuality, and the place of the feminine in poetry repeatedly arose through his engagement with Chinese poetry and the practice of translation itself. As we shall see in the next chapter, Pound also pursued these concerns in his next major achievement in translation, the *Homage to Sextus Propertius*. Though ultimately less radical than *Cathay* in its challenge to conventional notions of translation as a literary mode, the *Homage* nevertheless departs in its own significant ways from translation orthodoxy. And the clamorous critical outrage it has elicited since its publication in 1919 has tended to obscure both the larger significance and the extent of its own investigation into the relationship between gender and poetry. Moreover, as I will discuss in chapter three, this association between translation as a literary mode and matters of gender came to operate within Modernism at large, enabling another writer and translator, H. D., to establish and advance the terms of her own vision of the relationship between poetry and the feminine. Poundian apologetics notwithstanding, *Cathay* must be read as one of his first forays in the oldest war of all, a conflict that continued to be waged on several fronts over the course of the Modernist period by means of translation.

Chapter Two

"My genius is no more than a girl"
Exploring the Erotic in Pound's
Homage to Sextus Propertius

I

In the introduction, I briefly discussed the treatment of Pound's *Homage to Sextus Propertius* as exemplary of the way criticism of Modernist translation has proceeded in large measure along distinctly undertheorized and even ahistorical lines. To expand upon this somewhat more fully: ever since its initial, partial publication in the March 1919 edition of Harriet Monroe's *Poetry*,[1] the *Homage* has elicited a sustained debate over its putative qualities as either an overly "free" distortion or a creatively "faithful" reproduction in English of Sextus Propertius's original Latin odes. Appearing almost immediately, in the very next issue of *Poetry* in fact, the first of these denunciations came from the University of Chicago classicist William Gardner Hale, who set the tone for an entire strain of criticism of Pound's efforts as a translator of Propertius by indicting all of the obvious liberties that the Modernist poet took with the original Latin text in producing his *Homage* simply as grammatical mistakes. Summarily declaring that "Mr. Pound is incredibly ignorant of Latin," Hale referred to "about threescore errors" in just the four published sections alone out of the twelve comprising the entire poem.[2] He went on to enumerate several specific "howlers" that he found particularly egregious, and these have become virtually obligatory points of discussion for all subsequent commentators on Pound's achievement in the *Homage*. I myself will attempt to address the larger significance of some of these notorious "errors" later in this chapter. For now I want merely to say that, despite (or perhaps more accurately, precisely because of) all its stark poetic insensitivity and rigid theoretical conservatism, Hale's screed effectively constrained criticism of the *Homage* for a long time to seemingly endless debate over the question of whether Pound's efforts merit the designation of "translation," as if the meaning of, that is the practices and procedures subsumed under, that term were permanently and universally fixed, not subject to historical development or alteration under the different forces of evolving literary conceptions, and as if the *Homage* itself did not contribute to a reconfiguring of the very dimensions of "translation" as a literary mode during the Modernist period.

Alongside the numerous, academically based philological attacks issued by Hale and others against Pound for his unconventional treatment of Propertius, various more broadly minded critics have also extended praise to the *Homage* for successfully conveying different qualities of the original elegies apart from their sheer semantic content, thus illustrating the split between "scholarly" and "artistic" approaches to translation that the Modernists helped to perpetuate through their unorthodox methods. Among these include, perhaps not surprisingly, T. S. Eliot, who again proved himself one of Pound's staunchest and most sympathetic readers when he wrote to explain why he decided to omit the *Homage* from his edition of *Ezra Pound's Selected Poems* (1928):

> I was doubtful of its effect upon the uninstructed, even with my instructions. If the uninstructed reader is not a classical scholar, he will make nothing of it; if he be a classical scholar, he will wonder why this does not conform to his notions of what translation should be. It is not a translation, it is a paraphrase, or still more truly (for the instructed) a *persona*. It is also a criticism of Propertius, a criticism which in a most interesting way insists upon an element of humour, of irony and mockery, in Propertius, which Mackail and other interpreters have missed. I think that Pound is critically right, and that Propertius was more civilized than most of his interpreters have admitted; . . . I felt that the poem, *Homage to Sextus Propertius*, would give difficulty to too many readers: because it is not enough a "translation," and because it is, on the other hand, too much a "translation," to be intelligible to any but the most accomplished student of Pound's poetry.[3]

Within this group finding significant, positive value in Pound's treatment of Propertius, which also includes R. P. Blackmur,[4] J. P. Sullivan has written the most thorough analysis of the *Homage* in its complex intertextual relation to the original Latin love elegies out of which it arose, and his *Ezra Pound and Sextus Propertius: A Study in Creative Translation* (1964) remains the essential work on that subject. From Sullivan's point of view, the *Homage* does indeed both constitute and largely succeed as a "translation," though one after the fashion of Johnson's *Vanity of Human Wishes* and Fitzgerald's *Rubáiyát* rather than of the more conventional, doggedly semantic sort, as the virtual invention of a generic category in his title suggests. In broadening consideration of the various ways Pound at once illuminates and imaginatively reproduces different aspects of Propertius while purposefully deviating from his literal meaning, such critics have provided a healthy corrective to the myopic philological dogmatism of Hale and others like him. As Sullivan wisely points out, "Were Pound as 'incredibly ignorant of Latin' (in Hale's words) as to make *unintentionally* the bloomers Hale accuses him of, he would not have been able to read Propertius at all or get anything like the sense out of his elegies that he actually does."[5]

Yet, for all the crucial insights and balanced linguistic assessment that critics such as Eliot, Sullivan, and others have offered into Pound's intentions and achievement in the *Homage*, they have remained fundamentally bound within the terms of debate as originally set forth by Hale. Failing to move beyond the basic question of "accuracy," they address neither the specific personal nor the broader cultural significance of Pound's expressly unorthodox treatment of Propertius. As a result, they fail to recognize the way Pound carries forward the inquiry he began in *Cathay* into the relationship between gender and writing in his own conception of poetry specifically through a radical approach to translating the love elegies of Propertius, which in turn helped to redefine the very parameters of translation itself as a mode of literary production in English. Indeed, Eliot's terminological waffling and Sullivan's coinage in their respective attempts to characterize the nature of Pound's accomplishment point directly to the extent to which the *Homage* sorely challenges, and thereby expands, a traditional notion of translation understood primarily in terms of the reproduction of semantic meaning from one language into another.

Accordingly, this aspect of the work has caused the most enduring difficulties, and more recent critics have employed various strategies in an attempt to resolve the issue of categorical identity. Donald Davie has gone so far as to try to avoid the problem altogether by defining it away, calling the *Homage* strictly an original poem.[6] Somewhat less extremely, Ron Thomas has taken up Eliot's tack and emphasized the function of "Propertius as dramatic mask" for Pound.[7] And finally, employing George Steiner's capacious definition for verse translation, which itself undoubtedly owes something to Pound's diverse and generative efforts in this arena, Daniel M. Hooley has most recently argued that the *Homage* remains "a poem [for] which a poem in another language . . . is the vitalizing, shaping presence; a poem which can be read and responded to independently, but which is not ontologically complete, a previous poem being its occasion, begetter, and in the literal sense, *raison d'être*."[8] Nevertheless, Hooley rightly sees that "Pound's redoubtable creative energies push translation to its conceptual limits."[9] Through such strategies, these critics have finally managed to shift the grounds of discussion away from the intractable problem of the generic status of the *Homage* to the thematic import of Pound's engagement with the amatory elegies of Propertius. Thus Thomas offers a tripartite explanatory scheme: "First, the poem reflects Pound's antiromantic rejection of his own earlier aesthetic treatment of Propertius in *Canzoni*. Also, it represents Pound's satiric reaction to contemporary pressures from pedants, poets, publishers, and, of course, the war (i.e., World War I) itself. Third, the *Homage* silhouettes an underlying crisis of aesthetic anxiety as Pound's secret inspiration for digging up Propertius in the first place."[10] Arriving at a slightly different, though broadly comparable, conclusion, Hooley argues that, "In this theme of love Pound was not interested. ... Pound saw an unacknowledged, perhaps more central, virtue in Propertius, his unmitigated loyalty to poetry itself and his desire to keep it free from the claims of the public and popular world. Pound saw 'love' in Propertius as essentially a metaphor for the poet's dedication to art."[11]

Hooley certainly advances criticism of the *Homage* by accommodating Pound's achievement to an established narrative about Modernist belief in the purity of art and the sanctified detachment of the artist from the tawdry concerns of the world. But as any number of more recent critics of Modernism have convincingly argued,[12] that narrative itself entails significant distortions, especially with regard to Pound and his repeated avowals (and efforts) "to COMMIT [himself] on as many points as possible."[13] Moreover, both Thomas and Hooley neglect to account for why Pound chose to pursue his satiric social or philosophical aesthetic concerns specifically through the medium of translation. After all, *Hugh Selwyn Mauberley* covers essentially the same thematic ground in the traditionally much more esteemed mode of original composition. Finally, in his sharply focused analysis based on the final section of the entire poem, Hooley replicates the tendency to examine Pound's diverse and numerous efforts at translation in almost complete isolation from one another (or, as in Thomas's case, at best only in relation to his renderings of other texts from the same language),[14] rather than as a fundamentally integral and even constitutive dimension of his entire career, as well as, indeed, that of Modernism as a whole. Consequently, as much of a definite improvement over previous criticism as he achieves, Hooley remains unable to clarify the particular importance of the *Homage* for Pound in his growth as a writer and especially an "original" poet. And neither he nor Thomas considers the significance of translation itself as a literary mode both within Pound's overall development and in the larger framework of Anglo-American Modernism.

In this chapter, therefore, I want to address all of these interrelated concerns by discussing the *Homage to Sextus Propertius* specifically in light of, on the one hand, Pound's immediately preceding feat of radical translation in *Cathay* and his exploration in that work of the place of women and women's voices in his own conception of poetry, and on the other, his subsequent use of translation in *The Cantos* as a fundamental technique of epic construction. Against this dual horizon, the *Homage* emerges as Pound's exploration of classical erotic verse and its attendant configuration of gender roles for poetry as a crucial step toward achieving an epic poetic stance. For over the course of the poem's twelve sections, Pound not only assumes, and thereby assesses, various traditional postures of masculine expression mapped by love poetry, but in doing so he also necessarily tests out the underlying model of their relation to the feminine for the process of literary production. Moreover, although throughout much of the poem he echoes, and even amplifies, Propertius's declared ambivalence toward the historical and mythic heroic themes typically associated with epic poetry as unsuited to his own particular genius, by its final section the *Homage* solidifies a conception of the erotic as both a logical precursor to and a driving force behind epic achievement. Such a framework helps to explain both the internal structure of the poem itself, as well as to clarify the specific importance of the *Homage* in the arc of Pound's overall career as the work most closely tied to the earliest, textually productive stages of his engagement with epic form at the time of the composition of the *Ur-Cantos*.[15] Finally, in demonstrating the enormous potential of translation as a literary mode for addressing issues of the relationship between gender and poetry within his own career, the *Homage* in turn arguably aided in making the practice of translation itself eminently recognizable to another writer of the period, as we shall see in chapter three, H. D., as a vital strategy for negotiating such concerns in her efforts to establish the terms of her own specifically feminine expressive modes and identity. In its complex attempt to define masculine and feminine poetic roles and its notorious generic (or more precisely, modal) ambiguity, then, Pound's radical treatment of Propertius displays the "irresolvable ambivalence toward powerful femininity"[16] that has been seen as characteristic of the Modernist attitude toward and concern with gender. But more important for my concerns here, the *Homage* also further particularizes that basic model by attesting to the capacity of translation during the Modernist period to serve as at once a conceptual and a practical means for individual writers to configure for themselves the relationship between gender and the process of literary production.

II

At one level, of course, it comes as little surprise that critics should for so long have given such time and attention to attempts at categorizing the *Homage* according to traditional notions of, in Eliot's words, "what translation should be." After all, Pound himself did nothing to help clarify matters. His private and public statements about the intentions underlying the work often frankly contradicted each other, thereby establishing fertile ground for virtually ceaseless debate. In a well-known letter of 1916 to Iris Barry, Pound writes of the prospective effort in terms betokening no radical ambition to engage in a kind of translation practice that would raise any controversy whatsoever. Dispensing a large dose of the sort of brashly didactic and sweeping educational advice for which he was becoming famous (not to say notorious), Pound offers a suggestion to Barry with both a rationale and a contingency plan that contains the seed of the *Homage*:

> You might learn Latin if it isn't too much trouble. If it is, I shall have to read a few Latin and Greek things aloud to you, and possibly try to translate 'em.
>
> The value being that the Roman poets are the only ones we know of who had approximately the same problems as we have. The metropolis, the imperial posts to all corners of the known world. The enlightenments . . .
>
> And if you CAN'T find *any* decent translations of Catullus and Propertius, I suppose I shall have to rig up something.[17]

But after the scathing negative criticisms issued by Hale and an anonymous reviewer in the *New Age*, as well as others,[18] following the early publication of the *Homage*, Pound began explicitly to renounce the term "translation" as an accurate description of his treatment of Propertius, therewith beginning a spate of defensive denials and equally caustic rebuttals that only served to confuse the issue further. In a 1919 letter to A. R. Orage, for example, he declared that "there was never any question of translation, let alone literal translation" (*SL*, 148–49) in his work on Propertius. Similarly, responding to another attack on the *Homage*, this one from one William Rowland Childe, as "so full of egregious blunders that a fourth-form boy would be whipped for the least of them,"[19] Pound wrote in 1920 that "Mr. Childe is in error when he states that I have published a translation of Propertius."[20] Again, in 1922 he explained to Felix Schelling: "No, I have not done a translation of Propertius. That fool in Chicago took the *Homage* for a translation despite the mention of Wordsworth and the parodied line from Yeats. (As if, had one wanted to pretend to more Latin that one knew, it wdn't have been perfectly easy to correct one's divergencies from a Bohn crib. Price 5 shillings.)" (*SL*, 178).

Despite abjuring the term "translation," however, Pound in the same letter both laid claim to having revealed something of (even academic) import about

Propertius and challenged the idea of the *Homage* as being simply his own "original" work:

> I do think, however, that the homage [sic] has scholastic value. MacKail (accepted as "right" opinion on the Latin poets) hasn't, apparently, *any* inkling of the *way* in which Propertius is using Latin. Doesn't see that S.P. is tying blue ribbon in the tails of Virgil and Horace, or that sometime after his first "book" S.P. ceased to be the dupe of magniloquence and began to touch words somewhat as Laforgue did. . . .
>   And "original"??? when I can so easily fit into the words of Propertius almost thirty pages with nothing that isn't S.P., or with no distortion of his phrases that isn't justifiable by some other phrase elsewhere? (*SL*, 178, 181)

Finally, even as late as 1931 Pound found himself defending the *Homage*. Responding to a letter by Harriet Monroe to the editor of the *English Journal*, he gave his most systematic answer to Hale's initial critique and the ensuing debacle. I quote the entire letter for the additional light it sheds on Pound's own sense of his achievement and the details of his practice in the *Homage*:

> Sir: it is fatiguing to argue about one's own work, but Miss Monroe's persistent errors seem to demand a reply.
>
> 1. Four sections of a poem written in 12 sections does not constitute a whole poem.
> 2. My *Homage to Sextus Propertius* is *not* a translation of Propertius.
> 3. I am unable to imagine a depth of stupidity so great as to lead Miss Monroe or the late Hale into believing that I supposed I had found an allusion to Wordsworth or a parody of Yeats in Propertius.
> 4. I did not at the time reply to Hale because I could not assume he had seen the entire poem.
> 5. Hale's "criticism" displayed not only ignorance of Latin but ignorance of English.
> 6. If Miss Monroe is unable to discover proof of Hale's ignorance I will (if any interest be now supposed to inhere in the subject) on receipt of a copy of Hale's "criticism" indicate his errors. Miss Monroe appears to preserve the superstition that a man is learned, or, *me hercule*, infallible *because* he is a professor.
>
> P. S. As Miss Monroe has never yet discovered what the aforementioned poem is, I may perhaps avoid charges of further mystification and obscurity by saying that it presents certain emotions as vital to men faced with the infinite and ineffable imbecility of the British Empire as they were to Propertius some centuries earlier, when faced with the infinite and ineffable imbecility of the Roman Empire. These emotions are given largely, but not entirely, in Propertius's own

terms. If the reader does not find relation to life defined in the poem, he may conclude that I have been unsuccessful in my endeavour. I certainly omitted no means of definition that I saw open to me, including shortenings, cross cuts, implications derivable from other writings of Propertius, as for example the "Ride to Lanuvium" from which I have taken a colour or tone but no direct or entire *expression*. (*SL*, 230)[21]

Thus, even as he retreated from any sort of explicit claim to "translation," Pound nevertheless consistently maintained, indeed insisted, on having largely achieved in the *Homage* the traditional ideal of translation, namely preserving all at once a thematic, tonal, as well as lexical "fidelity" to "Propertius's own terms." Every apparent concession to the wave of criticisms against the *Homage* brought with it an even more forceful counter-assertion by Pound justifying his achievement along different procedural lines.

I have indulged in rehearsing the famous early controversy surrounding the status of the *Homage* specifically in order to stress the extent to which Pound aggressively blurs any categorical distinction between "translation" and "original" composition by utilizing the reproduction of semantic meaning from a work in another language as a constitutive, and even primary, technique in the creation of a text with its own particular ambitions to cultural signification. For as his defiant admission about the various "means of definition" he used in producing the work makes clear, Pound sought in the *Homage* not simply to render, whether literally, freely, or otherwise, the mere semantic meaning of Propertius's *Elegiae*; rather, he employed translation as both a conceptual strategy and a concrete textual device to attempt to articulate a freshly vital "relation to life," to apply the achievement of Propertius to his own contemporary circumstances, to take an ancient text, in other words, and "Make it New." Ultimately, the *Homage* remains less radical in its departure from orthodox translation methodology than *Cathay*, since Pound actually could read the Latin with which he worked,[22] while he never really gained a functional, much less accurate, understanding of Chinese. On the other hand, with the famous exception of "The River Song," in which he mistakenly assimilated two poems into one, Pound generally respected the textual integrity of the individual Chinese lyrics he rendered in *Cathay*, whereas in his treatment of Propertius he frequently and quite freely stitched together parts of separate elegies to produce different sections of the *Homage*.[23] In any event, precisely because of the greater historical centrality of and consequent familiarity with the classics in the Anglo-American cultural tradition, the *Homage* aroused a hotter controversy. Accordingly, it presented a more immediately noticeable challenge to the conceptual dimensions, and therefore the practical constraints, of translation as a literary mode. It thus stands as one of the great ironies in the history of English literary translation that a work so initially and persistently reviled as the *Homage to Sextus Propertius* should have come to exert such an enormous impact on the transmission of the classics through its influence on the efforts of such subsequent figures as Robert Lowell and Louis Zukofsky, a matter that I will take up in greater detail in chapter seven.

Of course, as the above letters and other of his writings on the subject clearly indicate, a significant revisionist impulse informs Pound's treatment of Propertius. Exemplifying his notion of "Criticism by translation" (*LE*, 74), the *Homage* enacts an attempt at once to redefine the position of Propertius within the classical canon at the time in general and to recast the prevailing image of him as simply a romantic elegist who uncritically evinced the values and employed the language of sentiment in particular. Thus, in his reply to the anonymous review in *The New Age*, Pound scoffed at the dominant scholarly view of the Latin poet:

> given the "Ride to Lanuvium," even Professor MacKail [sic] might have suspected that there was something in Propertius apart from the smaragdites and chrysolites, and that this poet of later Rome was not steeped to the brim in Rossetti, Pater and Co., and that, whatever heavy sentimentality that was in Propertius's juvenilia, it is not *quite* the sentiment of thirteenth-century Florence decanted in the tone of the unadulterated Victorian period.[24]

And in the same letter, he openly ridiculed the established hierarchy of classical authors that conventionally celebrated Horace and Virgil when he posed the rhetorical question: "did Propertius who brought a new and exquisite tone into Latin...tremendously care for writing a language that was not the stilted Horatian peg-work or Georgian maunder of Maro?" (83). To put it another way, in these responses Pound challenges the reigning conception of Propertius in English at the time, a conception that itself arose as a result of the particular ideology of "fluency" that governed translation as a literary mode during the Victorian era.

To correct the ostensible errors or oversights in the accepted view of Propertius, Pound used all the "means of definition" mentioned above, as well as distortion of literal semantic meaning, to highlight tonal irony and amplify the themes of anti-imperialism and artistic independence. Critics have variously debated both the "accuracy" of Pound's unconventional interpretation and the extent to which he maintains the overriding amatory theme.[25] But as Ron Thomas aptly points out, whatever actual insights it affords into the original text, such a reading reveals as much or more about Pound and his concerns at the time of the *Homage* as it does about Propertius and his during Augustan Rome.[26] Consequently, Pound's treatment of

Propertius defies any easy categorization according to the simple binary opposition between "translation" (of whatever sort) and "original" composition. Instead, the *Homage* can perhaps be most productively conceived as a text wherein Pound carefully *orchestrates* certain themes already present in Propertius, some manifestly evident and others only latent, which he in turn manipulates and in some instances even inverts by various means to suit his own expressive purposes. Rather than simply a "faithful," "free," or even "creative" translation, the *Homage to Sextus Propertius* constitutes arguably the first of many Modernist works in which the *practice* of translation functions as a fundamental method of textual construction. In this respect, it also resembles a "parody" in the classical sense of *Parôdia*, or a "singing alongside" something else, the creation of different meanings to the same tune or words.

Far from merely splitting terminological hairs, this distinction focuses primary critical attention on the *Homage* itself instead of Propertius's Latin *Elegiae* as an ideal toward which Pound can at best only approach asymptotically. For Pound's text, constructed by means of translation, not only exhibits both its own internal structural logic and a particular dynamics of expression, but it conveys meaning at virtually every level of its engagement with its source, from instances of felicitous or "accurate" rendering to examples of egregious "mistranslation." Indeed, such a perspective offers a way to explain the broader significance of Pound's very decision to employ a writer famous for his romantic elegies as a mask or *persona*, since, given the considerable liberties he took with Propertius's literal meaning in the *Homage*, he could have conceivably appropriated the work of virtually any Latin poet and shaped its contents to suit, and thereby authorize, his own stated concerns about artistic independence and "the infinite and ineffable imbecility of...Empire." For in taking a Latin writer known almost exclusively as a love poet, who was at the same time much less renowned for his achievement in this arena than either Ovid or Catullus, as an instrument through which to voice his other thematic interests, Pound accomplishes at least two things. First, he indulges his iconoclasm by trumpeting his apparent independence from, as well as contempt for, the establishment values of canonical classical scholarship. In this regard, the *Homage* resonates with, and likely even helped to inspire, the views of other Modernists such as Yeats and H. D. in their own rejections of formal training in the classics as a barrier to authentic translation. Second, and more important for my purposes here, he implicitly examines the contemporary signifying potential available within the various conventions of classical erotic verse and its attendant deployment of masculine and feminine poetic roles. At the most basic level of its titular subject, then, the *Homage* advances the inquiry into the relationship between gender and poetry that Pound began in *Cathay* into the precise terms of a personally enabling ideological configuration between gender and poetry. This second aspect of the meaning of his engagement with Sextus Propertius as both a literary predecessor and a *persona* in the *Homage* underscores one of the functions of translation as a literary mode during the Modernist period to serve as at once a conceptual strategy and a practical technique for exploring, and indeed defining, the relationship between gender categories and the process of literary production.

III

From the very outset of the *Homage*, Pound displays his concern with assessing the current viability of the traditional arrangement of gender roles in classical erotic verse. Highlighting, and even amplifying, Propertius's own stated commitment in Latin to the love lyric as his most fitting and desired mode of expression, Pound begins the *Homage* with a treatment of the initial poem of Book III of Propertius's *Elegies*.[27] Starting with the opening lines of his source:

> Callimichi Manes et Coi sacra Philetae
> > in vestrum, quaeso, me sinite ire nemus.
> primus ego ingredior puro de fonte sacerdos
> > Itala per Graios orgia ferre choros.
> dicite, quo pariter carmen tenuastis in antro?
> > quove pede ingressi? quamve bibistis aquam?[28]

Pound establishes the unique terms of his own work in producing the loose, practically jaunty rendering:

> Shades of Callimachus and Coan ghosts of
> > Philetas
> It is in your grove I would walk,
> I who come first from the clear font
> Bringing the Grecian orgies into Italy,
> > and the dance into Italy.
> Who hath taught you so subtle a measure,
> > in what hall have you heard it;
> What foot beat out your time-bar,
> > what water has mellowed your whistles? (*I*, 207)

Clearly departing from any sort of typical translational idiom, and especially that of his immediate Victorian predecessors, Pound already exhibits the casual disregard for such grammatical niceties as number, case agreement, and accepted norms of semantic equivalence that so incensed Hale. As comparison with more conventionally accurate versions clearly shows, the original Latin refers to a single "shade," or "Manes," as well as to "rites" (for "sacra") instead of "ghosts." Moreover, "orgia" agrees with "Itala," and has a standard meaning of "mysteries" rather than the more sexually connotative "orgies," so that Propertius speaks of "bringing Italian mysteries [into the grove] in dances [i.e., poetic rhythms or meters] of Greece." Finally, though he conveys the basic pragmatic sense of the rhetorical questions in the last couplet of the opening Latin passage, Pound loosens the diction considerably, adding such colloquial, largely invented phrases as "time-bar," and "mellowed your whistles" for the decidedly more mundane *bibistis* (second-person plural for "did drink").

The sheer abundance and character of such "errors" together underscore that Pound definitely did not seek in the *Homage* to achieve any sort of precise grammatical accuracy, but rather to produce a distinctively ironic tone. More important, Pound's sharpest deviation from the literal meaning of the Latin, where he boasts of "Bringing the Grecian orgies into Italy/and the dance into Italy," magnifies the erotic charge carried by the English lines so that the *Homage* begins by tacitly claiming a connection between poetic vocation and ritual sexual (rather than spiritual) knowledge. Such an assertion already reflects a desire to establish an enabling, if decidedly traditional, configuration between masculine and feminine roles for the purposes of poetic expression. As I argued in the previous chapter, Pound's notoriously masculinist views about the gender of Modernist poetry did not emerge fully formed and then remain static, but rather grew increasingly virulent over the course of his career. Accordingly, then, such subtle, yet undeniable posturing about the esoteric sexual wisdom of the poet at the opening of the *Homage* represents less a solid conviction than an instance of exploratory bravado. For in the very glaring extremity of their departure from the strict semantic content of the original, these lines bespeak a response to persistent anxiety about the relationship between the masculine and feminine in poetry, an exaggerated declaration of belief put forth to allay a lingering uncertainty through sheer force of overstated will.[29]

A desire to assess the contemporary viability of different traditional postures of masculine poetic expression helps to explain both the overall tenor and several important details of Pound's treatment of Propertius throughout the rest of Section I. Thus he casts the Latin poet's exclamatory and distinctly figurative dismissal of war poetry in favor of his own finely polished amatory verse in the next couplet of III, i, "ah, valeat, Phoebum quicumque moratur in armis!/exactus in tenui pumice versus eat,"[30] in terms that present the aggressively martial form of masculine expression as terminally failing to evince an aesthetic of Imagist precision. Such repudiation assimilates Propertius's original contrast to Pound's own contemporary system of value, thereby indicating the extent of his own investment in the problem of deciding between the two poetic avenues. Moreover, in adding the phrase "as we know" to his rendering of the first line of the couplet, and in deviating markedly from the literal meaning of the second, Pound conveys an attitude of heavy ennui that produces the characteristic ironic tone of the *Homage*:

> Out-weariers of Apollo will, as we know, continue
>   their Martian generalities,
> We have kept our erasers in order.

Hence, too, Pound maintains and even extends Propertius's subsequent gentle mockery of officious imperial verse to include Empire itself, both of which, together with war poetry, constitute traditionally masculine domains of achievement:

> Annalists will continue to record Roman reputa-
>   tions,
> Celebrities from the Trans-Caucasus will belaud
>   Roman celebrities
> And expound the distentions of Empire.

And yet, a decided ambivalence colors the way Pound goes on to render Propertius's stated preference for love poetry over martial or imperial verse as the appropriate avenue for his own expression. Such uncertainty manifests not only in the tone that arises from his adoption of an ironic stance:

> I ask a wreath which will not crush my head.
>   And there is no hurry about it;
> I shall have, doubtless, a boom after my funeral,
> Seeing that long standing increases all things
>   regardless of quality.

It also marks the gusto with which Pound recounts various events of the Trojan conflict and attributes their enduring renown specifically to the efforts of Homer, rather than simply to the passage of time, as in the original:

> And who would have known the towers
>   pulled down by a deal-wood horse;
> Or of Achilles withstaying waters by Simois
> Or of Hector spattering wheel-rims,
> Or of Polydmantus, by Scamander, or Helenus and
>   Deiphobos?
> Their door-yards would scarcely know them, or
>   Paris.

> Small talk O Ilion, and O Troad
> twice taken by Oetian gods,
> If Homer had not stated your case![31]

Over and above its explicit statement, the tangibly vibrant tempo of this passage points to the well-known, monumental importance of the archetypal epic poet as an inspirational model for Pound, as well as for so many other Modernist writers, most obviously Joyce.[32] In this respect, Section I of the *Homage* reflects in miniature the conceptual problem driving the entire work, namely Pound's struggle to decide among various models of masculine achievement within his ongoing efforts to establish the terms of his own poetic expression.

Even more telling, perhaps, an overriding drive to determine the proper configuration between the masculine and feminine in his own conception of poetry provides a rationale for what has become the most infamous of Pound's many departures from the literal semantic meaning of Propertius in the *Homage*. I refer here to Pound's treatment of the couplet "Carminis interea nostri redeamus in orbem,/gaudet ut solito tacta puella sono," which correspond to the lines in Section I:

> And in the meantime my songs will travel,
> And the devirginated young ladies will enjoy them
> when they have got over their strangeness,

In his critique, Hale singled out this passage as "peculiarly unpleasant" and, giving the more conventionally literal translation, "Meanwhile let me resume the wonted round of my singing; let my lady, touched (by my words), find pleasure in the familiar music," he went on to argue that "Just possibly, though not probably, Propertius meant 'young ladies' rather than 'my lady.' But there is no hint of the decadent meaning which Mr. Pound read into the passage by misunderstanding *tacta*, and taking the preposition *in* as if it were a negativing part of an adjective *insolito*."[33]

For his part, Pound responded with both an ad hominem counter-attack against Hale and the entire system of Victorian aesthetics that he represented, as well as a defense, on the very grounds of Hale's challenge, of the ultimately more accurate grammatical and tonal precision of his own version:

> AND as for accuracy, what are we to say to the bilge of rendering "puella" by the mid-Victorian pre-Raphaelite slush of "my lady"?...
>
> I note that my translation "Devirginated young ladies" etc. is as literal, or rather more so than his. I admit to making the puella (singular) into plural "young ladies." It is a possible figure of speech as even the ass admits. Hale, however, not only makes the "girl" into "my lady," but he has to supply *something for her to be* "*touched* BY." Instead of allowing her to be

> simply *tacta* (as opposed to *virgo intacta*), he has to say that she is touched (not, oh my god, no not by the———of the poet, but by "my words"). Vide his own blessed parentheses. (*SL*, 149–50)

Over the years, both sides of the issue have been repeatedly argued without the establishment of a solid consensus.[34] But however one assesses the ultimate legitimacy of Pound's overtly sexualized rendering, his very predisposition to sensing the suggestive undertones of Propertius's diction, along with his patent willingness—even insistence—in calling attention to those possibilities through his unorthodox translation, together strongly indicate the depth of his concern in the *Homage* with (hetero)sexuality as it affords a powerfully enabling configuration of masculine and feminine roles for the purposes of poetic expression.

This effort to discover the terms of a proper conception of the relationship between gender and poetic production also clarifies the motivation behind such otherwise puzzling lines in Section I as:

> Yet the companions of the Muses
>   will keep their collective noses in my books,
> And weary with historical data, they will turn to my
>   dance tune.

For in this passage Pound not only departs significantly from the meaning of the original Latin, which merely reads: "at Musae comites et carmina ara legenti,/nec defessa choris Calliopea meis."[35] But in purposefully broadening the scope of Propertius's claim about the appeal of his verse with an invented disparagement of "historical data" as an appropriate subject for poetry, Pound voices a sentiment that stands in direct contrast, and possibly even contradiction, to his subsequent, monumental attempt in *The Cantos* to write a "poem including history." Furthermore, the sustained attention that Pound gives throughout the *Homage* to Propertius's concern with the dimensions of his reputation and the precise nature of his "genius" as a poet also betoken an interest in testing different traditional postures of masculine poetic articulation for both their personal and contemporary viability. Hence Pound concludes Section I without any major departures from or additions to Propertius's original paean to literary immortality:

> Flame burns, rain sinks into the cracks
> And they all go to rack ruin beneath the thud of the
>   years.
> Stands genius a deathless adornment,
>   a name not to be worn out with the years.

In Section II, Pound explicitly takes up the issue of "genius" and its relation to subject matter through his treatment of elegy III, iii, thereby continuing to probe the range of thematic and expressive possibilities of love poetry. In this elegy, Propertius recounts a dream wherein Apollo, the god of poetry, and Calliope, the muse of epic or heroic verse, both berate the poet for presuming even to think of venturing outside the domain of the erotic. The opening lines describe Propertius's vision of writing about such mytho-historical topics as the kings of Alba and their heroic deeds. As part of this vision, Propertius refers to one of his predecessors, the Latin poet Ennius, who wrote on such explicitly heroic and even imperial subjects as the military exploits of the Horatii and the Curian brothers, the famous delaying tactics of the general Fabius, various events of the Second Punic War, and the Roman victory over Hannibal. Pound's taste for this elegy indicates his concern at the time of the *Homage* over deciding for himself between historical epic poetry on the one hand and erotic verse on the other. Moreover, in the details of his rendering he both intensifies the mild irony of the original Latin and personalizes the situation depicted by Propertius. Thus in the opening lines of Section II, Pound employs careful word choice and repetition to mock the pretense to writing about history:

> I had been seen in the shade, recumbent on
> > cushioned Helicon,
> The water dripping from Bellerophon's horse,
> Alba, your kings, and the realm your folk
> > have constructed with such industry
> Shall be yawned out on my lyre—with such industry.

And whereas the original accurately presents Ennius as the one who produced works about different historical events, in the *Homage* Pound as speaker assumes the onus of authorship, going so far as to mention it twice, thereby revealing his concern with the problem:

> I had rehearsed the Curian brothers, and made
> > remarks on the Horatian javelin
> (Near Q. H. Flaccus' book-stall).
> "Of" royal Aemilia, drawn on the memorial raft,
> "Of" the victorious delay of Fabius, and the left-
> > handed battle at Cannae,
> Of lares fleeing the "Roman seat" . . .
> > > I had sung of all these
> And of Hannibal,
> > and of Jove protected by geese.

Smaller deviations from the Latin, such as his invention of the parenthetical reference to the bookstall of Q. H. Flaccus, reflect and reinforce his perception of Propertius as a literary renegade who opposed the imperial sycophancy of Horace and Virgil.[36]

In contrast, Pound's treatment of the speeches by Apollo and Calliope in which they urge Propertius to dismiss thoughts of writing about heroic subjects adheres fairly closely to the strict semantic content of the Latin, as for example the lines:

> And Phoebus looking upon me from the Castalian
>   tree,
> Said then "You idiot! What are you doing with
>   that water:
> "Who has ordered a book about heroes?
>   "You need, Propertius, not think
> "About acquiring that sort of a reputation."

Similarly, Calliope declares later in Section II:

> "Content ever to move with white swans!
> "Nor will the noise of high horses lead you ever to
>   battle;"

Such localized "fidelity" to the literal meaning of Propertius further underscores that beneath the rampant irony and apparent flippancy of the *Homage* lies Pound's genuine concern over deciding between heroic epic and erotic lyric as models for his own masculine poetic expression.

Of the departures from the Latin that Pound does commit in these parts of Section II, one in particular has inspired repeated criticism and so deserves specific comment, namely his rendering of:

> "quippe coronatos alienum ad limen amantes
>   nocturnaeque canes ebria signa morae
> ut per te clausas sciat excantare puellas,
>   qui volet austeros arte ferire viros."[37]

Here, Calliope simply identifies the subjects about which Propertius will write, and in his treatment Pound produces one of his most famous "howlers" in the *Homage*:

> "Obviously crowned lovers at unknown doors,
> "Night dogs, the marks of drunken scurry,
> "These are your images, and from you the sorcer-
>   izing of shut-in young ladies,
> "The wounding of austere men by chicane."

As Hale accurately parses the error in his letter:

> Mr. Pound mistakes the verb *canes*, "thou shalt sing," for the noun *canes* (in the nominative plural masculine) and translates by "dogs." Looking around then for something to tack this to, he fixes upon *nocturnae* (genitive singular feminine) and gives us "night dogs"! I allow myself an exclamation point. For sheer magnificence of blundering this is unsurpassable. (p. 53)

Of course, from a strictly philological standpoint, Hale's analysis remains correct, if somewhat humorless, and no amount of grammatical contortion or reference to context can possibly redeem "Night dogs" as viable. But as Sullivan points out, Pound's invented image does possess "greater vividness" than the original line.[38] At the same time, Pound manages successfully to convey the basic pragmatic, as opposed to the strict grammatical, sense of the passage. He achieves this through quotation marks and tone rather than by explicit statement, as would have been the case had he rendered *canes* "accurately." Consequently, Pound's "mistake" here arguably stems at least in part from his commitment to a poetics of extreme verbal concentration and Imagist precision.[39] Moreover, in giving *canes* as "dogs" instead of "you will sing," Pound clearly "translates" on the basis of sound and aural similarity rather than strict grammatical relation and proper semantic equivalence, thereby opening up new avenues for translation itself as a literary mode. Similar, though less overtly "incorrect," examples in the passage include "austere men" for *austeros viros* (more typically "strict" or "stern men") and "sorcerizing" for *excantare* ("to charm forth") by means of the intermediary word "enchant." Thus, in the *Homage* Pound not only explores the range of possibilities of erotic verse, but in his manner of doing so he lays the foundation for such other feats of radical translation as Louis and Celia Zukofsky's remarkable, sound-based treatment of the odes of Catullus.

In Sections III and IV, Pound deepens his exploration into the possibilities of erotic poetry by assuming two conventional postures specifically identifiable with amatory verse, first the male lover who bemoans the unreasonable demands of his mistress, yet still extols the sanctity of his station, and second the paramour who seeks news of his beloved through an intermediary after one of their many quarrels. These parts of the *Homage* reflect Pound's engagement with the narrative dimensions of Propertius's *Elegies* and their poetic depiction of his tempestuous relationship with Cynthia. Appropriately, they each represent treatments of individual elegies as discrete poetic units, in particular III, xvi and III, vi respectively. Likewise, Sections I and II of the *Homage* both arise out of single elegies from Book III.

Beginning with Section V, Pound departs even more markedly from normal translation methodology by stitching together different segments from two separate elegies, II, x and II, i. Significantly, such a development in Pound's practice as a translator in the *Homage* coincides with the reappearance of the issue of choosing between heroic poetry singing the praises of war and Empire on the one hand and expressly personal erotic verse focusing on women on the other. Based on elegy II, x in which Propertius assumes an expressly Virgilian stance and celebrates the military exploits of Augustus, Section V opens with the announcement of an intention to take up the stately subject of imperial achievement and leave behind the lesser concerns of love. But in accord with his perception of an ironic strain running throughout the *Elegies*, Pound undercuts such a portentous ambition by putting into quotation marks Propertius's own self-deprecating justifications of his efforts in this unfamiliar arena:

> Now if ever it is time to cleanse Helicon;
> to lead Emathian horses afield,
> And to name over the census of my chiefs in
> the Roman camp.
> If I have not the faculty, "The bare attempt would
> be praise-worthy."
> "In things of similar magnitude
> the mere will to act is sufficient."
> The primitive ages sang Venus,
> the last sings of a tumult,
> And I also will sing war when this matter of a girl is
> exhausted.

Similarly, Pound ridicules the manner of imperial verse by casting Propertius's declarations in a mocking tone: "Oh august Pierides! Now for a large-mouthed/product."

For Parts 2 and 3 of this Section, Pound draws from the earlier elegy II, i, wherein Propertius explains his predilection for love poetry and avows his distaste for heroic themes. Such an immediate contrast with the sentiments expressed in Part 1 further undermines Propertius's stated intention to write in praise of Empire. But this juxtaposition of opposite views does more than merely reflect an ironic reading of the Latin poet. Equally important, it signifies Pound's own concern with assessing the differences between heroic epic and erotic lyric and their attendant configurations of gender categories for the process of poetic production. Thus, Part 2 opens with a proposition about the relationship between gender and poetry:

> Yet you ask on what account I write so many love-
> lyrics
> And whence this soft book comes into my mouth.

> Neither Calliope nor Apollo sung these things into
>   my ear,
>   My genius is no more than a girl.

Indeed, through his treatment of Propertius in the immediately succeeding lines, Pound at once offers and entertains a virtual theory of the feminine origins of poetry, as well as a conception of the erotic as rivaling, and even surpassing, the grandeur of epic and its traditional focus on masculine heroic achievement:

> If she with ivory fingers drive a tune through the
>   lyre,
>   We look into the process.
> How easy the moving fingers; if hair is mussed on
>   her forehead,
> If she goes in a gleam of Cos, in a slither of dyed
>   stuff,
> There is a volume in the matter; if her eyelids sink
>   into sleep,
> There are new jobs for the author;
> And if she plays with me with her shirt off,
>   We shall construct many Iliads.
> And whatever she does or says
>   We shall spin long yarns out of nothing.

Of course, such a vision hardly delineates a radical notion of either the category of gender itself or the role of the feminine within the process of literary production. After all, Pound merely invokes a decidedly conventional, indeed ancient, arrangement in positioning the woman as the source of poetic inspiration based precisely on her status as an object of male sexual desire. Nevertheless, with their clear focus on mapping a place for the feminine within the domain of poetry, these lines underscore the poet's concern throughout the *Homage* with discovering the terms of a personally enabling conception of the relationship between gender and poetic expression. And in doing so, they confirm the capacity of translation as a literary mode during the Modernist period to function as a manifold strategy for negotiating that concern. For Propertius's twin conceits about the feminine origins of his "genius" as a poet and the epic dimensions of eroticism offered Pound a powerful, if staunchly traditional, configuration of masculine and feminine poetic roles for poetry to set against that of heroic verse celebrating military achievement and Empire. Thus, while he rearranges the original order of the Latin lines in his treatment of this passage, Pound adheres closely to their basic semantic meaning. Hence, too, the conclusion to this section in the very brief Part 3, which not only ironizes conventional heroic masculine values by deploying them in an erotic context, but also establishes an explicit opposition between erotic and epic versions of the feminine:

> It is noble to die of love, and honourable to remain
> > uncuckolded for a season.
> And she speaks ill of light women,
> > and will not praise Homer
> Because Helen's conduct is "unsuitable."

Accordingly, then, Section V marks the crucial point in the development of the *Homage* when Pound expressly conjoins the issues of genre and gender. And this, in turn, defines a logic that enables him ultimately to recuperate heroic epic for his own masculine poetic expression by locating its origins in erotic desire rather than martial accomplishment and imperial celebration.

Fittingly, in Section VI Pound offers his most pointed critique of military achievement by treating lines from three separate elegies (II, xiii; III, iv; and III, v) in which Propertius, respectively, anticipates his own death, sings the praises of a planned war by Caesar, and, contrastingly, declares his own worship of peace. Strategically interweaving lines from each, Pound begins the section by marking imperial conquest as futile, since death ultimately erases the significance of any difference between victor and vanquished:

> When, when, and whenever death closes
> > our eyelids,
> Moving naked over Acheron
> Upon one raft, victor and conquered together,
> Marius and Jugurtha together,
> > one tangle of shadows.
>
> Caesar plots against India,
> Tigris and Euphrates shall, from now on, flow at
> > his bidding,
> Tibet shall be full of Roman policemen,
> The Parthians shall get used to our statuary
> > and acquire a Roman religion;
> One raft on the veiled flood of Acheron,
> > Marius and Jugurtha together.

In contrast, Pound declares poetry the realm of lasting achievement through his rendering of Propertius's fantasy about his own funeral rites, which, though modest and simple, nevertheless display sufficient ceremony by virtue of his literary accomplishment:

> The perfumed cloths shall be absent.
> A small plebeian procession.
> > Enough, enough and in plenty

> There will be three books at my obsequies
> Which I take, my not unworthy gift, to Persephone.

This common theme of death then raises the issue of commemoration, which becomes in the *Homage* not just an ingenious way to rebuke Cynthia for her fickle treatment of the poet while living, as in the original, but also a manner of poetic utterance that allows for both the expression of desire and an engagement with history and myth. Hence the distinctly elegiac note that colors the treatment of Propertius's admonition at the end of Section VI:

> You, sometimes, will lament a lost friend,
>   For it is a custom;
> This care for past men,
>
> Since Adonis was gored in Idalia, and the Cytherean
> Ran crying with out-spread hair,
>   In vain, you call back the shade,
> In vain, Cynthia. Vain call to unanswering shadow,
>   Small talk comes from small bones.

For the next three sections of the *Homage*, Pound again assumes conventional amatory postures. And appropriately enough, he returns to the practice of treating individual elegies, even going so far as to spread a single long elegy (II, xxviii) over the space of Sections VIII and IX. In Section VII Pound plays the triumphant lover who announces his joy and exults in the details of a night with his mistress.[40] At the opposite end of the emotional spectrum, the following two sections trace the course of the poet's emotions as he responds to his mistress falling victim to and then recovering from a grave illness. In Section VIII, he ironically addresses Jove and attempts through sarcastic humor to convince the gods to spare her life. And Section IX veers from despair to relief as he first vows to follow his mistress should she die, then appeals to the gods of the underworld to release her,[41] and, finally, playfully chides her to attend to her various obligations, which she has incurred as a result of her recovery, most notably "The ten nights of your company you have/promised me." The extreme conventionality of these sections illustrate the thoroughness with which Pound explores in the *Homage* the range of possibilities of erotic verse and its configuration of masculine and feminine poetic roles.

But if these sections signal Pound beginning to perceive the limits of a strictly amatory stance, Propertius's raptures also offer a conceptual genealogy for epic that liberates it from the establishment function of extolling imperial dominion or military conquest, thereby making it available as a vehicle for Pound's own masculine poetic expression. So in Section VII, a celebration of the power of love invokes two different mythic tales:

> "Turn not Venus into a blinded motion,
>   Eyes are the guides of love,
> Paris took Helen naked coming from the bed of
>   Menelaus,
> Endymion's naked body, bright bait for Diana,"
>   ————such at least is the story.

Pound's characteristic irony in the last, invented line notwithstanding, this passage establishes sexual desire as the originating force behind the events leading to epic.[42] In doing so, it outlines a vision that preserves the status of epic as masculine expression, while at the same time expunging the taint deriving from its use as an instrument of empire. Such a conception of the foundations of epic charts a path for Pound to move beyond the strictly erotic postures of the *Homage* and into engagement with myth and history in *The Cantos*.

Whereas the middle parts of the *Homage* focus on the most intimate occasions of erotic expression, the final three sections turn to the more social situations of love poetry, thus attesting to the broadened focus of Pound's evolving concern. So the fantasy sequence opening Section X, which assimilates II, xxixA and B, shifts to touch upon the dual themes of jealousy and imagined infidelity, both of which imply a third party within the erotic situation. And in Section XI, Pound confronts the extremes of eroticism as a poetic strategy by weaving together lines from three elegies (I, xv; II, xxxA; and II, xxxii) in which Propertius bemoans the torments of love. Combining the opening and closing lines of elegy I, xv, Part 1 of this section presents the ultimate consequences of the affair as decidedly negative, with the speaker himself embodying a warning:

> The harsh acts of your levity!
>   Many and Many.
> I am hung here, a scare-crow for lovers.

Following this, Part 2 offers an even more vehement depiction of the insidious power of love taken from elegy II, xxxA and rendered accurately:[43]

> Escape! There is, O Idiot, no escape,
>   Flee if you like into Ranaus,
>   desire will follow you thither,
> Though you heave into the air upon the gilded
>   Pegasean back,
> Though you had the feathery sandals of Perseus
> To lift you up through split air,

> The high tracks of Hermes would not afford you
> shelter.
> Amor stands upon you, Love drives upon lovers,
> a heavy mass on free necks.

In the course of constructing this emotional drama, Pound again incorporates a passage mentioning the events leading to the Trojan War. And he makes this reference even more explicit by naming Helen, where the original identifies her only as "Tyndaris," that is, "Tyndareus' daughter":

> A foreign lover brought down Helen's kingdom
> and she was led back, living, home;

Such a persistent concern with Helen and the genesis of the Trojan War betokens the evolution of Pound's interest in the *Homage* from the erotic to the origins of epic.

Concluding the entire sequence, Section XII takes up various thematic strands initially laid down throughout the earlier parts of the *Homage* to close out Pound's exploration of erotic poetic conventions. Most relevant to my concerns in this chapter, Pound goes out of his way to revive the mockery of epic through his treatment of Propertius's elegy II, xxxiv, in which the Latin poet first berates his friend Lynceus for trying to steal away Cynthia, then discourses on the significance of love poetry. Thus, as others have clearly shown,[44] Pound reverses Propertius's original praise of Virgil, giving instead a stinging parody of imperial epic:

> Upon the Actian marshes Virgil is Phoebus' chief of
> police,
>   He can tabulate Caesar's great ships.
> He thrills to Ilian arms,
>   He shakes the Trojan weapons of Aeneas,
> And casts stores on Lavinian beaches.
> Make way, ye Roman authors,
>   Clear the street, O ye Greeks,
> For a much larger Iliad is in the course of construc-
> tion
> (and to Imperial order)
> Clear the streets, O ye Greeks!

Similarly, Pound turns Propertius's celebration into mockery of even the impulse to write epic, inventing an allusion to ensure that no one misses the joke:

> Go on, to Ascraeus' prescription, the ancient,
>   respected, Wordsworthian:

And finally, overt "mistranslation" converts Propertius's original admiration for Virgil into bilious sarcasm. Yet even in their most overt departures from the semantic meaning of the original Latin, Pound's lines avow the power of sexual desire to give rise to poetic expression:

> Like a trained and performing tortoise,
> I would make verse in your fashion, if she should
>   command it,
> With her husband asking a remission of sentence,
>   And even this infamy would not attract
>   numerous readers
> Were there an erudite or violent passion,
> For the nobleness of the populace brooks nothing
>   below its own altitude.
> One must have resonance, resonance and sonority
>   ... like a goose.

Such a sense of the generative power of the erotic that arises from a distortion of original meaning underscores Pound's concern with (hetero)sexuality as a configuration of masculine and feminine roles for poetry throughout the *Homage*. And this, in turn, sheds a revealing light on the significance of the opening lines of Section XII, where Pound condenses, but otherwise accurately renders, Propertius's resigned response to the dangers of love in II, xxxiv:

> Who, who will be the next man to entrust his
>   girl to a friend?
> Love interferes with fidelities;
> The gods have brought shame on their relatives;
> Each man wants the pomegranate for himself;
> Amiable and harmonious people are pushed incon-
>   tinent into duels,
> A Trojan and adulterous person came to Menelaus
>   under the rites of hospitium,
> And there was a case in Colchis, Jason and that woman in Colchis;
> And besides, Lynceus,
>   you were drunk.

Pound's basic semantic accuracy here results in yet another reference to the (sexual) origins of the Trojan War, as well as a new one to the tale of Jason and Medea, itself one of the subjects of another epic poem, the *Argonautica* by Appollonius Rhodius.[45] Accordingly, then, these lines not only reiterate Pound's preoccupation with the erotic and its configuration of masculine and feminine poetic roles throughout the *Homage*. They also solidify a conception of sexual desire as the ultimate foundation for heroic action. In doing so, they provide a way for Pound to assume an epic stance by preserving an expressly masculine position of poetic expression, but one not constrained by the obligation to celebrate empire or military achievement. As he undoubtedly knew, this vision of the erotic as the foundation for epic also lies at the heart of Ovid's *Metamorphoses*. Ultimately, through his efforts in the *Homage*, Pound arrives at a conception of love poetry as the logical precursor to heroic epic, a notion that has its own roots in the very myths that he would use to attempt to explain history in *The Cantos*. After all, in classical mythology, Erato is Calliope's older sister.[46]

IV

Following his engagement with Propertius, Pound became much more dogmatically certain in his views about both poetry itself and women, as well as about the place of women in poetry. The contemporary satire of *Hugh Selwyn Mauberley* and the schematization of myth and history in *The Cantos* at once bespeak and arise from the confidence in having discovered a comprehensive position of masculine poetic articulation. Indeed, as we shall see presently, Pound soon came upon the occasion of another feat of translation to issue one of his most overtly masculinist statements about the relationship between gender and writing. Thus, the *Homage* marks not only a transition between Pound's early lyric concerns and the epic, historical ones of *The Cantos*, but perhaps even more tellingly, a crucial moment in the development of his sexist views about gender and its role in the process of poetic production. For in both cases, he got from one point to the other by fully exploring, and thereby exhausting for himself, the conventions of erotic verse through the act of translation.

Among Pound's early poetic achievements, *Cathay* and *Homage to Sextus Propertius* have consistently aroused the most passionate responses, typically effusively positive for the former, and frequently caustically negative for the latter. For each of these works, praise or censure generally arises from judgments based on its status specifically as a translation. Yet in both works, Pound departs radically from, and thereby expands the possibilities of, conventional translation methodology. In *Cathay*, he renders works from a language of which he possessed no (and finally never really gained any) formal knowledge. And in the *Homage*, he freely violates both the original textual organization and the strict semantic meaning of Propertius's *Elegiae*. Accordingly, then, the differential responses to these two works stem at least in part from the asymmetrical levels of knowledge about, as well as, implicitly, respect for, the Chinese and Latin cultural traditions respectively on the part of Western critics, a matter of such depth and moment that it deserves its own treatment in a separate essay. More directly relevant to the concerns in this study, however, in both works translation functions as at once a conceptual and a concrete textual strategy to explore the "proper" configuration of gendered roles in the process of poetic production. In *Cathay*, Pound considers the place of women and women's voices in his own conception of poetry. And in the *Homage*, he not only selects a love poet as both his subject and *persona* in the work, but in his rendering he focuses on the matter of love poetry and its ostensible superiority over epic. Thus, these two texts also participate in the ongoing attempts at the time to compose the idea of gender itself and to define its relationship to literary creation. Such a confluence of subject matter and compositional technique in Pound's two most renowned and important early achievements begs for more of an explanation than merely an appeal to stunning coincidence. Together, *Cathay* and the *Homage to Sextus Propertius* indicate a fundamental connection between translation as a literary mode and issues of the relationship between gender and poetry during the Modernist period. As we shall see in the following chapter, such a connection also underlies and helps to clarify specific details in H. D.'s development as both a Modernist and a self-consciously woman poet.

Chapter Three

"from Greece into Egypt"
Translation and the Engendering of H. D.'s Poetry

I

In the "Translator's Postscript" to his 1922 rendering of Rémy de Gourmont's treatise on sex, the *Physique de l'Amour*, Ezra Pound offers one of his most infamous speculations about the evolution of human creativity:

> It is more than likely that the brain is, in origin and development, only a sort of great clot of genital fluid. . . . This hypothesis . . . would explain the enormous content of the brain as maker or presenter of images. . . . I offer an idea rather than an argument, yet if we consider that the power of the spermatozoide is precisely that of exteriorizing a form, and if we consider the lack of any known substance in nature capable of growing into brain, we are left with only one surprise, or rather one conclusion, namely, in the face of the smallness of the average brain's activity, we must conclude that the spermatozoic substance must have greatly atrophied in its change from the lactic to coagulated and hereditarily coagulated conditions. . . . There are traces of [this idea] in the symbolism of phallic religions, man really the phallus or spermatozoide charging, head-on, the female chaos. Integrations of the male in the male organ. Even oneself has felt it, driving any new idea into the great passive vulva of London, a sensation analogous to the male feeling in copulation.[1]

Though he pretends to "offer an idea rather than an argument," and though, only a little later in the "Postscript," he makes an explicit gesture toward parity and "for the sake of symmetry ascribe[s] a cognate role to the ovule" (*NPL*, 150), Pound was clearly trying to revive for the sake of Modernism, as well as to assimilate to the discourse of the relatively new science of evolutionary biology, one of the oldest and most persistent tropes in Western culture, namely the traditional conception of artistic creation as an essentially male act, one that substitutes for, rivals, and ultimately even surpasses the female capacity for biological reproduction.[2]

Nor was Pound unique, or even original, among his Modernist contemporaries in linking artistic creativity to male sexual physiology and masculine experience. The aggressively masculinist view of literary production at which he arrived after his explorations in *Cathay* and the *Homage to Sextus Propertius*, most nakedly evident in his 1958 assertion that "Poetry speaks phallic direction," merely constitutes one particularly candid example of the implicitly sexualized and often polemical textual strategies by which such male writers as Eliot, Stevens, Hemingway, Williams, and Lawrence, together with Pound himself, all sought to transform the literary landscape as they both received and perceived it, waging, in Gilbert and Gubar's influential phrase, a "war of words" against the domestic and relentlessly sentimental idioms and sensibilities of their enormously popular and culturally dominant literary predecessors, women writers like Sara Teasdale, Elinor Wylie, Mrs. (Lydia) Sigourney and, in England, Mrs. Felicia Hemans. Indeed, feminist criticism has for some time now argued that many of the aesthetic strategies typically identified with canonical (male) Modernism—the use of ancient myths as an organizing framework and the cultivation of an impersonal, allusive, and deeply learned style, for example—represent calculated responses to and vehement reactions against the "astonishing rise of both critically and culturally successful women of letters throughout the middle and late nineteenth century in England and America."[3] More recently, second- and third-wave feminist critics have complicated the simple, antagonistic structure of this argument and viewed Modernist formal innovation by *both* male and female writers as enacting, in Marianne DeKoven's words, "irresolvable ambivalence" and "irreducible self-contradiction" in response to the prospect of wholesale social revolution, embodied in the Anglo-American social–political sphere by the "two forces of socialism and feminism."[4] From all of these perspectives, however, the category of the feminine and its relation to literary production together stand out as central problematics within the development of Anglo-American Modernism.

Thus, at the same time as their male contemporaries battled what one historian has termed "the feminization of American [and one might add here, British] culture,"[5] Modernist women writers also sought alternatives to nineteenth-century visions of the feminine and of its role in the creation of literary texts. Consequently, as Albert Gelpi has written, "For women like Hilda Doolittle, Marianne Moore, and Amy Lowell, trying to define themselves as poets between 1910 and 1920, there seemed no available female predecessors—only their struggling selves."[6] To make matters worse, such women could hardly turn to their fellow (male) Modernists for easily congenial models of poetic self-creation. For as Pound's example alone makes abundantly clear, the ongoing debate about the gendered nature of literary creation quite frankly, and often vigorously, devalued the category of the feminine, casting it as something to be rejected and, ultimately, overcome. Even as formidable a figure as Amy Lowell, arguably the most actively influential poet of her day, conceived of writing poetry as an essentially masculine activity. So in "The Sisters," her 1925 monologue lamenting the difficulties of being both a woman and a poet, Lowell perceives a contradiction between these two crucial aspects of her self, a contradiction that drives her to "wonder what it is that makes us do it,/Singles us out to scribble down, man-wise,/The fragments of ourselves."[7]

In her complaint, Lowell expresses the fundamental dilemma facing Modernist women writers and especially poets. For as much as they too rejected the examples and assumptions of their nineteenth-century female predecessors, Modernist women writers could hardly accept the masculinist theories of literary production being advanced by their male colleagues without seriously undermining their own claims to equal poetic status and closing off entire realms of their own experience to literary treatment. Confronted with this kind of conceptual double bind in their attempts to define and establish themselves as writers, Modernist women poets faced, to recontextualize one of the lines from "Sage Homme," Pound's comedic and gender-crossing poem about his role in the "birth" of T. S. Eliot's *The Waste Land*, the problem of "nuptuals [sic] thus doubly difficult"[8] in the creation of their own poetic modes and identities. Indeed, much of the implicit drama of poetry written by women in the twentieth century lies in the differing responses to just this challenge, the various strategies women have deployed in confronting, circumventing, or capitulating to the conception of poetry as an essentially male activity.

Yet, as pervasive as the masculinist notions about poetry were, and as entrenched as they would become over the course of the Modernist period, the very terms of the theories themselves implied questions about other modes of literary production, which in turn raised possibilities for alternative conceptions. Thus if, according to the ascendant heterodoxy of the times, original, "Modern" poetry, indeed all truly innovative writing, was, in the words of T. E. Hulme, "the expression of virile thought,"[9] then what was the gender inflection of an act like translation in which a translator "merely" converts the work of another writer into a different language? Does the transformation of a poem, for example, from its original language into another constitute a full-blown masculine activity, an act of "exteriorizing a form" out of the "female chaos" of another linguistic medium? Or is translation only a debased form of "manly" poetic activity, the brain in the act of translation serving as a kind of feminized transforming or incubating crucible for the "spermatozoide" of the original work? Or, even more strangely, is the act of linguistic transformation more closely akin to asexual reproduction, a kind of parthenogenesis of new, but still fundamentally related artistic forms?

While these questions were never explicitly articulated by Modernist writers and translators themselves, they nevertheless delineate a set of concerns about translation as a literary mode that derives logically from and isolates a critical ambiguity within the masculinist sexual poetics of Modernism.[10] And, paradoxically perhaps, this ambiguity helps to explain the abiding concern with gender and the particular dynamics underlying the most renowned feats of Modernist translation. Thus, as I argued in the previous chapters, through both his choice of which poems to translate and many of the specific details of his renderings of the Chinese lyrics contained and glossed in the Fenollosa notebooks, Pound offered in *Cathay* an extended meditation upon the place of women and of women's voices in his own conception of poetry. Similarly, his *Homage to Sextus Propertius* represents much more than just a selective and frequently poorly executed rendering of the Roman poet's odes. Rather more meaningfully, the sequence can be better understood as enacting Pound's personal inquiry into the Modernist viability of erotic verse, his individual test of the poetic proposition: "My genius is no more than a girl."

If these examples of Pound's efforts as a translator suggest the ambiguously gendered status of the practice of translation within the logic of male Modernists' attempts to establish a masculinist poetics, then H. D.'s achievement demonstrates the extent to which translation as a literary mode also functioned during the period as at once a textual and a conceptual strategy by which to contest the very (gendered) ways Modernist poetry itself could be conceived and (re)produced. Like Pound, her early poetic mentor, one-time fiancé, and life-long friend, H. D. devoted considerable and sustained time and energy to the practice of translation, rendering over the course of her career a number of texts from various (though mainly Greek) sources. As early as 1915, a year before the appearance of her first book of original poems, *Sea Garden*, H. D. published her *Choruses from Iphigeneia in Aulis* as No. 3 of the *Poet's Translation Series*; and three years later, in 1918, she added to the reprint of that work several choruses from another Euripidean drama, *Hippolytus*. Through these efforts, she joined with her husband, Richard Aldington, along with several others who produced volumes in this series, thus demonstrating the importance of translation itself as a mode of literary production during the early Modernist period. In *Heliodora* (1924), her third volume of verse, H. D. not only included as essential parts of several poems fragmentary translations from various Greek epigrammatic poets, but she also rendered the opening of the first book of Homer's *Odyssey*, as well as the first long chorus of Euripides' *Ion*. And in

Red Roses for Bronze (1931), there appeared three substantial translation sequences, again all from dramas by Euripides: "Choros Translations from *The Bacchae*," "Sea-Choros from *Hecuba*," and "Choros Sequence from *Morpheus*." Finally, in 1937, all of these efforts culminated in the publication of her most ambitious feat of translation—*Euripides' Ion, Translated with Notes*.

In producing these various renderings, H. D. participated in the Modernist redefinition of both the requirements and the proper methods of translation by treating works from a language for which she never received any formal training and only ever gained at best an amateur's knowledge. Even such informal knowledge makes her less radical than Pound in his most significant departures from established translation orthodoxy, as in *Cathay*, since she did in fact learn Greek to some extent. Still, she too pushed the conceptual boundaries of translation practice beyond merely the "accurate" reproduction of semantic meaning, and she also apparently used various intermediary sources as aids in her renderings.[11] Moreover, as we shall see, together with Pound and Yeats, she went so far as to reject classical erudition as a barrier to authentic translation, and she openly flaunted her departures from accepted translation practices. Unlike her male contemporaries, however, H. D. figured her rejection of classical scholarship in expressly gendered terms.[12] Thus, her engagement with the practice of translation ties in directly to her own sense of herself as a Modernist woman writer.

In addition to producing actual texts and cultivating a radical methodology, H. D. repeatedly, if never systematically, theorized the special significance of translation as a distinct literary mode. Indeed, in two of her novels, *Palimpsest* (1926) and *Bid Me to Live (A Madrigal)* (1960),[13] the practice of translation plays a crucial role in the evolution of the respective central female characters, serving as the mechanism by which Hipparchia and Julia Ashton each initiates her journey toward self-fulfillment and the discovery of her own feminine voice and language. Throughout the greater part of her career, then, translation constituted for H. D. a critical (in all senses of that word) literary practice, one that at once reflected and contributed to her overall development as a writer.

Despite both the extent and duration of her efforts as a translator, however, critics have largely ignored the specific, generative importance of translation as a literary mode in the trajectory of H. D.'s poetic evolution. Even as they have broadened the scope of her reputation in recent years by drawing attention to her other literary efforts, including her prose fiction and unorthodox critical writings, as well as her engagement with other cultural media such as film,[14] critics have persisted, either implicitly or explicitly, in relegating H. D.'s numerous translations to a place of at best secondary importance within her diverse body of work. As a result, they have failed to recognize the fundamental importance for H. D. of translation itself as both a conceptual framework and a concrete textual practice in her efforts to establish herself as both a Modernist and a woman poet. In what follows, I want to address this critical oversight by discussing the crucial role of translation as a literary mode within H. D.'s entire career, how it provided a means both to establish the terms of her relationship to the predominantly male classical tradition from which she drew so much inspiration and to conceive an alternative to the expressly masculinist theories of literary production being put forth by her male contemporaries, many of whom, like Pound, Richard Aldington, and D. H. Lawrence, she knew intimately, and genuinely, if not always uniformly and unproblematically, admired.

Of course, to say that the specific importance of the practice of translation to H. D. has gone largely unacknowledged does not mean that critics have ignored her various treatments of Greek works altogether. Understandably, perhaps, the manifest idiosyncrasies of her translations in terms of both style and form have prompted a wide range of responses. And as with criticism of Modernist translation generally, these responses have followed two main conceptual lines, each with its own distinct limitations. In the first of these approaches, critics with their own significant investment in the classics have remained firmly bound in the age-old binary opposition between "fidelity" and "freedom," and they have sought to evaluate the "appropriateness" or "accuracy" of her treatment of such figures as Euripides. Yet their assessments have been markedly divergent, and even contradictory. Thus, for example, Douglass Bush complained early on about her translations in particular that "alterations of detail are everywhere and the total effect is not Euripidean; Euripides was an ancient Greek, not a Modern Imagist."[15] Comparably, objecting to H. D.'s presentation of "Greek tragedy as a sustained lyric," Richmond Lattimore characterized her *Ion of Euripides, Translated with Notes* as a "pseudomorph."[16] At the other end of the spectrum of these sorts of responses, D. S. Carne-Ross has more recently extended high praise to H. D., and in particular to her "fragmentary sketches from the *Iphigenia in Aulis*," for having "suggested certain elements in the Greek lyric better than they have ever been suggested before or since."[17] The stark incommensurability of these evaluations highlights the fundamental limitations of this approach. For all their ostensibly strict philological precision and intimate familiarity with the classical tradition, the implicitly normative dimension of such judgments, both positive and negative, of H. D.'s achievement as a translator has precluded consideration of the larger significance of translation itself as a literary mode, that is, of the various types of conceptual and cultural work that it both performs and enables, within the development of H. D.'s individual career, as well as, indeed, that of Modernism as a whole.

The other principal approach to H. D.'s translations has been employed by critics focused more specifically on assessing her achievement strictly as a poet. Accordingly, they have regarded H. D.'s different renderings primarily as instruments for illuminating her "original" work, as mere epiphenomena, in other words, of her sustained engagement with the classics, or as a transparent medium for conveying the influence of classical writers. Thus Vincent Quinn implicitly relegates H. D.'s translations to secondary, almost ephemeral status when he writes that her "interest in the classics would have almost inevitably involved some translating, whether she chose to publish the results or not."[18] Vigorously disputing Quinn's finally dismissive judgment of H. D. as a poet, more recent critics working from or inspired by feminist perspectives have nevertheless quietly accepted his assumptions about the (un)importance of the practice of translation itself within her career. So Louis Martz, Rachel Blau Duplessis, Susan Gubar, and Diana Collecott have more recently all written specifically on H. D.'s transformative renderings of Sappho, but their concerns have been thematic rather than either technical or generic.[19] That is, they have rightly recognized the importance of Sappho as both a textual source and an ancient lesbian literary inspiration to H. D. in the Modernist poet's efforts to establish her own poetic voice, yet they have generally neglected her translations as such, considering neither the details of her treatment of different writers, nor the larger significance of her conception of translation as a literary mode to her overall development. Even Eileen Gregory, whose *H. D. and Hellenism: Classic Lines*[20] offers the most recent and thorough examination of H. D.'s engagement with the classics, including her translations of Greek writers ranging from Sappho, Theocritus, and Homer to Euripides, organizes her discussion around specific figures and their influence on and treatment by H. D. In doing so, she continues to cast the practice of translation itself as ancillary to, rather than fundamentally intertwined with and indeed constitutive of, her overall development.

In both approaches, censure, praise, or significance arises from the observation that H. D.'s translations (too) closely resemble her own poems. At one level, to be sure, critics have been right in noting the remarkable consistency of style and concern between H. D.'s treatment of other writers and her own "original" work. In fact, Vincent Quinn is probably correct in his assertion that "if she had not acknowledged the original text, a reader would easily accept these translations as original work."[21] Compounding matters, H. D. repeatedly employed translation as a *technique* in the construction of her own "original" poetry, thereby further underscoring the deep connection in her practice as a writer between the two modes of literary production. Unfortunately, for critics of either approach, that similarity has completely defined the meaning of H. D.'s translations to their ultimate detriment. For evaluationists such as Bush, Lattimore, and Carne-Ross, it makes or breaks her translations qua translation depending upon the particular critic's contingent conception of "Greekness," of the supposedly essential qualities of the original source text and the ostensible appropriateness of H. D.'s chosen style to those perceived qualities. For critics such as Quinn, Duplessis, and even Gregory, on the other hand, that similarity merely emphasizes the uniqueness and power of her poetic vision. Regardless of their ultimate assessments, however, critics have so far all categorically subordinated H. D.'s translations to her "original" poetry, tacitly assuming that her practice as a poet enlivened, or infected, her efforts as a translator. Yet, as I will show, both the intensity and duration of her commitment to translation as a literary mode belie any such simple categorical distinctions. Indeed, it stands as one of the larger goals of this study to reverse the habitual subordination of translation to other modes of literary production, especially, but not only, in discussions of Modernism.

II

From the time she began to write seriously, during her brief stay at Bryn Mawr, H. D. found in the practice of translation an introduction to the poetic. In a letter written in the late 1920s to Glenn Hughes, editor of the University of Washington Chapbooks series (which brought out Pound's first complete translation of the classic Confucian treatise on government, the *Ta Hio*)[22] and author of the first book-length study of Imagism as a poetic movement, H. D. recalled her earliest significant literary efforts:

> ... of course I scribbled a bit, adolescent stuff. My first serious (and I think, in a way, successful) verses were some translations I did of Heine (before I was seriously dubbed "Imagist"). I think they were very lyrical in their small way, but of course, I destroyed everything. I also did some verse-translations of the lyric Latin poets at Bryn Mawr, vaguely, but nothing came of them. I do not think I even submitted them to the college paper. I do recall, however, how somewhat shocked I was to be flunked quite frankly in English. I don't know why I was surprised. I really did like all those things, even when they were rather depleted of their beauty, *Beowulf* and such like. I suppose that was one of the spurs toward a determination to self-expression.[23]

If these were somewhat inauspicious beginnings for the person who would become one of the most important Modernist woman poets, H. D.'s retrospective account of her early literary apprenticeship nevertheless reveals the extent to which she first began to develop a sense of herself as a writer specifically through the practice of translation. Not only did she come to consider her initial, even if only partially successful, poetic accomplishment to be a set of translations; in addition, another act of translation, this one of "the lyric Latin poets," came to be associated in her mind with, and perhaps even helped to ease the sting of, a critical confrontation with the literary tradition she at once genuinely admired and actively sought to engage. And as H. D.

herself noted, this confrontation served as "one of the spurs toward a determination to self-expression." Thus, from the earliest stages of her career, translation constituted for H. D. not just a means of achieving the poetic, but even more important, a strategy for negotiating her relationship to the cultural patrimony of her mother tongue.

While Heine and the lyric Latin poets would not themselves prove to be lasting influences for H. D., translation continued to play a vital role in the development of her own poetic craft and identity, serving as both a means of gaining access to important sources of inspiration and as a model for the act of writing itself. After her academic debacle at Bryn Mawr, where she left after only three semesters due to "illness,"[24] H. D. came to focus her attention on the classics, reading translations of and eventually herself translating Latin and especially Greek texts. Coinciding with the revival of interest in Greek and Latin literature that took place at the beginning of the twentieth century, H. D.'s early interest would become a life-long fascination that would leave its mark on almost all of her work.[25] As Eileen Gregory succinctly notes, "H. D.'s hellenism is the major trope or fiction within her writing, providing her orientation with historical, aesthetic and psychological mappings."[26] During this time, after having left Bryn Mawr in 1906, H. D.'s "engagement" with the classics included reading such works as Bulwer-Lytton's *The Last Days of Pompeii*, Andrew Lang's rendition of Theocritus (brought to her by Ezra Pound), and the prose translations of various Greek texts done by Gilbert Murray. In addition, after having honed her own skills, H. D. also began devoting considerable time and energy to translating various Greek texts herself, first in America and then with even greater dedication after moving to London in 1911.

More than just a transparent mechanism for pursuing her interest in the classics, however, translation as a literary mode provided H. D. with both the material and, even more important, the concept for her first published poems, whose "discovery" and subsequent promotion by Ezra Pound has become (thanks largely to the efforts of Hugh Kenner) one of the canonical founding moments of Modernism, the apocryphal tale of the creation of Imagism in the tea-room of the British Museum in October of 1912. Recalling the incident some forty-six years later in *End to Torment* (1958), her memoir of the early years of her relationship with Pound, H. D. described the scene in her typically charged fashion:

> "But Dryad," (in the Museum tea room) "this is poetry." He slashed with a pencil. "Cut this out, shorten this line. 'Hermes of the Ways' is a good title. I'll send this to Harriet Monroe of *Poetry*. Have you a copy? Yes? Then we can send this, or I'll type it when I get back. Will this do?" And he scrawled "H. D., Imagiste" at the bottom of the page.[27]

It is ironic, as well as a marker of the general success of the masculinist critical framework of Modernism, that H. D.'s own account of this formative event has helped to establish the canonical, deeply gendered critical views of both her and Pound: he, the explorer and discoverer of hidden talents, a kind of literary Odysseus, the figure with whom he would eventually begin *The Cantos*; and she, the quiet, unassuming, exquisitely focused, but essentially limited Imagist poet, or, as Pound himself came disparagingly to refer to her in 1920, "that refined, charming, and utterly narrow-minded she-bard, 'H. D.' " (*SL*,157). More to the point, while the full story behind the creation of Imagism as a poetic movement remains significantly more complex than most readers have assumed,[28] the episode in the British Museum tea-room nevertheless illustrates the tangled web of social and sexual forces within which H. D. first struggled to establish herself as a poet. It thereby also indicates the way translation as a mode of literary production served to help her begin discovering her own avenues of expression by modeling a writing practice through which she could gain access to the authority of the classical tradition, while at the same time preserving the importance of her own role and the integrity of her voice in the transmission of that tradition.

Pound's genuinely sincere praise not only launched H. D.'s official career as a writer, helping her to complete her break with the psychological and emotional restrictions of her family's expectations and her prospective life in America, but it also constituted a subtle act of appropriation, one whereby he at once solidified his own position as the arbiter of early Modernist poetic taste and cast H. D. as the perfect exemplar of a movement he would later claim to have founded. Indeed, in scrawling "H. D., Imagiste" beneath her poems, Pound essentially created and authorized Hilda Doolittle's public identity as a poet, the initials serving as both the authorial tag for nearly all of her work and as the hieroglyphic and anagrammatic inspiration for the majority of the names of the central personae of her poetry and prose.[29] H. D. herself came to recognize both the originary and repressive dimensions of Pound's early influence and of his efforts on her behalf when she wrote that, "To recall Ezra is to recall my father" (*ETT*, 48), a deftly formulated acknowledgment that encodes in the psychoanalytic terms with which she would become so deeply familiar the difficulties she faced in her early attempts to establish her own poetic identity and manner without either falling back upon the modes and sensibilities of nineteenth-century female poetesses or falling prey to masculinist ideas about poetry being advanced by her male contemporaries.

While it remains unclear exactly how many poems Pound saw that day in the British Museum tea-room in 1912, as well as precisely how he "edited" them, all the lyrics that H. D. came to refer to as "my first authentic verses" together illustrate the ways in which the practice of translation functioned for her, from the earliest stages of her career, as a manifold writing strategy for negotiating the challenges of being both a Modernist and a woman poet. More specifically, "Hermes of the Ways," "Priapus" (subtitled "Keeper of Orchards" and later collected and known simply as "Orchard"), and "Epigram," which as Pound promised soon appeared in *Poetry* in January 1913, all arose out of H. D.'s encounter with *The Greek Anthology*, a diverse collection of epigrams, inscriptions, epitaphs, songs, and prayers dating from the fifth century B.C. through the sixth century A.D., which was compiled and edited in 1301 by the scholar Maximus Planudes.[30] Together with Richard Aldington, whom she married in October of 1913, and sometimes Pound, H. D. had been reading and translating from the collection since soon after arriving in London and meeting her future husband.[31] And another poem H. D. counted among her earliest, "Acon," which appeared somewhat later, in the February 1914 issue of *Poetry*, bearing the epigraph "After Johannes Baptista Amaltheus," H. D. herself described as a "transposition from that Renaissance Latin book."[32] Indeed, the introductory caption to her first published poems in the January 1913 issue of *Poetry* magazine underscores the constitutive inter-relationship, for H. D., between the ostensibly distinct processes of original composition, translation, and critical interpretation, describing them collectively as "Verses, Translations and Reflections from 'The Anthology.' "[33]

The most famous of these poems, "Hermes of the Ways," for example, represents H. D.'s interpretive transformation of an epigram by Anyte of Tegea, a female Greek poet who lived in Arcadia, according to the best scholarly estimations, during the third century B.C. Consisting of a single quatrain, Anyte's poem is an inscription for a fresh-water spring and probably appeared with a statue of Hermes, serving in his capacity as the patron god of travelers, and hence of roads or ways. In 1915, Richard Aldington published a literal translation of this epigram in *The Egoist*, also entitled "Hermes of the Ways," and H. D. apparently contributed to that rendering.[34] Aldington's version thus points to an effort at revising a masculinist literary economy as one of the motivations underlying the composition of H. D.'s poem. More important for my purposes here, it also provides a uniquely incisive gauge for evaluating the process by which H. D. transformed the original Greek epigram into the first public articulation of her own poetic voice. Aldington's version reads as follows:

> I, Hermes, stand here at the cross-roads by the wind beaten orchard, near the hoary-grey coast;
> And I keep a resting-place for weary men. And the cool stainless spring gushes out.[35]

In contrast to the reputation that she came to develop for a persistent, even relentless, concision, H. D.'s "Hermes of the Ways" expands considerably upon the Greek original.[36] Most important, she shifts the center of poetic articulation from the overseeing god who keeps "a resting-place for weary *men*" (emphasis added) to an ambiguously gendered, deeply human subject. Instead of merely reiterating the simple, conventionalized utterance of the original poem, "Hermes of the Ways" opens with a vivid act of perception. As befits the initiatory Imagist poem, a radical instant of vision gives rise to poetry:

> The hard sand breaks,
> and the grains of it
> are clear as wine.
>
> Far off over the leagues of it,
> the wind,
> playing on the wide shore,
> piles little ridges,
> and the great waves
> break over it.

This constitutive act of seeing itself bespeaks a complex matrix of feeling and experience, and the poem moves quickly to its real, emotional subject. The speaker expresses a weathered familiarity with the patron god of travelers, symbolized by the silent, unmoving statue standing before her (him?) at the confluence of a variety of natural forces and exacting landscapes, thereby revealing her own personal history of extensive travel and wandering:

> But more than the many-foamed ways
> of the sea,
> I know him
> of the triple path-ways,
> Hermes,
> who awaits.
>
> Dubious,
> facing three ways,
> welcoming wayfarers,
> he whom the sea-orchard
> shelters from the west,
> from the east
> weathers sea-wind;
> fronts the great dunes.

Where the Greek poem (as Aldington's literal version makes clear) presents the divinely inspired utterance of the statuary god, H. D. takes her own experience as a translator as the conceptual basis for her poem, and she imagines a physical and psychological context within which someone might have read Anyte's poem in its original form, just as she herself had done as it appeared in "The Anthology." At one level, of course, H. D.'s most renowned early lyric merely recapitulates the Modernist fascination with classical mythology in general, and with the Greek tradition in particular. Over and above its thematic content, however, the poem demonstrates the generative conceptual importance for H. D. of translation as a concrete writing practice. For, though not a translation in the literal sense, "Hermes of the Ways," like a translation, has as its founding imaginative moment the act of reading the Greek original, which allows H. D. to tap the authority of a preexisting work, while at the same time opening a space for her own personal expression.

In the second part of the poem, the speaker turns her attention to the "cool stainless spring" that was the occasion for Anyte's original epigram and to the "twisted" but stubbornly resilient life that it sustains with its "sweet" water. Such vitality contrasts with the salty, destructive force of the sea and its waves.

>   Small is
>   this white stream,
>   flowing below ground
>   from the poplar-shaded hill,
>   but the water is sweet.
>
>   Apples on the small trees
>   are hard,
>   too small,
>   too late ripened
>   by a desperate sun
>   that struggles through sea-mist.
>
>   The boughs of the trees
>   are twisted
>   by many bafflings;
>   twisted are the small-leafed boughs.
>
>   But the shadow of them
>   is not the shadow of the mast head
>   nor of the torn sails.

The stunted trees and the gnarled, untouched apples attest to the beauty that can survive even under the harshest conditions, and by noticing them, the speaker affirms both her ability and her determination to experience the joys and satisfactions of her own life despite its emotional, as well as physical, demands. Though she faces the difficulties of wandering, the shadows of her life, like those of the trees she sees, are "not the shadow of the mast head/ nor of the torn sails" that reveal and herald the death of sailors, fellow travelers like herself, but ones who must endure without the renewing vitality and beauty of the earth. The poem ends by invoking Hermes, the god whose patience and protection affords such boons as the spring that sustains life at the harsh junction of land and sea.

> Hermes, Hermes
> the great sea foamed,
> gnashed its teeth about me;
> but you have waited,
> where the sea-grass tangles with
> shore-grass.[37]

In the final stanza, the speaker addresses directly the very god whose original utterance, in the form of Anyte's epigram, provided the basis for H. D.'s poem. By explicitly invoking the god who was the inspiration for the poem she came to translate and later to transform into her own, H. D. at the end of "Hermes of the Ways" simultaneously gives thanks for and enacts the process of her own poetic self-creation.

Seen in the light of its originary pre-text, "Hermes of the Ways" reveals the complex textual negotiations by which H. D. began to shape her identity as a woman poet even as she had to operate within the already developing masculinist critical framework of Modernism. It illustrates how she sought to connect herself as a modern woman writer to an ancient Greek female poet (and to the attendant poetic tradition that Anyte implicitly represents), while at the same time struggling to find her own personal and artistic way amid the contending and interconnected social, familial, and sexual forces in her life at the time. The feelings of isolation and resolve underlying the poem's sparse, Imagist detail provide an illuminating commentary on H. D.'s experience as a recent American expatriate living in England, who was embroiled, between 1911 and 1913, in ending one heterosexual relationship that, having begun in late adolescence, had reached the point of engagement (with Pound), beginning another that would soon result in marriage (with Aldington), and in coming to terms with the social and emotional consequences of her first, and in many ways most enduring, lesbian passion (with Frances Gregg).[38]

Moreover, in addition to the "romantic" roles they played in her life, Pound and Aldington also together mediated H. D.'s exposure to the established literary tradition and, as the Museum tea-room episode makes abundantly clear, to the contemporary marketplace through which the three of them would come to help define one of the principal strands of Modernist poetry. Pound had read William Morris and other Pre-Raphaelite poets aloud to H. D. during their youthful and physically innocent trysts in the woods around Philadelphia. He also brought her, in addition to Lang's *Theocritus*, volumes of Swedenborg, Ibsen, and Shaw, among others (*ETT*, 22–23, 39). And of course, it was through Pound's position as the foreign correspondent for *Poetry* that H. D. gained the opportunity for publication. Similarly, it was with Aldington and his more developed knowledge of classical languages that H. D. read and translated from *The Greek Anthology* and derived material for her "first authentic verses" that Pound would send to Harriet Monroe.

On one level, then, insofar as an act of translation provided both its compositional and conceptual basis, "Hermes of the Ways" merely crystallizes and repeats the various ways in which at the earliest stages of her career, H. D.'s relationship to poetry and to the process of her own poetic self-creation was mediated by external (male) voices and other texts. At the same time, though, the poem illustrates the way translation also functioned for H. D. as a writing strategy by which she could challenge, or at least circumvent, the obstacles to her development as a woman poet posed by the aggressively masculinist poetics that were being advanced by her poetic mentors and colleagues. For in the act of translation that preceded the writing of "Hermes of the Ways," H. D. found not only a concrete textual method of forging a link with an ancient literary foremother, but also a way of securing for herself and her own voice a vital place in the creation of a Modernist feminine poetic practice.

If "Hermes of the Ways" shows H. D.'s resolve in the face of an unknown emotional and poetic terrain, then "Priapus," the other poem of the three that first appeared in the *Poetry* of January 1913 that she thought enough of to retain in subsequent collections of her work, indicates the extent to which, in her early poetry, H. D. also worked within Victorian notions about women as passive, suffering vessels whose depths of feeling provide both the impetus and the justification for poetic outbursts of lyric and passionate intensity. But whereas the nineteenth-century women poets against whom she, together with her fellow, male Modernists, were in many ways reacting (Mrs. [Lydia] Sigourney, for example) gloried in the limited realm of the domestic and in "the sufferings of motherhood on earth for the ultimately triumphant reunion with husband and offspring in heaven,"[39] H. D. explicitly confronts the primal fascination and danger of sexuality, rather than sublimating such feelings into the sanctified conventions of matrimony and maternity. Thus, even though "Priapus" (or "Orchard," as it came to be known) depicts an instance of female sexual subjugation, or to use Rachel Blau Duplessis's influential term, "romantic thralldom,"[40] the poem itself represents an attempt to expand both the conceptual boundaries of modern poetry and, by implication, the role of the feminine in modern writing generally.

Conceived as a kind of offertory prayer to the Greek god of fertility, Priapus, the son of Dionysus and Aphrodite, and thus the very incarnation of ecstatic carnal play, "Priapus/Keeper of Orchards" presents an erotically charged landscape at once alluring and perilously captivating:

> I saw the first pear
> as it fell—

> the honey-seeking, golden-banded,
> the yellow swarm
> was not more swift than I,
> (spare us from loveliness)
> and I fell prostrate
> crying:
> you have flayed us
> with your blossoms,
> spare us the beauty
> of fruit trees.
>
> The honey-seeking
> paused not,
> the air thundered their song,
> and I alone was prostrate.

Overwhelmed by the beauty of her surroundings and by her own susceptibility to such sensual delights, the feminine speaker of the poem begs protection ("spare us from loveliness") at once by and from the god presiding over the fecund sexuality of the garden that both incites and captivates her, her pleas merely underscoring the depth of her subjugation. Priapus was traditionally depicted in sculpture as a small twisted male figure with an enormous penis, or even more simply, as just a phallus, images that Pound likely had in mind when he came to refer to "the symbolism of phallic religions" in his "Postscript" to *The Natural Philosophy of Love*. Thus, the speaker falls down quite literally before the naked symbol of an imposing, even predatory, male sexuality. Even as the bees, in whose social organization innumerable male drones serve an absolutely dominant female queen, function naturally within the environment buzzing with the power of the male god, the speaker demonstrates the unique intensity and fragility of her own response to his divine sexual providence: "the yellow swarm/was not more swift than I,/... and I alone was prostrate."

In the second half of the poem, the speaker addresses the "rough-hewn/ god of the orchard" directly, seeking to placate him with an offering of nuts and various split and fallen fruits, the traditional symbols of femininity having evolved into images of the speaker's own imminently overripe sexuality:

> O rough-hewn
> god of the orchard,
> I bring you in offering—
> do you, alone unbeautiful,
> son of the god,
> spare us from loveliness:
>
> these fallen hazel-nuts,
> stripped late of their green sheaths,

> grapes, red-purple,
> their berries
> dripping with wine,
> pomegranates already broken,
> and shrunken figs
> and quinces untouched,
> I bring you as offering. (*CP*, 28–29)

Ironically, her gifts of appeasement merely confirm the ultimate certainty of her subjugation, for she offers herself in the "shrunken figs/and quinces untouched," the exhausted yet still unconsummated fruits of the garden. In "Priapus," feminine sexual subjugation stands as the only conceivable alternative to a sterile virginity, and the poem at once narrates and performs the feminine speaker's transformation from an unfulfilled virginal figure into the willing participant in the ceremony of her own sexual sacrifice.[41]

Like "Hermes of the Ways," "Priapus" modulates from a heightened moment of perception into the direct invocation of a masculine statuary divinity. This basic structural homology points to a fundamentally similar mechanism of inspiration through H. D.'s readings of, reflections on, and attempts to translate the epigrams contained in *The Greek Anthology*.[42] Thus, "Priapus" too bears the marks of H. D.'s efforts as a translator, and thereby indicates the way the practice of translation served as a conceptual and compositional foundation for the first enduringly successful articulations of her own poetic voice. And this becomes all the more apparent when one recalls that the third, though least well-known of the poems with which H. D. made her debut as a poet, entitled "Epigram," was expressly conceived as an attempt to compose "After the Greek."[43]

For many years, H. D.'s reputation as a poet suffered (somewhat unfairly) from a perceived lack of both thematic and technical range in her work. To be sure, "Hermes of the Ways" and "Orchard" together already reveal the spectrum of emotions that H. D. would exhibit in her early poetry: on the one hand, a stalwart, even fierce, determination in the face of physical and psychological challenges; and on the other, a primal fascination with the dangers and delights of sexuality, all expressed through tersely structured evocations of an assortment of (mostly female) mythic personae and classical landscapes. The poems of her first three volumes, *Sea Garden* (1916), *Hymen* (1921), and *Heliodora* (1924), collectively illustrate H. D.'s examination, via an insistent classicism, of the varieties of feminine psycho-sexual experience.

At the same time as she pursued such imaginative and aesthetic avenues in her poetry, H. D. also continued to practice translation as a major literary mode in its own right in the years following her poetic debut in 1913, producing, as I mentioned earlier, versions of a number of classical Greek texts and publishing them separately as well as together with her original poems in

Heliodora. In doing so, she found in the practice of translation much more than just a mere technique for exercising her interest in the classics. Rather, translation as a mode of writing embodied for H. D. a vital strategy by which she could both challenge masculinist conceptions of culture and of the gender of literary production, as well as cultivate her own Modern feminine poetic practice. And this, in turn, led to the increasingly important and complex interactions between her efforts as a translator and her continuing development as a poet.

III

H. D. specified the importance of translation to her growth as a writer when she came in her fiction to review and narrate the history of her own poetic evolution. As Susan Stanford Friedman notes, H. D. sought in her novels "to retell, reorder and thereby recreate her own 'legend'" (Friedman, *Dictionary* 131). So in "Hipparchia," the initial section of her first novel, *Palimpsest* (1926), the titular heroine (as is typical in H. D.'s novels, a thinly veiled mask for the author herself) begins as both a colonial subject and courtesan. Tellingly, however, she initiates her journey out of this doubly muted condition and toward the discovery of her own voice imbued with revolutionary feminine power by attempting to translate a song by Moero from Greek into Latin. This effort occasions a critical insight into the constraints of Latin itself, the language not only of her sexual and economic oppressor, Marius Decius (Richard Aldington in a toga), but also, on a larger scale, of the Roman Empire that threatens to destroy her native Greek culture:

> The translation in the heavier language read faulty, repetitive. . . . What the Greek could manage with his honeyed delicacy of curious vowel syllable, the foreign tongue was forced to contrive by neat fitting of pallid mosaic. . . . The translation into Latin was the dark sputtering of an almost extinguished wick in an earth bowl which before had shown rose in alabaster. . . . As soon think of putting the run and vowelled throat of a mountain stream into chiseled stone, as to translate the impassive, passionate yet coldly restrained Greek utterance into this foreign language. . . . Sappho in Latin. It was (now she came to reconsider it) absolute desecration. It was desecration to translate it. She decided not to re-render the hyacinth on the mountain side. She would let that rest flawless. She would quote it entire in Greek. The Greek words, inset in her manuscript, would work terrific damage. She almost saw the Dictator's palace overpowered by it. (*Palimpsest*, 72–73)

Hipparchia's attempt to render the song by Moero leads her to reconsider not only the advisability but even the possibility of translating another poem, one by the female poet Sappho, "which had long escaped her," and this in turn brings her to perceive in the latter Greek poem itself the capacity to "work terrific damage" on the repressive, patriarchal political and literary structures of Rome. Thus, even though Hipparchia believes it impossible, indeed "absolute desecration," to render Greek poetry justly in the "pallid mosaic" of Latin, her experience nevertheless serves to indicate the general meaning of H. D.'s extended and intense hellenism, a matter that other critics have discussed at length. More important for my purposes here, however, her experience also reveals the crucial significance of the practice of translation itself to her development as a writer. For as both the occasion and the method by which Hipparchia comes to recognize the critical, feminine power of the "impassive, passionate yet coldly restrained Greek" of the Sapphic poem, translation represents at once a strategy and a mode of writing that enables her to perceive and, even more importantly, to begin conceiving for herself an artistic identity unconstrained by the categories and assumptions of a masculinist literary culture.

Over and above its critical function of releasing or exposing energies and precedents capable of toppling the repressive structures of patriarchy, the practice of translation itself engenders a writing process that unites poetic insight with an expressly feminine manner of linguistic (re)production. In *Bid Me to Live (A Madrigal)*, the writer heroine, Julia Ashton (again, H. D. in thin disguise), attempts to render a chorus-sequence from an unidentified Greek play. Her effort serves as a prelude to the final section of the novel in which she resolves her insecurities about both her own sexuality and talent by coming to terms with the deeply compelling, yet sexist philosophy of her friend and artistic rival and opposite, Rico (H. D.'s portrait of D. H. Lawrence, who played the same role in her own life). Unlike her fictional antecedent, Hipparchia, Julia does not doubt the capacities of English as a proper medium for the Greek work, and her approach to the task records a virtual theory of translation as a uniquely generative literary mode:

> She was self-effacing in her attack on those Greek words, she was flamboyantly ambitious. The words themselves held inner words, she thought. If you look at a word long enough, this peculiar twist, its magic angle, would lead somewhere, like that Phoenician track, trod by the old traders. She was a trader in the gold, the old gold, the myrrh of the dead spirit. She was bargaining with each word.
>
> She brooded over each word, as if to hatch it. Then she tried to forget each word, for "translations" enough existed, and she was no scholar. She did not want to "know" Greek in that sense. She was like one blind, reading the texture of incised letters, rejoicing like one blind who knows an inner light, a reality that the outer eye cannot grasp. She was arrogant and she was intrinsically humble before this discovery. Her own.

Anyone can translate the meaning of the word. She wanted the shape, the feel of it, the character of it, as if it had been freshly minted. She felt that the old manner of approach was as toward hoarded treasure, but treasure that had passed through too many hands, had been too carefully assessed by the grammarians. She wanted to coin new words. (*Bid Me to Live*, 162–63)

The figurative details and overall trajectory of this passage together exemplify the way in which H. D. viewed and engaged in the practice of translation as much more than just the transfer of semantic content from one language to another. Rather, it embodied for her a special engagement with language itself that created an opportunity to Modernize and to transform tradition, a chance at once to revive a Hellenic literary patrimony and to reconfigure the very (gendered) terms of its authority. In seeking to reveal the "inner words" contained in the words of the foreign language, Julia attains through the practice of translation to the mystical vision that lies at the heart of H. D.'s notion of poetic activity, which Robert Duncan has described, in terms strikingly resonant with the dynamics of translation, as entailing the conversion "into human language a word or phrase of the great language in which the universe itself is written" (28) (c.f. Gregory, 141–42).[44] Moreover, the evolution within this passage of Julia's technique as a translator, from a masculinist poetics of "attack on those Greek words," to a method of productive exchange in her "bargaining with each word," and finally to an explicitly reproductive and feminine process as she "brooded over each word, as if to hatch it," indicates the extent to which translation as a literary mode delineated for H. D. a writing practice that serves at once to critique masculinist constructions of both knowledge and literary production and to engender alternatives to such conceptions. Thus, Julia tries "to forget each word," because she does "not want to 'know' Greek in that sense," which is perhaps the Biblical sense. Instead, she seeks to discover a mode of expression untainted by masculinist ideals of sexual mastery informing conventional "translations" (and, indeed, any feat of literary creation), "the old manner of approach." Julia's "discovery" of a visionary blindness, then, plays upon the age-old image of poetic consciousness as a way of returning critically to the most famous blind poet of all and to the very metaphorical foundations of the Western poetic tradition. Finally, Julia's desire "to coin new words" out of "the shape, the feel" and "the character" of the words of the Greek, which invokes the decidedly conventional equation between literary and chrematistic production reflects the way the practice of translation involved for H. D. a complex of primary perceptions and experience that could itself serve as the foundation for a new poetry.[45]

As these episodes from her novels make clear, then, H. D. regarded translation not merely as a procedural artifact of her interest in the classics, as most critics have implicitly asserted, but rather as a critically important compositional process and conceptual strategy in her effort to establish herself as a woman poet within the evolving masculinist literary culture of Modernism. Moreover, such a *theory* of both the enormous revisionary and originary possibilities deriving from translation helps at once to explain H. D.'s considerable and sustained efforts as a translator, as well as to clarify the larger polemical and ideological dimensions of her radical *methods*. As I mentioned earlier, these methods have elicited repeated criticisms such as those issued by Bush and Lattimore. Yet such philologically based dismissals epitomize precisely the deeply conservative, narrowly semantic conception of the practice of translation that H. D., along with several other of her fellow Modernists, most notably Ezra Pound and William Butler Yeats,[46] explicitly rejected. So in the "Preface" to the first edition of her *Choruses from Iphigeneia in Aulis*, H. D. first sought to extend the boundaries of the practice of translation as a literary mode beyond the limits of merely semantic equivalence, arguing that a "literal, word-for-word version of so well-known an author as Euripides would be useless and supererogatory."[47] Moreover, in a clear reference to the poetic manner of "the most conspicuous Greek propagandist of the day,"[48] Gilbert Murray (whom T. S. Eliot would also come to dismiss as a translator in his essay "Euripides and Professor Murray"), she declared that "a rhymed, languidly Swinburnian verse form is an insult and a barbarism."[49] Instead, H. D. held, "the rhymeless hard rhythms" in her own translation "would be most likely to keep the sharp edges and irregular cadence of the original."[50]

But whereas Pound and Yeats repudiated traditional approaches to translation in order to establish and justify their own masculine authority, H. D. had to face the added burden of articulating a new method of translation in terms that would underwrite her efforts to establish herself as both a Modernist and a woman poet. Thus, in the "explanatory notes" punctuating her complete rendering of the *Ion*, she asserted that in the practice of translation direct, physical experience plays as important a role as linguistic competence:

> We may relegate the boy, Ion, to the dust heap and parse his delicate phrases till we end in a mad house. It will bring us no nearer to the core of Greek beauty. Parse the sun in heaven, distinguish between the taste of mountain air on different levels, feel with your foot a rock covered with sea-weed, one covered with sand, one worked and marbled by the tide. You cannot learn Greek, only, with a dictionary. You can learn it, with your hands and your feet and especially with your lungs. (*Ion*, 16)

For H. D., genuine translation, that is, translation that penetrates to "the core of Greek beauty," involves, indeed requires, a physical engagement with the world as much as a mental one with the word. Grounded in her belief that Nature constitutes a language that can itself be read (and the significance of which manifests in and can therefore be "carried over" into different individual human languages), H. D.'s conception of the proper method of translation underlies the marked (and remarked upon) idiosyncrasy of her various renderings of and from Greek texts. Thus, in discussing her treatment of the initial dialogue between Kreousa and Ion in her *Ion of Euripides, Translated with Notes*, H. D. could admit, and even flaunt, the sharp stylistic difference between her translation and the Greek original, while still maintaining the former's essential accuracy: "The broken, exclamatory, or evocative *vers-libre* which I have chosen to translate the two line dialogue, throughout the play, is the exact antithesis of the original. Though concentrating and translating sometimes, ten words, with two, I have endeavored in no way, to depart from the meaning. . . . There are just under a hundred of these perfectly matched statements, questions and answers. The original runs as a sustained narrative."[51]

Accordingly, at the levels of both theory and method, H. D. engaged in translation as a strategy for directly renewing Hellenic culture, while at the same time configuring and presenting that culture in a way that would put her on equal footing with her male contemporaries. Moreover, and just as important, in their very form, they register her polemic against approaches to the practice of translation that, in her view, themselves derive from and help to perpetuate a patriarchal conception of tradition by adhering to a deeply conservative ideal of authenticity that, among other things, emphasizes knowledge of the Word over personal, bodily experience. In this regard, H. D. can be seen as anticipating much of the work done by French feminist thinkers of the 1970s and their critiques of phallogocentrism.[52] Through translation, both in her choice of texts and in her radical methods as a translator, H. D. sought not simply to revive the tradition of the classics, but to reconfigure the very gendered nature of its authority.

IV

The virtual theory of translation adumbrated in her fiction, together with the unorthodox methodology outlined in her various prose statements, shed a revealing light on the stakes involved in H. D.'s actual renderings of Greek works, where, just as in her poetry, she addresses issues of sexuality and identity. To be sure, as Duplessis, Gregory, and others have rightly seen, her impulse and abiding dedication to translation can in part be understood as a desire for a writing process through which she could recover and renew a feminine literary tradition stretching back to antiquity that could both validate and inspire her own efforts as a Modernist woman poet. Yet the extreme selectivity and radical formal innovation of her practice as a translator together emphasize that H. D. engaged in translation not merely to invoke a feminine heritage, but actively to reconfigure the largely masculine classical tradition to meet and authorize her particular needs. Thus, she recuperates Euripides as a figure for her efforts, configuring him as "a white rose, lyric, feminine, a spirit" (*Vision*, 32) (c.f. Gregory, 179–231); and in selecting and rendering passages from his dramas, she created texts that reiterate the concerns, thematic as well as formal, of her poems, while at the same time partaking of the authority of the classics. The opening to H. D.'s version of the "Chorus of the Women of Chalkis" from *Iphigeneia in Aulis*, for example, recalls the emotionally charged, liminal landscape depicted in "Hermes of the Ways" and several other of the lyrics in *Sea Garden*:

> I crossed sand-hills.
> I stand among the sea-drift before Aulis.
> I crossed Euripos' strait—
> foam hissed after my boat.
>
> I left Chalkis,
> My city and the rock-ledges.
> Arethusa twists among the boulders,
> Increases—cuts into the surf. (*CP*, 71)

Similarly, the plaintive questions asked by the "Chorus of Troizenian Women" in H. D.'s selections from the *Hippolytus* ring with a deep and personal acuteness, published as they were, in 1918, just as the succession of traumatic events that marked her individual experience of the war years was coming to a head. These events included her miscarriage in 1915 and the ensuing host of physical, emotional, and sexual difficulties; her protracted marital problems with Richard Aldington; the loss of her brother Gilbert in the trenches in France; the death of her father in response to that tragedy; and her radically different, yet in their own ways equally intense relationships, with D. H. Lawrence, which, while profoundly intimate, was apparently platonic, and Cecil Gray, which resulted in the birth of her daughter, Perdita.

> Or is it that your lord,
> born of Erechtheus,
> the king most noble in descent,
> neglects you in the palace
> and your bride-couch
> for another in secret?
> Or has some sea-man,
> landing at our port,
> friendly to ships,
> brought sad news from Crete?
> For some great hurt

>   binds you to your couch,
>   broken in spirit. (*CP*, 87)

Rather than cede the domain of classical literature to her contemporaries like Pound, Eliot, and Joyce and their attempts to establish a masculinist literary culture, H. D. expressly employed translation as a means to pursue her belief in the classics as both a precedent and a source of inspiration for a feminine literary conception distinct from the sentimental modes of her immediate female predecessors.

Nor did H. D. only translate writers, like Euripides, whom she could construe as exemplifying a feminine sensibility. In fact, as a translator, she even came to treat an author whom several of her male contemporaries had taken as one of the cornerstones of their own efforts to create an expressly masculine Modernism. Just as Pound and, in his own way, Joyce both did, H. D. translated Homer, producing in 1920 a version of approximately the first 100 lines of *The Odyssey*. While her own epic ambitions do not culminate until the 1950s in *Helen in Egypt*, H. D.'s rendering of the opening of *The Odyssey* illustrates the way in which she employed translation as a conceptual and practical strategy for exploring, and indeed even actively reimagining, the relation between the category of the feminine and the classical tradition. For in her engagement with one of the master texts for (male) Modernism, H. D. sought through the scope and form of her translation to recalibrate the sexual economy of the heroic epic (and, by extension, of Modernism itself) by focusing on and bringing out the feminine presence in the Western archetypal masculine text.

Beginning with the invocation to the Muse and continuing through to Athena's departure from the council of the gods to rouse Telemachos into action and thereby initiate the actual narrative line of *The Odyssey*, H. D. confronts Homer more as an obligatory rival than as either congenial model or inspiring predecessor (c.f. Gregory, 173–78). Throughout her translation, she departs radically from the formal dimensions of the original, breaking the hexameter of the Greek, eliding many of the discursive, formulaic epithets applied to the various gods and mortals, and even eliminating a large section of the Prooemium. Clearly H. D. agreed with Pound when he declared that "English translators [of Greek] have gone wide . . . in trying to keep every adjective, when obviously many adjectives in the original have only melodic value" (*LE*, 273). But the specific details of her rendering fall into a pattern indicating that H. D.'s motivations as a translator were as much ideological as aesthetic.

Thus, for example, she gives the ten lines of the opening Prooemium as follows:

>   *Muse,*
>   *tell me of this man of wit,*

> who roamed long years
> after he had sacked
> Troy's sacred streets. (CP, 94)

By cutting the hexameter flow of the original epic lines down to the charged, "broken" pulse of her own free-verse style, H. D. compresses *The Odyssey* to fit the mold of a lyric, the form whose history as a vehicle of feminine expression she had added to through her own early poetic efforts.[53] In addition, the actual poetic articulation of the lines themselves emphasizes the importance of feminine inspiration to the genesis of epic. Where the original begins by announcing its theme of masculine heroic adventure with "Ανδρα," H. D. calls attention in her translation to the ultimately feminine source of epic by placing the Muse, instead of either "the man" or, as many other translators have done, the traditionally male bard, at the outset of the poem.[54]

Beyond the formal arrangement of the lines, H. D. also reconfigures the traditional gender economy of the opening by completely eliminating in her translation the remaining eight lines of the Prooemium, which summarize Odysseus's adventures and establish him as a sympathetic hero. Rather than follow the original and its mention of the death of Odysseus's comrades for their transgressions against Helios (a deity who, in other contexts, loomed large for her),[55] H. D. resumes her translation from line eleven, the point at which Calypso enters the narrative, and several of her decisions as a translator can perhaps be best understood as attempts to amplify the feminine presence within the epic:

> All the rest
> who had escaped death,
> returned,
> fleeing battle and the sea;
> only Odysseus,
> captive of a goddess
> desperate and home-sick,
> thought but of his wife and palace;
> but Calypso,
> that nymph and spirit,
> yearning in the furrowed rock-shelf,
> burned
> and sought to be his mistress;

In rendering line thirteen of the original, H. D. gives "νόστου κεχρημένον ἠδ ἐγυναικὸς" (*Loeb*, 12) as "thought but of his wife and palace." Richmond Lattimore's literal translation of this segment reads, "longing for his wife and homecoming" (27). By substituting the concrete "palace" for the abstract noun "νόστου" ("homecoming"), H. D. not only lends an Imagist precision to her version, but she also implicitly asserts the epic dimensions of Penelope's unnarrated experience. For in emphasizing the specific architectural location to which Odysseus desires to return, rather than merely mentioning the act of his homecoming, H. D. calls attention to the site of Penelope's own epic struggle to stave off her numerous and persistent suitors during her husband's twenty-year absence. Moreover, in line fifteen, which reads "ἐν σπέσσι γλαφυροῖσι, λιλαιομένη πόσιν εἶναι,"[56] H. D. replaces the Greek word for "husband," πόσιν, with "mistress," centering her locution around Calypso and her role in the relationship rather than around Odysseus. Justification for this choice may have come from the word πότνι, the feminine form of πόσισ ("husband"), usually translated "mistress" or "queen," that is used to describe Calypso herself in the previous line. But whether H. D. was inspired in her translation by the appearance of this word in line fourteen, or simply committed a grammatical error (an unlikely possibility since, whatever level of Greek she had attained by 1920, she could have easily consulted any number of other more literal or scholarly sources for guidance and corrected such a "mistake" had she wanted to), her substitution effects, even if only momentarily, a shift in the focal character for the poem.

Throughout the remainder of her treatment, H. D. stays fairly close to the basic semantic content of the original, departing at various points from the exact wording or grammatical construction of the Greek, but never again so significantly as in the opening fifteen lines. However, the manner in which she concludes her rendering further underscores that H. D. did not seek in her encounter with Homer merely to produce an updated, Imagist version of the opening of *The Odyssey*. For she imposes a visual and verbal closure upon her rendering that encodes a subtle critique of the sexual politics informing the masculine epic tradition. Ending with lines ninety-six through ninety-eight, H. D. finishes her partial translation as if it were a complete poetic unit unto itself, separating and italicizing the final stanza (just as she did with the opening Prooemium) and employing a repetition of the final image to achieve a kind of formal poetic resolution:

> *She spoke*
> *and about her feet*
> *clasped bright sandals,*
> *gold-wrought, imperishable,*
> *which lift her above sea,*
> *across land stretch*
> *wind-like,*
> *like the wind breath.*

In the original, this passage comprises the opening three lines of a transitional interlude that describes Athena's preparations as she departs from the council of the gods, where she has argued for Odysseus finally to be able to return home, to go to Ithaka so that she can incite Telemachos to confront the suitors and begin searching for his lost father. Thus, H. D. leaves off precisely at the point at which the epic takes up the expressly masculine narrative of Telemachos's paternity quest, and she ends her translation with an image signifying the power of feminine divinity. In doing so, she implicitly asserts the centrality of Athena to the epic as the instigating force behind both Odysseus's homecoming and Telemachos's growth into manhood (c.f. Gregory, 173–78). Simply entitled "Odyssey," her rendering constitutes much more than simply an idiosyncratic, Modernist treatment of the first ninety-eight lines of Homer's poem. Rather, as a textual articulation of her critical engagement with the very embodiment of the masculinist heroic literary tradition, as well as, indeed, one of the foundations for the Modernism within which she struggled to establish her practice as a woman writer, H. D.'s partial and deeply personal translation represents an attempt to discover the means by which she could claim epic itself as a vehicle of feminine poetic expression. Some critics have viewed H. D.'s early lyric strategies as representing a rejection of epic as a product and an instrument of patriarchal ideology (c.f. Duplessis 1986, 20). But her version of the opening of *The Odyssey* indicates that she also early on both recognized and coveted its immense poetic and cultural authority. It was through the practice of translation that she first found a way to assimilate epic to her own purposes by breaking its form and realigning its narrative focus, and thus begin to make her way toward *Helen in Egypt*.[57]

V

Originally published in the first edition of *Heliodora* (1924), "Odyssey" exemplifies the evolving importance of translation as a distinct mode of literary production within H. D.'s development as a writer, as well as, more particularly, a poet. For not only did she include her renderings from various Greek works together with her verse beginning specifically with *Heliodora*, but she also came to employ translation as a constitutive *technique* in the composition of her own "original" poems.[58] H. D. herself calls attention to this in the prefatory "Note" to *Heliodora* when she identifies the different sources for a number of her efforts: "The poem Lais has in italics a translation of the Plato epigram in the Greek Anthology. Heliodora has in italics the two Meleager epigrams from the Anthology. In Nossis is the translation of the opening lines of the Garland of Meleager and the poem of Nossis herself in the Greek Anthology" (*Heliodora* 1924).

Not coincidentally, all of these poems containing translations as basic elements present women occupying different roles in the act of literary creation, and together they form an interwoven sequence that systematically explores, and implicitly seeks improvement upon, traditional postures for the feminine within the process of poetic production.[59] A lament for the lost allure of an aging, epic (indeed, Helen-ic) beauty, "Lais" concerns a woman as the traditional object of poetic depiction. In "Heliodora," which recounts the efforts of two poets striving to distinguish themselves in the realm of poetry, the woman serves as inspirational muse. And "Nossis" celebrates a woman as herself a powerful poet capable even of sexually arousing the very wax upon which she writes her erotic verses. As a group, these three poems make up H. D.'s most direct, formally innovative and sophisticated lyric response to the conceptual double bind she faced in her struggle to define and establish herself as both a Modernist and woman poet. For they at once evince and openly hazard the fundamental contradiction of that double bind in seeking to represent the dimensions of feminine poetic identity through male personae. And in each one, an act of translation provides the means for H. D. to surmount that contradiction, serving as a compositional strategy by which she assimilates the masculine tradition of writing about women with her own project of writing as a woman.

So, for example, in "Lais" H. D. joins her rhapsody on the themes and images in Plato's epigram together with the epigram itself rendered into English. In doing so, she creates a composite text that illustrates the history of women in poetry precisely in order to reconfigure that history and imagine a female poetic subject independent of a masculinist ideology of beauty. Organized in eight stanzas, the poem begins with a pointed renunciation of one of the traditional accouterments of feminine cosmetic beauty:

> Let her who walks in Paphos
> take the glass,
> let Paphos take the mirror
> and the work of frosted fruit,
> gold apples set
> with silver apple-leaf,
> white leaf of silver
> wrought with vein of gilt. (*CP*, 149)

Repeated imperatives to Aphrodite underscore the vehemence of the emotion, but the lavish description of the mirror itself bespeaks a deep attachment, as well as indicates an abiding concern with precise detail that renders each excruciating realization of lost beauty into a subject for poetry. A series of questions reveals each traumatic marker of age, and the first half of the poem ends with a depiction of both physical decline and emotional bereavement:

> Did she deck black hair
> one evening, with winter-white
> flower of the winter-berry,
> did she look (reft of her lover)
> at a face gone white
> under the chaplet
> of white virgin-breath?

But rather than foreclosing the possibility for further poetic treatment, as would be the case in a traditional masculinist aesthetic economy, in "Lais" the loss of beauty merely occasions the development (or at least the assertion) of a distinct feminine identity. Thus, in its second half the poem shifts from the indirect narrative modes of the imperative and interrogative to the direct, declarative presentation of the titular female subject. After two stanzas explaining that "Lais, exultant, tyrannizing Greece" now "has left her mirror" because of lost beauty, a third stanza describes the woman who, though no longer beautiful, nevertheless finds the capacity to move beyond emotional devastation:

> Lais has left her mirror,
> for she weeps no longer,
> finding in its depth,
> a face but other
> than dark flame and white
> feature of perfect marble.

After attaining to the expression of a feminine poetic subject not defined solely[60] in terms of the category of physical beauty, "Lais" culminates with "a translation of the Plato epigram in the Greek Anthology," a change in presentational modes that H. D. not only announces in her prefatory "Note," but one that she also explicitly marks within the poem itself, visually (by means of italics) as well as verbally (through her own parenthetical interjection):

> *Lais has left her mirror,*
> (so one wrote)
> *to her who reigns in Paphos;*
> *Lais who laughed a tyrant over Greece,*
> *Lais who turned the lovers from the porch*
> *that swarm for whom now*
> *Lais has no use;*
> *Lais is now no lover of the glass,*
> *seeing no more the face as it once was*
> *wishing to see that face and finding this.*

In itself, this epigram merely recapitulates a masculinist poetic economy in that it focuses upon its female subject only and precisely to the point of declaring her loss of beauty. Assimilating the original through the practice of translation and deploying it as the conclusion of her own poem, however, H. D. openly displays the genealogy of "Lais," thereby constructing a literary history that recuperates Plato's epigram as a source and inspiration for her attempt at giving expression to a Modernist feminine poetic identity. Thus, in "Lais," translation serves as a means by which H. D. creates a compound text wherein she synthesizes the classical, masculine history of writing about women with her own Modernist feminine poetic practice.

Just as she incorporates a rendering of Plato's epigram in "Lais" to confront and redefine the treatment of women as objects of poetic depiction, so, in "Heliodora," H. D. translates "the two Meleager epigrams from the Anthology" as a way of assuming the authority of the classical male poet in order to assert the originary importance of the feminine in its traditional role as inspirational muse. Voiced in the persona of one of its two male participants, "Heliodora" narrates a competition between brother poets, each seeking to achieve eternal fame and genuine poetic originality by finding images and words of praise adequate to the woman of the poem's title. After trading locutions over the course of several stanzas, the unnamed speaker acknowledges the superiority of his rival's verses and, at once deeply moved and covetous of the other's poetic gift, he seeks to recover his pride by questioning the importance of a single human girl in comparison to the divine inspirational power of the nine muses:

> Let him take the name,
> he had the rhymes,
> "the rose, loved of love,
> the lily, a mouth that laughs,"
> he had the gift,
> "the scented crocus,
> the purple hyacinth,"
> what was one girl to the nine? (*CP*, 153)

In response, the speaker's friend and rival, who turns out to be Meleager, merely presents his poems. At the climax of "Heliodora," H. D. once again employs translation to incorporate the work of a classical male poet into her own and to put its authority to her own purposes. Meleager's epigrams help to establish a role of genuine importance for the feminine in the process of poetic production by demonstrating the capacity of a human woman, even a "girl faint and shy," "to vie with the nine" as a source of inspiration and, by extension, of poetry itself.

> He said:
> "I will make her a wreath;"

he said:
"I will write it thus:

I will bring you the lily that laughs,
I will twine
with soft narcissus, the myrtle,
sweet crocus, white violet,
the purple hyacinth, and last,
the rose, loved-of-love,
that these may drip on your hair
the less soft flowers,
may mingle sweet with the sweet
of Heliodora's locks
myrrh-curled."
(He wrote myrrh-curled,
I think, the first.)

At the end of "Heliodora," the speaker meditates upon the achievement of his friend as they part company, recognizing the way in which Meleager has permanently altered the art of poetry (and even his own habits of perception) with his lines of Imagist intensity. The poem concludes, then, through a complex logic with H. D. demonstrating her own poetic power and authority by asserting the originary significance of the writer whose image and even text she has cast in her own idiom by means of translation:

I watched him to the door,
catching his robe
as the wine-bowl crashed to the floor,
spilling a few wet lees,
(ah, his purple hyacinth!)
I saw him out of the door,
I thought:
there will never be a poet
in all the centuries after this,
who will dare write,
after my friend's verse,
"a girl's mouth
is a lily kissed."

Never another poet, that is, until H. D. herself; and in taking Meleager's voice through the practice of translation, she not only claims for women a constitutive role in the act of literary creation, but, in doing so, she also proves her claim to the status of poet.

In "Nossis," H. D. once again both incorporates part of a text by Meleager and dramatizes a debate between two males. Unlike "Heliodora," however, this last of her trio of lyrics concerning the different roles occupied by women in the process of poetic production also contains a translation of "the poem of Nossis herself in the Greek Anthology" and takes as its subject the classical female writer for whom the poem is titled. At the outset an unnamed speaker challenges the admiration Meleager has for Nossis as a poet by ridiculing her achievement and crudely reducing her to the status of a receptacle for male sexual desire:

> I said:
> "a girl that's dead
> some hundred year;
> a poet—what of that?
> for in the islands,
> in the haunts of Greek Ionia,
> Rhodes and Cyprus,
> girls are cheap."

Meleager answers by lamenting the masculine tendency, as embodied in his friend's cheap taunt, to obscure the accomplishments of women and by declaring a desire for "a garden" to commemorate Nossis, as well as several of her sister poets. The speaker comes to learn that, rather than wishing for an actual horticultural enclosure where he can, in Adamic fashion, engage in the traditionally masculine act of creating language by naming each flower, Meleager has in his *Garland* anthology transmitted the work of various female poets and offered in the medium of their own accomplishment an appropriate floral tribute to each of them, thereby preserving their memory against the obscuring ignorance of masculine history. Reciting Meleager's preface to his *Garland*, the speaker then realizes that Nossis does indeed possess such power as a poet that her words actually arouse and soften the wax upon which she writes; and he quotes a lyric by the poet herself (through H. D.'s act of translation) that rejects conventional tropes praising Love merely to demonstrate the staggering depths of her own desire and devotion:

> *"Who made the wreath,*
> *for what man was it wrought?*
> *speak, fashioned all of fruit-buds,*
> *song, my loveliest,*
> *say, Meleager brought to Diocles,*
> *(a gift for that enchanting friend)*
> *memories with names of poets.*
> *He sought for Moero, lilies,*
> *and those many,*
> *red-lilies for Anyte,*
> *for Sappho, roses,*
> *with those few, he caught*
> *that breath of the sweet-scented*

> *leaf of iris,*
> *the myrrh-iris,*
> *to set beside the tablet*
> *and the wax*
> *which Love had burnt,*
> *when scarred across by Nossis:"*

when she wrote:

> *"I Nossis stand by this:*
> *I state that love is sweet:*
> *if you think otherwise*
> *assert what beauty*
> *or what charm*
> *after the charm of love,*
> *retains its grace?*
>
> *"Honey," you say:*
> *honey? I say "I spit*
> *honey out of my mouth:*
> *nothing is second-best*
> *after the sweet of Eros."*

Ending with the same lines by which it began, the poem charts the transformation of its speaker from a sarcastic skeptic of Nossis's power as a poet to a fellow devotee who shares Meleager's admiration for her and understands the nearly mystical rejuvenatory power of his words of praise:

> I thought to hear him speak
> the girl might rise
> and make the garden silver
> as the white moon breaks,
> "Nossis," he cried, "a flame."

In "Nossis" H. D. attempts to map a revisionary history of poetic influence in which women give inspiration to men based not only on their status as objects of desire, but also through their own poetic mastery. And if the content of Nossis's epigram from *The Greek Anthology* recapitulates the conventional association between female poets and themes of love and loss, H. D. precisely through her act of translation nevertheless simultaneously offers a precedent for her own ambitions as a woman poet and justifies those ambitions by modernizing the achievement of her classical predecessor and assimilating it to her own expressive manner.

Together, these three poems indicate some of the writers from which H. D. drew both challenge and inspiration as she engendered the Greek tradition to underwrite her efforts as a self-consciously woman poet. In particular, Meleager's dual presence in both "Heliodora" and "Nossis" as at once a source and a persona in their respective dramas attests to his significance for H. D. as a classical male poet who "offered a constructive model of gender relations in culture which at the same time did not ignore the possibility of a chivalric iconisation of woman—the best, one might argue, of both possible worlds, of both discourses" (Duplessis 1986, 22). More important for my purposes here, however, as a group, "Lais," "Heliodora," and "Nossis" demonstrate the fundamental practical and conceptual importance of translation as a strategy by which H. D. sought actively to configure the relationship between the feminine and poetic production.

In the years following the publication of *Heliodora* in 1924, H. D. continued to engage in translation as a vital practice of her own expression, publishing three substantial translation sequences from dramas by Euripides in *Red Roses for Bronze*, "Choros Translations from *The Bacchae*," "Sea-Choros from *Hecuba*," and "Choros Sequence from *Morpheus*," as well as, in 1937, a complete version of *Euripides' Ion, Translated with Notes*. Inasmuch as these works were produced during H. D.'s supposedly "fallow" period during the 1930s, they represent an important bridge between her earlier lyrics and her later magisterial achievements in verse. As such, they indicate the continuing importance of translation as a literary mode to H. D.'s development as a writer, and therefore warrant a reexamination of their considerable formal idiosyncrasies in light of her conception of translation as a critical practice through which she sought to engender alternatives to masculinist constructions of literary production (c.f. Gregory, 183–90 and 205–18).

VI

Up to this point, I have concentrated on those works in which H. D. employed translation as a *practical* technique in the creation of literary texts, both her translations per se and her own "original" poems. I would like to conclude by pointing out a moment that suggests how translation continued to play a crucial *conceptual* role in the process of her poetic development. At the beginning of *Helen in Egypt*, a work that has been recognized as a Modernist attempt at "creating a women's mythology" (Friedman, "Mythology"), H. D. reveals the classical Greek precedents and mythic threads out of which she came to weave her "own cantos" (*ETT*, 32):[61]

> We all know the story of Helen of Troy but few of us have followed her to Egypt. How did she get there? Stesichorus of Sicily in his Pallinode, *was the first to tell us. Some centuries later, Euripides repeats the story. Stesichorus was said to have*

been struck blind because of his invective against Helen, but later was restored to sight, when he reinstated her in his Pallinode. *Euripides, notably in* The Trojan Women, *reviles her, but he also is "restored to sight." The later little understood* Helen in Egypt, *is again a Pallinode, a defence, explanation or apology.*

According to the Pallinode, *Helen was never in Troy. She had been transposed or translated from Greece into Egypt. Helen of Troy was a phantom, substituted for the real Helen, by jealous deities. The Greeks and the Trojans alike fought for an illusion.* (Helen, 1)

Though brief and clearly introductory, this initial argument to *Helen in Egypt* nevertheless maps the principal dimensions of H. D.'s manifold accomplishment. Most obviously, it illustrates her ardent classicism. In addition, these two paragraphs also reflect the extent to which male writers, in particular Euripides, and their views of women functioned for H. D. throughout her career as both inspiration and challenge. On a more formal level, as the opening to perhaps her single greatest poetic achievement, this passage demonstrates H. D.'s commitment to prose as a vital medium of expression and underscores the fundamental inter-relationship between her considerable prose fiction texts and her more renowned poetry. Indeed, one of the chief distinctions of *Helen in Egypt* lies in the way it sustains an epic momentum as well as a lyric intensity throughout by modulating between the expository prose arguments and the terse, emotionally charged poetic passages of each of its sections. Finally, the opening to *Helen in Egypt* indicates how translation continued to function for H. D., even late into her career, as a conceptual strategy for configuring the relationship between gender and artistic production; for H. D.'s assertion that Helen "had been transposed or translated from Greece into Egypt" articulates a metaphorical structure for the mythical event constituting the very foundation for *Helen in Egypt*, a text that attempts to transform the mythic female figure who lies at the heart of the masculine literary tradition so many male Modernists were trying to revive and extend (Helen of Troy) into the embodiment of a Modernist feminine poetic practice (Helen in Egypt).

As it does with so many of her other, more well-known concerns and predilections, then, *Helen in Egypt* culminates H. D.'s long-term engagement with translation. In this engagement, translation served a range of crucial functions. In the earliest stages of her development, it provided an introduction to the poetic. More than simply an exercise in apprenticeship, however, translation played a number of important roles throughout H. D.'s efforts as a writer. As a literary mode, it embodied a strategy through which she began to conceive an artistic identity unconstrained by the categories and assumptions of a masculinist literary culture. Indeed, as she theorized it, translation itself engenders a writing process that unites poetic insight with an expressly feminine manner of linguistic (re)production. As a concrete writing practice, moreover, it provided a means not only to renew a feminine literary tradition stretching back to antiquity, but also to reconfigure the gendered nature of the largely masculine classical tradition, the authority of which so many of her male contemporaries were attempting to put to their own purposes. And as a conceptual framework it provided the metaphorical foundations for arguably her most enduring poetic achievement.

Pound's (in)famous early achievements in *Cathay* and the *Homage to Sextus Propertius* together with H. D.'s sustained engagement in rendering various Greek texts collectively demonstrate how translation functioned during the Modernist period as at once a concrete and conceptual strategy for exploring and even actively configuring the relationship between gender and literary production. Perhaps of even more lasting importance, through their efforts they redefined the operative parameters of translation as a literary mode, both obviating thorough knowledge of the source language as a requirement and, as a corollary, expressly pushing the boundaries of the practice beyond merely the "accurate" reproduction of semantic meaning. In saying this, I do not mean to suggest that Pound and H. D. worked together in some kind of conscious partnership toward any of these goals. Despite their long, and at times intimate, association with each other and each other's work, the differences between their views, especially on the issues of gender and its relation to poetry, remain at least as important as their similarities or shared beliefs. However, the *consequences* of their efforts as translators reinforced each other and had similar effects for the subsequent practice of translation as a literary mode in English.

Momentous as they are, however, these achievements do not exhaust either the significance or the developments in translation during the period of Anglo-American Modernism. As we shall see in the following section, both Yeats and Pound also employed translation as a crucial means for addressing issues of nation in both cultural and political terms. For Yeats, translation plays a pivotal role in the formation of a national Irish dramatic culture, and his versions of both *King Oedipus* (1928) and *Oedipus at Colonus* (1932) represent important stages in his pursuit of that goal. Comparably, Pound came at once to consider and to practice translation as a means for establishing a just government through his renderings of several Confucian philosophical classics. Moreover, through their work as translators, they not only solidified the redefinition of translation as a literary mode, under which we still largely operate today, but they also came to expand the terms of their own poetics. And all of these efforts helped to make the age of Anglo-American Modernism truly an "age of translations."

Part II

Translation and Politics

Chapter Four

"Uplift our State"[1]
Yeats, Oedipus, and the Translation of a National Dramatic Form

I

With major achievements of various sorts ranging from the late nineteenth century to almost the middle of the twentieth, William Butler Yeats stands as the first, and in many ways most successful, of the polymath geniuses of Anglo-American Modernism.[2] Poet, playwright, propagandist, philosopher of the occult, and politician, among other things, Yeats also helped to make the Modernist period in English "an age of translations" by producing renderings of both *King Oedipus* (1928) and *Oedipus at Colonus* (1934), which to this day remain compelling for their charged diction and powerful, stately rhythms. The ongoing effectiveness of these works, especially that of their language, eloquently registers the extent to which contemporary aesthetic values remain deeply rooted in the standards and practices first set forth by the Modernists. In addition to such specifically dedicated feats of translation per se, Yeats also explicitly practiced translation as a form of poetic composition, concluding both "A Man Young and Old" and "A Woman Young and Old," the final sequences from arguably his two finest collections of verse, *The Tower* (1928) and *The Winding Stair and Other Poems* (1933), with poetic renderings of choral odes from *Oedipus at Colonus* and *Antigone* respectively. Much more than just belated exercises of apprenticeship, as their appearance at the very height of his career alone suggests, these acts of translation of and from the tragedies of Sophocles culminate a more than quarter-century engagement with the practice of translation as a strategy for establishing the terms of an expressly national culture in the face of the hybrid cultural situation of modern Ireland, an engagement that unfolded primarily within the context of Yeats's attempt to establish an Irish national theater and native dramatic form. Indeed, over and above his efforts specifically as a translator, Yeats participated in the Modernist revolution in translation as a literary mode through his varied reflections upon both the larger significance and proper method of translation as a constitutive practice in the formation of an authentic modern Irish culture. Thus, as with virtually all forms of cultural production in which he took an interest, Yeats viewed translation not simply as a casual literary practice, but as a crucially important one with profound national cultural, social, and political implications.

Over the years, the subject of Yeats's politics, and in particular his engagement with ideologies of nationalism, has generated considerable discussion. Indeed, something of a controversy began with Conor Cruise O'Brien's now famous critique of the writer's political views as elitist and authoritarian and his "true" nationality as Anglo-Irish Protestant.[3] Responding to these assertions, critics have for some time debated the content of Yeats's political opinions, with some echoing O'Brien's indictments, while others have defended him as either a "genuine" Irish nationalist or as a liberal humanist and individualist.[4] Another approach has been to trace his development from Irish nationalist to Anglo-Irish reactionary.[5] With the advent of post-colonial cultural theory, which has offered fresh perspectives on the terms and significance of nationalism as a cultural and political ideology, critics have shifted the grounds of debate slightly, while continuing to operate within an evaluative scheme of praise and censure. Thus, Edward Said has valorized Yeats as a "poet of decolonization,"[6] while Seamus Deane and Richard Kearney have each issued critiques of Yeats's nationalism as a particularly harmful sort with foundations in mystification, myth, and even blood sacrifice.[7] Most recently, some critics have begun to move beyond such ultimately reductive partisan judgments to analyze the various strategies by which Yeats participates in the discourse of Irish nationality and national culture. So David Lloyd has offered a remarkable discussion of Yeats's later poetry "as constituting in its very extremities a profound interrogation of the process of foundation by which states come into being, a process predicated on a performative violence which his own poetry dramatically appropriates."[8] And in *Yeats's Nations*, Marjorie Howes has produced the most thorough-going and nuanced examination of "the particular structures of his various conceptions of Irishness, their relation to social, political and cultural discourses, and their changes and continuities over time."[9] Throughout their diverse and sometimes conflicting assessments, however, all of the critics addressing the issues surrounding Yeats's politics have focused virtually exclusively on his "original" poetry and plays, completely ignoring his lengthy, if comparatively attenuated, engagement with translation as a mode of cultural production.

Within the field of Translation Studies, moreover, Yeats's work as a translator has gone similarly unnoticed. In *Translating Ireland: Translation, Languages, Cultures*, Michael Cronin offers the most extensive survey of the importance of translators for "the emergence and development of different cultures in Ireland" from the Middle Ages to the contemporary moment;[10] yet even he makes no mention of Yeats's own efforts in this arena. At one level, of course, this comes as little surprise. After all, unlike Pound, Yeats did not achieve his considerable reputation to any significant degree, if at all, through his efforts as a translator. Indeed, by the time of the publication of *King Oedipus* in 1928, Yeats had long since established himself as arguably the preeminent poet of his era writing in English. Due at least in part to his monumental status as an "original" writer, discussions of Yeats's translations have remained limited to textual histories and thematic analyses aimed at showing how his renderings of Sophocles recapitulate the concerns he explored in his own verse and drama.[11] For all their detailed philological insight and local utility, however, existing studies have perpetuated a longstanding prejudice by uncritically assuming the secondary, and even derivative, status of translation as a mode of literary production, a trait they share with more overtly "political" approaches to Yeats's diverse body of work. Yet numerous theorists have convincingly argued for the primary, generative significance of translation as a cultural practice in various contexts and, more particularly, as the work of Michael Cronin amply demonstrates, Yeats's engagement with literary translation participates in a more than thousand-year history in which "translators as inventive mediators have shaped every area of Irish life for centuries" (Cronin, 1). At least as important as these general theoretical and historical considerations, Yeats himself, as we shall see, considered translation absolutely crucial to the constitution of a healthy and distinctive Irish national culture. This helps to explain both his early interest in staging *Oedipus Rex* for the Irish National Theater and why he again took up and finally completed his own renderings of both Oedipus plays at the very height of his career, after having let them fall aside for more than a decade. Accordingly, then, I want in what follows to bring these various separate strands of Yeats criticism together with the results of recent work in Translation Studies in order to trace the development of Yeats's conception of the significance of translation as a mode of literary production, from a necessary task of negotiating the rift between the Gaelic roots and English realities of modern Ireland to a vital instrument, in the form of his renderings of *King Oedipus* and *Oedipus at Colonus*, for critiquing the monolithic, exclusionary version of national culture promulgated by the Irish Free State after its establishment in 1922. Along the way, showing how a key Modernist writer at once conceived and engaged in different particular feats of translation as a means of expressly political action, I hope in this chapter to contribute to ongoing discussions about the relationship between national formations and various modes of literary production.[12]

II

Though he would not himself actually become a translator until many years later, Yeats helped to lay the foundation for a Modernist redefinition of the cultural and practical meaning of translation as a mode of literary production when he came, relatively early in his career, to regard and espouse it as one of the most important means by which Ireland could establish its own particular identity amid the crowd of world contemporary, and even historical, cultures. In his eyes, translation as a literary mode provided a way to reconcile the Gaelic roots of Irish culture with its "raw modern English" realities. Such a view underwrites, for example, his response to Lady Augusta Gregory's *Cuchulain of Muirthemne* (1902), and it helps to explain the uncharacteristic hyperbole with which he begins his response to the collection of Irish folktales concerning the men of the Red Branch of Ulster that she arranged and put into English. So telling is his reaction that I repeat it here from the Introduction: "I think this book is the best book that has come out of Ireland in my time. Perhaps I should say that it is the best book that has ever come out of Ireland; for the stories it tells are a chief part of Ireland's gift to the imagination of the world—and it tells them perfectly for the first time."[13]

At the simplest level, Yeats offers his friend, fellow Protestant Celtic revivalist, and eventual patron lavish praise for renewing these legends and making such artifacts of Ireland's cultural heritage more accessible (and, as we shall see momentarily, more presentable) by dressing them in the hegemonic language of her current social circumstances. Such enthusiasm registers in part Yeats's discomfort with, if not opposition to, the implicit cultural exclusivity of the Gaelic League and its efforts to reestablish the dominance of the language of Ireland's pre-colonial past. For in asserting that Lady Gregory had taken the stories that "are a chief part of Ireland's gift to the imagination of the world" and "[told] them perfectly for the first time," Yeats situates Irish cultural production within a global context and quietly insists upon the capacity of English to serve as a medium of specifically Irish expression. Indeed, he even suggests that translation improves upon the tales themselves by enabling the achievement of perfection in the process of retelling them in English.

Even more important than the renewal of indigenous Irish legends or folktales, then, Yeats finds Lady Gregory's real accomplishment in the expressly and intensely literary quality of her method as a translator, a method marked by two characteristics also distinguishing Modernist poetic practice: compression and rhythmical invention. Contrasting Lady Gregory's efforts with those of previous translators from the Gaelic, Yeats discerns and endorses an approach to translation that does not end merely with the "accurate" reproduction of semantic content from one language to another, but rather entails a manifold process of narrative concentration, selection of appropriate detail, and rhythmic adequation. He thereby promotes translation as a form of literary production fundamentally comparable, if indeed not equivalent, to poetic composition. Yeats himself would eventually come to follow such a procedure for his own renderings of Sophocles, though in his own way and for decidedly different reasons:

> Translators from the Irish have hitherto retold one story or other from some one version, and not often with any fine understanding of English, of those changes of rhythm that are changes of the sense. They have translated the best and fullest manuscripts they knew, as accurately as they could, and that is all we have the right to expect from the first translators of a difficult and old literature. But few of the stories really begin to exist as great works of imagination until somebody has taken the best bits of many manuscripts. Sometimes, as in Lady Gregory's version of *Deirdre*, a dozen manuscripts have had to give their best before the beads are ready for the necklace. It has been as necessary also to leave out as to add, for generations of copyists, who had often but little sympathy with the stories they copied, have mixed versions together in a clumsy fashion, and every century has ornamented what was once a simple story with its own often extravagant ornament. We do not perhaps exaggerate when we say that no story has come down to us in the form it had when the story-teller told it in the winter evenings. Lady Gregory has done her work of compression and selection at once so firmly and so reverently that I cannot believe that anybody, except now and then for a scientific purpose, will need another text than this, or than the version of it the Gaelic League is about to publish in Modern Irish. (*Exp.*, 3–4)

The plans of the Gaelic League to publish a Modern Irish version of *Cuchulain of Muirthemne* hint at the sharply bifurcated approach to national culture formation that has marked Irish literary production since at least the mid-nineteenth century and the efforts of the Young Ireland movement.[14] On the one hand, figures such as Dr. Douglas Hyde insisted on the need to reclaim Gaelic as the principal medium of cultural commerce in the effort to establish an authentic Irish national culture, while on the other, Yeats together with other monoglot English speakers maintained at least the practical necessity of allowing for the possibility of using their "mother tongue" as an appropriate vehicle for Irish culture.[15] It remains beyond the scope of the present study to give a full account of this long controversy, as well as of the various efforts by members of the Irish Literary Revival to render indigenous texts into English and to produce new literary works in Gaelic itself. However, as Michael Cronin has convincingly shown, translation remained a crucial activity for both sides of the debate.[16] Hence, most important of all for Yeats, Lady Gregory had come through the process of translation to discover a language, Hiberno-English, rooted firmly in and therefore uniquely suited to the expression of Irish experience, a vitally hybrid language that registers a synthesis between the resources of Gaelic and the dominant, but by no means uncontested, medium of English. Indeed, as he tells it, Yeats's own early efforts at reviving the Irish cultural past through narrative (presumably in *The Celtic Twilight* [1893]) merely prepared him to recognize not simply the value of Lady Gregory's achievement as a translator, but more important, the significance of translation itself as a crucially generative practice in the establishment of a distinctly modern Irish culture. Well before Mikhail Bakhtin published his theory of the novel as a genre that arises from and reflects the polyglot conditions of a given society,[17] Yeats considered translation a practice that provided a way to resolve the conflict in modern Ireland between English and Gaelic:

> Perhaps more than all she has discovered a fitting dialect to tell them in. Some years ago, I wrote some stories of medieval Irish life, and as I wrote I was sometimes made wretched by the thought that I knew of no kind of English that fitted them as the language of [William] Moriss's prose stories—the most beautiful language I had ever read—fitted his journeys to woods and wells beyond the world. I knew of no language to write about Ireland in but raw modern English; but now Lady Gregory has discovered a speech as beautiful as that of Morris, and a living speech into the bargain. As she moved about among her people she learned to love the beautiful speech of those who think in Irish, and to understand that it is as true a dialect of English as the dialect that Burns wrote in. It is some hundreds of years old, and age gives a language authority. We find in it the vocabulary of the translators of the Bible, joined to an idiom which makes it tender, compassionate, and complaisant, like the Irish language itself. It is certainly well suited to clothe a literature which never ceased to be folk-lore even when it was recited in the Courts of Kings. (*Exp.*, 4)

Through the specific example of Lady Gregory's efforts, then, Yeats came to recognize and promote translation as a constitutive writing practice that, among other things, made available a language offering a way to meet one of the most enduring challenges confronting Irish literary culture, the contradiction of presenting Irish subject matter through the established and effectively inescapable medium of English, a language tainted by its history in Ireland as an instrument of colonial domination and native cultural displacement.[18] As Yeats himself suggests, such a situation imposed emotional as well as artistic difficulties for him in particular, inasmuch as he did not posses Gaelic to any significant degree and in any case deeply revered the poetic tradition and capacities of English. To be sure, the decidedly conventional metaphor of clothing he employs in the final sentence of the above passage even suggests that Yeats felt Irish literature could only be made presentable to the eyes of the world dressed in the lineaments of some form of English.[19] In this respect, Yeats's thinking on translation at this point remains solidly traditional, premised on a belief that translation as a mode of writing does not fundamentally alter an original work, but rather merely updates it by fitting it with more contemporary and fashionable garb. No doubt this view arose at least in part as a self-serving justification for Yeats's own inabilities with Gaelic. And yet, he also recognized the inherent problems, both political and conceptual, of using English to write about Ireland. In a speech given in New York in 1903–4, Yeats recalled the early impact that the Gaelic language movement had on his sense of relevance and utility as a writer: "When this Gaelic movement first arose, it seemed to people like me, who had to do our work in English, that there was no work at all for us to do in Ireland. At first it looked as if there was only one task and that was to set everyone to work learning Irish."[20] And in the *Samhain* of 1903, he addresses the contradictions of writing about a free and culturally independent Ireland in the language of its domination, as well as the constraints such a tradition places on the possibilities of true artistic innovation. Contrasting his own efforts with those of the Gaelic writers, Yeats laments, "we who write in English have a more difficult work, for English has been the language in which the Irish cause has been debated; and we have had to struggle with traditional phrases and traditional points of view" (*Exp.*, 104).

Nevertheless, despite any uncertainties he may have harbored about the politics of English as a medium for Irish expression, or perhaps more precisely because of them, Yeats began to advocate the practice of translation as an essential component in an overall national Irish cultural program. Indeed, reviewing the year's activities of the Irish Literary Theatre in the *Samhain* of 1902, he goes so far as to openly urge one of his most distinguished and successful contemporaries, Dr. Douglas Hyde, who co-founded the Gaelic League and led the cultural separatist effort of "de-anglicisation," to focus more of his efforts on producing additional translations from Gaelic. Again invoking the example of the King James Bible in England,

Yeats explicitly asserts a connection between translation and the foundation of a national literature:

> I wish . . . that [Dr. Hyde] could put away from himself some of the interruptions of that ceaseless propaganda, and find time for the making of translations, loving and leisurely, like those in *Beside the Fire* and the *Love Songs of Connacht*. . . . Above all I would have him keep to that English idiom of the Irish-thinking people of the West which he has begun to use less often. It is the only good English spoken by any large number of Irish people to-day, and we must found good literature on a living speech. English men of letters found themselves on the English Bible, where religious thought gets its living speech. Blake, if I remember rightly, copied it out twice, and I remember once finding a few illuminated pages of a new decorated copy that he began in his old age. Byron read it for the sake of style, though I think it did him little good; and Ruskin founded himself in great part upon it. Indeed, we find everywhere signs of a book which is the chief influence in the lives of English children. The translation used in Ireland has not the same literary beauty, and if we are to find anything to take its place, we must find it in that idiom of the poor, which mingles so much the same vocabulary with turns of phrase that have come out of Gaelic. (*Exp.*, 93–94)

Inasmuch as it serves as the mechanism by which a living, native speech becomes a vehicle for written expression through the rendering of indigenous folk-tales and songs, translation lays the foundation, in Yeats's eyes, for a distinctly modern and Irish, rather than simply traditional Celtic, literature. As a literary mode, translation afforded Yeats a way to assimilate the Gaelic tradition, from which he was linguistically excluded, to his own, English-language based conception of a national Irish culture.[21]

At the same time that he encouraged "internal" translation, or the rendering of works between the operative languages within the country, as a way for Ireland as a whole to recognize, renew, and remain true to its Gaelic roots without forsaking either the realities or the benefits of English, Yeats also viewed "external" translation, or the rendering of works from other languages, as a means by which to cultivate and to gauge Irish achievement against the examples of great civilizations past and present, thereby making it essential to the formation of a distinctive modern national culture. Indeed, evolving primarily within the context of his enormously diverse efforts on behalf of modern Irish theater, this particular aspect of Yeats's thought on translation ultimately led to his versions of both *King Oedipus* and *Oedipus at Colonus*. But long before he undertook to translate Greek tragedy himself, Yeats bestowed upon translation a central role in the program of the various phases of the Irish Dramatic Movement, through which he, along with other such luminary figures as

Lady Gregory, Edward Martyn, George Moore, and Frank and Willie Fay, together sought to make drama a vital form of modern Irish cultural life. So, in the prospectus for the Irish Literary Theatre that appeared as the initial *Samhain* in 1901, Yeats implicitly underscores the importance of the practice of translation as an instrument in the formation of a national identity when he lays out the internationalist ambitions of the stock company of the Theatre:

> [The company] would perform plays in Irish and English, and also, it is proposed, the masterpieces of the world, making it a point of performing Spanish, and Scandinavian, and French and perhaps Greek masterpieces rather more than Shakespeare. ... It would do its best to give Ireland a hardy and shapely national character by opening its doors to the fours winds of the world, instead of leaving the door that is towards the east wind open alone. Certainly, the national character, which is so essentially different from the English that Spanish and French influences may well be more healthy, is at present like one of those miserable thorn-bushes by the sea that are all twisted to one side by some prevailing wind. (*Exp.*, 75–76)

Again, for Yeats translation strengthens Irish cultural identity against undue Anglo-Saxon influence by making possible the performance of masterpieces from other countries and traditions. Here, Yeats's sense of nationalism links up with the internationalism so characteristic of Modernist writing in general, suggesting one of the reasons why translation came to occupy such an important role throughout the period. But even more important than for the performance of foreign plays, translation stands as a necessary precondition for achieving a mature Irish drama. Making it his own point to insist that "It is of the first importance that those among us who wish to write for the stage should study the dramatic masterpieces of the world" (*Exp.*, 78), Yeats goes on to assert that "the moment we leave even a little the folk-tradition of the peasant, as we must in drama, if we do not know the best that has been said and written in the world, we do not even know ourselves" (*Exp.*, 80). The strong echo here of part of Matthew Arnold's definition of culture indicates the depth of Yeats's allegiance to an English literary tradition. Moreover, it reveals a distinctly conservative strain in his thought about both the proper sources and functions of culture in the establishment of a national Irish cultural identity, something that has frequently led to charges of elitism. But whereas Arnold saw foreign cultures and traditions as important for the *maintenance* of English culture against the rising dangers of philistinism and anarchy, Yeats saw the wealth of literary achievement from around the world as necessary to the *constitution* of a modern Irish cultural identity. The difference between Arnold and Yeats in this regard attests to the necessarily different meanings of internationalism within a colonizing as opposed to a colonized context. And with respect to the practice of translation in particular, Arnold, as I mentioned in the introduction, insisted upon a scholarly foundation for the practice. By contrast, as we shall see, in his own efforts Yeats specifically eschewed such a requirement, which marks his practice as distinctly Modernist. Hence, within the aestheticist logic of his particular brand of cultural nationalism, true knowledge of the Self requires an engagement with the multi-dimensional Otherness of foreign cultures. And insofar as it at once embodies and makes possible such an engagement, translation as a literary mode, especially the translation of foreign drama, represented to him not just a mechanical procedure of linguistic conversion, but a fully literary practice that contributed to the development of an authentic modern national Irish culture. So, even though his own efforts as a translator did not culminate until the 1920s, Yeats was arguably the first major Modernist writer to seriously consider translation a primary and generative literary practice, thus helping to initiate the Modernist revolution in translation.

III

From relatively early on in his career, then, Yeats conceived of translation not just as a literary exercise, but as a form of political action as well; and the extraordinarily drawn-out process that finally issued in his 1928 version of *King Oedipus* began, fittingly enough, with an expressly and perhaps even crudely political desire to stage the play, which had been banned in England at the time by the censor due to its depiction of incest, as a way to trumpet Irish intellectual and artistic sovereignty. Long after the fact, after even its earliest performance at the Abbey Theatre on December 7, 1926, and its publication two years later, Yeats gave two accounts of how he came to write his *Sophocles' King Oedipus*, and it seems useful to quote both of them at length in order to understand his methods and motivations as a translator. Read a few days earlier from the Belfast studio of the BBC as an introduction to the broadcast of the play that took place six days later, Yeats's first account appeared in the September 12, 1931, edition of the *Irish Weekly and Ulster Examiner*:

> Nearly thirty years ago I was at the Catholic University of Notre Dame at Illinois. I had come there to give a lecture about Irish literature, and stayed for a couple of days. A certain monk, specially appointed, I think, to look after the guests, was the best of companions, and told me a great many exciting things about his monastery, about the Irish in America, and about his own thoughts.

The thing that stayed longest in my memory was that "Oedipus the King" had just been performed there under the auspices of his University. "Oedipus the King" was at that time forbidden by the English censor, and I thought that if we could play it at the Abbey Theatre, which was to open on our return, we might make our audience proud of its liberty, and take a noble view of the stage and its mission.

Some three or four years passed, and I began my version with the help of Mr. Nugent Monk [sic], who was at the time helping us at the Abbey, and has since established a famous theatre in Norwich, and a young Greek scholar, then one of our actors, but now a Circuit Judge; and half a dozen translations. Sometimes I went on to the stage and spoke a sentence to be sure that it was simple enough and resonant enough to be instantaneously felt and understood in every part of the theatre. I did not want to make a new translation for the reader, but something that everybody in the house, scholar and pot-boy, would understand as easily as he understood a political speech or an article in a newspaper. The subject matter might be strange and sometimes difficult, but no word might be strange or difficult, nor must I tire the ear by putting those words in some unnatural order.

I finished my first rough draft and began to look for an actor, but before I had found one the English censor withdrew its ban, and when the pleasure of mocking it and affirming the freedom of our Irish uncensored stage was taken from me, I lost interest. I put it into a file with my letters and forgot it, and then four or five years ago my wife found it and persuaded me to finish it and put it on to the Abbey Stage.[22]

Yeats's second account capped his last American lecture tour, appearing in the *New York Times* on January 15, 1933. Perhaps having learned that Notre Dame is not in Illinois, Yeats did not venture to name its location:

When I first lectured in America thirty years ago, I heard at the University of Notre Dame that they had played *Oedipus the King*. The play was forbidden by the English censorship on the ground of its immorality; Oedipus commits incest; but if a Catholic university could perform it in America my own theatre could perform it in Ireland. Ireland had no censorship, and a successful performance might make her proud of her freedom, say even, perhaps, "I have an old historical religion moulded to the body of man like an old suit of clothes, and am therefore free."

... When I got back to Dublin I found a young Greek scholar, who, unlike myself, had not forgotten his Greek, took out of a pigeonhole at the theatre a manuscript translation of *Oedipus* too complicated in its syntax for the stage, bought Jebb's translation and a translation published at a few pence for dishonest schoolboys. Whenever I could not understand the precise thoughts behind the translator's half Latin, half Victorian dignity, I got a bald translation from my Greek scholar. I spoke out every sentence, very often from the stage, with one sole object, that the words should sound natural and fall in their natural order, that every sentence should be a spoken, not a written sentence. Then when I had finished the dialogue in the rough and was still shrinking at the greater labour of the choruses, the English censor withdrew his ban and I lost interest.

About five years ago my wife found the manuscript and set me to work again and when the dialogue was revised and the choruses written, Lady Gregory and I went through it all, altering every sentence that might not be intelligible on the Blasket Islands.[23]

In their thorough, textual study, *W. B. Yeats: The Writing of Sophocles' King Oedipus*, David R. Clark and James B. Maguire have enumerated the various inaccuracies of times, places, and persons that riddle these two accounts.[24] Reconstructing from contemporary documents the entire process through all its fits and starts, they have corrected Yeats's memory lapses, understandable after such a long period, and shown that he did not actually begin to make his own version of *Oedipus Rex* until 1912, though he was interested in producing the play from 1904 onward, as soon as he returned from his first American lecture tour. His faulty, imprecise memory notwithstanding, however, these accounts not only reveal the particularities of Yeats's individual practice as a translator, as well as illuminate certain general trends in the practice of translation as a mode of literary production during the Modernist period as a whole, but they also indicate, in a way that Clark and Maguire seem to have underestimated, the duration and intensity of Yeats's personal engagement with the idea of translation as such. For whenever he actually began himself to translate, as soon as he began seriously to consider staging *Oedipus Rex* at the Abbey Theatre, he necessarily had to confront the questions of translation, questions that he would resolve to his own satisfaction only after a quarter-century had passed.

First, his repeated descriptions of how he very often "went on to the stage and spoke a sentence to be sure that it was simple enough and resonant enough" underscores the extent to which Yeats practiced translation within the parameters of his goals and ambitions as a dramatist and man of the theater. Indeed, over and above the initial cachet of affording him the opportunity to mock English cultural parochialism, translating *Oedipus Rex* enabled Yeats ultimately to give direct and concrete expression to his life-long reverence for the tradition of classical Greek drama, and especially tragedy, upon which he based so many of his theatrical conceptions. In a letter written to Dorothy Wellesley shortly before his death, Yeats declared, "the Greek drama alone achieved perfection," adding that "it has never been done since; it may be thousands of years before we achieve that perfection again."[25] Even so, as James Flannery has written, quoting Yeats's "Commentary on the Three Songs to the Same Tune," "Yeats dreamed of creating an Irish equivalent of the Theatre of Dionysus, a national theatre in which the people would watch 'the sacred drama of its history, every spectator finding self and neighbour, finding all the world there as we find the sun in the bright spot under the looking glass'."[26] Here, the political intentions behind Yeats's early attempt at translation coincide with the larger social purposes he had in mind for the theater, namely to forge a sense of national identity and community, grounded in a process of critical self-scrutiny, through the agency of (symbolic) drama. As Marjorie Howes summarizes, "Yeats's gradual rejection of Celticism and the intensification of his interest in the theatre signaled a shift towards a mode of engagement with the question of Irish nationality that emphasizes the creation and definition of national community."[27] Here Yeats anticipates and even extends Benedict Anderson by including translation among the forms of cultural production that contribute to the development of an expressly national identity. Hence his goal of producing a translation that could be understood as easily as "a political speech or an article in a newspaper," two forms directly related to the establishment and growth of a national collectivity.[28] In addition, on a more technical level, his insistence upon the constraints of verbal utterance as a guiding principle for his translation matches the changes Yeats was seeking to introduce into his verse at about this time, changes that, interestingly enough, he labeled as the introduction of a "theatrical element."[29] Such a correspondence emphasizes the underlying unity of Yeats's diverse efforts as a writer, and furthermore anticipates, as we shall see, the way in which translation would come to serve as a form of poetic composition in the sequences "A Man Young and Old" and "A Woman Young and Old."

Second, and perhaps most significant with regard to the history of translation in English as a literary mode, the actual procedure Yeats outlines in these accounts, the practice of sifting through and weighing different preexisting translations, whether in textual or verbal form, against each other in order to arrive at a new, composite version more closely resembles a form of Barthesian bricolage than any traditional conception of translation, which emphasizes direct engagement with an original foreign text by a single individual. Fully a year before the first of his three winters at Stone Cottage with Pound, where the younger poet worked on the notebooks of Ernest Fenollosa to produce *Cathay*, the first genuine achievement of Modernist translation,[30] Yeats's initial, abortive practice as a translator of *Oedipus Rex* marks an embryonic form of a distinctively Modernist sense of translation as a literary mode, constituting a fundamental break with the conventions of the past. For even when they have been most intensely personal and, some might say, assimilative, as in the cases of Dryden and Pope, it could always be assumed that English translators had full and formal command of the languages from which they translated.[31] By contrast, Yeats freely admits to having "forgotten his Greek" (in fact, as with Hebrew, he never really knew it), yet feeling no compunction whatsoever in proceeding with his translation. Indeed, in both accounts of his procedure as a translator he even goes so far as to make of his ignorance a virtue, suggesting that his lack of classical training actually enabled him to penetrate through the deadening layers of scholarship and, in particular, Latinate culture that have accumulated over the course of history to better express the essential core of Greek sensibility, which he sees as fundamentally similar to that of the Irish. In the *Irish Weekly and Ulster Examiner* he declares,

> I think those great scholars of the last century who translated Sophocles into an English full of Latinised constructions and Latinised habits of thought, were all wrong—and that the school-masters are wrong to make us approach Greek through Latin. Nobody ever trembled on a dark road because he was afraid of meeting the nymphs and satyrs of Latin literature, but men have trembled on dark roads in Ireland and in Greece. Latin literature was founded on documents, but Greek literature came like old Irish literature out of the beliefs of the common people.[32]

Comparably, in the *New York Times* account he writes, "being an ignorant man, I may not have gone to Greece through a Latin mist. Greek literature, like old Irish literature, was founded upon belief, not like Latin literature upon documents. No man has ever prayed to or dreaded one of Virgil's nymphs, but when Oedipus at Colonus went into the Wood of the Furies he felt the same creeping in his flesh that an Irish countryman feels in certain woods in Galway and in Sligo."[33] Needless to say, perhaps, one ought not uncritically to accept Yeats's claims about having been able to reveal some putatively essential quality of the original Greek work because of his lack of formal classical training. After all, his statements clearly function in part as convenient self-justification for his own limitations as both a classicist and a polyglot. Nevertheless, with the truly momentous gesture of retrospectively valorizing his own ignorance, Yeats provides the terms by which to recognize the way he too helped to free literary translation from the requirement of formal knowledge of the source language, thereby casting it as a practice grounded in intuition and poetic sensibility rather than either scholarly training or linguistic ability. In this, he matched Pound and H. D. in redefining the conditions of possibility for translation as a mode of literary production. Indeed, he likely even gained from Pound's quite visible examples in *Cathay* and the *Homage to Sextus Propertius* the necessary confidence in the viability of such a method finally to complete his own renderings of Sophocles. Unlike his two younger contemporaries, however, because his goals as a translator remained one of communication rather than either visionary exploration or transformation, Yeats never went so far as to regard the word itself as the proper focus of translation, holding instead to the more traditional unit of the sentence.[34]

Of course, Yeats did not pursue his interest in *Oedipus Rex* exclusively, or even primarily, as a vehicle through which to reconceptualize the parameters of translation as a literary mode. Rather, as noted above, his engagement with the play began through a desire to produce a version of it for the Irish stage as a way to ridicule English social conservatism, thereby signifying a distinctive Irish cultural sensibility and generating a concomitant sense of national pride. Toward this end, from around the close of 1904 Yeats sought out several potential candidates who actually knew Greek and could provide an English translation for an Irish production. The most distinguished of these was Gilbert Murray, at the time the preeminent literary translator of Greek drama. In his letter to Murray, dated January 24, 1905, Yeats reiterates his goals of mocking English censorship and also contributing to the cultural formation of the Irish nation by staging a performance of *Oedipus Rex*:

> Will you translate Edipus Rex for us? We can offer you nothing for it but a place in heaven, but if you do, it will be a great event. Our company are excited at the idea. The Fays have read it, and believe we can give a fine performance. There is no censor here to forbid it as it has been forbidden in England. It is much better worth writing for us than for Granville Barker. Nothing has any effect in England, but here one never knows when one may affect the mind of a whole generation. The country is in its first plastic state, and takes the mark of every strong finger. We have a beautiful little theatre and can stage it well. Do not ask us to play Euripides instead, for Euripides is rapidly becoming a popular English dramatist, and it is upon Sophocles that we have set our imaginations. Besides, I am always trying to persuade Ireland, which does not understand the game, that she is very liberal, abhor[s] censors[,] delights in the freedom of the arts, is prepared for anything. When we have performed Edipus the King, and everybody is proud of having done something which is forbidden in England, even the newspapers will give [up] pretending to be timid.[35]

Yeats's appeal to Murray emphasizes the degree to which he understood the project of staging *Oedipus Rex*, as well as the project of translation generally, in expressly cultural nationalist terms. For even if his thinking on the matter operates via a crude (and perhaps even objectionable) binary opposition between essential Irish and English attitudes, it nevertheless casts the practice of translation as a vital instrument in the formation of an Irish national identity that "is very liberal, abhor[s] censors[,] delights in the freedom of the arts, is prepared for anything." Indeed,

Murray declined the invitation to render the play in terms that reveal the extent to which overtly nationalist conceptual schemes governed the thinking on cultural matters, including translation of foreign works: "I will not translate the Oedipus Rex for the Irish Theatre, because it is a play with nothing Irish about it: no religion, not one beautiful action, hardly a stroke of poetry."[36]

In his early desire for Murray as the translator for his production of *Oedipus Rex*, Yeats gives an idea of just how far he would eventually come from the point at which he first considered staging the play and thus began to confront the terms and possibilities of translation as a literary mode. For not only was Murray far from radical in his practice as a translator, but he came to embody precisely the kind of essentially conservative approach to translation that such expressly Modernist figures as Pound, H. D., and even T. S. Eliot aggressively denounced as tending to bury the vital essence of Greek literature beneath layers of classical learning, allowing moribund scholarship to replace true, mystical insight.[37] As his later comments make clear, Yeats came largely to share these views of both Greek literature and the practice of translation.

But in 1905, he had yet to begin to undertake, or even to think seriously about, redefining the cultural space of translation. Nor was Gilbert Murray the only person he approached about making a translation of *Oedipus Rex* around this time. Yeats also asked both Oliver Gogarty (the man who served as Joyce's model for "Buck Mulligan" in *Ulysses*) and William Kirkpatrick Magee ("John Eglinton") to produce versions for a possible stage production.[38] For various reasons, none of these avenues proved in the end successful, or perhaps more precisely, satisfactory, and after several more years during which he compared various other existing translations, including ones by Whitelaw and Plumptre, Yeats finally settled, in November of 1909, on the version by R. C. Jebb as "much the best"[39] for the planned Abbey Theatre performance of *Oedipus Rex*. After working for two more years together with Nugent Monck in an abortive attempt to present the play, however, Yeats found Jebb, too, wanting, though it would serve as the foundation from which he would begin making his own version in early 1912.

In his much belated accounts of how he came to write his translation of *Oedipus Rex*, Yeats recalls that when "the English censor withdrew his ban, and when the pleasure of mocking it and affirming the freedom of our Irish uncensored stage was taken from me, I lost interest." Not surprisingly, perhaps, this represents something of a simplification. For, as Clark and Maguire have astutely noted, the Lord Chamberlain lifted his stricture against *Oedipus Rex* in 1910 when he licensed the poet Herbert Trench to stage a production that never actually made it to the boards, some two years before Yeats began corresponding to friends about making his own version; and they have further shown that Yeats did not give up his ambitions either to produce or to translate the play until several months after the opening of yet a different production in 1912, Max Reinhardt's staging of *Oedipus Rex*, which featured, ironically enough, the rendering by Gilbert Murray published in 1911.[40] Thus, Yeats's abandonment of his plans in mid-stream should not be taken simply, as he himself later came to assert, as a loss of interest in either the play or, even more significantly, the project of translation itself. Rather, perhaps all the more revealing of his personal investment in the idea, it suggests a crisis of confidence on the part of Yeats in his own talents as both a producer and a translator when confronted with the apparently greater resources and, at the time, more esteemed abilities in these two respective areas of Reinhardt and Murray.[41]

Nevertheless, Yeats's stated reason for why he abandoned his initial plans to stage *Oedipus Rex* underscores the fundamentally political terms in which he viewed the significance of translation as a literary mode. Moreover, it suggests the evolving social intentions behind his engagement with a single historical text with its own defined system of semantic meaning. For by the time he again took up and finished his rendering of the play, after a fourteen-year hiatus, the conditions of his involvement with the project of creating a national culture had necessarily altered with the establishment of the Irish Free State in 1922 and its subsequent pursuit of an intensely conservative, explicitly Catholic cultural and political agenda. In her defense of his political record as a senator from 1922–28, Elizabeth Cullingford has shown how Yeats consistently worked against the dominant nationalist and Catholic majority by opposing such measures that promoted "compulsory Gaelic, the refusal of divorce and censorship."[42] In other words, the terms of Yeats's pursuit of a cultural nationalism through the practice of translation had changed from one of resistance to an external, colonial ruler (England) to one of opposition to an internal, repressive government. This made the choice of a foreign drama all the more relevant, since it was no longer a question of defending a notion of indigenous Irish culture, but rather one of challenging an increasingly rigid and exclusivist conception of that culture. Accordingly, then, Yeats's *King Oedipus*, which was first performed at the Abbey Theatre in December of 1926 and subsequently revised and published in 1928, not only reflects the developments in translation as a literary mode that took hold during the Modernist period. Equally significant, it also illustrates the concerns and capabilities of Yeats himself during the most intensely productive period of his late career by registering his increasing sense of alienation from the deeply conservative, largely Catholic conception of national culture promulgated by the Free State government. Within this context, the practice of translation functioned for Yeats as a vital means of national critique by enabling the deployment of a culturally authoritative foreign dramatic work to stage his own conception of at once the tragic political fate and the attendant social isolation of a heroic individual. And this significance, in turn, helps to explain why Yeats came to employ translation as a method of textual production in his own "original" poetic composition.

IV

On a personal level, *King Oedipus* (as Yeats called his translation) reveals, in the words of Frederic Grab, "a desire to stress the relevance of Greek drama to Irish culture; a fascination with Oedipus as 'subjective' hero of an irrational historical age; and an identification with Oedipus as a persona of Yeats's own old age through which he could unite tragedy and joy, and fuse the violence of the body and the immortality of the soul into an image of permanence and transfiguration."[43] In light of Yeats's deep and sustained involvement with issues of national Irish culture, especially as a Free State Senator during the period he again took up and completed his renderings of Sophocles, such thematic concerns also entail a distinct sociopolitical dimension. Yeats himself emphasized the fundamental interconnection between his diverse activities and interests, when, in his essay "If I Were Four and Twenty" (1919), he described his early effort to unify his "interest in a form of literature, in a form of philosophy, and a belief in nationality" (*Exp.*, 263), further declaring that "now all these are, I think, one, or rather all three are a discrete expression of a single conviction" (*Exp.*, 263). Marjorie Howes has thoroughly discussed how "the essay recommends unity to the Irish nation—cultural, emotional, logical, religious—but the solutions it offers constantly reinscribe division and defeat," thereby illustrating "the structures of ambivalence in Yeats's Anglo-Irish nationality and the constructions of family, sexuality and genealogy that embody and support them."[44] Comparably, through its broad themes of parricide, hubris, and incest, through its overall tenor of tragic irony, and in various specific details of its language, Yeats's presentation of *Oedipus Rex* in *King Oedipus* constitutes a thinly veiled, Jamesonian "national allegory" that outlines a deeply troubled and conflicted vision of state social organization. By enabling the renewal and deployment of a classical literary precedent, translation serves for Yeats at this point in his career the paradoxical function of offering access to a foundation for a conception of history and society as foundationless and predicated on violence. In this regard, translation operates in much the same way as his occult studies.

Working from Jebb's rendering, which offered basic semantic accuracy, but employed a markedly Victorian standard of fluency, Yeats set down in his preface to *King Oedipus* the principles to which he held in his efforts as a translator: "I put readers and scholars out of my mind and wrote to be sung and spoken. The one thing that I kept in mind was that a word unfitted for living speech, out of its natural order, or unnecessary to our modern technique, would check emotion and tire attention."[45] Such an insistence on specifically verbal expressivity, modern syntax, and absolute stylistic currency underscores Yeats's desire not simply to revisit and rejuvenate an ancient classical text, but also to maximize its potential applicability within his own contemporary social circumstances. Thus, whereas Jebb clearly proceeds from an urge to reproduce the semantic content of Sophocles' tragedy as completely and as accurately as English allows, Yeats suffers no compunction whatsoever in shaping and modifying the system of meaning defined by the original (and approximated in Jebb's version) according to his own ends and Modernist stylistic predilections. Far more than just an idiomatic, or even meaningfully idiosyncratic, version of *Oedipus Rex*, Yeats's *King Oedipus* exemplifies an expressly Modernist practical convergence between translation and "original" composition. Yeats himself touted this dimension of his achievement as a translator when, as she recalled in her journal, he said to Lady Gregory, "with your help I have made the Edipus a masterpiece of English prose."[46] The difference in expressive modes notwithstanding, *King Oedipus* exhibits from its opening scene the compression and rhythmical invention so characteristic of Modernist verse technique, and for which, as will be recalled, Yeats praised Lady Gregory's *Cuchulain of Muirthemne* when he first came to reflect upon the meaning and practice of translation as a literary mode. So, for example, in the opening exchange between Oedipus and the Priest of Zeus, Yeats not only condenses his source in order to make it suitable for dramatic utterance, but he also thereby advances a specific interpretation of the play. Here is Jebb's full rendering of the first fifty-seven lines of Sophocles' tragedy, with bracketed passages indicating ones omitted by Yeats:

> Oedipus: My children, latest-born to Cadmus who was of old, why are ye set before me thus with [wreathed] branches of suppliants, while the city reeks with incense, rings with prayers [for health] and cries of woe? [I deemed it unmeet, my children, to hear these things at the mouth of others, and have come hither myself, I, Oedipus renowned of all.] Tell me, then, thou venerable man—[since it is thy natural part to speak for these—in what mood are ye placed here, with what dread or what desire?] Be sure that I would gladly give all aid; hard of heart were I, did I not pity such suppliants as these.

136   Translation and the Languages of Modernism

> Priest of Zeus: Nay, Oedipus, ruler of my land, thou seest of what years we are who beset thy altars,—some, nestlings still too tender for far flights,—some, bowed with age, priests, as I of Zeus,—and these, the chosen youth; while the rest of the folk sit with wreathed branches in the market-places, [and before the two shrines of Pallas, and where Ismenus gives answer by fire.]
>
> For the city, as thou thyself seest, is now too sore vexed, and can no more lift her head from beneath the angry waves of death; a blight is on her in the fruitful blossoms of the land, in the herds among the pastures, in the barren pangs of women; [and withal the flaming god, the malign] plague, [hath swooped on us, and] ravages the town; [by whom the house of Cadmus is made waste, but dark Hades rich in groans and tears.]
>
> It is not as deeming thee ranked with gods that I and these children are suppliants at thy hearth, but as deeming thee first of men, [both in life's common chances, and when mortals have to do with more than man:] seeing that thou camest to the town of Cadmus, and didst quit us of the tax that we rendered to the hard songstress; [and this, though thou knewest nothing from us that could avail thee, nor hadst been schooled; no, by a god's aid, 'tis said and believed, didst thou uplift our life.]
>
> And now, Oedipus, king glorious in all eyes, we beseech thee, all we suppliants, to find for us some succor, whether by the whisper of a god thou knowst it, or haply as in the power of man; [for I see that, when men have been proved in deeds past, the issues of their counsels, too, most often have effect.]
>
> On, best of mortals, again uplift our state: On, guard thy fame,—[since now this land calls thee savior for thy former zeal; and never be it our memory of thy reign that we were first restored and afterward cast down; nay, lift up this State in such wise that it fall no more!]
>
> With good omen didst thou give us that past happiness; now also show thyself the same. [For if thou are to rule this land, even as thou art now its lord,] 'Tis better to be lord of men than of a waste: since neither walled town nor ship is anything, if it is void and no men dwell with thee therein.[47]

Yeats's considerably condensed version reads much more smoothly and powerfully:

> Oedipus: Children, descendants of old Cadmus, why do you come before me, why do you carry the branches of suppliants, while the city smokes with incense and murmurs with prayer and lamentation? I would not learn from any mouth but yours, old man, therefore I question you myself. Do you know of anything that I can do and have not done? How can I, being the man I am, being King Oedipus, do other than all I know? I were indeed hard of heart did I not pity such suppliants.
>
> Priest: Oedipus, King of my country, we who stand before your door are of all ages, some too young to have walked so many miles, some—priest of Zeus such as I—too old. Among us stand the pick of the young men, and behind them in the market-places the people throng, carrying suppliant

branches. We all stand here because the city stumbles toward death, hardly able to raise up its head. A blight has fallen upon the fruitful blossoms of the land, a blight upon flock and field and upon the bed of marriage—plague ravages the city. Oedipus, King, not God but foremost of living men, seeing that when you first came to this town of Thebes you freed us from that harsh singer, the riddling Sphinx, we beseech you, all we suppliants, to find some help; whether you find it by your power as a man, or because, being near the Gods, a God has whispered to you. Uplift our State; think upon your fame; your coming brought us luck, be lucky to us still; remember that it is better to rule over men than over a waste place, since neither walled town nor ship is anything if it be empty and no man within it.[48]

The differences between these two renderings attest to Yeats's considerable success in making his translation "something that everybody in the house, scholar and pot-boy, would understand as easily as he understood a political speech or an article in a newspaper." Through the techniques of omission and compression, Yeats transforms Jebb's archaic vocabulary, diffuse images, and awkward constructions into clear, hard, and precise Modernist prose. So, for example, in the opening speech by Oedipus, Jebb's "I deemed it unmeet, my children, to hear these things at the mouth of others, and have come hither myself, I, Oedipus renowned by all" becomes the much more pointed and direct, "I would not learn from any mouth but yours, old man, therefore I question you myself." Moreover, the vague metaphor at the beginning of the Priest's response, "nestlings too tender for far flights," hardens into a straightforward assertion of fact: "some too young to have walked so many miles." Similarly, the overwrought description of the plague and its effects simplifies to the plain statement, "plague ravages the city;" and Yeats simply eliminates the extremely convoluted declaration of the Priest, "for I see that, when men have been proved in deeds past, the issue of their counsels, too, most often have effect."

More significant than simply improving the dramatic flow, Yeats also advances a specific interpretation of the play and its titular protagonist, one that does not entirely accord with the details of the original. Eliminating mention of the tragic hero's success in confronting beings "more than man" and of the "god's aid" that helped him defeat the Sphinx, Yeats emphasizes Oedipus's status as a mortal, rather than semi-divine, entity. And even though the Priest appeals to him as one who is "near the Gods," Yeats's Oedipus nevertheless appears through his earlier victory simply as "not God but foremost of living men," one who contains within himself all of the qualities necessary to conquer the Sphinx and subsequently save the city of Thebes a second time. Thus, the suppliants beseeching Oedipus do not "beset thy altars," but rather "stand before your door." Moreover, the citizens of Thebes gather only "in the marketplaces," Yeats having cut the references to "the two shrines of Pallas" and the river Ismenus. By eliminating such specific markers of cultural difference, Yeats suggests that neither the hero nor the people of the play differ too significantly from the Irish people themselves, to whom he wanted to make the play not only intelligible, but also directly and socially relevant. Such a motivation also informs other changes Yeats makes to Jebb. So, a little later in the opening scene of the play, Jebb presents Creon's answer to one of the King's questions about the murder of his predecessor and unrecognized father as, "such things were surmised; but, Laius once slain, amid our troubles no avenger arose."[49] In his treatment, Yeats not only smooths out the wrenched syntax, but in doing so he clearly evokes recent national Irish political terminology in which the Anglo-Irish War from early 1919 to July 1921 had been euphemistically referred to as the "troubles":[50] "such things were indeed guessed at, but Laius once dead no avenger arose. We were amid our troubles."[51] No doubt Jebb's choice of such vocabulary, as well as his decision throughout the play to render πολισ as "state" rather than "city," helped to make his version appealing to Yeats in the first place. Still, Yeats's changes serve to highlight the applicability of the play to a specifically Irish cultural and political context.

These modifications from the early part of the play exemplify the procedure that Yeats follows over the course of *King Oedipus*. In general, he tightens the rhetoric of individual characters and quickens the dramatic tempo of the tragedy as a whole, all the while striving to emphasize the fundamental similarity between Greek and Irish sensibilities. In his otherwise beneficial process of concentration, however, Yeats does elide some of the subtleties contained in the original that are preserved in Jebb's more literal translation. Thus, in omitting Oedipus's curse of himself at lines 249–51 (Jebb gives these lines as, "and for myself I pray that if, with my privity, he should become inmate of my house, I may suffer the same things which even now I called down upon others"), Yeats loses the dramatic irony that attends to the hero's subsequent recognition that "no mouth but my own has laid this curse upon me" (Yeats's translation of ll. 819–20). Even more significant, perhaps, is the loss of Jocasta's glorification of Chance as the principle guiding the lives of men at ll. 977–83 (Jebb's version reads, "Nay, what should mortal fear, for whom the decrees of Fate are supreme, and who hath clear foresight of nothing? 'Tis best to live at random, as one may. But fear not thou touching wedlock with thy mother. Many men ere now have so fared in dreams also: but he to whom these things are as nought bears his life most easily"). Though he does render Jocasta's earlier disparagement of oracles (at ll. 946–49 and ll. 952–53), by eliminating her climactic assertion, Yeats gives up one of the key dynamics of the original wherein the final revelation of the omniscience of the gods demonstrates the ultimate failure of this position. On the whole, these changes to Jebb (or, depending on one's perspective, departures from the original) diminish the narrative tension within the play by making the tragic outcome seem that much more inevitable. Yet precisely in doing so, they correspondingly amplify the allegorical potential of the drama. Indeed, given its eminent place within the classical canon, it seems very likely that Yeats simply assumed on the part of the audience a full knowledge of the plot line of *Oedipus Rex* in planning the intended effects of his rendering.

Such an assumption also helps to explain the reason behind the theme Yeats most consistently downplays in his translation, namely Oedipus's incestuous marriage. Perhaps as his own concession to dominant Catholic moral sensitivities, Yeats almost systematically cuts references to this aspect of Sophocles' tragedy, including Tiresias's prediction at lines 420–25 ("And what place shall not be harbor to thy shriek, what of all Cithaeron shall not ring with it soon, when thou hast learnt the meaning of the nuptials in which, within that house, thou didst find a fatal heaven, after a voyage so fair?") and at 457–60 ("And he shall be found at once brother and father of the children with whom he consorts; son and husband of the woman who bore him; heir to his father's bed, shedder of his father's blood"). Also gone are Oedipus's confession at 821–22 ("and I pollute the bed of the slain man with the hands by which he perished") and his question at line 976 ("But sure I must needs fear my mother's bed?"), which elicits the previously mentioned glorification of Chance by Jocasta. All these omissions notwithstanding, however, Yeats does not attempt to disguise this incest that lends the play so much of its visceral force and horror. Indeed, in his rendering of the final ode he even goes so far as to embellish the chorus' graphic lines on Oedipus's marriage; and at line 1403, he alters Jebb's rather innocuous "marriage-rite that gave me birth" to the distinctly more precise, and therefore disturbing, "marriage-bed that gave me birth." In thus carefully managing the most potentially controversial dimension of the play, which could easily have distracted attention away from its equally, if not more, troubled depiction of the foundations of political power, Yeats casts his rendering of *Oedipus Rex* as an authoritative depiction of national state formation.

With the exception of the final scene, Yeats works his greatest changes upon Jebb in the choral odes that punctuate the dialogue of the play. Rendered into verse rather than prose, these choral odes clearly illustrate the way in which the practice of translation converged for Yeats upon "original" poetic composition. For not only does Yeats make his most marked formal departure from Jebb in rendering the odes as rhymed stanzas, but in them he also strays in significant ways from the semantic content of his source, often modifying the meaning of Jebb's translation to bring it more in line with his own conception of the play, as well as the themes and ideas he was exploring in his own poetry around this time. Moreover, at least since he first expressed a desire to stage *Oedipus Rex* in the *Samhain* of 1904, Yeats had associated the Greek Chorus with the Irish people themselves.[52] Thus, his treatment of the choral odes both illustrates Yeats's interpretation of the play as an allegory of the troubled foundations of state power, and also, therefore, underscores the way he practices translation as a means of national critique.

In the first ode (ll. 151–205) as rendered by Jebb, the chorus expresses the communal sorrow of the *polis*, describing its woes and calling upon Apollo, Athena, Artemis, and even Bacchus to deliver them from the pestilence ravaging Thebes. In his own translation, however, Yeats offers a prayer for the defeat of death. Whereas Jebb's chorus gives voice to grief, Yeats's seeks transcendence. So, for example, in rendering the first strophe, Jebb preserves the fear of the unknown as the motivating force behind the ode: "O sweetly-speaking message of Zeus, in what spirit hast thou come from golden Pytho into glorious Thebes? I am on the rack, terror shakes my soul, O thou Delian healer to whom wild cries rise, in hold fear of thee, what thing thou wilt work for me, perchance unknown before, perchance renewed with the revolving years; tell me, thou immortal Voice, born of Golden Hope!" (31–33). By contrast, Yeats assumes the awaited news from the oracle at Delphi will be a "message of disaster," thereby amplifying the terror of the ode with images that recall that "rough beast, its hour come round at last" of "The Second Coming" (1928).[53] Bernard Krimm has shown how "The Second Coming" represents a response to the anarchic violence of the Anglo-Irish War.[54] Consequently, such a similarity attests not only to the national political concerns informing Yeats's treatment of this choral ode, but also to the apocalyptic nature of his vision of politics:

> What message come to famous Thebes from the Golden House?
> What message of disaster from that sweet-throated Zeus?
> What monstrous thing our fathers saw do the seasons bring?
> Or what that no man ever saw, what new monstrous thing?
> Trembling in every limb I raise my loud importunate cry,
> And in a sacred terror wait the Delian God's reply. (306)

As these lines might suggest, Yeats's real interest in this ode lay in expressing the emotions that derive from a confrontation with divine power. Thus, he entirely omits strophe and antistrophe two, which describe the travails of the stricken city and reveal the profound grief of its people. Instead, Jebb's translation of strophe three, which begins, "and grant that the fierce god of death, who now with no brazen shields, yet amid cries of battle, wraps me in the flame of his onset, may turn his back in speedy flight from our land" (37), serves as the basis from which Yeats develops his version of the ode from the second stanza onward. Focusing in upon those elements from the original ode that deal with the god of death, Yeats depicts the citizens of Thebes as defiant in the face of imminent, and unavoidable, doom. Speaking of the god of Death, the chorus invokes Apollo and Zeus to come to their aid in the third stanza, which ends with an allusion to one of Yeats's predecessors, John Donne, in defying the limits of mortality:

> Hurry him from the land of Thebes with a fair wind behind
> Out on to that formless deep where not a man can find
> Hold for an anchor-fluke, for all is world-enfolding sea;
> Master of the thunder-cloud, set the lightning free,
> And add the thunder-stone to that and fling them on his head,
> For death is all the fashion now, till even Death be dead. (306–7)

In his treatment of the second choral ode (ll. 463–512), Yeats departs even more radically from his source, which expresses the uncertainty of the people of Thebes as they reflect upon the immediately preceding conflict between Tiresias and Oedipus. In Jebb's version of strophe and antistrophe two, the chorus speaks of its "foreboding" and "lack of clear vision," and ends with the assertion that "until I see the word made good, never will I assent when men blame Oedipus." Apparently operating based upon a full knowledge of the outcome of the play, and thus unconcerned with the validity of prophecy as a mode of human knowledge, Yeats completely omits these sections, focusing instead on the mystical associations of the oracle itself mentioned in Jebb's antistrophe one: "Yea, newly given from snowy Parnassus, the message hath flashed forth to make all search for the unknown man. Into the wild wood's covert, among caves and rocks he is roaming, fierce as a bull, wretched and forlorn on his joyless path, still seeking to put from him the doom spoken at Earth's central shrine: but that doom ever lives, ever flits around him" (73–75). Where Jebb concentrates on the search for the "unknown man" who is the source of defilement, and hence of the city's woes, Yeats apparently finds greater interest in the mention of "earth's central shrine," an elaborate description of which ends his treatment of the ode:

> That sacred crossing-place of lines upon Parnassus' head
> Lines that have run through North and South, and even through
>   West and East,

> That navel of the world bids all men search the mountain wood,
> The solitary cavern, till they have found that infamous beast. (311)

The final image here again recalls "The Second Coming" and gives further illustration of the way in which translation functioned for Yeats as an avenue to explore his own concerns about the foundations of power.

The third choral ode (ll. 863–910) also takes as its central theme the question of divine prophecy and its truth. An extended warning against the hubris for which Oedipus would become so famous in the Aristotelian interpretation of the play, this ode ends at antistrophe two, which Yeats almost completely eliminates in his rendering, with the chorus calling upon Zeus to enforce the prediction of the oracles:

> No more will I go reverently to earth's central and inviolate shrine, no more to Abae's temple or Olympia, if these oracles fit not the issue, so that all men shall point at them with the finger. Nay, king,—if thou art rightly called,—Zeus all-ruling, may it not escape thee and thine ever-deathless power!
>
> The old prophecies concerning Laius are fading; already men are setting them at nought, and nowhere is Apollo glorified with honours; the worship of the gods is perishing. (123)

In contrast to such piety, Yeats was always more interested in the power of an individual personality, and so his version sustains a tension between, on the one hand, the immutable decrees of divine will, and on the other, the compelling example of dedicated human action. Thus, in rendering antistrophe one, Yeats alters the tone of pious sermonizing in Jebb's version: "insolence breeds the tyrant; Insolence, once vainly surfeited on wealth that is not meet nor good for it, when it hath scaled the topmost ramparts, is hurled to a dire doom, wherein no service of the feet can serve. But I pray that the god never quell such a rivalry as benefits the State; the god will I ever hold for our protector" (119). All mention of gods in the final lines having been expunged, Yeats's rendering expresses a Romantic faith in personality by maintaining the value of ambition even in the face of divine sanction against hubris:

> A man becomes a tyrant out of insolence,
> He climbs and climbs, until all people call him great,
> He seems upon the summit, and God flings him thence;
> Yet an ambitious man may lift up a whole State,
> And in his death be blessed, in his life fortunate. (317)

Yeats's attraction to Fascist politics perhaps finds an early expression in the convictions that led him to transform Jebb and produce these lines.[55]

In his treatment of the relatively short fourth ode (ll. 1086–109), Yeats gives further illustration of the way in which he practiced translation as a means of pursuing his own concerns as a writer. Here, Jebb gives a chorus that joyfully anticipates the revelation of Oedipus's birth, speculating excitedly about the possibilities represented by the mystery of his parents. For Yeats, by contrast, the revelries "in the hidden glen" hold interest for their own sake and not simply because of their ultimate issue. Focused on the result rather than on the mystery of such a meeting, Jebb's version of the antistrophe takes the problem of Oedipus's birth as its principal concern: "Who was it, my son, who of the race whose years are many that bore thee in wedlock with Pan, the mountain-roaming father? Or was it a bride of Loxias that bore thee? For dear to him are all the upland pastures. Or perchance t'was Cyllene's lord, or the Bacchants' god, dweller on the hill-tops, that received thee, a new-born joy, from one of the Nymphs of Helicon, with whom he most doth sport" (145–47). For Yeats, however, the dynamics of the encounter, rather than its outcome, seem to be the main point of poetic interest:

> Who met in the hidden glen? Who let his fancy run
> Upon nymph of Helicon?
> Lord Pan or Lord Apollo or the mountain Lord
> By the Bacchantes adored? (321)

Just as in "Leda and the Swan" (1928), which appeared in *The Tower* during the same year that Yeats published his version of *Oedipus Rex*, the essential mystery (and violence) of a divine intercession into the world of mortals provides both the motivation and the interrogative form for these lines. Moreover, they arguably anticipate such poems at the end of Yeats's career as "News for the Delphic Oracle" (1938–39) in which the poet glories in sensual fulfillment. In modifying Jebb, Yeats not only departs from the strict content of *Oedipus Rex*, but he actively shapes the tragedy to suit his own purposes.

Similarly, in parts of the final ode (ll. 1186–222), Yeats looks forward to his own late poetic development. This ode charts the life of Oedipus as a paradigm of human misfortune, and through strophe and antistrophe one Yeats does not depart significantly from Jebb. In his treatment of strophe two, though, Yeats adds considerable graphic detail to Jebb, whose language at this point, one suspects, Yeats had in mind when he wrote in his *New York Times* article about other "translators' half Latin, half Victorian dignity." Jebb's version of strophe two reads as follows: "But now whose story is more grievous in men's ears? Who is a more wretched captive to fierce plagues and troubles, with all his life reversed? Alas, renowned Oedipus! The same bounteous place of rest sufficed thee, as child and as sire also, that thou shouldst make thereon thy nuptial couch. Oh, how can the soil wherein thy father sowed, unhappy one, have suffered thee in silence so long?" (157–59). Yeats at once condenses, makes more explicit, and extends the images and metaphors underlying Jebb:

> But, looking for a marriage-bed, he found the bed of his birth,
> Tilled the field his father had tilled, cast seed into the same
>   abounding earth;
> Entered through the door that had sent him wailing forth. (323–24)

Although he cut several references to Oedipus's terrible marriage at several earlier points in the play, at this moment of climax Yeats emphasizes and even draws out all of its incestuous horror. Such fascination with the details of physicality clearly looks forward to the Yeats of *Last Poems*, and indicates the way in which translation functioned for Yeats as a generative practice in his overall development as a writer. Within the context of the play itself, this sharply rendered final ode calls acute attention to the grievously vexed foundations of human affairs, especially in the realm of politics.

The five choral odes notwithstanding, Yeats's most drastic departures from Jebb occur in his rendering of the conclusion of the play, which provides perhaps the most powerful demonstration of how Yeats considered translation not simply an exercise in literary approximation or homage, but a primary mode of literary production with its own unique capacity for broader social, and even political, signification. By the accounting of Frederic Grab, Yeats omits a total of 81 lines from the final 233 lines of the play, and he moves an additional 12 far from their original position.[56] Beginning with the second *kommos* of the play (ll. 1297–368), Yeats eliminates several expressions of grief by both the chorus and Oedipus himself, including the lamentations that follow upon the reappearance of Oedipus from the palace after having put out his eyes:

> O dread fate for men to see, O most dreadful of all that have met mine eyes! Unhappy one, what madness hath come to thee? Who is the unearthly foe that, with a bound of more than mortal range, hath made thine ill-starred life his prey?
>
>   Alas, alas, thou hapless one! Nay, I cannot e'en look on thee, though there is much that I would fain ask, fain learn, much that draws my wistful gaze,—with such a shuddering does thou fill me! (169–71)

In addition, Yeats cuts Oedipus's response to this demonstration of communal commiseration, in which, for the first time in the play, the king gives up any semblance of self-control:

> O these horrors of darkness that enfoldest me, visitant unspeakable, resistless, sped by a wind too fair!

> Ay me! and once again, ay me!
> How is my soul pierced by the stab of these goads, and withal by the memory of sorrows! (173)

By eliminating so much of the emotionally charged *kommos*, Yeats modifies the expressive dynamics of the original play (kept intact in Jebb), presenting both an Oedipus who regains control over his feelings of loss much more quickly than his previous incarnation, as well as a chorus that sits in harsher judgment of their fallen king. Yeats's other changes reinforce this impression. So, for example, in Yeats's version the chorus, rather than Oedipus, declares, "It had been better if that herdsman had never took your feet out of the spancel or brought you back to life." Moreover, Oedipus's self-reproach at lines 1357–66 (ending "...if there be yet a woe surpassing woes, it hath become the portion of Oedipus"); his first request to Creon to be cast from Thebes (ll. 1436–46), since he has been revealed as "the parricide, the unholy one"; and his request at line 1467 "to indulge my grief" by touching his children; all these disappear in Yeats's translation. At the end of the play, then, Yeats offers a vision of Oedipus as a man whose first concern when faced with the return of Creon, the brother-in-law who is to replace him as the king of Thebes, is not for himself or his lost position, but for his children, a hero at once less despairing and more concerned with the proper handling of his political authority and attendant responsibilities than the original model. Correspondingly, Yeats's chorus gives less sympathy to their fallen king, and the ending of the play suggests their function, in Yeats's conception of the tragedy, as the ironic and detached commentators on the frailty of human achievement by the relentless, implacable rhythm of the repeated phrases and strong rhymes of their final lines:

> Make way for Oedipus. All people said,
> "That is a fortunate man";
> And now what storms are beating on his head!
> "That is a fortunate man";
> Call no man fortunate that is not dead.
> The dead are free from pain. (328)

In *King Oedipus* Yeats ventures much more than simply either to get behind the half Latin, half Victorian dignity" of Jebb or to reproduce all the details and nuances of Sophocles. Rather more significantly, in producing (in both senses of the word) a version of *Oedipus Rex* "for the Modern Stage," Yeats sought to intervene in the articulation of Irish national culture by assimilating a universally renowned and, in his eyes, fundamentally congenial example of foreign dramatic achievement that could underwrite his own deeply troubled vision of political power as founded on violence and haunted by the specter of problematic generation. In other words, in *King Oedipus* Yeats attempted to create a text that manages to partake of the authority of Sophocles' tragedy, while exemplifying the discipline of his own expressly Modernist literary principles and conveying his own occult notions of state organization. Yeats's departures from his source and, consequently, from the original in *King Oedipus*, then, express not only aesthetic or practical concerns, but ideological ones as well. And his indirect, composite method as a translator does not just reflect his ignorance of Greek (though it does that certainly), but more important, it also bespeaks a distinctly Modernist conception of both the function and the parameters of translation itself as a literary mode.

Indeed, far from questioning the validity of his approach, Yeats only became more ambitious in his subsequent effort as a translator. Writing to Olivia Shakespear in early 1927, Yeats reports, "My work on *Oedipus at Colonus* has made me bolder and when I look at *King Oedipus* I am shocked at my moderation. I want to be less literal and more idiomatic and modern."[57] Thus, rather than being merely peripheral achievements, or ancillary to his original dramatic works, both of Yeats's translations from Sophocles stand as central efforts in his attempt to establish an Irish national theater and dramatic form. Moreover, Yeats himself considered them the most important contributions to Irish dramatic culture he had made up to that point. In another letter written while in the midst of working on his second feat of translation, Yeats speaks about his satisfaction at the prospect of completing his version of *Oedipus at Colonus* and describes his feelings about the significance of his efforts as a translator: "I shall be much more content with my work for the Abbey when this play is finished. I shall have done my part in creating a repertory, & without going outside my professed work in life."[58]

In his own estimation, then, Yeats felt that he came largely to fulfill his ambitions as a dramatist expressly through the practice of translation. Thus, his versions of the Oedipus plays not only reflect his fascination with Greek culture in general, and with Sophocles in particular, but they demonstrate the extent to which he conceived of (and engaged in) translation as crucial to the definition of a national culture by enabling the assimilation of works of international stature to a specifically Irish social and linguistic context. But rather than belabor the point by enumerating the various departures he made from his sources in rendering *Oedipus at Colonus*, I want to conclude this chapter with a glance at two instances in which Yeats employs translation expressly as a means of poetic composition, thus illustrating a practice characteristic of Modernism as a whole that is one of the principle concerns of this study.

V

As noted earlier, Yeats presented his treatment of choral odes from *Oedipus at Colonus* and *Antigone* respectively as the culminating lyrics for the complementary series of short poems known as "A Man Young and Old" and "A Woman Young and Old." Each of these sequences has been extensively discussed, both for their meaning as individual works and for their structural importance as the respective conclusions to what have come generally to be regarded as Yeats's two finest poetic achievements, the "masculine" collection *The Tower* and its subsequent, "feminine" counterpart *The Winding Stair and Other Poems*.[59] Rather than enter precipitously into an already substantial conversation about the thematic and social significance of these brief poems, I want instead simply to show how, occupying such crucial positions in his two most esteemed volumes of verse, "From 'Oedipus at Colonus'" and "From 'The Antigone'" together underscore the evolving importance of translation as a literary mode for Yeats over the course of his development as a writer and, more specifically, as a poet. Indeed, on a larger scale, explicitly breaking down the distinction between genres, as well as crossing over temporal and linguistic boundaries, these short poems emblematize (to use a particularly Yeatsian term) the significance of translation as a constitutive practice within the field of Modernist poetry as a whole.

Last of the eleven poems comprising the sequence, "From 'Oedipus at Colonus'" ends "A Man Young and Old" on a paradoxical note of defiant fatalism, a gesture made all the more powerful by the invocation of classical authority enacted in the title. A rendering of the third *stasimon* of Sophocles' *Oedipus at Colonus*, "From 'Oedipus at Colonus'" presents the moment of the play at which, in Yeats's own words, "the tragedy of the old wandering man is described and his fate summed up."[60] As in his versions of the two Oedipus plays themselves, Yeats based his efforts in "From 'Oedipus at Colonus'" on the translation of R. C. Jebb, which reads as follows:

> strophe: Whoso craves the ampler length of life, not content to desire a modest span, him will I judge with no uncertain voice; he cleaves to folly. For the long days lay up full many things nearer unto grief than joy; but as for thy delights, their place shall know them no more, when a man's life hath lapsed beyond the fitting term; and the Deliverer comes at the last to all alike,—when the doom of Hades is suddenly revealed, without marriage—song, or lyre, or dance,—even Death at the last.
>
> antistrophe: Not to be born is, past all prizing, best; but, when a man hath seen the light, this is next by far, that with all speed he should go thither, whence he hath come.

> For when he hath seen youth go by, with its light follies, what troublous affliction is strange to his lot, what suffering is not therein?—envy, factions, strife, battles and slaughters; and, last of all, age claims him for her own,—age, dispraised, infirm, unsociable, unfriended, with whom all woe of woe abides.
>
> epode: In such years is yon hapless one, not I alone: and as some cape that fronts the North is lashed on every side by the waves of winter, so he also is fiercely lashed evermore by the dread troubles that break on him like billows, some from the setting of the sun, some from the rising, some in the region of the noon-tide beam, some from the gloom-wrapped hills of the North.[61]

In the final, published version of his poem, Yeats freely deviates from the order and content of Sophocles' ode, mixing elements from the different parts, extending certain ideas, eliminating various images, while creating others in lines that have no apparent precedent in the original, all in addition to updating Jebb's Victorian mannerisms to a direct, if at some points turgid, Modernist idiom. Beginning with a distinct improvement over Jebb's prolix opening, the first two stanzas correspond roughly to the original strophe, though they also include elements from the antistrophe, as well as a line from the otherwise missing epode, which clarify the imaginative situation in the absence of any dramatic context:

> Endure what life God gives and ask no longer span;
> Cease to remember the delights of youth, travel-wearied aged man;
> Delight becomes death-longing if all longing else be vain.
>
> Even from that delight memory treasures so,
> Death, despair, division of families, all entanglements of mankind
>   grow,
> As that old wandering beggar and these God-hated children know. (210)

The initial imperatives lend intensity to the direct address of Oedipus in the first stanza, while the immediate shift to the withering third-person reference to "that old wandering beggar" and his "God-hated children" (which do not appear in the original) in the second creates a dynamic in which the poem subtly, but explicitly, broadens its range of concern from the blinded King's individual situation to the scope of a universal condition, thereby transforming the portentousness of Jebb into a tone of tragic gravity. Moreover, Yeats intensifies certain sentiments of the original. Where Jebb gives "the long days lay up full many things nearer unto grief than joy," Yeats specifies, "even from that delight memory treasures so/Death, despair, division of families, all entanglements of mankind grow," perhaps taking his cue for the form, though not the exact constituents, of the series from the "troublous affliction[s]" listed in Jebb's version of the antistrophe.

Containing images from the end of the strophe together with the first-person voice that does not appear until the opening of the epode in Jebb, the third stanza of "From 'Oedipus at Colonus'" represents a striking synthesis of disparate elements taken from the original into an unprecedented poetic unit that nevertheless conveys important aspects of Sophocles' thought, and even manages to produce a paradoxical image distinctly applicable to Oedipus's plight—the image of a bridal bed combined with a death bed:

> In the long echoing street the laughing dancers throng,
> The bride is carried to the bridegroom chamber through torchlight
>   and tumultuous song;
> I celebrate the silent kiss that ends short life or long. (226)

And derived from the beginning of the antistrophe, the fourth and final stanza achieves an oblique reference to Sophocles himself and ends the poem on a note of gaiety that defies the gravity of the nihilism expressed within it:

> Never to have lived is best, ancient writers say;
> Never to have drawn the breath of life, never to have looked into
>   the eye of day;
> The second best's a gay goodnight and quickly turn away. (227)

Clearly, "From 'Oedipus at Colonus'" operates more as a poem in itself or as an adaptation of Sophocles than as a translation in any conventional sense. Indeed, manuscripts show that Yeats never intended to preserve the order of the original ode, opening several initial drafts with a rendering of the "cape" simile that occupies so much of the original epode.[62] And in a letter to Olivia Shakespear, he reveals just how conscious he was of deviating, not just from the order of the ode, but also from other, subtler qualities of the Greek language itself, producing instead a distinctly "English" effect. Writing about the concluding line of "From 'Oedipus at Colonus,'" Yeats admits, "the last line is very bad Grecian but very good Elizabethan and so it must stay."[63] Moreover, the rhythm of the poem constitutes Yeats's own unique achievement. It begins in each triplet stanza with a fairly straight six-beat iambic line, then swells in the second to a considerably longer, sprung-rhythm line of seven beats with several extra syllables, and then subsides again to another fairly regular six-beat iambic line. Such periodicity gives formal expression to the rhythm implicit in Oedipus's story as a tragic hero, with its succession of a steady rise to power in Thebes, the consequent discovery of his real history and all the ensuing complications, and his final demise as dramatized in the play from which Yeats took this ode.[64] Yeats could not have gotten this rhythm from Jebb, as his version of the ode (and, indeed, of the entire play) is in prose, and it remains doubtful how much he could have gotten, even with the help of a trained scholar, from the original Greek. In writing "From 'Oedipus at Colonus,'" then, Yeats proceeded more as a poet than as a translator. Yet, by means of its title, it bills itself as a translation, and as a text, it depends for its function within "A Man Young and Old" upon its status as a reproduction of part of Sophocles' play. For it not only consecrates the mythological references made in two other poems in the sequence, Number VI "His Memories" and Number X "His Wildness," but in doing so it raises the power of the sequence as a whole (as well as of Yeats's imagination) to the level of archetype by casting an authoritative example of classical drama as at once its fulfillment and the confirmation of the scope of its themes. Thus, translation serves as the conceptual, if not necessarily procedural, underpinning for "From 'Oedipus at Colonus.'"

In much the same way, Yeats wrote "From 'The Antigone'" as the conclusion to "A Woman Young and Old." The only actual result of a once considered version of the entire play,[65] "From 'The Antigone'" adapts the famous fourth choral ode (stasimon III), also known as the éros" chorus, in which the group of Theban elders sings in awed and even fearful respect to erotic Love and its power to overcome any human schemes of order in causing son (Haemon) to revolt against father and King (Creon) on behalf of beloved and betrothed (Antigone). Though he knew of and probably used other versions of the play in writing "From 'The Antigone,'" including a French rendering by Paul Masqueray[66] and one in English by Lewis Campbell,[67] Yeats again based his efforts significantly on the translation of R. C. Jebb, whose version reads as follows:

> strophe: Love, unconquered in the fight, Love, who makest havoc of wealth, who keepest thy vigil on the soft cheek of a maiden; thou roamest over the sea, and among the homes in the wilds; no immortal can escape thee, nor any among men whose life is for a day; and he to whom thou hast come is mad.
>
> antistrophe: The just themselves have their minds warped by thee to wrong, for their ruin: 'Tis thou that hast stirred up this present strife of kinsmen; victorious is the love-kindling light from the eyes of the fair bride; it is a power enthroned in sway beside the eternal laws; for there the goddess Aphrodite is working her unconquerable will.
>
> epode: But now I also am carried beyond the bounds of loyalty, and can no more keep back the streaming tears, when I see Antigone thus passing to the bridal chamber where all are laid to rest.[68]

Again, in his treatment of this ode, Yeats departs in significant ways from the original, preserving the basic order of images, but completely altering the mood and ultimately even the sentiments expressed within it.

Whereas the group of elder statesmen making up the chorus in the *Antigone* fearfully acknowledges Love and Aphrodite as divine and unconquerable forces capable of driving even the gods themselves to madness and ruin, Yeats celebrates Love, invoking it to redeem the mundane and cosmic orders alike by throwing everything into a glorious chaos. Corresponding to the original strophe and antistrophe, the first two stanzas of "From 'The Antigone'" derive much of their details from cues within Jebb's translation, but they express ecstatic joy rather than fear:

> Overcome—O bitter sweetness,
> Inhabitant of the soft cheek of a girl—
> The rich man and his affairs,
> the fat flocks and the fields' fatness,
> Mariners, rough harvesters;
> Overcome gods upon Parnassus;
>
> Overcome the Empyrean; hurl
> Heaven and Earth out of their places,
> That in the same calamity
> Brother and brother, friend and friend,
> Family and Family,
> City and city may contend,
> By that great glory driven wild.

Rather than name Love explicitly, Yeats invents the apposition "O bitter sweetness,"[69] which recalls "Love's bitter-sweet" from an earlier poem in the sequence, Number VIII "Her Vision in the Wood," thereby stressing the integration of "A Woman Young and Old." Moreover, he transforms the original conception of Love as a cruel and invincible warrior who "keepest thy vigil on the soft cheek of a maiden" ready to ambush unsuspecting victims into a much more poignant and vulnerable entity as the "inhabitant of the soft cheek of a girl," locating it in a place emblematic of human fragility rather than insidiously malevolent power. "From 'The Antigone'" ends "A Woman Young and Old" with an authoritative gesture toward Greek culture, raising the unnamed, presumably Irish, subject of the sequence to the level of myth, and the diction of these first two stanzas echoes other poems in which Yeats also compares actual historical Irish women to mythic figures. So, the call for Love to "hurl/Heaven and Earth out of their places" recalls the lines from "No Second Troy" (1910) in which the poet wonders about that Modern Helen, Maud Gonne, who would "have taught to ignorant men most violent ways/Or *hurled* the little streets upon the great, Had they but courage equal to desire" (emphasis mine). Similarly, the final line of the second stanza employs the same phrasing as when Yeats comes upon a youthful incarnation of the same woman who filled his younger days with misery and violent emotion in "Among School Children" (1928): "And thereupon my heart is driven wild: She stands before me as a living child."

With such allusions coursing just beneath the surface of the poem, it makes sense that Yeats stays fairly close to Jebb in the ending to "From 'The Antigone,'" which closes "A Woman Young and Old," as well as the entire volume *The Winding Stair and Other Poems*, on a profoundly mixed emotional note, one blending reverence, admiration, and wrenching grief:

> Pray I will, and sing I must
> And yet I weep—Oedipus' child
> Descends into the loveless dust.

Fittingly, it was Ezra Pound, the preeminent theorist and practitioner of Modern translation, who suggested the revisions that resulted in the final, published version of "From 'The Antigone'." Such a pedigree serves to highlight the stakes involved in examining Yeats's poetic transformations of Sophoclean choral odes in both "From 'Oedipus at Colonus'" and "From 'The Antigone'."[70] For, in and of themselves, these poems may seem slight in comparison to his major, original works. Yet, together they illustrate the way in which translation came to occupy a place of great importance within Yeats's efforts as a writer. Indeed, according to Ellmann, Yeats spent five months of 1935 in Majorca with swami Shri Purohit translating the ten principal *Upanishads*.[71] To be sure, Yeats was not Pound, nor even H. D. He only came to practice translation fairly late in his career, and in the end his output as a translator remains decidedly modest, both in scope and volume. Still, as the first Modernist writer to bestow upon translation as a literary mode a central role in the process of national culture formation by espousing the practice in his early critical writings as a crucial means for establishing a distinctly Irish cultural identity through both the "internal" poetic rendering of indigenous, pre-colonial Gaelic works and the "external" rendering of foreign landmark texts against which Irish achievement might be measured, and therefore cultivated; in subsequently engaging in translation as an instrument of national critique by producing deeply personal, yet powerful, renderings of both *King Oedipus* and *Oedipus at Colonus* aimed at revealing the vexed foundations of state power; and, finally, in expanding the procedural limits of translation both in his treatment of Sophocles and in writing the poems that conclude his two most important verse collections, Yeats helped at once to usher in and carry forward the age of Anglo-American Modernism as "an age of translations."

Chapter Five

"better gift can no man make to a nation"
Pound, Confucius, and the Translation of
Politics in *The Cantos*

I

In 1945, when his long-standing dream of witnessing the establishment of a truly "just" government had definitively crumbled with the defeat of Fascist Italy and the ignominious death of his contemporary political hero Mussolini, Ezra Pound wrote his celebrated, and controversial, "Pisan Cantos" while incarcerated at the U.S. Army Detention Training Center just north of Pisa. Within the same makeshift notebook he used to compose arguably his single most renowned poetic achievement, on the reverse side of the pages onto which he copied out his own poetry in fact, Pound also produced highly unconventional English renderings of two books from the Confucian tradition of social and political thought, the 大學 (*Da Xue*), which he called *The Great Digest* (1947), and the 中庸 (*Zhong Yong*), to which he gave the decidedly idiosyncratic title *The Unwobbling Pivot* (1947).[1] The intimate, textual proximity within this notebook of such ostensibly disparate examples of Pound's accomplishment as a writer betokens much more than either mere coincidence or even basic material necessity. In the broadest terms, these opisthographic manuscript pages give starkly vivid testimony to the central importance of translation as a mode of literary production within Anglo-American Modernism that is the principal concern of this study. More particularly, they illustrate the fundamental interconnection between Pound's goals, and even methods, as a poet and his diverse, frequently unorthodox practice as a translator. Indeed, throughout *The Cantos* in particular translation serves as both a means and theme of the poem itself. Thus, in Canto I Pound launches his "poem including history" (*LE*, 86) by at once presenting a version of the *Nekuia* episode from Book 11 of the *Odyssey* and explicitly invoking one of his predecessors, Andreas Divus Justinopolitanos, out of whose 1538 Latin crib for Homer's epic he actually worked to develop his treatment. Additionally, as we shall see, over the course of his more than forty-year attempt to distill and synthesize the religious, aesthetic, and political insights from various different world cultures and languages, Pound not only employs translation as a technique of poetic composition, but he comes to view a particular form of the practice as a model for the process by which to establish the *paradiso terrestre*. Finally, and most directly relevant to my concerns in this chapter, the heavily worked notebook illustrates the deep, constitutive link between Pound's engagement with Confucianism and Confucian texts through the practice of translation and both the expressly political ambitions and much of the radical formal armature of his most sustained, and in many ways problematic, poetic endeavor, *The Cantos*.

In contrast to Yeats, Pound never successfully gained access to any conventional political power, even that relatively attenuated sort wielded by a largely oppositional minority Senator in an immediately post-colonial government for a still-dependent country. Like his older contemporary, however, Pound believed in a fundamentally organic conception of society and the State, which helps to explain their shared attraction to Italian Fascism and to Mussolini in particular, though these attractions differed significantly in both content and duration.[2] As part of his organicist belief, Pound came over the course of his career to insist upon a fundamental connection between the cultural and political realms, a connection most apparent, and important, in the medium of language. For him,

> Language is not a mere cabinet curio or museum exhibit. It does definitely function in all human life from the tribal state onward. You cannot govern without it, you cannot make laws without it. That is you make laws and they become mere mare's nest for graft and discussion. "The meaning has to be determined," etc. ...As language becomes the most powerful instrument of perfidy, so language alone can riddle and cut through the meshes. Used to conceal meaning, used to blur meaning, to produce the complete and utter inferno of the past century...against which SOLELY a care for language, for accurate registration by language avails. (*LE*, 76–77)

Put another way, Pound considered language the most powerful and enduring tool with which people shape their lives and the life of society as a whole, for good or for ill. Consequently, unlike his predecessors the Symbolists (and their Modernist inheritors Eliot and Stevens), Pound never thought of great literature, and especially poetry, as an idealized retreat from, or replacement for, the harsh, and even banal, realities of the world. Instead, he saw poetry in particular as the most effective means for revealing the insights and promoting the values necessary for the creation of a society that could meet all the needs, social as well as spiritual, of its citizens. Accordingly, *The Cantos* represent Pound's nearly life-long attempt to write a poem that conveys the political and religious "truths," which could provide the basis for an earthly paradise, to create a language that could "riddle and cut through the meshes."

Alongside his belief in the expressly political significance of poetry, Pound also held that Confucian social thought had identified the governmental principles essential to a just, harmonious society, and in the "Four Books" of this tradition—the 大學 (Da Xue), usually known in English as *The Great Learning*, the 中庸 (Zhong Yong), typically given as *The Doctrine of the Mean*, the 論語 (Lun Yu), *The Analects*, and the 孟子 (Meng Zi), or *The Book of Mencius*—he felt that he had discovered the "key to the peace of the world,"[3] or the "blueprint for a world order."[4] Rightly so, readers have long recognized the central place that Confucianism holds in the "hierarchy of values"[5] Pound seeks to delineate in *The Cantos*, a place that became increasingly important as the poem developed, until it eventually drove him to multiply the very linguistic codes he felt it necessary to employ in his "poem including history." As a social philosophical system that, he believed, had been proven effective in the real arena of Chinese history, Confucianism provided Pound not only with a sense of the precise political role he could play as a poet; perhaps even more important, it offered a conceptual foundation upon which to structure the heterogeneous mass of religious, historical, and even economic material he sought to incorporate into his epic, as well as, in the form of Canto XIII and the "Chinese History Cantos" (Cantos LIII–LXI), a significant portion of that material itself. Thus, as Michael Bernstein concisely notes, "one could summarize the Confucian element in *The Cantos* as [Pound's] most determined attempt to show a concrete, historical embodiment of his intuitions, to prove by specific examples that a worthwhile state can be established on the basis of an ethic unencumbered by Judaeo-Christian notions of man's innate sinfulness, and the related assumption that life on earth is a pilgrimage to, or preparation for some other, higher existence."[6]

> And Kung gave the words "order"
> and "brotherly deference"
> And said nothing of the "life after death." (XIII, 59)

But Pound's engagement with Confucianism, and consequently the different ways in which this philosophical tradition informs both the values and structures of *The Cantos*, remains inextricably bound together with the development of his practice as a translator. For in his effort to produce a vital new *paideuma* of culture and history, Pound depended explicitly on translating and incorporating parts of Confucian, as well as other, texts as a means of investing his own "poem of some length"[7] with the cultural and historical authority to which it aspired, indeed required, if it was to succeed in its own expressly social aims. Even more important, while Pound's *belief* in Confucianism never wavered, his *understanding* of the exact nature of its political wisdom went through significant changes as he acquired different versions of various texts, and as he came to develop notions about the monumental importance of the vast differences he perceived between Chinese "ideogrammic" writing and Western alphabetic scripts.

As part of this evolution, together with utilizing Confucian ethics and historiography as a support for his greatest poetic project, Pound also gave over the course of his career various separate translations of different Confucian works. In addition to *The Great Digest* and *The Unwobbling Pivot* already mentioned, these include a semantically conventional rendering through an intermediate French source of the 大學 (Da Xue) in 1928, which, following tradition at the time, he called *The Great Learning*; a version of the 論語 (Lun Yu), or *The Analects* (1950); and even a complete, though highly unorthodox edition of the 詩經 (Shi Jing), or *The Book of Odes*, to which he gave the rather lengthy title *The Classic Anthology Defined by Confucius* (1954). Together, these translations at once reflect and embody Pound's deepest conviction that precise language constitutes the most effective means of both pursuing political reform and, therewith, ensuring social harmony. In doing so, they comprise the most systematic expression of his life-long attempt to demonstrate an ethical and governmental system, and, what he eventually came to see as even more important, a vital mode of written signification, upon which a "just" society could be built. Indeed, over the ten-year span between the disaster at Pisa in 1945 and the publication of "Section: Rock-Drill" of *The Cantos* in 1955, Pound's Confucian renderings known as *The Great Digest*, *The Unwobbling Pivot*, *The Analects*, and *The Classic Anthology Defined by Confucius* were the only new works by him to appear in book form, thereby indicating the extent to which during this period translation even came to replace poetry as his principal avenue of literary, and therefore political, activity.[8]

Despite their crucial place within the arc of his career, however, Pound's renderings from the Confucian canon have up to this point garnered relatively little critical attention. For reasons including both methodological restraint and disciplinary conservatism, critics have largely neglected to address either the details or the broader importance of Pound's various Confucian translations. On the one hand, most critics ignorant of Chinese have, understandably, simply felt unqualified to comment at all. Ironically, though, Pound himself undertook all of his translations of Confucian texts with only ever at best a deeply flawed understanding of their source language.

Indeed, as previously discussed, like so many other Modernist translators working from various languages, he considered his lack of formal training a distinct advantage in his efforts to penetrate to the "true" meaning of the originals. On the other hand, those few who have possessed "proper" language skills have concentrated their efforts virtually exclusively on assessing the "quality" and "accuracy" of Pound's renderings from the 詩經 (Shi Jing), or *The Book of Odes*, presumably because of their more readily apparent connection with his other achievements as a poet.[9] In doing so, however, such commentators have uncritically adhered to a categorical separation between poetry and social philosophy that Pound consistently challenged throughout much of his career as a writer, and especially in his manifold engagement with Confucian texts. As a result, Pound's expressly philosophical Confucian translations known as *The Great Digest*, *The Unwobbling Pivot,* and *The Analects* have been seriously overlooked.

The major exception to this general pattern, Mary Patterson Cheadle has recently given in her *Ezra Pound's Confucian Translations* (1997)[10] an admirably complete history of Pound's belief in and engagement with Confucianism, together with detailed explication and discussion of each of his principal renderings of Confucian texts. In addition, she also fully enumerates the deployment of Confucian concepts and terms in *The Cantos*. As she rightly sees, "Without an understanding of the Confucian translations it is impossible to arrive at a clear and comprehensive understanding of Pound's long, metamorphic career or of *The Cantos* that are its achievement."[11] For all her remarkable thoroughness, however, Cheadle too readily employs Sullivan's conceptually limited category of "creative translation."[12] She thereby fails to realize the status of translation as a primary mode of Modernist literary production in its own right. As a result, her principally thematic and biographical focus precludes adequate recognition of the specifically *generative* importance, and therefore the expressly political meaning in this context, for Pound of translation itself as a mode of literary production, how the very effort to render "accurately" what he saw as the precise meaning of Confucian wisdom led him not only to modify his understanding of Confucianism as a whole, but perhaps even more dramatically, to alter repeatedly the very formal dimensions of *The Cantos*.

Accordingly, then, I want to discuss the political commitment of *The Cantos* by examining Pound's Confucianism. But rather than simply reiterate the well-known *fact* of his belief, I shall focus on the *dynamics* and *logic* attendant upon the development of his understanding of Confucian thought by tracing the evolving process through which he sought to convert into English and to assimilate into *The Cantos* the mode of thinking contained in this "record of a very great sensibility" (*GK*, 232, 255). In this way, I hope to demonstrate the fundamental importance of translation as a mode of cultural production for both the definition of Pound's political ideology and the formal articulation of that ideology in his "poem including history." And this, in turn, will hopefully further illustrate the importance of translation itself as an avenue of political engagement during the period of Anglo-American Modernism. Because ultimately, Pound considered the "ideograms" in which the Confucian texts were written to be inseparable from the wisdom of the political doctrines they contained. Such a view helps to explain the startling proliferation of Chinese characters in *The Cantos*, especially those in late sections like "Rock-Drill" and "Thrones," parts of Pound's poem that to so many seem (with some justification) willfully esoteric and perhaps even maliciously obscure. In addition, I want to consider the ways in which Pound's conception of the task of "translating" and assimilating the Confucian texts illuminates some crucial aspects of his economic thought. For Pound saw Confucianism as a "totalitarian"[13] system, one that had successfully integrated all the spheres of human society, from government to economics and taxation, to ethics and religion, to the proper use of language itself.

II

From the earliest stages of his interest in Confucianism, Pound admired what he saw as the expressly political emphasis of this social philosophical system, the attention it gives to matters concerning people in relation to one another rather than simply as isolated beings. One of the first times that Pound mentions Confucius in his published work comes in the early polemical essay "Provincialism the Enemy," which appeared serially in A. R. Orage's Guild Socialist weekly *The New Age* during the summer of 1917. Contrasting him with the "profound philosophic genius" of the "irresponsible Galilean," Christ, Pound writes of Confucius and Confucianism, "It is a statesman's way of thinking. The thought is for the community. Confucius' constant emphasis is on the value of personality, on the man's right to preserve the outlines of personality, and of his duty not to interfere with the personalities of others" (*SP*, 193).

Pound's almost obsessive focus here on the "value of personality" reveals the particular emphases of his early political thinking more than it does a subtle understanding of Confucian social doctrine, since this philosophy posits a complex relationship between the needs and traits of individuals and the context of ritual social behavior, designated as lí (禮).[14] Such a conception of Confucianism, and the related idea of "community" as simply a collection of individuals who only require freedom from one another rather than as a unit of social organization with its own, synergistic dynamics, together reflects the "cult of personality" that dominates Pound's work during this time.[15] Nonetheless, written about 1923 and technically the first of his "Confucian translations," Canto XIII is perhaps Pound's earliest attempt to provide *The Cantos* with an explicitly articulated philosophical grounding. If the "Malatesta Cantos" constitute Pound's most thorough examination of the "factive personality" and of its potential as a guiding structural principle for the development of *The Cantos*, then Canto XIII can be seen as his attempt to validate through the auspices of an independent system of social and political thought, his own belief, asserted in the final lines of "Provincialism the Enemy," that "Civilization is made by men of unusual intelligence" (*SP*, 202).

In Canto XIII Pound translates several passages from the version of the Confucian texts he had been reading since at least 1913, J. P. G. Pauthier's French translation of the "Four Books"—the 大學, translated by Pauthier as *La Grande Étude*, the 中庸, or *L'Invariabilité Dans Le Milieu*, the 論語, or *Les Entretiens Philosophique*, and the 孟子, the *Meng-Tseu*—which was published in 1841 and entitled *Doctrine de Confucius: Le Quatre Livre de philosophie morale et politique de la Chine*.[16] Thus, like most of Canto I, Canto XIII actually constitutes a translation of another, intermediary translation, though Pound never explicitly acknowledges his source for this canto as he does at the opening of the poem when he names Andreas Divus. This indicates that the activity of translation interested him less than did the Confucian doctrines themselves, or at least what he could make of them. Indeed, Canto XIII is perhaps the first among the early Cantos to be absolutely clear in its values and assertions, lacking as it does any non-English phrases or sudden changes in mythological or historical reference. Moreover, despite (or perhaps because of) the relative accessibility of Pauthier's French, Pound selectively translates his source so as to emphasize those aspects of Confucian thought that supported his own theories about "personality" as a vitally important political category, as both a fundamental right that must be preserved by any just government and as the foundation upon which any such government must itself be based.

Adapting a passage from the 大學 (I, 4), or *La Grande Étude* as he knew it 1923, Pound presents a concise summary of Confucian political wisdom.

> And Kung wrote on the bo leaves:
> If a man have not order within him
> He cannot spread order about him;
> And if a man have not order within him
> His family will not act in due order;
> And if the prince have not order within him
> He cannot put order in his dominions. (XIII, 59)

As the sinologist Angus Graham has explained, Confucianism holds that "the social order derives through the family from the self-cultivation of individuals."[17] The prince's relationship to his subjects is perfectly analogous to a father's relationship to his children; and subjects must pay the same respect to their princes as children to their fathers. Moreover, personal virtue, especially that of a ruler, constitutes the basis for the stability of society as a whole. Thus, fitting in to his established organicist predispositions, Confucianism not only confirmed Pound's belief in the value of "personality" as a political right, but it also maintained that "personality" itself was the ultimate source of political rectitude. But the 大學 and Pauthier's French translation *La Grande Étude* pursue the logic of this "politics of personality," specifying that self-cultivation, or "personal order," arises from the efforts of people "à rendre leurs intentions pures et sincères" and "à perfectionner le plus possible leurs connaissances morales."[18] Pound's interpolation of the Confucian account of the genesis of social order, remaining as it does at the general level of personal, familial, and statal "order," reveals the relative simplicity of his early understanding of Confucianism. In his various subsequent renderings of the 大學, which I will be examining in much greater detail later in this chapter, Pound translates the entire Confucian formula for achieving social stability, and the differences between his versions of this passage show the great changes in his own Confucianism, and the political development of *The Cantos* as a whole.

But more than simply selecting passages from the "Four Books" that confirmed his own theories about the political function of "personality," Pound even went so far as to omit certain parts from his translations of different passages of the Confucian books so as to bring them more into accord with his own thinking. For example, the longest single passage that Pound took from Pauthier's version of the "Four Books" comes from *Les Entretiens Philosophique* (XI, 25), and it opens Canto XIII. The passage concerns the responses that four disciples give when Confucius asks, as Pauthier gives it, "Nous ne somme pas connus. Si quelqu'un vous connaissait, alors que feriez vous?" (We are not known. If someone [a ruler] were to know you, then what would you do?) (*Pauthier*, 162, brackets mine). Each of the four disciples answers with a different proposition for achieving social order, and Pound incorporates the first three responses into Canto XIII without any significant changes.

> And Tseu-lou said, "I would put the defences in order,"
> And Khieu said, "If I were lord of a province
> "I would put it in better order than this is."
> And Tchi said, "I would prefer a small mountain temple,
> with a suitable performance of the ritual,"   (XIII, 58)

Pauthier gives the response of the last disciple as follows:

> Le disciple ne fit plus que de tirer quelques sons rares de sa guitare; mais ces sons se prolongeant, il la déposa, et, se levant, il répondit respectueusement: Mon opinion diffère entièrement de celles de me trois condisciples. ...Le printemps n'étant plus, ma robe de printemps mise de côté, mais coiffé du bonnet de virilité, accompagné de cinq ou six hommes et du six ou sept jeunes gens, j'aimerais à aller me baigner dans les eaux de l'Y, à aller prendre le frais dans ces lieux touffus où l'on offre les sacrifices au ciel pour demander la pluie, moduler quelques airs, et retourner ensuite à ma demeure.
>
> Le Philosophe, applaudissant a ces paroles par un soupir de satisfaction, dit: Je suis de l'avis de *Tian*. (*Pauthier*, 163)
>
> [The disciple did no more than to pluck a few occasional notes on his lute; but with the sounds still echoing, he set it down, and, rising, he answered respectfully; My opinion differs completely from that of my three co-disciples. ... Spring being past, my spring gown put aside, but covered with my man's hat, accompanied by five or six men and six or seven young lads, I would like to go and bathe in the waters of the Yi, to take in the fresh air where one offers sacrifices to heaven to ask for rain, to chant some songs, and then return to my home.
>
> The sage, approving these words by a sigh of satisfaction, said: I agree with Tian] (My translation)

Pound shortens this passage considerably in composing Canto XIII and, more importantly, he subtly modifies its significance by eliminating Kung's explicit agreement with the fourth disciple Tian.

> And Tian said, with his hand on the strings of his lute
> The low sounds continuing
>   after his hand had left the strings,
> And the sound went up like smoke, under the leaves,
> And he looked after the sound:
>   The old swimming hole,
> "And the boys flopping off the planks,
> "Or Sitting in the underbrush playing mandolins."
>   And Kung smiled upon all of them equally. (XIII, 58)

The rhythms of these lines and the images that Pound added recall many of the poems of *Cathay* [c.f. especially "The Beautiful Toilet"], and together with the colloquial tone of Tian's response, they represent the conversion of prose into the rigors and possibilities of *The Cantos*' developing poetic form. Such a choice of register, moreover, suggests perhaps a desire for wider comprehensibility, which further underscores his investment in Confucianism.[19] But more than simply changing Pauthier's French into English poetry, Pound deliberately omits Kung's endorsement of Tian's response, and thus portrays a Confucius who validates each of the disciples' answers "equally." Moreover, Pound completely ignores the latter part of this chapter of *The Analects* wherein Confucius exposes the false humility of the first three disciples.[20] Pound edits his translation to make the philosopher of Canto XIII someone who, like he himself, believes in the irreducible element of "personality." Pound only includes that part of this passage from *The Analects* corroborating his own beliefs.

> And Thseng-sie desired to know:
> "Which had answered correctly?"
> And Kung said, "They have all answered correctly,
> "That is to say, each in his nature." (XIII, 58)

Pound's practice as a translator in Canto XIII ought not be seen so much as bad or misguided as simply motivated by his existing desires as a poet. And my point here is not to criticize Pound for failing to give a "faithful" rendition of Pauthier's version of the Confucian texts. As I have already shown, Pound was always too cognizant of the differences between languages to believe in any simplistic notion of translational equivalence, to believe that either Pauthier or he himself could translate the Confucian texts without some kind of fundamental alteration of significance. Rather, I simply want to point out that the separate passages from the Confucian books out of which Pound made Canto XIII were selected because they confirmed Pound's already established views. Moreover, parts of these passages were strategically changed or omitted, and many of the images, and of course the rhythms, are simply Pound's own inventions. All these specific details indicate the degree to which Canto XIII represents an early attempt by Pound to incorporate into *The Cantos* a coherent and authoritative philosophical grounding that corroborated his own intuitions, especially those about the political importance of "personality."

III

Pound's reading in Confucianism did more than simply reiterate his own political assumptions, however, and it was from this philosophical tradition that he came to develop a sense of the vital political role he himself could play specifically as a writer, something he often doubted. Because Confucianism holds that social order could be achieved by any ruler who understood and practiced the doctrines written down by the Sage, poets and other such guardians of the Confucian textual and cultural tradition thus fulfilled the expressly political and high moral purpose of instructing those in power. Perhaps even more important, in the Confucian social vision, poets and philosophers held a position from which they could genuinely affect the fate of a nation. By contrast, most of Pound's early prose on the political function of the arts is marked by a deep sense of the artist's critical estrangement from the power centers of society. Even as he sought to define "what position the arts are to have in the ideal republic" (*LE*, 41), Pound persisted in characterizing artists, and writers in particular, as the "antennae of the race," or as "voltometers and steam-gauges" (*LE*, 58), or in other words, as perceptual or admonitory components of the body politic or social machine, but incapable by themselves of effecting social change. Even as late as 1927, in a short essay entitled "The State," Pound lamented the specific inability of artists to change their political world in any timely or intentional way: "The artist, the maker is always too far ahead of any revolution, or reaction...for his vote to have any immediate result" (*SP*, 215). This much has been well established. Less recognized, however, is the fact that later that same year, Pound decided to undertake a full translation of the Confucian text he knew through Pauthier as the *Ta Hio*, or *The Great Learning*, and both his decision to render the whole work into English and his own comments about the work show him beginning to develop a sense of the possibility that the individual artist (translator) could in fact contribute directly to the field of politics. Despite his reputation as someone who always maintained a conviction in his own ability (indeed, responsibility) to help direct affairs of state, Pound did not arrive at this belief until the late 1920s. And, moreover, it was specifically as a translator, and not, as Bernstein has claimed, as a poet, that Pound first came to believe that his voice could in fact have direct and momentous political consequences.

Pound's first complete translation of the 大學, published in 1928 and entitled *Ta Hio: The Great Learning*, amounts to a semantically conventional rendering of Pauthier's French text, though about this time he had obtained an anonymous bilingual version of Legge's English translation of the "Four Books."[21] Accordingly, the *Ta Hio* reads more like a nineteenth-century Rationalist treatise on government than like any of Pound's other, usually highly polemical political essays, including his later translation of this same and two other Confucian books. This difference points to a fundamental conservatism marking Pound's efforts as a translator of Confucius at this point in his career; for it illustrates the extent to which he adopts the prevailing standard of "fluency" for rendering the works of the Sage at the time, a standard deriving, no less, from the values of nineteenth-century French Enlightenment culture and its corresponding semantic equivalent in English. As we shall see, in later versions of the Confucian books, Pound explicitly rejected this approach. At any rate, Pound offered the *Ta Hio* as a substitute for his literary autobiography, which Glenn Hughes originally had solicited for the University of Washington Chapbooks series. Just before publication, Pound decided to omit a preface he had already written for this version, a preface in which he argues that the principles articulated in the *Ta Hio* could be beneficially applied to the American political scene. Indeed, Pound's own description of his version of the work as "Newly rendered into the American Language," which appears on the pamphlet's cover, indicates the degree to which he specifically targeted his translation at his own country. In the letter in which he asks Hughes not to publish the preface, Pound demonstrates that he was beginning in discontinuous moments to see his own role as translator as a kind of Confucian advisor to those in power, the modern "princes" and governmental administrators. He writes to Hughes,

> On reading over my translation of the *Ta Hio*, it strikes me that the acrid and querulous preface I had sketched is a bloody impertinence and that any attempt to force local application, talk about need of present America, etc., bloody bureaucracy, etc. etc., would be damned impertinence. I mean tacking my bloomink preface onto the work itself. …
>
> Re the preface to the *Ta Hio*: I don't think I ought to use Kung as a shoe-horn for a curse on American state Dept. and the Wilson-Harding Administrations, etc. At least thass [sic] the way I feel this A.M. (*SL*, 213–14)

Despite this recantation, such remarks show that by 1928, Pound was in fact well on his way to being convinced that Confucian principles could serve as much more than simply a philosophical grounding for *The Cantos*. In his mind they provided a standard of governmental wisdom against which he could measure any state or administration throughout history. Indeed, the variability of opinion to which Pound alludes in the above letter would swing back in the other direction, and, less than seven months later, in May of 1928, he wrote to René Taupin, "I have mentioned Gourmont, and I have just given a new version of the *Ta Hio* of Confucius, because I find in it formulations of ideas that seem to me useful for civilizing America (tentatively). I value good sense rather than originality (whether Rémy de G.'s or Confucius')" [*SL*, 217, translation mine].[22] All this helps to indicate the degree to which Pound saw the Confucian texts as correctives to the political problems in America, and by extension the world, and his translation of the *Ta Hio* as the essential guide to reform.

Throughout the 1930s Pound continued to declare his Confucianism and to pursue his studies of Confucian texts through the different versions of the "Four Books" he had obtained. Indeed, by 1934 Pound had come to believe in Confucianism so deeply that one of the answers he gave to T. S. Eliot's long-standing question, "What does Mr. Pound believe?," was the richly succinct statement, "I believe the *Ta Hio*" (*LE*, 86). Moreover, he also continued to affirm the importance of translating Confucian texts themselves, even going so far as to say in 1937, after having already written Cantos XLII-LI, "If my version of the *Ta Hio* is the most valuable work I have done in three decades I can only wait for the reader to see it. And for each to discover its 'value' to the 'modern world' for himself" (*SP*, 75). Pound's reluctance to proselytize about what he saw as the fundamental value of the Confucian texts reflects perhaps his continued adherence to the Imagist poetic principle of "direct treatment of the thing," this time "objective," which prohibited him from making any "emotional" endorsements of this philosophy. Nevertheless, such a statement stands as remarkable testimony both to the value he saw in Confucian social thought and to the fundamental political importance of translation itself as a mode of cultural production. Moreover, Confucian thought, this time in the form of Confucian historiography, came to occupy the center of Pound's concerns in *The Cantos*, thereby fundamentally altering the governing poetics of his epic. What was begun in 1923 with Canto XIII, developed in 1928 with his first full translation of the *Ta Hio*, and underlined in his remark to Eliot in 1934 comes to the center of Pound's work in 1938 with the writing of the "Chinese History" and "Adams Cantos."

As I mentioned earlier, Pound believed in the absolute validity of Confucian political principles, and further that the history of China itself had proven the effectiveness of those principles, something which he most clearly asserts in the introductory "Note" to his second English translation of the 大學, or *The Great Digest*, as he would come to call it.

> [Confucius'] analysis of why the earlier great emperors had been able to govern greatly was so sound that every durable dynasty, since his time, has risen on a Confucian design and been initiated by a group of Confucians. China was tranquil when her rulers understood these few pages. When the principles here defined were neglected, dynasties waned and chaos ensued. The proponents of a world order will neglect at their peril the only process that has repeatedly proven its efficiency as social coordinate.[23]

While his claims for Confucianism are of course hardly adequate to the complexities of Chinese political history, Pound's belief that Confucian doctrines had been proven effective in a genuine historical reality drove him to alter fundamentally the poetics of *The Cantos*. Most readers have complained that the "Chinese History" and "Adams Cantos," which together comprise the single largest division of the entire poem, seem to degenerate into tedious, as well as apparently endless, lists of positive and negative examples of governmental action, without any compelling narrative or lyrical evocations that enliven the earlier parts of Pound's poem.[24]

            a.d. 317   HOAI TI was deposed, MIN TI taken by tartars
                        made lackey to Lieou-Tsong of Han
                        TçIN TCHING cared for the people,
                        TçIN NGAN died of tonics and taoists
                        TçIN HIAO told a girl she was 30
                            and she strangled him
            a.d. 396   (piquée de ce badinage) he drunk at the time.
                        Now was therefore SUNG rising. (LIV, 282)

And yet such dull, almost incantatory passages as this remain fundamentally important to the political intent of *The Cantos*, and they are intended to show the kind of historical assessment afforded by Confucian thought. As most readers of *The Cantos* already know, Pound's principle source for the "Chinese History Cantos" was Pere Joseph Anne-marie de Moyriac de Mailla's *Histoire Générale de La Chine* (13 vols. Paris, 1777–1783). De Mailla's work is itself a French version of the Manchurian translation of a Confucian history text, the *T'ung-Chien Kang-Mu* (通鑑綱目), or "The Outline and Digest of the Comprehensive Mirror," compiled by the Sung dynasty scholar and neo-Confucian Chu Hsi (A.D. 1130–1200) from an earlier and much more detailed history called the Tzu-Chih T'ung Chien (資治通鑑), or the "The Comprehensive Mirror for the Aid of Government." John J. Nolde explains that the T'ung-Chien Kang-Mu "is really a guide for Statesmen, a Cautionary Tale, designed to instruct emperors and ministers in the operation of good government."[25] And Pound clearly wanted the "Chinese History Cantos" to provide just such an illustration of the "eternal principles" of social organization for the leaders of his own time. Several critics have already addressed the influence of Confucian history on both the function and dynamics of these parts of *The Cantos*, and I do not want to duplicate their excellent work here.[26] Instead I want to focus on a heretofore unexamined aspect of the "Chinese History" and "Adams Cantos": the dynamics of Pound's several references to one Confucian doctrine in particular, a doctrine that, as I shall argue, helped him to find the poetic and political terms necessary both for maintaining his belief in the ultimate possibility of a *paradiso terrestre* and for continuing *The Cantos* even after the fall of Fascist Italy and his own incarceration in the U.S. Army Detention Training Center at Pisa, the doctrine of 正名, or the "Rectification of Names."

The importance of the doctrine of the "Rectification of Names" to *The Cantos* stems not simply from the number of times it appears in the poem—in fact there are more explicit references to it, both in the form of the Chinese characters and in various transliterations, than any other Confucian or Chinese terms. More important, the doctrine gave Pound a conceptual framework for extending his poetics beyond the confines of Western, alphabetic languages while still maintaining, indeed intensifying, his commitment to a socially effective verse, for developing a sense of poetry that collapsed the distinction between words and actions.[27] Even from his initial readings of the Confucian books through Pauthier, the doctrine of 正名 must have seemed to Pound a validation of his own belief that the precise use of language could have profound political effects, and its importance to him can be seen in that he decided to open the *Guide to Kulchur* with a translation of the passage from *The Analects* in which this doctrine is explicitly articulated. In this passage (*The Analects* XIII, 3), Confucius answers a question about the first action he would take as a government administrator, saying, 必也, 正名乎, or in Pound's final complete version of *The Analects* published in 1950, "Settle the names (determine a precise terminology)" (*CON*, 249). Confucius goes on to delineate the consequences of failing to do this. Again I quote from Pound's 1950 translation:

> 5. If words (terminology) are not (is not) precise, they cannot be followed out, or completed in action according to specifications.
> 6. When the services (actions) are not brought to true focus, the ceremonies and music will not prosper; where rites do not flourish punishments will be misapplied, not make bullseye, and the people won't know how to move hand or foot (what to lay hand on, or stand on).
> 7. Therefore the proper man must have terms that can be spoken, and when uttered be carried into effect; the proper man's words must cohere to things, correspond to them (exactly) and no more fuss about it. (*CON*, 249)

Confucius holds that the intimate connection between language and the various objects, activities, and roles in society it ostensibly represents serves as the foundation for a proper state, a unified community in which every aspect of society, from religious observance and the arts (ceremonies and music) to governmental regulation (punishments), is joined into an organic and self-sustaining whole, a vision of society that undoubtedly appealed to Pound. The conception of language underlying this doctrine, according to the philosopher Herbert Fingarette, "is not merely an erroneous belief in word-magic or a pedantic elaboration of Confucius' concern with teaching tradition," nor does it contain "a doctrine of 'essences' or Platonic Ideas, or analogous medieval-age neo-Confucian notions"; rather the call for a Rectification of Names as the basis for a proper government stems from the recognition that the "correct use of language is constitutive of effective action."[28] Because names identify the various roles that individuals must fulfill, and further, because the definitions of those names indicate the different responsibilities involved in those roles, the definitive normalization of language becomes a political necessity. Confucius recognizes language as the medium in which social relationships are registered and maintained. Thus for him (as well as for Pound), language both reveals and possesses political significance. Moreover, precisely because language has such political importance, its correct usage comprises an aspect of upright ethical behavior. The 君子, or "proper man" as Pound translates this term, must use language precisely, neither using the established terms loosely, nor speaking of things he does not know, or cannot or will not do. His "words must cohere to things, correspond to them (exactly) and no more fuss about it." Confucianism envisions a human society based upon concerns at once sacred and political in which each citizen is reciprocally responsible for maintaining the community through fulfilling their various roles and using the communal language precisely, or in other words, by *enacting* the connection between words and social reality. Indeed, the essential unity of religious, political, and ethical concerns in Confucianism, mediated through language, constitutes one of the cornerstones of Pound's deep attraction to this philosophical-social system.

The doctrine of 正名, then, serves as a concrete, governmental policy responding to the political importance of language, and it gave formal expression to Pound's already established belief in the explicitly beneficial political function of Flaubertian stylistic precision. Concluding a review of Joyce's *Ulysses* in 1922, almost a year before he first began to incorporate Confucian thought into his developing poem, Pound declared, "The *mot juste* is of public utility. I can't help it. I am not offering this fact as a sop to aesthetes who want all authors to be fundamentally useless. We are governed by words, the laws are graven in words, and literature is the sole means of keeping these words living and accurate" (*LE*, 409).[29] Confucianism not only recognized the political and ethical dimensions of language, it also incorporated that understanding into the very fabric of its social philosophy, expressly calling for the "Rectification of Names" as a necessary condition for establishing a just government.

The initial impact of this Confucian doctrine on Pound's poetry can be seen in the "Chinese History" and "Adams Cantos," both written in 1938, where the 正名 characters themselves appear as emblems marking the "Confucian" wisdom of different leaders who recognized that a care for language and its use must be basic governmental, as well as aesthetic, concerns. In Canto LX, for example, Pound uses the 正名 characters to identify the wisdom of the Manchurian Qing dynasty emperor K'ang-hi (Kang Xi), who understands the specifically political importance of mastering cultural documents and of knowing a people's history. Among a large host of other cultural translations and exchanges with European culture through the

French Jesuits at his court, this exemplary ruler of Manchurian heritage "Had history translated to Manchu. Set up board of translators" (LX, 332). Pound also cites this ruler demonstrating "Confucian" wisdom in his decree

> qu'ils veillèrent à la pureté du langage
> et qu'on n'employât que des termes propres
> (namely CH'ing ming)
> 正　名　(LX, 332–33)

[that they watched over the purity of the language and that one should use only suitable terms.]

The translation of Chinese history into the Manchurian language, ordered by K'ang-hsi, that Pound mentions in this passage from Canto LX actually refers to the Manchurian text de Mailla translated into French as the *Histoire Générale de la Chine*, which in turn gave Pound the material for the "Chinese History Cantos" themselves. Indeed, as John J. Nolde explains, "de Mailla said that he chose the Manchu text because it, in turn, had been designed, upon the orders of Emperor K'ang-hsi as an instruction manual for the Manchu people into the mysteries of Chinese civilization—exactly what de Mailla was trying to do for Europe (*Histoire*, I, Preface, xlvii, lxviii) and Pound for his generation."[30] While it remains unclear how much Pound knew of the complicated genealogy of his source, such a layering of references within his own poem suggests that he recognized the *Histoire Générale* as only a link in a long chain of translations and compilations intended to delineate the eternal principles of good government, of which *The Cantos* were only the latest addition (edition). Thus, when Pound transcribes part of the *Histoire* (Vol. IX, 361) directly into the "Chinese History" cantos, he not only alludes to the source for his own poetry, as in the reference to Andreas Divus in Canto I, but he also emphasizes that the act of translation itself functions as an important tool in the creation of the ideal state. This represents a logical extension of the collaborative approach to translation that Pound first adumbrated in *Cathay*. Moreover, by quoting in the French of his source K'ang-hsi's decree about the need for precise language, Pound enacts the very process of translation within the economy of his own poem, and dramatizes its importance in the acquisition of political wisdom. The 正名 characters that Pound adds to the passage explicitly equate K'ang-hsi's declaration with Confucian doctrine, and thus indicate the foundation of the Manchurian emperor's beneficent reign.

Pound recognizes that Chinese leaders are not the only ones to demonstrate such "Confucian" wisdom, however, and in the "John Adams" cantos the 正名 characters appear several times, marking in Canto LXVIII, for example, the wisdom of the American president and his desire

> to show U.S. the importance of an early attention to language
> for ascertaining language.
>
> 正名   Ching
>
> Ming
>
> (LXVIII, 400)

In many respects Pound's method of composing the "John Adams" cantos was essentially the same as he used in the "Chinese History" series, transcribing and adapting large sections of the ten volumes of *The Works of John Adams* edited by John's grandson Charles Francis Adams. Indeed, the speed with which these lengthy groups were composed (Pound began the sections in 1938 and the whole set was ready for publication by March of 1939), indicates the similarity between these two groups. Little has been made about the relationship between the "Chinese History" and "Adams" cantos, Kenner giving probably the conciset explanation that "John Adams came out of the world that discovered China."[31] While it remains beyond the scope of this chapter to address all the specific complexities of these sections of *The Cantos*, I want to point out that the appearance of the 正名 characters coincides exactly with the shift in Pound's actual mode of poetic production from lyrical (and narrative) evocations of his social and political views to explicitly didactic transcriptions of "historically grounded" examples of governmental action (both wise and foolish). Indeed, in the 1940 edition of "The China Cantos," the 正名 characters appear on the title page, serving as the governing emblem for the entire section of the then latest installment of Pound's "poem including history."[32] In later editions and in the current text, the 正名 characters have been moved forward in the poem and now conclude the *Fifth Decad* at the end of Canto LI, where they signal the shift in Pound's poetics. The values of the poem remain essentially the same, but the mode of *evaluation* changes between the end of the *Fifth Decad* and the onset of *Chinese History*, and the 正名 characters provide a kind of visual bridge between the two kinds of poetic judgment. In Cantos XLV and LI in the *Fifth Decad*, for example, Pound condemns "Usury," a social practice, because it is "Contra Naturam" (XLV, 230) and because it substitutes "Whores for Eleusis," (XLV,230, LI, 250). The 正名 characters, by contrast, correspond to the concrete legislative details out of which Pound constructs the "Chinese History" and "Adams" cantos, representing a specific legislative action that could prevent the spiritual violations of an unjust government that allows usury to flourish. 正名, or the Rectification of Names, constitutes for Pound the most basic tenet of Confucian religio-political doctrine because it addresses the foundation upon which a just society and unified community could be built: language itself. And once a precise terminology is determined, once the correspondence between language and social reality has been "rectified," proper government, according to Confucian thought and to Pound as well, becomes a matter of upright ethical behavior, of individuals enacting and perpetuating the connection between signifier and social signified mandated by the Rectification of Names.

1. Duke Ching of Ch'i asked Kung-tze about government.
2. Kung-tze replied: Prince to be prince; minister, minister; father, father; son, son. (*The Analects* XII,11, *CON*, 246).

Confucianism, and the doctrine of 正名 in particular, did more than simply give Pound the means to identify examples of governmental wisdom throughout many historical periods. The appearance of the 正名 characters, or "ideograms" as Pound conceived of them, not only coincide with the explicit ideology and didacticism of the "Chinese History" and "Adams Cantos," but they also mark a further basic expansion of the poetics of *The Cantos* as a whole, an expansion that helps to explain both the proliferation of Chinese "ideograms" later in the poem and why Pound came to translate several Confucian texts in their entirety rather than satisfy himself with simply incorporating their wisdom into his own poetic work.

In the "Malatesta Cantos" Pound included large blocks of prose in his poem, juxtaposing one literary medium to the other, thereby making, in the words of Michael Bernstein, "one of the decisive turning points in modern poetics, opening for verse the capacity to include domains of experience long since considered alien territory."[33] Similarly, but even more radically, when he places the 正名 "ideograms" at the end of Canto LI, the first Chinese characters to appear in *The Cantos*, Pound makes the process of written signification itself a subject for poetic treatment.[34] Because Pound believed that Chinese "ideogrammic" writing encoded meaning in a fundamentally different way than English, or any Western, alphabetic script for that matter, the Chinese "ideograms" throughout *The Cantos*, beginning with the invocation of the doctrine of the Rectification of Names by the 正名 characters, all implicitly raise the question of how different written conventions convey meaning differently.

Initially, however, Pound did not fully exploit what he saw as the latent significance of the "ideogram," explaining the function of non-English languages in the "Chinese History" and "Adams Cantos" primarily as a kind of embellishing visual apparatus: "Other foreign words both in these two decades and in earlier cantos enforce but seldom if ever add anything not stated in the english, though not always in lines immediately contiguous to the underlining" (256). Throughout the pre-Pisan sequences, then, Pound emphasizes the visual appearance of the Chinese "ideograms" over their semantic content. Nonetheless, only a few months before he began composing the "China" and "Adams" sequences, through a close examination of Legge's bilingual edition of the "Four Books," combined with his long-dormant understanding of the "ideogram" that he had derived from Ernest Fenollosa, Pound came to see the Chinese written character as itself a fundamental part of Confucian political wisdom, which helps to explain why he began to incorporate "ideograms" into *The Cantos* in earnest beginning in Canto LII.

In an essay on Mencius, written in 1938, Pound describes the single most important moment in the development of his practice as a translator, and therefore in his understanding, of Confucian thought:

> During August and the first half of September 1937, I isolated myself with the Chinese text of the three books of Confucius, Ta Hio, Analects and the Unwavering Middle, and that of Mencius, together with an enormously learned crib, but no dictionary. ... When I disagreed with the crib or was puzzled by it I had only the *look* of the characters and the radicals to go on. And my contention is that the learned have known too much and *seen* a little too little. Such of 'em as knew Fenollosa profited nothing.
>
> Without knowing at least the nature of the ideogram I don't think anyone can suspect what is wrong with their current translations. Even with what I have known for some time I did not sufficiently ponder it. (*SP*, 82, emphasis mine)

In other words, Pound came not only to believe in the absolute validity of Confucian political doctrines such as 正名, the Rectification of Names, but also that the Chinese "ideograms" in which those doctrines were written themselves encoded some kind of vital truth in the way they represented meaning. Again and again, Pound touted the superiority of Chinese "ideogrammic" writing, even going so far as to declare this "method" the governing structural principle of *The Cantos*; and critics have debated exhaustively about the applicability of the "ideogrammic method" to Pound's actual poetic practice, as well as about the degree and accuracy of his understanding of the Chinese language itself.[35] Rather than enter what has for some time been an unprofitable discussion, I want instead to trace the effect that Pound's ideas about the Chinese written language had on his understanding of Confucianism and, in turn, on the political underpinning of *The Cantos* as a poem dedicated to changing the political realities of its world.

IV

It is well known that Pound derived his understanding of the Chinese written language from Ernest Fenollosa, whose *The Chinese Written Character as a Medium for Poetry* he edited and first had published in his own collection of essays *Instigations* in 1920, though over the course of studying various Chinese texts he did obtain several Chinese/English dictionaries by several sinologists with varying degrees of linguistic sophistication.[36] Following Fenollosa, Pound believed in the innate poeticity of Chinese writing, that Chinese "ideograms" and the sentences made from them are "vivid shorthand pictures of actions and processes in nature" (*CWC*, 21). Western languages, which all use alphabetic scripts, depend on sound as an intermediary between written words and their meanings. Chinese "ideograms," by contrast, represent meaning directly, circumventing, even obviating, sound.[37] Complex or abstract notions, in this view, are represented in Chinese writing by combining or juxtaposing the different, basic pictograms in order to suggest a relationship. Pound's favorite example of this method was Fenollosa's imaginary etymology for how the "ideogram" for "red" might be composed out of "the abbreviated pictures" of

> ROSE   CHERRY
> IRON RUST FLAMINGO[38]

Pound believed, then, both that there was a natural and direct connection between Chinese writing and the world it sought to represent, that "ideograms" were "natural symbols," and that they conveyed meaning in a fundamentally different way than Western languages, through the process of metaphor, "the use of material images to suggest immaterial relations" (*CWC*, 22).[39] Sinologists have long debated the nature of the Chinese written language, and current scholarship rejects Fenollosa's "ideogrammic" interpretation of Chinese characters, arguing instead that they function "grapho-phonetically," with one part of the character indicating an approximate syllabic and tonal pronunciation, and the other part, or radical, indicating a general semantic field to which the word as a whole refers.[40]

Despite (or perhaps because of) this misunderstanding of the basis of Chinese writing, Fenollosa, in his underlying theory of language, reiterates the Romantic understanding of the fundamentally metaphoric operation of language in general, holding that "The whole delicate substance of speech is built upon substrata of metaphor," and further that "Poetry only does consciously what the primitive races did unconsciously" (*CWC*, 22–23), namely, use language in its originally metaphorical and concrete way.[41] Chinese writing is superior to Western alphabetic scripts in Fenollosa's view, then, because in its mode of symbolization, its method for encoding meaning, "the etymology is constantly visible" (*CWC*, 25). Whereas the Western phonetic word utilizes arbitrary markings to denote sound, and therefore "does not bear its metaphor on its face" (*CWC*, 23), in Chinese "ideograms," "the lines of metaphoric advance are still shown, and in many cases are actually retained in the meaning" (*CWC*, 25). "Ideograms" preserve the history of their own conceptual development in their very form, and so could never be evacuated of the vitality and poetry implicit in the process of signification itself. They retain "the creative impulse and process, visible and at work" (*CWC*, 25).

Accordingly, then, Pound uses "ideograms" throughout the *The Cantos* not only to signify different aspects of Confucian wisdom such as 正名, or the "true//definition" as he calls it in Cantos LXVI, but, equally important, to illustrate the kind of thought processes that underlie the ideogram as a linguistic sign. The Confucian wisdom presented in the "Chinese History" and "Adams Cantos," and most powerfully symbolized by the doctrine of the Rectification of Names, then, involves not just a finite number of vitally important political and ethical precepts, but also a particular mode of representation as well. The Chinese language, as Pound understood it, was itself part of what made Confucianism so deeply compelling. Thus he could claim in 1942, in the essay originally addressed to the Italian people and sent to Mussolini, *Carta di Visita*, that "One cannot get the full meaning [of the Confucian books] without analyzing the ideograms" (*SP*, 332). And he several times expressed the desire to issue bilingual editions of the Confucian texts, so that readers could perceive the significance of the "ideograms" for themselves.[42] Eventually Pound succeeded in publishing bilingual editions in both Italian and English of two of the "Four Books," the 大學 and the 中庸, and the *en face* Chinese versions represent essential components of these texts.

All this helps to underscore the fundamental importance of the "ideogram," beginning as early as Canto LI, to the entire project of *The Cantos*, something that Pound confirms in a letter written to the Japanese poet Katue Kitasono in 1940 in which he states, "Ideogram is essential to the exposition of certain kind of thought. ... At any rate I need ideogram. I mean I need it in and for my own job" (*SL,* 347). The Chinese "ideograms" in *The Cantos* provide examples of "language charged with meaning to the utmost possible degree" (*LE*, 23); and as such they serve as models for a form of linguistic representation ideally suited to the founding of a just state. In Pound's eyes, Confucianism had not only determined that the Rectification of Names had served as the basis for all the just and benevolent dynasties throughout Chinese history, and would do the same for the West if it were applied rigorously, but the texts of this tradition illustrated in the very sign system in which they were written the lines along which just such a rectification ought to take place.[43]

Thus, in Canto LIII when he lists the many positive accomplishments of the Shang dynasty emperor Tching Tchang (Cheng Tang), who reigned from 1766 to 1753 B.C., Pound not only cites the Chinese ruler's slogan as a precedent to his own famous aesthetic dictum, but he includes the Chinese characters for the saying alongside the English in the body of the text. And the Chinese slogan, in turn, gives rise to the further articulation of the lines through Pound's Fenollosan analysis of the character for "new" (新), which he reads "ideogrammically" as the pictograph for "axe" (斤) placed next to those for "tree" (木) and "pile of logs" (立):

> Tching prayed on the mountain and 新 hsin[1]
>   wrote MAKE IT NEW
>   on his bath tub
>   Day by day make it new
>   cut underbrush
>   pile the logs
>   keep it growing.
>   Died Tching aged years an hundred, 日 jih[4]
>   In the 13th of his reign . (LIII, 264–65)[44]

And in Canto LXIII of the "Adams" series, Pound pointedly incorporates the "rectification" ideogram into his transcription of John Adams's praise for a book on jurisprudence, Van Muyden's *Short Treatise on the Institutions of Justinian*:

> Van Myden *editio terza* design of the book is
> exposition 正 of technical terms (LXIII, 352)

V

After the "Chinese History" and "Adams Cantos," Pound came to focus even more intently upon the doctrine of 正名 and upon examples of Chinese "ideograms" as the keys to political harmony, though the range of his references to Confucian texts expanded dramatically. In "A Visiting Card" (1942), for example, Pound gives what he considers the foundation of order, a paraphrase of the doctrine of the Rectification of Names: "Towards order in the state: the definition of the word" (*SP*, 333). The historical circumstances of World War II, including the fall of the Fascist government in Italy and the overall defeat of the Axis powers, the ignominious execution of Mussolini, a man in whom Pound had publicly expressed an almost religious faith since the early 1930s, and his own incarceration at the U.S. Army Detention Training Center (DTC) at Pisa in May of 1945, together combined to shatter the expatriate American poet's dream that a truly just government and Confucian paradise could actually be established in the modern West. Nevertheless, Pound maintained and continued to espouse his belief that the Confucian texts did in fact contain the answers to the world's political problems.

>   but to keep 'em three weeks   Chung 中
>   we doubt it
>   and in government not to lie down on it
>   武
>   the word is made
>   perfect
>   better gift can no man make to a nation
>   than the sense of Kung fu Tseu
>   who was called Chung Ni
>   nor in historiography nor in making anthologies. (LXXVI, 454)

It has been for some time now a critical commonplace that in the "Pisan Cantos," Pound abandons the dream of an earthly paradise, and instead delves deeply into personal reminiscences and visions in order to create the luminous moments of his poetry. But as Peter Nicholls has rightly observed, "the 'heroism' and 'courage' for which the sequence has been praised often entail a holding-fast to those very ideas for which most critics are keen to see the poet 'transcend.'"[45] In other words, even at his most contrite and self-evaluative moments, Pound continues to maintain a positive link between his poetic work and his political ideals. As the passage from the "Pisan Cantos" cited above makes clear, even after his incarceration at the DTC, even after the fall of the state he saw as the one most likely to resurrect the stability and justice enjoyed by the best Chinese dynasties, Pound still believed in the explicitly political value of Confucius's writings, though their application might have to be deferred. But because he had to confront a markedly changed world political reality, and perhaps even more important, a radically restricted sense of political possibilities, occasioned by the fall of the Axis powers, Pound also had to reevaluate his own understanding of the relationship between China's "exemplary" political history and the details of Confucian governmental wisdom. Thus he explicitly rejects the poetics of the "Chinese History" and "Adams Cantos," both of which were engendered at least in part by the social possibilities Pound saw embodied in Mussolini's Fascist regime: "nor in historiography nor in making anthologies." I would argue, however, that it was specifically through a complete reexamination of the Confucian texts, in light of both the doctrine of 正名 and Fenollosa's understanding of the nature of the "ideogram," that Pound discovered the confidence and the philosophical support necessary to continue seeing poetry and politics as two fundamentally linked activities, indeed, to continue the very project of *The Cantos*, even in the face of his own disastrous historico-political circumstances.

Even before his imprisonment in the DTC, Pound had begun to reconceive his own Confucianism in light of Fenollosa's analysis of the "ideogram," which, as the passage from his 1938 essay on Mencius cited above shows, he thought he had failed to "sufficiently ponder" in his initial 1928 translation of the 大學, or the *Ta Hio* as he then called it. And even as he confronted and lamented the failure of his own political ideals in the "Pisan Cantos," Pound was completing a second English translation of the *Da Xue* (大學) while imprisoned at the DTC, one that in his own view adequately rendered the conceptual underpinnings of the "ideograms" signifying the most important Confucian terms, thereby maintaining, or perhaps even reviving, their explicitly political usefulness to the modern world. Hence in the passage from the "Pisan Cantos" above, Pound puns on the double meaning of the word "sense." For not only would he attempt to make a "gift" to the world of the "sense," or "meaning," of Kung fu Tseu through the medium of his own Confucian translations; but in making these translations he would try to communicate the "sense," or "sensibility," underlying that meaning by reproducing the way in which, as he saw it, the Chinese language operated. Pound's detailed examination of Legge's bilingual edition of the "Four Books" that occurred in August and September of 1937 culminated in 1945 at Pisa in a fundamental rethinking of his Confucianism.

Given Pound's complex understanding of the Confucian texts themselves, his belief that there was an intimate, constitutive relationship between the language in which they were written and the political "truths" they contained, the very task of translation itself would have appeared to be utterly impossible even as it seemed to become absolutely necessary. Such a conundrum might bring to mind more recent Derridean or deManian articulations of the logical contradiction that lies at the heart of translation as a mode of writing; but it differs significantly from these latter-day expressions of paradox because it remains grounded in the specificity of Pound's (largely mistaken) perception of the Chinese written language and its difference from Western alphabetic scripts, rather than any trans-lingual or trans-historical conception of translation as such. Indeed, in the *Guide to Kulchur*, Pound hints at what must have struck him as the basic impossibility of "translating" the Confucian texts. Clearly linking the "Four Books" with his own extremely complex and explicitly political notions about the nature of poetry, Pound declares, "Apart from the Four Classics: *Ta Hio* ('Great Learning'), *The Standing Fast in the Middle*, the *Analects*, say the three classics, or tack on Mencius, and Papa

Flaubert, certain things are SAID only in verse. You can't translate 'em" (*GK*, 121).⁴⁶ If the things "SAID" in verse could not be translated into prose, what prospects were there for "carrying over" the significance of the Confucian texts into Italian or English, languages that encoded meaning in a radically different way than Chinese? In a sense, as he attempted to translate a Confucian text, Pound would have to read pictorial symbols, as in a painting, and convert them into a written system that conveys sonic information, as in musical notation, all the while trying not to lose any "meaning" in the process, a concern all the more troubling given his belief that the Confucian texts did in fact contain the wisdom necessary to create order in the world, if only they were "read," that is viewed and understood "properly" by the "proper" people.

The "answer" to this problem lay in not simply rendering the established Italian or English semantic equivalents of the various Confucian terms, but in attempting to translate those terms in the very way in which they had been conceptualized, in "rectifying" the Confucian terms themselves and recognizing the way in which they were defined by their constituent, "ideogrammic" parts. Since the "ideogram" 德, for example, "wore its etymology on its face," providing an image of the way in which the idea had been originally conceptualized, it would be completely inaccurate, and therefore politically disastrous, to translate it simply as "le principe lumineux de la raison que nous avons reçu du ciel," or as "virtue" as Pauthier and Legge respectively had done. As Pound describes the situation in the "Terminology" page of *The Great Digest*, "To translate this simply as 'virtue' is on par with translating rhinoceros, fox and giraffe indifferently by 'quadruped' or 'animal' (*CON*, 21). The proper method for translating 德 was to examine the "ideogram" itself in order to determine the metaphorical and poetic underpinning of the Confucian conception of "virtue." Doing so, Pound arrives at a translation that emphasizes self-reflection and dynamism: "What results, i.e., the action resultant from this straight gaze into the heart. The 'know thyself' carried into action. Said action serving to clarify the self-knowledge" (*CON*, 21). In Fenollosan terms, the etymology for the character derives from the combination of the radical for "action," or "two men walking" (彳), together with that for "eye" (目) turned on its side, which signifies a gaze, placed over the radical for "heart" (心). To Pound, then, Confucian "virtue" is not simply an abstract quality, but a mode of behavior that derives from careful self-examination and that, in turn, promotes and deepens the self-examination that is its source. It is a kind of automatically renewing mode of behavior. It is not an exterior set of precepts imposed by society, but an integral part of every person that requires genuine action to become manifest. In order to "rectify" his own understanding of Confucian wisdom, Pound examined all the "Four Books" in such "ideogrammic" detail, producing in the process the fullest expression of his mature understanding of Confucian governmental wisdom, *The Great Digest*.

Still often translated as *The Great Learning*, the Confucian text known in Chinese as the 大學, according to Wing-tsit Chan, "gives the Confucian educational, moral and political programs in a nutshell, neatly summed up in the 'three items' and the 'eight steps.' "[47] Chu Hsi, the Sung dynasty scholar and neo-Confucian who compiled the text that Pound and his cribs Pauthier and Legge all used, asserts in the preface to the work, which Pound includes in *The Great Digest*, that the 大學 "is the critical study for whomso would pass the gate into virtue. ... the Analects and the Book of Mencius are subsequent" (*CON*, 25). The expressly social and political focus of the 大學 helps to explain why Pound decided to retranslate this text before attempting to render any other Confucian books, as well as why he chose first to translate it into Italian, a task that he completed well before the end of World War II, even going so far as to send a copy of the *Studio Integrale* to Mussolini in February of 1943. This, along with the pair of "Italian Cantos" written in 1944 and only relatively recently published with the whole body of Pound's long poem, together indicate the depth of Pound's commitment to Fascist Italy. Similarly, the fact that Pound completed his second English version of the 大學 while still imprisoned at the DTC indicates the degree to which he maintained, even after the loss of his dream of a *paradiso terrestre*, both a strong political motivation for his work and a belief in the potential social efficacy of Confucianism itself. If, as I have argued, Pound saw the doctrine of 正名 as a specific governmental policy recognizing that precise language must serve as the foundation of any just government, then his translation of the 大學 known as *The Great Digest* constitutes his attempt to reconcile this doctrine with a more fully articulated Confucian theory of proper social development than appears in *The Analects*, where the doctrine of the Rectification of Names makes its only explicit appearance. As such, *The Great Digest* represents that point in the evolution of Pound's aesthetico-political thinking when the activity of translation itself became an explicitly political strategy, rather than simply an aesthetic procedure for investing *The Cantos* with its own, wide-ranging cultural authority. For in retranslating the 大學, Pound tried not only to give the "sense" of the text's political insights, but also to reveal the conceptual operations of "the very great sensibility" (*GK*, 255) that had identified these "eternal rules" of good government.

VI

The 大學 is separated into two main divisions, the first a short passage traditionally attributed to Confucius (though modern scholars dispute this)[48] as handed down by one of his disciples, Thseng Tseu; and the second section, comprised of ten chapters of commentary, these having been recorded by Thseng's own pupils, in which he expands upon and clarifies the meaning of various phrases in the first section, or the "canon" as Pound reverentially calls it within the text of *The Great Digest*. In compiling the text that Pound was to use some eight centuries later, Chu Hsi added his own commentaries to Thseng's clarifications. These several layers of tradition contained within the work itself no doubt appealed to Pound, confirming the "truth" of the Confucian social principles by demonstrating the text's continued currency over the course of many dynasties. In his own attempt to renew the world through a fresh rendering of the 大學, Pound added his own commentaries upon the text, usually in the form of Fenollosan etymologies, thus placing himself firmly within the tradition of the Confucian poet/sage who offers political advice to those in power.

Before 1937 Pound had always referred to the 大學 as either the "Ta Hio" (Pauthier's transliteration of the Chinese title, which he adopted for his own 1928 translation of the text) or as "The Great Learning" (Legge's English translation). Pound's decision to retitle his second English translation of the text reflects the way in which he had come, through a careful examination of the Chinese characters themselves in light of Fenollosa's analysis of the "ideogram," to reconceptualize the very mechanics of the Confucian social program. In the Chinese "ideogram" conventionally rendered as "learning" (學), Pound saw the "pictograms" for a "mortar" (臼) placed over that for a "child" (子). He also interpreted the (丿) symbols inside the upper half of the character (𠂇) as abbreviated versions of the (米) "pictogram," the symbol for "rice" or "cereal foods" generally. Thus he explicates the first two characters of the text, which also comprise the work's title as "The great learning [adult study, grinding corn in the head's mortar to fit for use]" (*CON*, 27). To Pound, the superposition of the "mortar and corn" over the "child" (學) provided insight into how the Chinese had originally conceptualized the mental, abstract operation of "learning." It was, according to this kind of analysis, fundamentally akin to basic agricultural and alimentary processes. Needless to say, perhaps, such a vision has little to do with accepted notions about the etymology of this character. Yet philological accuracy matters less here than the logic of Pound's approach to translation, and his interpretation of the 學 ideogram no doubt at once arose in part from and thus naturally appealed to his underlying organicist conception of state formation. Thus, in order to reproduce the same kinds of conceptual associations that he saw at work in the Chinese title, Pound chose the English word "Digest," which can also refer to either bodily or mental functions. Even in the title of *The Great Digest*, Pound tries to indicate and to reproduce—in other words, to translate—the kind of thinking he saw contained in the original Chinese text.

Just as he attempts to match the conceptual dynamics of the original title as he perceived them, Pound also tries to expose the conceptual underpinnings of the body of this text, which offers the clearest and most succinct articulation of the Confucian social vision. In 1928, Pound gave in the *Ta Hio* basically a semantically conventional English translation of Pauthier's nineteenth-century French version of the Confucian governmental classic. For example, the passage from the 大學 that delineates the "eight steps" to social harmony comes out in the *Ta Hio* colored by a high Rationalist idiom:[49]

> 4. The ancient princes who wished to develop and make apparent, in their states, the luminous principle of reason which we receive from the sky, set themselves first to govern well their kingdoms; those who wished to govern their kingdoms well, began by keeping their families in order; those who wished good order in their families, began by correcting themselves; those who wished to correct themselves tried first to attain rectitude of spirit; those who desired rectitude of spirit, tried first to make their intentions pure and sincere, attempted first to perfect their moral intelligence; the making as perfect as possible, that is, the giving fullest scope to the moral intelligence (or the acquaintance with morals) consists in penetrating and getting to the bottom of the principles (motivations) of actions.[50]

As I noted earlier, this is one of the passages that Pound adapted for the composition of Canto XIII, the first full tribute to Confucian wisdom in *The Cantos*; and we can see here how Pound's Confucianism was affected by the vocabulary and implicit limitations of his earliest sources. Indeed, as many people have already perceived, much of the bias in Pound's Confucianism, the most notorious example of which is the overt and often brutal prejudice he displays against Buddhism and Taoism in the "Chinese History" cantos, can largely be attributed to the nineteenth-century origins of both Pauthier and de Mailla (and to a lesser degree even to Legge), though it is also true, as Michael Bernstein has persuasively argued, that "the Taoist and Buddhist emphasis on a struggle between a higher soul and a corrupt or 'illusory' world would have displeased Pound *irrespective* of De Mailla's polemics, and even independent of Pound's allegiance to Confucianism."[51] In any case, for *The Great Digest*, Pound examined the 大學 in deep Fenollosan detail, rejecting what must have seemed to him around 1945 the vague, Enlightenment idiom of his first translation, which he had derived from Pauthier and found confirmed in Legge. Instead of simply repeating such uninstructive phrases as "the luminous principle of reason" and "to make their intentions pure and sincere," Pound sought to ground his new version of the Confucian "blueprint" for society in the precise and concrete imagery of the original Chinese "ideograms," a method of translation that he believed would render the path to social harmony perfectly clear, and so that much easier to follow. In this work, Pound undertakes a radical approach to translation, one enabled by his own lack of formal knowledge of Chinese, with the conviction that it would ensure the legibility and, moreover, the political effectiveness of the text. *The Great Digest*, then, blurs any clear distinction between "translation" and "original" composition because it operates according to its own, largely imaginative logic. Nevertheless, Pound *intended* it as the clearest, most concrete articulation possible of Confucian political thought.

In order to perceive the particular logic of *The Great Digest*, it will be necessary to examine the Chinese text from which Pound derived his mature understanding of Confucian social wisdom. Confucius's account of the genesis of social order reads as follows:

古之欲明明德於天下者，先治其國，欲治其國者，先齊其家，

欲齊其家者，先脩其身，欲脩其身者，先正其心，欲正其心者，

先誠其意，欲誠其意者，先致其知，致知，在格物。物格，而后知至，

知至，而后意誠，意誠，而后心正，心正，而后身脩，身脩，

而后家齊，家齊，而后國治，國治，而后天下平。[52]

Pound felt that Fenollosa's analysis of the "ideogram" provided the means to uncover the precise conceptual underpinnings of this text, which had mapped for China the road to peace; and the details of Pound's translation in *The Great Digest* stem from his "ideogrammic" reading of the Chinese characters in this passage. Pauthier and Legge, whose versions Pound had used both as sources for his Confucianism and as cribs for his translation, each proved adequate up to a point, but neither had been able to "penetrate the secretum' (*GK*, 145). Pound wanted his translation to reproduce the thought processes represented in the Chinese characters themselves. Accordingly, *The Great Digest* retains all the basic contours of the 大學, and Pound retains the Confucian assertion of a fundamental organic connection between all the different levels of human life, from the spiritual to the moral to the political, which as I have shown was one of the aspects of this philosophical system that first attracted him; and he gives a conventional rendering of the text's emphasis on the universal importance of individual development 自天子，以至於庶人，壹是皆以脩身爲本, or, "From the Emperor, Son of Heaven, down to the common man, singly and all together, this self-discipline is the root" (*CON*, 33). But Pound also sought to identify the specific actions involved in the Confucian notion of "self-discipline," and he saw the explanation of this ideal in the phrase 欲脩其身者，先正其心，欲正其心者，先誠其意, which Legge translates as, "Wishing to cultivate their persons, they first rectified their hearts. Wishing to rectify their hearts, they first sought to be sincere in their thoughts." The 正, or "rectification," "ideogram" in this social equation arguably suggested to Pound that there was a basic connection between the Confucian process of self-discipline and the act of 正名, or the "Rectification of Names," which had played such a large role in the "Chinese History" and "Adams" cantos. Pound no doubt saw this suggestion confirmed in the 大學 when he analyzed the next step in the program: 誠其意. Pound saw in the 誠 "ideogram," which is usually translated as "sincerity," the character meaning "to perfect" (成) placed next to the "pictogram," or radical for "word" (言). Thus he explicates this character as "The precise definition of the word, pictorially the sun's lance coming to rest on the precise spot verbally. The right hand of this compound means: to perfect, bring to focus" (*CON*, 20).[53] And in the "ideogram" usually given as "intentions," 意, Pound saw the pictogram for "music" (音) placed over the pictogram for "heart" (心), so he translates this as the "inarticulate thoughts [the tones given off by the heart]" (*CON*, 31). For Pound the Confucian process of self-discipline is an essentially poetic operation, and *The Great Digest* contends that the *paradiso terrestre* depends ultimately on the precise use of language.

> 4. The men of old wanting to clarify and diffuse throughout the empire that light which comes from looking straight into the heart and then acting, first set up good government in their own states; wanting good government in their own states, they first established order in their own families; wanting order in the house, they first disciplined themselves; desiring self-discipline, they rectified their own hearts; and wanting to rectify their own hearts, they sought precise verbal definitions of their inarticulate thoughts [the tones given off by the heart]; wishing to attain precise verbal definitions, they set to extend their knowledge to the utmost. This completion of knowledge is rooted in sorting things into organic categories.
> 5. When things had been classified into organic categories, knowledge moved toward fulfillment; given the extreme knowable points, the inarticulate thoughts were defined with precision [the sun's lance coming to rest on the precise spot verbally]. Having attained the precise definition [*aliter*, this sincerity], they then stabilized their hearts, they disciplined themselves; having attained self-discipline, they set their own houses in order; having order in their own homes, they brought good government to their own states; and when their states were well governed, the empire was brought into equilibrium. (*CON*, 29–33)

The values articulated here reflect an augmentation or reinterpretation of an ideal of precise language and its potential political consequences that stretches all the way back to Pound's Imagist phase. Moreover, as Mark Morrison has argued, other Modernists like Ford Maddox Ford anticipated Pound in casting precise use of language as necessary to peace and good government.[54] Accordingly, then, in this passage Pound's early Imagist aesthetic, his belief in the important political functions of language (most concisely emblematized by the Confucian doctrine of 正名 and confirmed here), his "ideogrammic" understanding of the Chinese written character, and his overriding belief in the historically proven effectiveness of Confucian social wisdom, all came together to form a single, unified approach to poetry and social action. Through his reading of the 大學, Pound came to see his own poetic practices as the most significant and enduring political work he could do. Exactly because he sought in *The Cantos* to use words as precisely as possible, or to 誠其意, he felt he was taking the first step to bringing peace to the world. And *The Great Digest* represents his attempt to bring to the West not only the great social insights of Confucius, but also the revolutionary political possibilities implicit in the "ideogram" itself as a form of representation, a form that helps to preserve the capacity of language as an agent of social change because it constantly reveals the dynamics of its own operation, because it always shows *how*, as well as *what*, it means. Thus in the lines from the "Pisan Cantos" cited earlier, Pound links the 誠 "ideogram" with his declaration of the explicitly political value of Confucian "sense." For Pound, Confucian social doctrine and the "ideograms" through which it was expressed together formed a profoundly illustrative articulation of the political function of precise language. And this arguably enabled him to discover the terms by which again to take up his "poem including history" after abandoning it for several years after his incarceration at Pisa and afterward.

VII

Such a development in Pound's understanding of Confucianism radically altered the poetics of *The Cantos* written after Pisa.[55] Instead of documenting the history of a foreign country, or anthologizing the writings of an American president as in the "Chinese History" and "Adams" series, Pound came to focus on examples of the precise use of language as themselves the keys to social reform. Thus in "Rock Drill" and "Thrones" he gives finely nuanced linguistic analyses of such social, moral, and legal texts as Leo the Wise's *Eparch's Book*, the Confucian *Sacred Edict*, and Sir Edward Coke's *Institutes of the Laws of England*. For Pound, these texts all provide vivid illustrations of how a few carefully chosen words, especially in the context of such important spheres as economics and law, sufficed to lay the foundation for an enduring and just society. Pound came to see and to describe the language of a fair legal and economic system as equivalent to, indeed constituent of, poetry itself. Thus in a famous passage in "Thrones," Pound explicitly links the realms of chrematistics (the study of money) and poetry, through a reading of Alexander Del Mar's *The History of Monetary Systems*.

> Coins struck by Coeur de Lion in Poitou,
> Caxton or Polydore, Villon: "blanc",
>   a gold Bacchus on your abacus,
> Henry Third's second massacre, wheat 12 pence a quarter
> that 6 4/ths pund of bread be a farden
> Act 51, Henry Three. If a penny of land be a perch
>   that is grammar
> nummulary moving towards prosody
> πρσόδος φόρων ἡ επέτειος. (XCVII, 671)[56]

Moreover, the veritable explosion of Chinese "ideograms in the late *Cantos*, especially in "Rock Drill," also stems from Pound's holistic (and linguistic) understanding of the Confucian social program. The "ideogram" represents a form of written language ideally suited to ensuring that language would be used in an accurate and concrete way. Indeed, for Pound in the late *Cantos*, the various "ideograms" not only symbolize the political importance of a precise language, as in earlier parts of the poem, but they also embody the very kind of perception Pound thought necessary for a new, Confucian civilization. "Ideograms" preserved the basic mystery and sanctity of the true social order. They involve a particular mode of signification, and so required "great labor to attain the secretum" of political wisdom that they expressed, remaining opaque symbols to those who had not been initiated into the Fenollosan rites of reading Chinese characters, and who therefore had not developed the right perceptual capabilities. (Thus as early as Canto LIII, Pound explicitly links Confucianism and the pagan religion of the Eleusinian mysteries: "Kung and Eleusis/ to catechumen alone" [LIII, 272]). And yet, because they were based upon the concrete particulars of Nature, "ideograms" remain potentially legible to anyone who could swiftly perceive the relationships between the depicted elements. Thus they automatically excluded the "lazy" or the "unworthy," while remaining open to anyone possessing the right "sensibility," regardless of whether they could read Chinese or not (c.f. *Gaudier-Brzeska*, *CWC*, 30–31n, *et passim*). In this respect, they underwrite a politics based on a hierarchy of abilities, which has its connection to Pound's attraction to Fascism. Thus he opens "Rock Drill" with an "ideogram" and an acknowledgment of the role that "ideogrammic" perceptions played in Chinese political history.

LING[2]

靈

Our dynasty came in because of a great sensibility. (LXXXV43)[57]

Couvreur's trilingual edition of the *Chou King*, "The History Classic," served as the main source for Cantos LXXXV and LXXXVI, and the very heavy presence of Chinese characters in these two cantos shows how much Pound saw Confucian wisdom as inseparable from the "ideograms" themselves. Only a few pages later, he underscores the fundamental importance of the "ideogram" to the very semiotic fabric of *The Cantos* as a whole.

But if you will follow this process

德

not a lot of signs but the one sign. (LXXXV, 546)

Indeed, according to Kenner, Pound had prepared for the "last" Canto a page of sixteen "ideograms" blocked into a square, without translation, but with standard Mandarin pronunciations, the sixteen "ideograms" Pound found 'most interesting'." Kenner somewhat overstates the case when he claims "Chinese has advantages; you cannot make an English poem out of the 16 words you find most 'interesting.'"[58] Only in a poem as widely ranging and as explicitly concerned with finding the "right" language, in other words only in *The Cantos*, could such an asyntactic assemblage be considered poetry. But for Pound it obviously was, and this anecdote goes a long way in illustrating the degree to which by the final stages of his long poem including history, Pound had come to model his own poetry after the appearance, the conceptual structure, and, perhaps most wishfully of all, what he considered the genuine social efficacy of the "ideogram." This form of representation came to embody for him the luminous union of a genuine social *praxis* and the very idea of poetry itself.

Finally, because of the privileged status they achieve in the late *Cantos* as the language of exactitude and authority, the "ideogram," and Pound's understanding of Confucianism in general, provide an illustrative contrast to the often frustrating complexities (or inconsistencies) of his economic thought. For along with the profusion of "ideograms" in the late *Cantos*, there is a concomitant increase in "Rock Drill" and "Thrones" of the explicitly economic concerns that had for so long occupied his voluminous prose writings, often centering on "money" as the linchpin to a proper economic order. As several people have rightly understood,

Pound's real interest lies in chrematistics rather than economics proper, something that he concisely confirms in the 1944 essay "Gold and Work": "All trade hinges on money. All industry hinges on money. Money is the pivot. It is the middle term. It stands midway between industry and work. The pure economic man does not exist, but the economic factor, in the problem of living, exists. If you live on clichés and lose your respect for words you will lose your 'ben dell' intelleto'" (*SP*, 342).[59] The explicit association here of money with debased language points to an important but often confusing aspect of Pound's thought. Pound believed that like all other social phenomena, the idea of "money" needed to be "rectified," to be properly defined, in order to initiate a proper economics: "We will never see an end to ructions, we will never have a sane and steady administration until we gain an absolutely clear conception of money" (*SP*, 290). To Pound the crucial fact about money, something obscured by such economic practices as the gold standard, was that money had absolutely no inherent value, that it was only a facilitator of exchange, an artificially established unit of measure. "Money is a measure. It is a warning or a notification of the amount the public owes to the bearer of the coin or note. 'Not by nature but by custom, whence the name NOMISMA'" (*SP*, 329).[60] Pound invokes Aristotle here to support his conception of money as an arbitrary, conventionalized system of representation, rather than, like anything people could use, having value in and of itself. While it goes beyond the scope of this discussion to evaluate the accuracy of Pound's theory of money, it remains clear that in its function only as a medium of exchange, a system for a particular type of interaction, money is for Pound analogous to written language, and in particular to Western, alphabetic forms. Money, like words, was not the "thing-in-itself," but only a means to facilitate its apprehension in an accepted order of signs and equivalencies. Money is thus a kind of debased, semiotic code that needed to be recognized as such, while nevertheless somehow linked with the very real processes of the world in which it operated. For Pound the ideal money would be value-less, while simultaneously coupled to the true sources of value, human effort and Nature. Thus, in advocating both "work money," in which conventional coin was replaced by a "certificate of work done," and Gessell's "stamp-scrip" currency, wherein money depreciated at a fixed rate in order to promote circulation and prevent hoarding, Pound was trying to establish a connection between what he saw as the arbitrary, too easily manipulated system of money and the realities of the natural world, to normalize the entire monetary code against the standard of Nature. Economics and language are two analogous systems whose constituent elements (money and written forms) both needed to be based on the world they sought to represent. And in the late

Cantos, Pound holds up the "ideogram" as the ideal condition to which both money and written language should aspire. A proper economics is, like poetry, the perfect alignment of human semiological effort with the forces of Nature, and for Pound in the late *Cantos*, the "ideogram" represents the epitome of both poetry, and the proper system of signs that would be the essence of a rectified money.

Pound always linked his poetry with his politics, and any attempt to examine one without the other would not only contradict Pound's own views, but also be missing the very motivational force behind *The Cantos*. For Pound's greatest dream was that he could, by poetic composition, usher in a new civilization. The Confucian texts provided him with a source text for much of the ideals offered in the poem, and indeed, the very act of translation became for him an explicitly political, as well as poetic, mode. Even more significantly, the "ideogram" came to be the very source of Pound's faith in the social possibilities of language, and in so far as it did, it represents the point where poetry met the world and the poet himself. As Pound himself liked to quote from the Confucian tradition from which he had gained so much for his poem, "A man's character is known from his brush-strokes." (*SP*, 210, see also *GK*, 91).

Part III

Translation and Language

Chapter Six

"transluding from the Otherman"
Translation and the Language of *Finnegans Wake*

I

More than sixty years after its publication in 1939, *Finnegans Wake* remains a towering mystery, casting its enormous and obscuring shadow over our collective understanding of the Modernist period. The considerable and still growing mass of commentary that has accumulated over the even longer time since it began appearing piecemeal in 1924 under the provisional title *Work in Progress*, some of it instigated by Joyce himself,[1] has done much to illuminate its purposefully murky interior. Yet the book persists as a blank spot, a nebulous zone of imposing and inchoate darkness, on virtually every map of Modernism. Indeed, for some, it has come to represent a crucial test for any account of Modernist literature. So, Terry Eagleton has asserted that any theory of Modernism, or indeed of literature in general, must at some point come to grips with, or else come to grief over, *Finnegans Wake*.[2]

The great difficulty, as well as glory, of Joyce's final work lies, of course, in its utterly distinctive expressive medium, which finds no genuinely comparable, much less equivalent, style throughout the range of Anglo-American Modernist literary production. Unfortunately, though not altogether surprisingly, responding in often ingenious ways to the interpretative challenges posed by the uniqueness of its constituent idiom, critics have implicitly marginalized *Finnegans Wake*, tacitly approaching and promoting it as an exception to, rather than a profoundly inflected expression of, Modernist textual practices and concerns. Indeed, such exceptionalist thinking has even been apparent within specifically Joycean circles, and been extended to the body of criticism surrounding Joyce and to readers of *Finnegans Wake* in general. Thus, for example, in *Reauthorizing Joyce* (1988), Vicki

Mahaffey at once diagnoses and reproduces this tendency when she advises that, "I do not as a rule include criticism of the *Wake* as part of what I am calling 'mainstream' criticism of Joyce; readers of the *Wake* comprise an atypical subcategory of Joyce criticism that is often far from 'mainstream.'"[3] Strangely, the text considered by many central to a full understanding of Modernism has largely been treated by the very group most dedicated to the study of its author as an anomaly in the course not just of the Modernist period as a whole, but even of Joyce's individual career. In this chapter, I hope to contribute to a resolution of this critical disjunction by taking up Eagleton's challenge and examining Joyce's efforts as a writer in light of the Modernist revolution in translation as a mode of literary production, the principle dimensions and consequences of which I have been attempting to map. For just as Yeats, H. D., and, most especially, Pound each discovered new avenues for their own poetic expression specifically by reformulating the dominant principles for translating works from other languages into English, so Joyce, in the novel that would occupy him for the final sixteen years of his productive life, effectively translates English itself into a different language through exploiting the capacities of some sixty other human languages, thereby expanding the boundaries of novelistic representation. From such a perspective, rather than simply as the period's most singular (and therefore inexplicable) discontinuity, *Finnegans Wake* can be understood in positive terms as the most rigorously pursued, but obverse, expression of the Modernist attempt to expand the possibilities of English by multiplying and, even more importantly, redefining its points of contact with other languages and cultures. Indeed, within the particular context of his own evolution, Joyce's ultimate and most radical achievement culminates a life-long engagement with the limits, both internal and external, of his own native tongue as a system for representing and conveying meaning. Speaking during the earliest stages of his work on *Finnegans Wake* to his friend, the Swiss sculptor August Suter, Joyce himself announced his entry into a region of thought and activity that overlaps in large degree with the domain of translation when he said, appropriately enough, in French, "Je suis au bout de l'anglais."[4]

Even more than *The Cantos*, that other great Modernist undertaking in which the multiplicity of its constituent languages at once reflects an abiding thematic concern and plays a crucial role in the formal articulation of the text, *Finnegans Wake* problematizes the dynamics of its own apprehension. The staggering, though by no means capricious opacity of its verbal texture inspires, indeed requires, the development of a new mode of reading, the cultivation of a set of semantic strategies significantly different from those necessary for comprehending English.[5] Characterizing the phenomenology of Joyce's final style, Jean Michel Rabaté has compared the experience of reading *Finnegans Wake* to the process of learning a new language:

> one starts reading *Finnegans Wake* in much the same way as one learns a foreign language—that is by mastering the various linguistic rules, the polysemic procedures, the system of punning *double-entendre* which fuses different personalities, until the axes of a microcosm start giving shape to what slowly dawns on the reader as an equivalent of the world, when he grasps that the irreducible indeterminacies are meant to mirror a cosmological concept.[6]

Though he does not invoke the term "translation" explicitly, Rabaté's description nevertheless resonates with, and perhaps even owes something to, the views of another critic, Fritz Senn, who employs the process of translation as at once a metaphor and a practical "portal of discovery" for the multiple purposes of describing the act of reading Joyce's works, particularly *Ulysses* and *Finnegans Wake*, of revealing the complex operations of his procedures as a writer, and of repositioning readers in their relationship to language itself, something he sees as one of the most important effects of Joyce's writing in general.[7]

Comparing renderings of *Ulysses* in various European languages, including Danish, French, German, Italian, Portuguese, Spanish, and Swedish, with the original in often excruciatingly fine detail, Senn turns the process of translation into an approach, a kind of methodology for exploring the systematicity of Joyce's novel. By demonstrating various felicities and failures of versions in different languages, and discussing the reasons for their shortcomings or successes, he charts the impulses and networks of verbal association that energize and organize *Ulysses* at both micro- and macroscopic levels. Using translation in a broader, conceptual sense to name the metaphorical basis of all language usage, Senn also argues that Joyce progressively instructs readers to recognize English itself as a foreign language, even if they themselves are native speakers, a process that finds its ultimate and most hyperbolic expression in *Finnegans Wake*. In his view, *Finnegans Wake* operates in the border region between human languages, and it constantly oversteps the essentially artificial (because invented) boundaries between them to offer new ways to both read and write about the world. In doing so, it remains untranslatable, but radically so, because it functions in ways that go beyond semantic relationship, ways that depend upon the specific configuration of the points of contact between English and the other languages out of which Joyce generates the style of *Finnegans Wake*.

Of all critics, Senn has been the one to recognize and explore the connection between Joyce's achievement as a writer and both the practice and the idea of translation, and my own concerns have been largely informed by his work. For all his critical sophistication and subtleties of insight, however, Senn neglects to consider the extent to which the conceptual foundation for his own deeply nuanced and highly elastic sense of translation itself finds its roots in the Modernist effort to rethink both the grounds and the methods of translation as a literary mode, a process to which, I would argue, Joyce himself contributed in his own, obverse way. Therefore, if in the pages that follow I retread some of the ground that Senn has already covered, my goal is neither simply to repeat nor refute his arguments, but rather to supplement them by exploring the homology between Joyce's career and the Modernist revolution in translation as a mode of literary production.

Both the intensity and diversity of effort that mark the Modernist concern with and practice of translation together bespeak a conviction that the establishment of personal and cultural identity requires engaging with the multiple Others of foreign languages and traditions, and defining a relationship to them. A similar belief in the constitutive power of the foreign can be seen at work throughout Joyce's writing and development. Indeed, in 1901, at the very outset of his attempts to cultivate a literary career, Joyce sought both to establish his own identity as a writer and to contribute to the formation of an Irish dramatic culture by confronting the foreign expressly though the act of translation, rendering two plays by the German dramatist Gerhart Hauptmann, *Before Sunrise* (*Vor Sonnenaufgang*) and *Michael Kramer*, and attempting to persuade the Irish Literary Theatre to perform them. Even more intensely than Yeats, who always maintained the importance of a native Gaelic dimension in the formation of a Modern Irish culture, Joyce upheld the necessity of Ireland looking to the Other of foreign masterpieces in order to learn how to establish its own cultural identity. For Joyce, that meant Continental drama, which, in his view, had found a successor to Ibsen in Gerhart Hauptmann.

Of Joyce's early attempts at translation, only his version of *Before Sunrise* has survived.[8] Clearly the work of apprenticeship, it distinguishes itself neither as a great translation in the conventional sense, on the order of Yeats's versions of the Oedipus plays, nor as a crucial point of technical or even thematic development within Joyce's individual career. Even so, it exhibits traits at once characteristic of the distinctly Modernist approach to translation and emblematic of the relationship to foreign languages, as well as to English, that Joyce would cultivate throughout his life. First, Joyce executed his translation without a complete working knowledge of German. Though he would come to learn German fluently later on in his life, in a textual note to his translation, Joyce admits that he simply employed asterisks where the Silesian dialect employed by Hauptmann proved "untranslatable."[9] As both Pound and Yeats would later come to argue in defense of their own efforts, Joyce obviously did not consider a thorough knowledge of the source language a requirement for translation. Ellmann suggests that one of Joyce's motivations for rendering Hauptmann's plays was "to improve his German,"[10] but Jill Perkins has argued, based upon her thorough study of the holograph, that "it is doubtful that [Joyce] had any working knowledge of the language prior to the translation."[11] In either case, Joyce proceeded under the expressly Modernist assumption that translation as a literary mode does not depend entirely, or even necessarily, upon the mastery of the original language. Its domain goes beyond the realm simply of linguistic competence. Unlike his contemporaries in other contexts, however, Joyce did not have the benefit of either previous translations from which to piece together his own, like Yeats, or thoroughly glossed notes by a trained scholar, as did Pound in his rendering of the poems in *Cathay*, so he had to muddle through as best he could. As a result, Joyce consistently departs from the exact semantic content of Hauptmann's original throughout his rendering, typically pruning away, or simply neglecting, phrases in the already elliptical dialogue. The cumulative deviations and omissions do not significantly reconfigure either the overall meaning or the dynamics of Hauptmann's play, though at various points they do result in certain moments of obscurity, confusions of fact, and slight alterations of character.[12] In contrast to Yeats, H. D., and Pound, Joyce never theorized his efforts as a translator in such a way as to make of his ignorance a virtue. Indeed, later in his life, he even went so far as to dismiss his early efforts as exercises with no value as translations. Hauptmann, he said, "would have a fit if they were published. I too."[13] Nevertheless, the approach he employs in his translation of *Before Sunrise* indicates that, by 1901, he had already begun exploring and, by implication, reconfiguring the standard conception of the relationship between English and other languages.

Joyce's treatment of the Silesian dialect in *Before Sunrise* underscores that he practiced translation not just as a mechanical operation of semantic conversion, but rather as a vehicle by which to explore the systematic resemblances and differences between German and English, as well as the relative conditions of dialects within each language. Throughout his translation, Joyce tends to formalize Hauptmann's German, even avoiding colloquialisms that carry over with a large degree of semantic precision into English. Thus, for example, among others, the phrase *hitzigen Zeit*, which translates literally into "hot-headed days," Joyce offers as youth's "incandescent period" (Act I, l. 156). Similarly, he gives *nun bist du ja im rechten Fahrwasser* ("you're on the right track") as "you're in the way of salvation" (III, 332–33). And most interestingly, when Hoffmann describes his business situation in Act III as *eine Hand wäscht die andere*, Joyce suppresses the insight into his business character by giving the phrase as "it's turn about among us" (III, 356). By contrast, in rendering the Silesian dialogue in the play, Joyce employs an Irish country dialect, or Hiberno-English, to match the status of the peasant tongue within the hierarchy of German linguistic culture. Here, Joyce does the opposite of what he did in translating the High German, becoming more figurative in his rendering, preferring pragmatic, rather than semantic, approximations. For *Stremer* (tramps), he uses "out o' works" (I, 473); *die iis geizig* (she's stingy) becomes "heart 'f a midge" (I, 477); *Räum ab!* (Clear away!) lengthens into "Clear the room! Every manjack a yez, clear!" (I, 704–5); and *Ich bin zwar sozusagen etwas herabjekommen* (It is true I have, so to speak, come down somewhat) takes on a more metaphorical tinge as "I'm really, so to speak, in low water myself just now" (IV, 81–82). Other examples abound. The difference between his approach to rendering the German and Silesian in *Before Sunrise* underscores that, in addition to wanting to expose Ireland to an example of modern Continental drama, Joyce pursued through the practice of translation a study of linguistic difference both within and between languages. In sum, then, for all its shortcomings and idiosyncrasies as a translation, Joyce's version of *Before Sunrise* attests to just how early he began to probe, like a translator, the relationship between languages as they converge and diverge in their conventions for expressing meaning, to apply the possibilities of a foreign language for the purposes of testing the expressive boundaries of English itself.

II

To be sure, Joyce's early translations of Hauptmann, which Ezra Pound later jokingly referred to as "juvenile indiscretions,"[14] merely manifest in a concrete textual way the formative roles that foreign languages and, by extension, the experience of linguistic difference played throughout his education and development as a writer. At Belvedere, and later at University College, Joyce studied Latin, French, and Italian. During the later stages of this period, he learned both Dano-Norwegian and German on his own to read Ibsen and Hauptmann respectively. He read widely in the languages for which he received formal training, including works by Flaubert, Verlaine, Huysmans, translations of Sudermann and Björnson in Italian, d'Annunzio, Ferdinando Paolieri, Fogazzaro, and, of course, Dante. Indeed, his dedication and interest in foreign languages became an integral part of Joyce's personal and familial identity. Ellmann reports that "John Joyce gave him money to buy foreign books whether or not the family had enough to eat."[15] Such a polyglot experience only became more profound, when, in 1904, at the age of twenty-two, Joyce fled Ireland for the European Continent, where he began the expatriation that would last the rest of his life in the city of Pola (now Pulj) teaching English for Berlitz. As John Paul Riquelme has noted, "Because of his employment by Berlitz, he was able to exchange language lessons with his colleagues and thereby extend his knowledge not just of one language, but of several, either simultaneously or in overlapping succession."[16] Moreover, the circumstances of Joyce's life, as he moved from Pola to Trieste, and then ten years later to Zürich and then finally, in 1920, to Paris, continually exposed him to a diversity of languages to reinforce his own experience as a polyglot. In Pola, he not only continued learning Italian from a colleague, but he could have heard, in addition, German and Serbian spoken by local residents. In Trieste, Joyce encountered an even wider array of languages and gained exposure to possibilities arising from their mutual interaction. Not only did he hear the special, Triestine dialect of Italian, but the diverse population of the city, which congregated there from Greece, Austria, Hungary, and Italy, further inflected the language with special pronunciations and the resources of their native languages. Joyce enjoyed his residence in such a Modern Babel, and took special pleasure in the consequences of its particular linguistic situation. In Ellmann's words, "The puns and international jokes that resulted delighted Joyce."[17] And in 1915, when he and his family moved to Zürich to avoid the depredations of World War I, Joyce found himself in both a city and a country that takes linguistic diversity as one of its fundamental conditions. Then, as well as now, German (both High- and Swiss-German), French, and Italian comprise the intertwined elements of Switzerland's linguistic fabric.

Joyce's life-long interest in languages other than English, as well as his physical exile from Ireland beginning in 1904, together betoken a profound alienation from his native tongue, which in turn provides a framework for understanding the remarkable process of stylistic development that culminates in the unique language of *Finnegans Wake*. At once an episode in and a narrative account of the origins of that development, *A Portrait of the Artist as a Young Man* explicitly depicts this condition of linguistic alienation. Speaking to the dean of studies of University College, who is British, Stephen thinks to himself:

> —The language in which we are speaking is his before it is mine. How different are the words *home, Christ, ale, master* on his lips and on mine! I cannot speak or write these words without unrest of spirit. His language, so familiar and so foreign, will always be for me an acquired speech. I have not made or accepted its words. My voice holds them at bay. My soul frets in the shadow of his language.[18]

The dangers of too readily identifying character with author notwithstanding, Stephen's musings underscore that for Joyce English constituted not just a simple medium of expression, but rather a matter of complex and abiding personal and cultural concern, one that he pursued primarily through the radically inspired formal dimensions of his major prose works. Thus, more than merely thematizing the dilemma of a Modern Irish subject's vexed relationship to English in *A Portrait of the Artist as a Young Man*, Joyce fashions both the style and the structure of the novel according to the several stages of Stephen's evolving mastery of English, thereby putting his own stamp on the linguistic instrument of British colonial domination. Indeed, Stephen's particular complaint about his, and his author's, mother tongue that "I have not made or accepted its words" contains an implicit promise, or perhaps threat, that finds its ultimate fulfillment in *Finnegans Wake*, where Joyce transforms English itself into a different language by exploiting the resources of some sixty other languages.

To say that Joyce's novels, especially *Ulysses* and *Finnegans Wake*, are in large measure "about language" has by now become a critical commonplace, but one that ignores the duration of his concern with his native tongue, as well as obscures both the variety and specificity of his strategies for negotiating that concern. For, as Fritz Senn has repeatedly shown, *Ulysses*, not to mention *Finnegans Wake*, defies translation because its diverse local and systematic effects depend upon the semantic, syntactic, and sonic particularities of English. Strictly speaking, though, this applies to every literary text in any language and has long constituted one of the grounds for declaring the "impossibility" of translation. More important, perhaps, like his Modernist contemporaries in their efforts as translators, Joyce simultaneously exposes and expands the boundaries of English specifically by exploring and progressively redefining its various axes of relationship to other languages and cultures. Thus, Joyce's achievement as a writer displays a profound structural affinity with the Modernist revolution in translation as a literary mode.

Long before he turned it into a basic principle of composition in *Finnegans Wake*, Joyce began to develop his fiction by making use of other languages and cultures in various ways to reshape the possibilities of expression in English. As early as "The Sisters," his first successful story and the opening episode in *Dubliners*, Joyce weaves expressly foreign elements into the fabric of his prose, calling attention to the different ways English intersects with and is in part shaped by other languages. Meditating on his friend's grave physical condition, the unnamed boy narrator forges a new system of connections within English by associating the word identifying Father Flynn's malady with two other words that each entered into the language from foreign cultural sources through the mechanism of translation: "Every night as I gazed up at the window I said softly to myself the word *paralysis*. It had always sounded strangely in my ears, like the word *gnomon* in the Euclid and the word *simony* in the Catechism."[19]

Citing the sources for these strange words, Joyce calls subtle attention to the practice of translation as a driving force within the evolution of English; and by not defining them, he confronts the reader with an experience similar to that of the boy narrator as he ponders the significance of the word *paralysis*, which itself derives from Greek roots meaning "a loosening beside." Over and above their immediate, local function in "The Sisters," these words serve an emblematic or symbolic purpose within *Dubliners* as a whole, describing the principle shortcomings of Joyce's subjects in their dealing with themselves and with the world at large. Invoked in its geometrical sense, a *gnomon* is that part of a parallelogram that remains after a similar parallelogram is taken away from one of its corners, and the term describes the absence or partiality that marks the lives of so many of the citizens of Joyce's Dublin. Similarly, *simony*, the worldly traffic in spiritual things, identifies the debasement at the heart of Irish religious life in Joyce's view, for which Father Flynn serves as a prime example and the sermon recounted in "Grace" gives explicit verbal expression. Later on in "The Sisters," Joyce depicts a different kind of transformation of standard English when Eliza mistakenly mentions "rheumatic wheels" (*D*, 17), instead of the proper "pneumatic." Her malapropism reveals her ignorance and provincialism, but it also looks forward to the kinds of procedures that Joyce would follow in transforming the system of reference in English itself in *Finnegans Wake*.

If Joyce problematizes English in *Dubliners* for primarily comic or satiric effect, in *A Portrait of the Artist as a Young Man*, he makes the process of learning language constitutive of identity by applying it as the guiding structural and stylistic principle of the novel. Stephen first gains a sense of himself through the idiomatic constructions of his father's story. "He was baby tuckoo" (*P*, 7). And the novel concludes with Stephen's highly personal use of English in his journal, where he attempts to define himself as an artist by authorial fiat, declaring his intention "to encounter for the millionth time the reality of experience and to forge the uncreated conscience of my race" (*P*, 252–53). Stephen's first attempt at song results in a different kind of, but no less dramatic, personalization of English: "*O, the green wothe botheth*" (*P*, 7). As he comes to acquire English, Stephen often confronts the strangeness of his native language, trying to understand its patterns of use and its connection to the world of sensation:

> Suck was a queer word. The fellow called Simon Moonan that name because Simon Moonan used to tie the prefect's false sleeves behind his back and

the prefect used to let on to be angry. But the sound was ugly. Once he had washed his hands in the lavatory of the Wicklow Hotel and his father pulled the stopper up by the chain after and the dirty water went down through the hole in the basin. And when it had all gone down slowly the hole in the basin had made a sound like that: suck. Only louder. (*P*, 11)

A little later on, the existence of foreign languages provides Stephen with a means by which he begins to ponder the equally fundamental, and interrelated, questions of divinity and identity. At such an early stage in his development, Stephen can only fall back on the tautology of his native tongue to resolve his confusion, but later on the mature Joyce would respond by blurring the distinctions between languages themselves.

> God was God's name just as his was Stephen. *Dieu* was the French word for God and that was God's name too; and when anyone prayed to God and said *Dieu* then God knew that it was a French person that was praying. But though there were different names for God in all the different languages in the world and God understood what all the people who prayed said in their languages still God remained always the same God and God's real name was God. (*P*, 16)

In tracing the process by which Stephen comes to master language, Joyce begins to defamiliarize English as a way, in Ezra Pound's words, to "Make it New." In an obverse, but nevertheless fundamentally related way, Pound and the other major Modernist translators attempted to reproduce the achievements of other cultures and languages, as a way of broadening the expressive possibilities of English. For Joyce, Greece provided the greatest source of inspiration and challenge, and *A Portrait* bears the marks of Joyce's Hellenism throughout, most notably in the highly improbable name of its Irish protagonist. The importance of the process of translation to the novel, however, can be seen perhaps most clearly in the strategic selection of the epigraph, which, as Joyce takes pains to note, comes from Book VIII of Ovid's *Metamorphosis: Et ignotas animum dimittit in artes*.[20]

Referring to Stephen's spiritual father and unlikely namesake, the phrase stems from a Latin text that is already a retelling, and therefore, at least figuratively if not actually, a translation of earlier Greek myths. Joyce never knew Greek, so the selection of texts for the epigraph may reflect mere expediency. Nevertheless, it inscribes the process of translation into the very opening pages of *A Portrait*, and points to the importance of translation as a conceptual impetus for Joyce's efforts, an importance that also manifests in the experience of the reader, who must also translate the phrase upon encountering it, whether by knowledge or appeal to guidebooks.[21] Likewise, in selecting *Ulysses*, which is the Latin version of the Greek name Odysseus, as the title for his next work, Joyce announces the relationship between the process of translation and his own Modernist retelling of *The Odyssey*. Thus, *A Portrait of the Artist as a Young Man* attests to Joyce's early engagement with the same issues that underlie the Modernist revolution in translation as a mode of literary production.

Ulysses marks Joyce's direct entry into a conceptual realm precisely homologous with that of Modernist translation, for in the novel he renders Homer's epic into the idiom of modern social and linguistic circumstances. Indeed, through his achievement, Joyce even played a part in the Modernist revolution in translation by inspiring Pound to revise *The Cantos* to open with a rendering of the Nekuia episode from *The Odyssey*.[22] But whereas Pound sought to renew language in his "poem including history" largely by translating fragments from numerous languages into English, Joyce, in "translating" *The Odyssey* into a Modern, Irish setting, probes the stylistic limits of English, thereby paving the way for his procedures in *Finnegans Wake*, where he applies the idea of translation not to another work, but to English itself. *Ulysses* broadens the scope of Joyce's concern from one individual consciousness and the development of a distinctive style to embrace a mature, if unlikely hero, as well as, indeed, an entire city, and the whole discursive breadth of English, from the intensely personal, as in "Proteus" and "Penelope," to its various social modes, as in "Aeolus," "Nausikaa," "Circe," and "Eumaeus," and including its different historical stages, as in "Oxen of the Sun." Tellingly, Joyce himself experienced the exhaustive or destructive ramifications of *Ulysses* in the act of writing. In a July 29, 1919, letter to Harriet Shaw Weaver, he declared that "the progress of the book is in fact like the progress of some sandblast.... and each successive episode dealing with some province of artistic culture (rhetoric or music or dialectic), leaves behind it a burnt up field."[23] Comparably, upon reading "Oxen of the Sun," T. S. Eliot is reported to have remarked that the episode reveals "the futility of all the English styles."[24]

Taking up where its predecessor leaves off, both in narrative and stylistic terms, *Ulysses* opens by resuming the story of Stephen's life and his evolving relationship with his native language. "Telemachus" and "Nestor" proceed in much the same manner as *A Portrait*, with an omniscient narrative voice tinged by Stephen's perceptions and habits of mind. In "Proteus," however, Joyce takes his first step toward redefining the limits of English by pursuing the stylistic principle of *A Portrait* to its logical extreme in the form of what has typically been called "stream of consciousness." As a fictional representation of Joyce's own early development, Stephen suffers a deep cultural alienation that he negotiates through an extensive interest in and familiarity with foreign languages and traditions, and his polyglot erudition contributes in large measure to the renowned, or perhaps notorious, density of the chapter. From the opening of "Proteus," Joyce begins to map for his readers the border of English by giving Stephen's thoughts in all their linguistic diversity. As in *The Waste Land*, foreign languages constitute an essential strand in the fabric of the text.

> Ineluctable modality of the visible: at least that if no more, thought through my eyes. Signatures of all things I am here to read, seaspawn and seawrack, the nearing tide, that rusty boot. Snotgreen, bluesilver, rust: coloured signs. Limits of the diaphane. But he adds: in bodies. Then he was aware of them bodies before of them coloured. How? By knocking his sconce against them, sure. Go easy. Bald he was and a millionaire, *maestro di color che sanno*. Limit of the diaphane in. Why in? Diaphane, adiaphane. If you can put your five fingers through it it is a gate, if not a door. Shut your eyes and see.
>
> Stephen closed his eyes to hear his boots crunch crackling wrack and shells. You are walking through it howsomever. I am, a stride at a time. A very short space of time through very short times of space. Five, six: the *Nacheinander*. Exactly: and that is the ineluctable modality of the audible. Open your eyes. No. Jesus! If I fell over a cliff that beetles o'er his base, fell through the *Nebeneinander* ineluctably![25]

Moreover, the interwoven density of his allusions to and through such temporally and culturally diverse figures as Aristotle, Jakob Boehme, Berkeley, Dante, and Gotthold Ephraim Lessing[26] in the above passage indicates the extent to which Stephen's considerable command of English itself derives from the efforts of others and achievements in other languages, which, especially in the case of Aristotle, he would have only been able to access by means of translation.[27] Going to the outermost limits of Joyce's accomplishment in *A Portrait*, "Proteus" operates in a space where English seamlessly intersects with various other languages.

With the appearance of Bloom, *Ulysses* moves definitively beyond *A Portrait* and the constraints of a single consciousness and its relation to language to begin encompassing the entire domain of English in its deployment as an instrument not just of individual expression or development, but also of social interaction and cultural production, conjugating through a series of stylistic modes, or discourses, from the journalistic to the literary to the scientific. The remarkable "odyssey of style" in *Ulysses*—to use Karen Lawrence's powerful phrase[28]—can be usefully understood as Joyce's attempt at once to resolve his own vexed relationship to his mother tongue and to redefine the terms of his cultural patrimony by systematically exploiting, and thus exhausting, the various resources and evolved conventions of English. The issues of maternity and the development of an expressly literary style come together in *Ulysses* most forcefully in "Oxen of the Sun," where Joyce presents a series of imitations parodying the evolution of English prose, from a "Sallustian-Tacitean prelude...to a frightful jumble of Pidgin English, nigger English, Cockney, Irish, Bowery slang and broken doggerel,"[29] as a sustained metaphor for the process of gestation. Set in the National Maternity Hospital, with the womb as its governing organ and mothers its symbol, "Oxen of the Sun" links literary and maternal production at virtually every level, and dramatizes the extent to which Joyce sought to conceive himself as a writer in *Ulysses* explicitly by coming to terms with his mother tongue, chronicling and incorporating its historical development into his own novel. As the parody of the Elizabethan "chronicle style" in the chapter puts it, "In woman's womb word is made flesh but in the spirit of the maker all flesh that passes becomes the word that shall not pass away" (*U*, 320).

The sense of stylistic exhaustion implied by Joyce's technique in "Oxen of the Sun," and silently embodied in the narrative of the chapter by Mina Purefoy, who has lain in labor and suffered "in throes now full three days" (*U*, 316), finds actual expression in the tired flabby prose of "Eumaeus," which mirrors the physical exhaustion Bloom and Stephen feel after the nightmare of "Circe." The first episode in the final section of *Ulysses*, "Eumaeus" marks the point in the novel where Joyce begins to resolve the theme of lost paternity, and throughout the chapter, Bloom displays a fatherly solicitude toward Stephen, ferrying him to "the propriety of the cabman's shelter, as it was called, hardly a stonesthrow away near Butt bridge where they might hit upon some drinkables in the shape of a milk and soda or a mineral" (*U*, 501), while speaking "a word of caution re the dangers of nighttown, women of ill fame and swell mobsmen" (*U*, 502), and warning that "the greatest danger of all was who you got drunk with" (*U*, 503). Moreover, the replacement of Stephen's actual father becomes explicit when the Simon Dedalus about whom Murphy the sailor inquires of Stephen turns out to be a sharpshooter who "toured the world with Hengler's Royal Circus" (*U*, 510). Proper paternity implies inheritance, and "Eumaeus" not only definitively establishes a relationship between Bloom and Stephen, but it inverts the values of the tradition that Joyce, in his earlier career and most notably in *A Portrait of the Artist as a Young Man*, upheld and even extended. For the utterly vapid idiom of the chapter erases the distinction between unique, individual expression and anonymous, formulaic discourse, between high literary style and cliché. Thus, through the exhaustion of English in "Eumaeus," Joyce redefines the terms of his own cultural patrimony.

At the same time that Joyce exhausts the possibilities of English as a medium of novelistic representation in *Ulysses*, foreign languages and different systems of semantic signification repeatedly function in the novel as avenues of contact between the various characters, thereby pointing the way to his procedures in *Finnegans Wake*. Thus, in "Calypso," Bloom translates "Metempsychosis" into plain words for Molly; and in "Lotos-Eaters," after reading his letter from Martha Clifford, he speculates about a language of flowers and translates the note into this new idiom: "Angry tulips with you darling manflower punish your cactus if you don't please poor forgetmenot how I long violets to dear roses when we soon anemone meet all naughty nightstalk wife Martha's perfume" (*U*, 64). Most tellingly, though, one of the subjects through which Bloom and Stephen make their most profound connection in "Ithaca" concerns their respective knowledge of ancient Hebrew and Irish. Even the detached, catechistic form of the chapter cannot obscure the importance of this event:

> What fragments of verse from the ancient Hebrew and ancient Irish languages were cited with modulations of voice and translation of texts by guest to host and host to guest?
>
> By Stephen: *suil, suil, suil arun, suil go siocair agus suil go cuin* (walk, walk, walk your way, walk in safety, walk with care).
>
> By Bloom: *kifeloch, harimon rakatejch m'baad l'zamatecjh* (thy temple amid thy hair is as a slice of pomegranate).
>
> How was a glyphic comparison of the phonic symbols of both languages made in substantiation of the oral comparison?
>
> By juxtaposition. On the penultimate blank page of a book of inferior literary style, entitled *Sweets of Sin* (produced by Bloom and so manipulated that its front cover came in contact with the surface of the table) with a pencil (supplied by Stephen) Stephen wrote the Irish characters for gee, eh, dee, em, simple and modified, and Bloom in turn wrote the Hebrew characters ghimel, aleph, daleth and (in the absence of mem) a substituted qoph, explaining their arithmetical values as ordinal and cardinal numbers, videlicet 3, 1, 4, and 100.
>
> Was the knowledge possessed by both of each of these languages, the extinct and the revived, theoretical or practical?
>
> Theoretical, being confined to certain grammatical rules of accidence and syntax and practically excluding vocabulary.
>
> What points of contact existed between these languages and between the peoples who spoke them?
>
> The presence of guttural sounds, diacritic aspirations, epenthetic and servile letters in both languages: their antiquity, both having been taught on the plain of Shinar 242 years after the deluge in the seminary instituted by Fenius Farsaigh, descendant of Noah, progenitor of Israel, and ascendant of Heber and Heremon, progenitors of Ireland: their archaeological, genealogical, hagiographical, exegetical, homiletic, toponomastic, historical and religious literatures comprising the works of rabbis culdees, Torah, Talmud, (Mischna and Ghemara), Massor, Pentateuch, Book of the Dun Cow, Book of Ballymote, Garland of Howth, Book of Kells: their dispersal, persecution,

survival and revival: the isolation of their synagogical and ecclesiastical rites in ghetto (S. Mary's Abbey) and masshouse (Adam and Eve's tavern): the proscription of their national costumes in penal laws and jewish dress acts: the restoration in Chanah David of Zion and the possibility of Irish political autonomy or devolution. (*U*, 563–64)

In depicting a moment during which Bloom and Stephen come together not just as individuals, but also as representatives of their respective races, this passage in "Ithaca" confirms that foreign languages represented for Joyce a means by which to overcome both specific personal and larger cultural constraints imposed by and associated with English. Moreover, it looks forward to the terms of Joyce's next achievement not least because it makes explicit reference to a place, "Adam and Eve's tavern," which subsequently appears in the very "first"[30] sentence of *Finnegans Wake*: "riverrun, past Eve and Adam's, from swerve of shore to bend of bay, brings us by a commodious vicus of recirculation back to Howth Castle and Environs."[31] "Adam and Eve's" was the name of a tavern in Dublin that also served as a front for an underground church established in 1618 by the Franciscans to circumvent the English attempt to suppress Catholic worship in Ireland during the sixteenth and seventeenth centuries. By invoking this establishment, yet transposing the elements in its name, at the very outset of *Finnegans Wake*, Joyce at once immediately locates readers within the vicinity of a site of Irish resistance to British colonial domination, and subtly indicates his goal in the novel of reversing the process of that domination, which has gone so far as to decree the vernacular in which its own resistance is articulated. Toward this end, Joyce develops the idiom for his final novel by thoroughly interweaving strands from some sixty different languages into the very fabric of English itself, thereby effectively translating it into a different language.

Finnegans Wake repeatedly asserts its difference from English, and the polyglot distinctiveness of its constituent language serves as one of the novel's abiding themes. Near the opening of the novel, for example, the *Wake* declares tauntingly that "Here English might be seen" (13, 1), but such a formulation merely implies that it might just as easily not, and later comes an explicit recognition that "however basically English" (116, 26) the language of the *Wake* may or may not be, it remains so fundamentally intertwined with other linguistic media that, ultimately, it speaks "in universal, in polyguttural, in each auxiliary neutral idiom, sordomutics, florilingua, sheltafocal, flayflutter, a con's cubane, a pro's tutute, strassarab, ereperse and anythongue athall" (117, 12–16). Similarly, in chapter II.i, "*The Mime of Mick, Nick and the Maggies*" is announced as "wordloosed over seven seas crowdblast in cellelleneteutoslavzendlatinsoundscript" (219, 28–29). And if the "*Mime*" spans the range of the Indo-European language family in what, according to the *Annotations*, Rev. John Roche called "The seven sister tongues,"[32] the letter that reappears throughout *Finnegans Wake* as a cipher for the novel itself appears, at least in an early manifestation, "written in lappish language with bursts of Maggyer" (66, 18–19), spanning the Finno-Ugrian languages, Lappish and Magyar, but also evoking German in its childish disregard both of conventional distinctions between languages and of the distinct conventions of language (*läppisch* in German means "childish"), as well as Latin in "lapsus linguae," or the slips of the tongue that accompany any attempt to read the *Wake* aloud, yet which also result from coincidental sonic connections between words and thus offer unforeseen avenues for producing meaning. Perhaps most militantly, the *Wake* exclaims in "Nightlessons" (II.ii), "None of your cumpohlstery English here!" (271, F3), where "compulsory English" comes clear as the domestic furniture of the mind for stuffed shirts and other such representatives and adherents of monolingual (and monolithic) constructions of national culture.

One of, if not the, great paradox of the *Wake* is, of course, that it primarily used English to assert the difference of its particular language. But if Joyce remains dependent on English for both the genesis and the impact of his final style, he redeems his claims of having transformed English by identifying in the novel his writing methods in terms that underscore the fundamental connection between his procedures in the *Wake* and the Modernist concern with and revolution in translation as a mode of literary production. Thus, he makes reference to the practice of "falsemeaning adamelegy" (77, 26), by means of which he displaces the Biblical Adam's place in ordering the world through language by bidding farewell in words to the system itself and opening its semantic structure to the influences of other languages and their attendant possibilities of expression and reference. Similarly, *Finnegans Wake* builds its own reality out of the "abnihilisation of the etym" (353, 22), a procedure that puts the novel in competition with the Biblical account of creation ex nihilo, and suggests the enormous power of such a linguistic strategy (the annihilation of the atom and the release of energy, for either destructive or constructive purposes, consequent to that act), while still acknowledging the inherently paradoxical nature of Joyce's endeavor ("atom" literally meaning in Greek "that which cannot be split"). Thus, *Finnegans Wake* can be understood as an elaborate investigation into "Epistlemadethemology for deep dorfy doubtlings" (374, 17–18), whereby Joyce sends a letter to the residents of his former city, "dear dirty Dublin," in order to refashion them, dispel doubts, and construct a new science of knowledge, all through recasting the language of their cultural and political disenfranchisement.

In his remarkable study of Joyce's "book of the dark," John Bishop has convincingly argued that Vico's greatest influence on Joyce stems not from the cyclical conception of history that concludes *The New Science* and organizes the surface of *Finnegans Wake*, but from the philosopher's exploration of primitive cognition through etymological reconstructions.[33] Joyce's decision to make etymons the building blocks of his final style highlights the inverse, but nevertheless fundamental, symmetry between his achievement in the *Wake* and the Modernist revolution in translation as a literary mode; for it amounts to an attempt to overcome the impoverishment of English and its historical legacy by reformulating it in relation to other languages. Thus, just as Pound, for example, redefines the principles for translating the Confucian classics into English in order at once to provide a "blueprint for civilization" and to articulate an idiom that would guarantee the vitality of that civilization, so Joyce, in the process of representing the night and the experience of sleep, synthesizes his mother tongue with some sixty other languages, thereby effectively translating English itself into a language never yet heard on earth. Pound's use of Fenollosa and Joyce's of Vico constitute structurally identical strategic responses to the demands of their obverse goals and concerns. Where Pound recognizes in *The Cantos*, "It can't be all in one language" (LXXXVI, 563), Joyce writes in *Finnegans Wake*, "We are once amore as babes awondering a wold made fresh where with the hen in the storyaboot we start from scratch" (336, 16–18). Indeed, translation makes an explicit appearance in *Finnegans Wake* as a process that becomes a form of narrative when the "Answering" voice in the "Question and Answer" chapter (I.vi) declares, "As none of you knows javanese I will give all my easyfree translation of the old fabulist's parable" (152, 12–13), and then proceeds to relate the tale of "The Mookse and The Gripes."

Of course, no word in standard English could entirely describe what takes place in the *Wake*, and this remains true for translation as well. Yet, here too Joyce provides a means for distinguishing between his procedures and the Modernist practice of translation. In the chapter known as "The First Watch of Shaun" (III.i), Shaun the Post, the aspect of HCE "representative of a letter-carrying and letter-conscious state of mind,"[34] boasts of his abilities in "transluding from the Otherman or off the Toptic" (419, 24–25). This phrase refers to, among other things, the "translations" of the nineteenth-century Irish poet/translator James Clarence Mangan, who often wrote original poems and appended phrases such as "from the Ottoman" or "from the Coptic" in order to "address the status of sources and origins,"[35] and undermine claims of authentic appropriation by which British colonial exploitation operated in both Ireland and Asia throughout the Victorian period. Joyce himself wrote an early essay in 1902 on Mangan, and he may well have recognized the political subtext of Mangan's efforts, inasmuch as he refers disdainfully to those who "have sought to discover whether learning or imposture lies behind"[36] the alleged translations. Within the context of the *Wake*, however, the model of translating from the Ottoman and from the Coptic becomes at once more profound, because more deeply foreign, and more digressive, arising from a generic "Otherman" and going "off the topic." The playful, yet no less disruptive, dimensions of Joyce's practice as a writer are captured in "transluding," which transforms translation into a form of play ("ludo" in Latin means "play"). Nevertheless, if Joyce reminds readers of how his own procedures differ from the practice of translation, *Finnegans Wake* as a whole remains a testament to the fundamental importance of translation, not just as a concrete textual practice in and of itself, but as both an instrument of composition and a driving conceptual force throughout the Modernist period, especially in its most extreme achievements.

Chapter Seven

"dent those reprobates, Romulus and Remus!"[1]
Lowell, Zukofsky, and the Legacies of Modernist Translation

I

Among the (American) writers of the post–World War II era, Robert Lowell and Louis Zukofsky stand out as the principal inheritors of the Modernist revolution in the theory, the practice, and, perhaps most important of all, the generative cultural possibilities of translation as a mode of literary production.[2] As "original" poets, of course, these two could hardly be more different. The nakedly emotive portraits, monologues, and reminiscences of *Life Studies* (1959) and *For the Union Dead* (1967), for example, resemble nothing so little as the mathematically rarefied celebrations of *A* (1959–72) and *80 Flowers* (1978). But in their efforts as translators Lowell and Zukofsky share a common lineage in the manifold and extensive liberties taken by their Modernist ancestors. And like two brothers with opposing temperaments, they each took their inheritance and pursued starkly different directions. No less audacious, but rather more savvy than his most notorious predecessor Ezra Pound, Lowell produced during the span of his career a number of decidedly "free" renderings of both poetic and dramatic works by various writers from several different European languages, at least one of which (Russian) he freely admitted to having no knowledge of at all.[3] Deriving a lesson in marketing, if not modesty, from Pound and the critical furor aroused by the *Homage to Sextus Propertius*, he gave the most significant and wide-ranging outcome of his engagement with translation as a mode of literary production the distinctly less confrontational title *Imitations* (1961). Taking the license in semantic freedom secured by his Modernist forebears, Lowell further explored the possibilities of translation as a principally creative, rather than simply derivatively mimetic, practice, employing it as an instrument of self-definition and personal expression.

Louis Zukofsky, on the other hand, took off from the radical conception of "fidelity" implicit in Pound's later approach to conveying the exact semantic meaning, at least as he saw it, of the Confucian classics and applied it instead to the domain of sound. In "How to Read" Pound had asserted that "melopoeia," or the "musical property" (25) of poetry, "is practically impossible to transfer or translate [. . .] from one language to another, save perhaps by divine accident, and for half a line at a time" (25). But in his unprecedented (within the tradition of English at least), largely "phonemic"[4] rendering of the odes of Catullus, Zukofsky sought to do precisely that on a large scale, attempting to reproduce the sound patterning, or the "music," of the Latin poet within an English semantic and phonetic framework. Over the course of his remarkable treatment, the practice of "translation" comes to serve as the lever by which to pry open the established syntactic constraints of English itself. As it happened, not surprisingly, Lowell earned readier critical acceptance, as well as even a degree of public acclaim, for his free, yet undeniably felicitous, *Imitations*, while Zukofsky drew mostly incomprehension and oftentimes even outraged dismissals. But history may well ultimately redeem Louis and Celia Zukofsky's *Catullus (Gai Valeri Catulli Veronensis Liber)* (1969) as the greater achievement, both for the way it expands the very parameters of translation itself as a mode of literary production and as a uniquely generative work in its own right.

Of course, despite his broad success, Lowell did not entirely escape attack for his procedures in *Imitations*. With a few notable exceptions,[5] early reviewers including such prominent figures as George Steiner, Louis Simpson, and Dudley Fitts, generally reacted with hostility, or at best condescension, to Lowell's numerous, as well as obvious, departures from the strict semantic content of the original poems from which he worked and to his corresponding tendency of producing his own, expressly personal tone. Thom Gunn, for example, complained bitterly: "Hugo's suave gestures similarly become spasmodic jerks, Villon takes on the flat clinical sound of the "confessional" poems in *Life Studies*, and others I am not able to read in the original, Homer and Pasternak for example, all speak with the unmistakable voice of Robert Lowell. Preserving the tone of most of these poets is, in fact, the last thing he has done."[6] In their negative responses, such critics treated *Imitations* as if it were just a loose set of conventional, semantically based translations, apparently ignoring the warning note sounded against this approach by the title of the volume, as well as in Lowell's careful, if somewhat confused, "Introduction," which I will discuss in greater detail momentarily. After this initial phase, however, readers began to distinguish more carefully between the creative and mimetic aspects of Lowell's efforts, thereby making it possible to endorse, or at least recognize, his achievement not as a translation in the conventional, semantically or pragmatically reproductive sense, but as a work with its own independent significance and meaning. Thus, Daniel Hoffman described *Imitations* as "a long, fragmented poem of the self, struggling in its engagement with history."[7] Comparably, in his essay "*Imitations*: Translation as Personal Mode," Ben Belitt argues, "the effect [of Lowell's volume] . . . is to draw the reader's attention constantly to the persona of the translator" (115).[8] Even more sympathetically, Richard Fein and Stephen Yenser have respectively traced the thematic and structural coherence of the volume, showing how it consistently explores such motifs as war, infinity, the quest, and nature within a "brilliantly chosen and scrupulously arranged . . . series of interrelated groups of poems which function in the manner of a narrative."[9]

Yet, even those responding positively to *Imitations* have differed incommensurably both about the specific "qualities" of Lowell's treatment of particular writers and over how to characterize his method generally. So Donald Carne-Ross confidently claims that Lowell's renderings from Baudelaire "stick so closely to the original, semantically and even rhythmically, without losing their own accent,"[10] as well as that "Thanks to Robert Lowell, poetic translation retains much of the importance which Ezra Pound won back for it."[11] By contrast, Burton Raffel declares with equal conviction both that "Autumn" (Lowell's version of Baudelaire's "Chant d'Automne") "is neither faithful nor Baudelaire," and that "I do not think *Imitations* is in fact translation."[12] Such flatly contradictory judgments underscore the fundamental theoretical limitations of an impressionistic, largely evaluative approach to translation. Moreover, they demonstrate the ongoing confusion over the "proper" procedural dimensions or boundaries of translation as a mode of literary production, an uncertainty brought on, or at least exacerbated, by the Modernists we have been examining and their remarkable, if oftentimes highly unorthodox, efforts as translators. Ironically, despite, or perhaps precisely because of, this conceptual muddle, *Imitations* earned Lowell a share of the Bollingen Prize for Translation in 1962.[13]

In Zukofsky's case, the responses to his treatment of Catullus have fallen along roughly comparable lines, though because of the greater eccentricity of his achievement the debate has taken place at a much shriller pitch. Attacks have been more vitriolic and defenses more extravagant. On the negative side, a number of reviewers and critics have issued broadsides against Zukofsky and his practice of "translating" based primarily on the "sound" of the Latin. Soon after its publication, Alan Brownjohn decried the work as "a crazy approximation of modern English" that "reads like hopeful stabs at unseen translation when one hasn't done the homework of the night before: knotted, clumsy, turgid, and ultimately silly." Echoing the tenor of Hale's early screed against Pound's *Homage*, he ultimately dismissed Zukofsky's effort as exhibiting "complete lunacy" and "unbelievable crankiness."[14] Similarly, in a now somewhat (in)famous response, Burton Raffel asked with almost outraged disbelief:

> To whom is this "translation" of Catullus . . . of any use? The Latinist can read Catullus in Latin; he does not need, nor presumably is he interested to read, that "o ventum horribilium atque pestilentem" can be aped (but not translated, no) as "o vent them horrible, I'm not quite, pestilent, mm." The non-Latinist wants to know, as well as he can, what Catullus said and how he said it. Can he get anything—*anything*—? from this?[15]

And most archly, Robert Conquest openly assumes the posture of moral and cultural indignation that stands implicit in the normative conception of his predecessors: "The Hun is at play—worse still, *at work*—among the ruins."[16] Even Andre Lefévere, who would eventually come to eschew a normative critical approach to translation as a literary mode, rejected Zukofsky's treatment of Catullus as a "childish game," giving a detailed critique of its limitations and excesses as a method.[17]

While others early on praised Zukofsky for his conceptual daring and poetic inventiveness, they also seemed to share a discomfort over his apparently casual disregard for conveying the basic semantic content of his source text, or even for producing something close to conventionally readable English. So, for example, Hugh Kenner wavered between a profound respect for the effort and an equally deep ambivalence over the demands made by the results:

> The structural eloquence is phatic, the Latin treated not only as a source of "meanings" but as a graph of breathings and intonations; the achieved English is irremediably strange; and the strangeness is accepted and turned into a virtue by the sheer scale of the enterprise, which (difficulty overcome) offers not just a few compliant instances, but Catullus whole, subdued after unimaginable trouble. A mad enterprise? yet it carries Pound's way with *The Seafarer*, or Joyce's with what you like, to its logical term. (1968, 113)

Likewise, even as he celebrates the achievement as similar in spirit and diction to both Joyce and even Shakespeare, Guy Davenport notes, "On every page we find ourselves looking for the place where Zukofsky has charmed his monstrous method into allowing the poet to get through a glorious passage on his lute unpestered."[18] And Zukofsky's friend (and sometime publisher) Cid Corman sought to defend the significance of the volume by sidestepping the issue of fidelity altogether: "There is no use in comparing these versions with any other versions of Catullus. ... The only accuracy must occur within the work itself as poetry."[19]

Going a significant step beyond these initial defenders, Burton Hatlen has given perhaps the most elaborate justification of Zukofsky's efforts as a translator, arguing not only that his unorthodox rendering of Catullus refuses "to pander to our fear of language, our hunger to escape from words into 'meanings,'" which reflects his "goal as a translator ... to establish the physical reality of his own English words, thereby also forcing us to come to terms with the physical reality of Catullus's ... Latin words"; perhaps even more radically, he also asserts that "if we are patient, we will discover that everything in this translation makes sense ... , in all possible meanings of that phrase," most especially in the "sense" of making "a pattern that the senses can apprehend with delight."[20] Working hard to redeem Zukofsky on both innovative as well as traditional grounds, Hatlen at one point even goes so far as to put forth the bold claim that "the translation unfolds, amplifies, explicates Catullus's Latin poem; but it is never false to the original," being "faithful to the sound as well as the sense of the original" (352). With the advent and dissemination of expressly post-Structuralist critical perspectives, Zukofsky's text has become even more legible, and its considerable (and notorious) eccentricities converted into positive traits through invoking their ostensible philosophical implications. Along these lines, Peter Quartermain has demonstrated the link between Zukofsky's procedures in his *Catullus* to Joyce's in *Finnegans Wake* and argued, "It is not, of course, that neither book is intelligible, but that they profoundly disturb our notions of intelligibility: like the world, the text must stubbornly resist the straightjacket of determined meaning and the singularity of intellectual order."[21] Finally, in situating Zukofsky's effort within the history of modern translators of Latin poetry, Daniel Hooley has given a discussion of the work that pertains most directly to my own concerns in this volume. Recognizing that the homophonic method "provides a system of relations which is precisely not ordinary semantic bartering but one that allows for an exploring, an enrichment, a building of word upon word" that produces "a compounding and deepening of meaning,"[22] he perceptively notes: "whereas ponies will feebly stand in for their original this translation insists on pulling us back in thought and time to the breath of the poem. Zukofsky's work enacts the process of poetic memory and demands that we undergo that same process" (68).

Both through carefully explicating individual translated odes and by indicating affinities between his achievement and those of other writers, these supporters have gone a long way in acquitting Zukofsky of the charges of pointless obscurity and even willful perversion of Catullus leveled against him by earlier critics. In particular, Hooley has done the most both to contextualize and to establish the internal logic of Zukofsky's thoroughly radical practice as a translator, rightly seeing that its conceptual impetus derives "most immediately from Pound who began to forge new connections between poem and translation, to break down the simple model of sense for sense" (66). Moreover, he has properly understood that, far from simply being meaninglessly indulgent, the homophonic approach actually "nudges the limits of translation beyond another frontier" (68). Still, for all their subtle interpretive skills and compelling local insights, even his staunchest and most recent advocates have yet to fully delineate the manifold ways Zukofsky at once builds upon and extends the efforts of his immediate predecessors, how his unique achievement embodies a logical culmination of the Modernist revolution in translation as a literary mode. As a result, they have failed to take full measure of his accomplishment as a translator. The debate surrounding Lowell's various renderings has likewise neglected to sufficiently address either the particular historical roots or the broader cultural meaning of his efforts in translation. In what follows, I want to close out the body of this study by briefly discussing the specific conceptions, in both procedural and theoretical terms, of translation itself that inform the respective practices of each of these writers. For in their achievements, they not only carry forward the Modernist redefinition of translation as a literary mode, but in doing so they also helped to establish the terms by which many of the most renowned contemporary translators engage in the practice not as an exercise in apprenticeship or as a form of cultural service, but rather as a privilege of established reputation and an alternative means of poetic expression. Accordingly, then, I do not intend in this final chapter to enter into what (it should by now be obvious) strikes me as the already tired and, even more important, fundamentally irresolvable debate over the putative "accuracy" or "fidelity" of the different renderings by either Lowell or Zukofsky. Instead, I want to focus primary attention on their controversial methods as translators precisely in order to trace how they each engage with and reconfigure the very parameters of translation as a mode of literary production.

II

Despite drawing the ire of more than a few critics holding to a narrowly mimetic, if never explicitly defined, understanding of the term, Lowell's procedures in *Imitations* for the most part fall well within the range of interlingual practices that have been discussed and performed under the rubric of "translation" over the course of English literary history. The volume takes its title, most obviously, from the third and freest category of the famous tripartite scheme Dryden articulated in the 1680 Preface to his *Ovid's Epistles, Translated by Several Hands* mapping different approaches to the task of rendering works from other languages into English: *metaphrase*, or "turning an author word by word, and line by line, from one language into another"; *paraphrase*, "or translation with latitude, where the author is kept in view by the translator, so as never to be lost, but his words are not so strictly followed as his sense, and that too is admitted to be amplified, but not altered"; and *imitation*, "where the translator (if now he has not lost that name) assumes the liberty, not only to vary from the words and sense, but to forsake them both as he sees occasion; and taking only some general hints from the original, to run division on the groundwork, as he pleases."[23] For Dryden, of course, this taxonomy serves the normative purpose of limiting the domain of "proper" translation to the more or less "faithful" reproduction of the "sense" of foreign writers. Hence he casts *imitation* in a distinctly negative light as "the most advantageous way for a translator to show himself, but the greatest wrong which can be done to the memory and reputation of the dead." By contrast, Lowell employs the term without a sense of moral taint, operating under a conception of translation that extends further than simply the "accurate" reproduction of semantic, or even pragmatic, meaning. Indeed, from the opening paragraphs of his "Introduction" to the volume, wherein he reveals his intentions and describes his methods in *Imitations*, Lowell begins to broaden the scope of translation beyond merely a mimetic or reproductive function:

> This book is partially self-sufficient and separate from its sources, and should be first read as a sequence, one voice running through many personalities, contrasts and repetitions. I have hoped somehow for a whole, to make a single volume, a small anthology of European poetry. The dark and against the grain stand out, but there are other modifying strands. I have tried to keep something equivalent to the fire and finish of my originals. This has forced me to do considerable rewriting.
> Boris Pasternak has said that the usual reliable translator gets the literal meaning but misses the tone, and that in poetry tone is of course everything. I have been reckless with literal meaning, and labored hard to get the tone. Most often this has been *a* tone, for *the* tone is something that will always more or less escape transference to another language and cultural moment. I have tried to write alive English and to do what my authors might have done if they were writing their poems now and in America. (xi) [emphasis in the original]

A number of things stand out as particularly noteworthy in this beginning to Lowell's "Introduction." First, his claim to a degree of textual autonomy for his series of renderings in *Imitations* as a "sequence" embodying its own internal coherence of voice already bespeaks his view of translation not primarily as a derivative mimetic practice, but rather as a distinct mode of literary production and even expression. Second, his desire "to make a single volume, a small anthology of European poetry" further emphasizes his expressly originary approach to translation by underscoring *selection* as a crucial aspect of his overall procedures. As might be expected for a book of "original" poems more than for one of conventional translations, Lowell strives for a thematic unity to complement that of voice. Even more revealing, perhaps, he then cunningly asserts that the effort "to keep something equivalent to the fire and finish of my originals...has forced me to do considerable rewriting." Behind such a claim stands the fundamental assumption of the incommensurable systematicity of different languages, or as Pound put it some thirty two years earlier in "How to Read" (and that I mentioned in the introduction to this study), the conviction that "Different languages—I mean the actual vocabularies and idioms—have worked out certain mechanisms of communication and registration. No one language is complete." By itself, of course, such a belief constitutes nothing new. It was already an ancient truism when Pound said it again in 1929. In fact, it represents one of the cornerstones of translation theory from at least the time of Cicero, when the Latin orator advised against strict word-for-word literalism. Thus, contrary to the assertions of some of his more rigidly dogmatic contemporary critics, Lowell's solidly traditional thinking about the relationship between different languages and the complex process of conveying the significance of a literary work from one to another situates his efforts in *Imitations* firmly within the established conceptual boundaries of translation.

At the same time, however, the very casualness of his admission, the remarkable ease with which he shifts from the terminology of mimesis in seeking to preserve "something equivalent to the fire and finish of my originals" to the expressly generative or revisionary activity of "rewriting" clearly signals his conception of translation primarily as a technique of independent textual construction, a notion that he inherited directly from his Modernist predecessors. Such a fundamentally generative vision of translation helps to explain the pragmatic, or as others might less generously call it, cynical, distinction he makes between idealistically capturing *the* tone of his originals and rather more cagily simply achieving *a* tone. Still, for all his Modernist sensibilities about the creative possibilities of translation as a mode of literary production, Lowell characterizes his approach to the practice itself in strikingly familiar terms: "I have tried to write alive English and to do what my authors might have done if they were writing their poems now and in America." As might be recalled, Dryden described his treatment of Virgil in precisely analogous terms, therewith indicating his desire to domesticate the Latin source text into the vernacular of his time. For his part, as we shall see, Dryden would not have sanctioned the degree of freedom that Lowell took with his originals in the effort "to write alive English." Even so, the basic similarity between their approaches to the task itself indicates the practically conservative strain that persists throughout Lowell's engagement with translation as a literary mode in *Imitations*, the complaints of various critics notwithstanding. After all, unlike Zukofsky, Lowell does not go so far as to venture through translation to challenge the very constraints of standard English itself. In short, then, even as he embraces a Modernist conception of the expressive possibilities of translation, Lowell nevertheless holds to an eminently conventional, which is to say semantically based, idea of the underlying principle for the actual practice.

These two perhaps slightly contrary impulses underwrite his ensuing critique of differing approaches to poetic translation. On the one hand, Lowell disparages formal literalists (he calls them "strict metrical translators") because of their implicit anachronism. For him, they "live in a world untouched by contemporary poetry." Consequently, "they are taxidermists, not poets, and their poems are likely to be stuffed birds." Thus Lowell considers "genuine" poetic translation a form of contemporary cultural engagement and stylistic currency a requirement for successful renderings. On the other hand, formally unconstrained treatments, or "translations into free or irregular verse," also fall short because "this method commonly turns out a sprawl of language, neither faithful nor distinguished, now on stilts, now low, as Dryden would say." In addition to currency, then, successful renderings must also exhibit an internal tonal consistency. Like his explicitly acknowledged neoclassical master in translation, Lowell attempts to steer a middle course between what he perceives as two extremes in order to justify and define his own practice. Yet in doing so, he casually elides the distinction that Dryden himself made between *imitation* and *paraphrase*, between overly free and properly respectful rendering. Instead, he articulates a model that derives from the Modernist practice of employing translation as a method of independent textual construction. Thus Lowell puts translation as a literary mode directly on par with original poetic composition: "I believe that poetic translation—I would call it an imitation—must be expert and inspired, and needs at least as much technique, luck and rightness of hand as an original poem." Such a conflation only became conceivable as a result of the Modernist rethinking of the significance of translation as a mode of literary production.

The actual extent of Lowell's distance from Dryden in this matter becomes clear when he enumerates his abundant departures from the strict semantic content and even formal arrangement of original poems from which he worked in *Imitations*, and this startlingly frank paragraph underscores his view of translation as by and large an alternative means of personal expression. While Dryden certainly would have agreed about the creativity necessary for successful translation, he would also have clearly disapproved both the number and the nature of Lowell's modifications to his originals, his apparently cavalier disregard for "the memory and reputation of the dead":

> My licenses have been many. My first two Sappho poems are really new poems based on hers. Villon has been somewhat stripped; Hebel is taken out of dialect; Hugo's "Gautier" is cut in half. Mallarmé has been unclotted, not because I disapprove of his dense medium but because I saw no way of giving it much power in English. The same has been done with Ungaretti and some of the more obscure Rimbaud. About a third of "The Drunken Boat" has been left out. Two stanzas have been added to Rilke's "Roman Sarcophagus," and one to his "Pigeons." "Pigeons" and Valéry's "Helen" are more idiomatic and informal in my English. Some lines from Villon's "Little Testament" have been shifted to introduce his "Great Testament." And so forth! I have dropped lines, moved lines, moved stanzas, changed images and altered meter and intent. (xii)

Ben Belitt has wryly observed that in the "Introduction," Lowell "delivers himself up to would-be assassins with the resolute fatalism of Caesar in the Roman Senate" (Belitt, 116). But his predilection for almost excruciating detail in this paragraph and its attendant tone of forthrightness seem at least as naïve and even gleeful as deliberate and resigned, and the genuine surprise he expressed in his letters about the vehemence of the negative reviews he received from critics with more rigid notions of translation suggests just how much he had simply assumed as a given the possibilities or freedom deriving from a Modernist conception of translation as itself a primary mode of literary production.[24] Such a feat of internalization helps to explain the simple candor with which he discusses his approach to Pasternak: "Pasternak has given me special problems. From reading his prose and many translations of his poetry, I have come to feel that he is a very great poet. But I know no Russian. I have rashly tried to improve on other translations, and have been helped by exact prose versions given me by Russian readers. This is an old practice; Pasternak himself, I think, worked this way with his Georgian poets" (xii).

While Pasternak may well have proceeded in this fashion "with his Georgian poets," it only really became a viable strategy in English after Pound, Yeats, and the other Modernists demonstrated its effectiveness, thereby definitively decoupling the linguistic and the expressly literary dimensions of translation as a mode of literary production. Through their aggressively non- and even anti-scholarly, yet undeniably committed and profoundly influential, approach to the practice, the Modernists writing in and into English, more than either Dryden or Pasternak, actually set the terms for Lowell's efforts in *Imitations*. And in turn, at least in part because of Lowell, actual knowledge of the original language of a source text remains unnecessary for the production of so-called translations of foreign works. Arguably, then, the real significance of his achievement lies less in the putative "accuracy" or "felicity" of his individual treatment of different writers than in the extent to which his openly free renderings at once register the impact of and perpetuate the Modernist revolution in translation as a literary mode, extending the horizon of the practice to make it available as an avenue of eminently personal expression.

The final paragraph of the "Introduction" highlights the abiding logical tension that ultimately enables Lowell's deeply personal approach to translation. In it, he both avows the fundamental uniqueness of his source poems in their original languages and claims the essential creative integrity of his own treatments of (or, perhaps more accurately, responses to) those works: "All my originals are important poems. Nothing like them exists in English, for the excellence of a poet depends on the unique opportunities of his native language. I have been almost as free as the authors themselves in finding ways to make them ring right for me" (xiii). Here Lowell openly courts contradiction by effectively declaring the basic untranslatability of his originals, their absolute interdependence with the specific material resources of their respective native linguistic media. But rather than consider this implicit condition of formal incompatibility between languages a disabling one, he takes it as authorizing both semantic invention and structural modification, or more simply, nearly complete freedom. And this, paradoxically perhaps, offers the means to achieve a comparability of effect based on personal response. Thus Lowell further extends the boundaries of translation as a literary mode by explicitly annexing several of the prerogatives of "original" composition. Both his general acclaim as a translator and the degree to which contemporary translators like Stephen Mitchell and W. S. Merwin have largely followed his example and even methods attests to the extent of his success. Yet, for all his audacity Lowell did hedge his claim to creative freedom with an "almost." Such a relatively minor, but obstinate qualification reflects the conceptual limits of his rethinking of the practice, for it demonstrates his continued adherence to the reproduction of semantic content, or at most pragmatic meaning, as the basis of translation as a literary mode. Hence, despite the mild controversy that he aroused, Lowell remains the more conservative inheritor of the Modernist revolution in translation. The decidedly more radical task of fundamentally altering the very principle for translation itself as a mode of literary production would be taken up and fulfilled, as I will now discuss, by one of Lowell's least read, but most daring contemporaries, Louis Zukofsky.

III

Composed over the span of seven and a half years and eventually published as a full, *en face* text in 1969, Louis and Celia Zukofsky's complete, mainly sound-based rendering of the odes of Catullus remains the most thoroughly unorthodox, yet still rigorously principled, performance thus far in the history of English literary translation.[25] Like anything genuinely radical, their achievement does not reject tradition outright, but rather engages it in a deep, if necessarily controversial, fashion. For the Zukofskys, that engagement involves confronting (one aspect of) the literary legacy of the classics through a reappraisal both of its living value as an authoritative cultural resource and of the established methods for its transmission. And this, in turn, entails for them redefining the very parameters of translation itself as a literary mode. As such, their *Catullus (Gai Valeri Catulli Veronensis Liber)* at once stems from and advances the Modernist revolution in translation along several fronts simultaneously. Yet, despite all the highly charged debate surrounding the work, neither its historical nor its contemporary significance has been sufficiently addressed, due in no small measure to an ongoing, collective failure on the part of readers, critics, and even translators themselves to recognize both the enormous importance and great potential of translation as itself a primarily generative mode of literary production.

Most immediately, perhaps, the very title of the volume betokens a distinct shift away from conventional notions of the operative terms for translation. By including the original language designation for the source text of their rendering, the Zukofskys quietly, yet insistently, denote a fundamental commitment to the Latin itself as a matter of basic concern within their effort of interlingual exchange, a dedication to the foreign tongue not merely as a transparent medium or passive vehicle for the conveyance of semantic content, but rather as a subject with its own productively meaningful specificity. Moreover, clearly deriving inspiration from the methodological precedent first set by Pound in *Cathay* and then subsequently reinforced throughout the Modernist period, especially in Pound's treatment of Confucian texts, they undertake (and therefore promote) the practice of translation as an expressly collaborative enterprise, explicitly sharing credit for the version. Indeed, in their actual mode of procedure, they absolutely decouple the linguistic and the originary or expressive aspects of translation. Thus Celia described the process she and Louis employed:

> I did the spade work. I wrote out the Latin line and over it, indicated the quantity of every vowel and every syllable, that is long or short; then indicated the accented syllable. Below the Latin line I wrote the literal meaning or meanings of every word indicating gender, number, case and the order or sentence structure. I used Lewis and Short *Latin Dictionary* (Oxford Un. Press) and

Allen & Greenough *Latin Grammar* (Ginn & Co.). Louis then used my material to write poetry—*good poetry*. I could never do that! I never questioned any of his lines, just copied his handwritten manuscript to facilitate the typing.[26]

The self-deprecatory posture she assumes notwithstanding, Celia not only delineates in this account the terms of her and Louis's operative conception of translation as a mode of literary production, but she also reveals the fundamental importance of her contribution to their joint project of rendering Catullus. In the strictest sense, her grammatical "spade work" actually made possible her husband's more esteemed "poetic" labors, literally establishing the conditions of his engagement with the original in all its sonic, as well as semantic and syntactic, complexity. For, in fact, Louis knew no Latin. Writing to Cid Corman during the early stages of their work on Catullus, Louis expressed a desire to understand Latin specifically because, he believed, it would help him to render his source in an unprecedented fashion: "dammit I wish I knew Latin, because I don't want to paraphrase. I want to transliterate."[27] Exactly how he envisioned such knowledge helping him to achieve his goals remains unclear. To be sure, it seems in retrospect that formal training would arguably have hindered more than helped him, since it would merely have worked to make him all the more cognizant of (and therefore potentially beholden to) the actual semantic content of the original, thereby wedding him all the more firmly to the limits of thematic paraphrase. But in any case, cleanly separating between the tasks of "faithful" or accurate semantic and grammatical reproduction on the one hand and expressly "free" or "creative" poetic treatment on the other marks the Zukofskys' approach as deeply rooted in the Modernist revolution in translation as a literary mode. Indeed, judging from the elementary nature of her cited references, it seems quite possible that Celia herself had little, if any, formal training in Latin, parsing out the Catullan odes with only the benefit of painstaking care and detailed perseverance. So the Zukofskys may well have undertaken their translation without any preexisting knowledge at all of the source language by either participant, an approach that carries even further the already considerable liberties of their Modernist predecessors who, perhaps more than anything else, obviated mastery of the original language as a requirement for translation.

Even more fully than these peripheral statements by both Celia and Louis, the dust jacket illustrations for the original Cape Goliard edition of their *Catullus (Gai Valeri Catulli Veronensis Liber)* give detailed visual evidence of the process that informs their radically unorthodox translation. Against a monochrome gray background, the front and back covers present photographs of a pair of pages from one of their spiral working notebooks, recto and verso respectively, which contain the notes for their

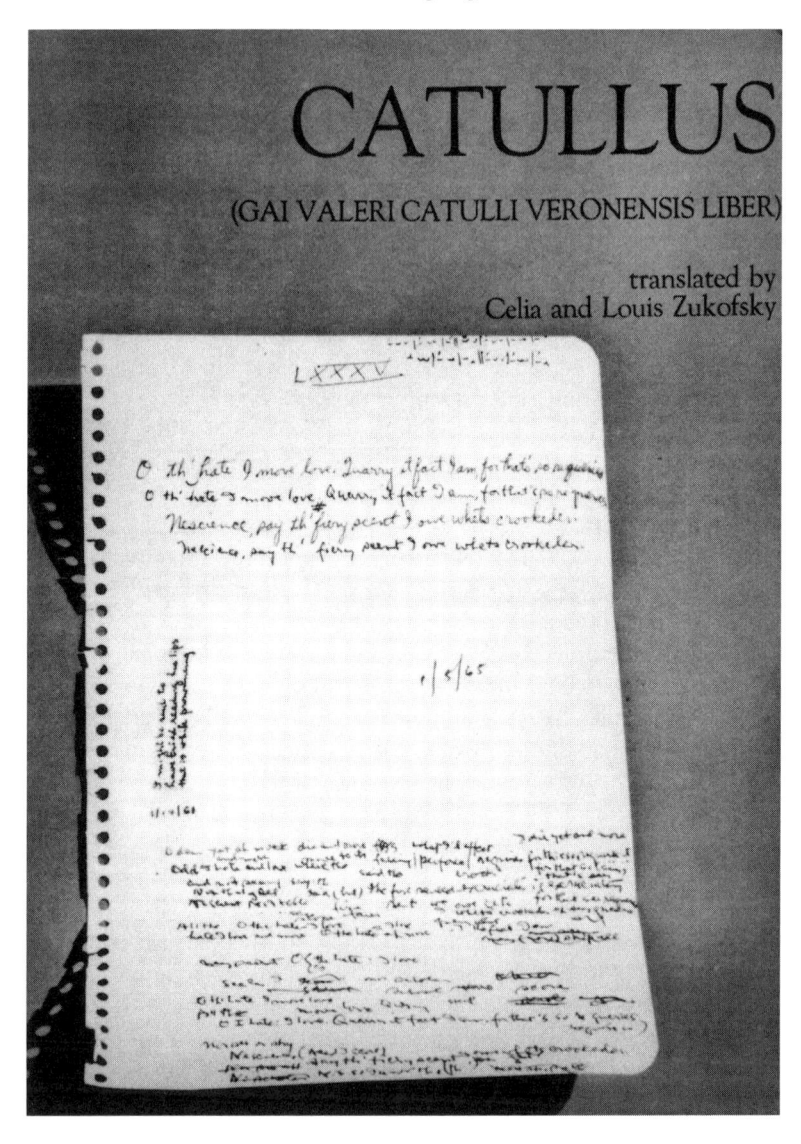

Figure 7.1

rendering of perhaps Catullus's most famous single distich, Carmen LXXXV, the renowned "Odi et amo." Together, these notes underscore that for all its manifest and even wild idiosyncrasies the Zukofskys' *Catullus* arises not out of perversity or mere capriciousness, but rather a thoroughly principled commitment to the original Latin work at virtually

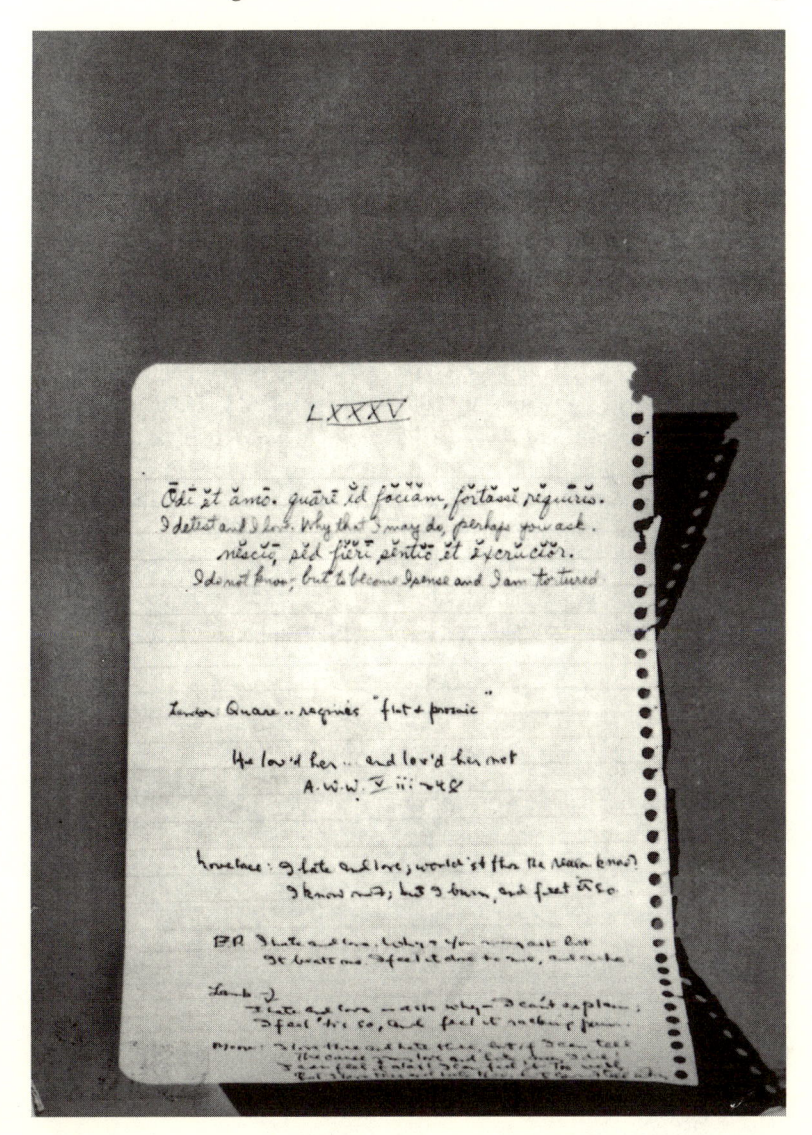

Figure 7.2

every conceivable level, including, most notably, the history of its transmission in English. On the front cover (see figure 7.1), Louis's treatment of Carmen LXXXV appears hand-written at the top of the photographed page, with Celia's fair-copy transcription done in the interlinear spaces above it. As an indication of the contents to follow, this rendering does little else but raise enormous questions. For the lines barely make any semantic sense at all, and the scribblings at the bottom of the page do nothing to help clarify their meaning. In this light, the puzzlement and even outrage that early critics felt seems quite explicable, and perhaps even legitimate. Clearly, this does not constitute "translation" by any conventional understanding of the term:

> O th'hate I move love. Quarry it fact I am, for that's so re queries
> Nescience, say th'fiery scent I owe whets crookeder.

But the front cover does provide a clue to the logic by which Zukofsky arrived at such a version. In a note oriented perpendicularly on the page and dated January 14, 1961, he explains: "I might be said to have tried reading his lips that is while pronouncing." In addition to this testimony regarding the crucial importance of sound in Zukofsky's approach, the notebook page on the back cover (see figure 7.2) of the volume attests to the basic rigor that underwrites this admittedly bizarre treatment, demonstrating its foundation in both the traditional methods and even the history of translation as a literary mode in English. For on that page appears the original Latin ode, written and scanned by Celia:

> LXXXV
> Ōdī ĕt ămō. quārē ĭd făcĭăm, fŏrtăssĕ rĕquīrĭs.
> nĕscĭō, sĕd fĭĕrī sĕntĭō ĕt ĕxcrŭcĭŏr,[28]

interlined with her strictly semantic rendering, which reads with the stilted rhythm and syntax of a commitment to conventional semantic literalism:

> 85
> I detest and I love. Why that I may do, perhaps you ask.
> I do not know, but to become I sense and I am tortured.

Moreover, Louis has copied out below several examples of the treatment of this ode over the course of English literary history, including adaptations by Landor (which he calls "flat and prosaic"), Shakespeare (from *All's Well That Ends Well*, V, iii, 48), and, most directly, conventional versions by Lovelace:

> I hate and love; would'st thou the reader know?
> I know not; but I burn, and feel it so;

Pound, or E. P.:

> I hate and love. Why? You may ask but
> It beats me. I feel it done to me, and ache;

Lamb:

> I hate and love—ask why—I can't explain;
> I feel 'tis so, and feel it racking pain;

and most melodramatic of all, Moore:

> I love thee and hate thee, but if I can tell
> The cause of my love and hate, may I die!
> I can feel it alas! I can feel it too well,
> That I love and hate thee, but cannot tell why.

So, as Celia's thorough supporting work and the several other versions of Carmen LXXXV contained on the notebook page make clear, Louis did not seek merely to produce an updated rendering of Catullus. After all, he had the necessary grammatical information at hand and had done sufficient research to accomplish this task. And in any case, Pound had already accomplished such a feat for this epigram as recently as 1963, employing, as the notes clearly demonstrate, a decidedly contemporary vernacular. Rather, Zukofsky undertook through his radical treatment to interrogate and reconceive the very terms of translation itself, employing sound rather than sense as the primary criteria upon which to base his rendering.

All of this helps to clarify the tremendous import of the terse "Translators' Preface" to the volume. Much shorter than Lowell's comparatively extended "Introduction" to *Imitations*, the Zukofskys' formal statement about their objectives nevertheless delineates a much more radical ambition and methodological procedure, as well as, therefore, a farther-reaching sense of the possibilities of translation as a literary mode. In a tone of almost deceptive modesty, they outline the terms of their unique undertaking: "This translation of Catullus follows the sound, rhythm, and syntax of his Latin—tries, as is said, to breathe the 'literal' meaning with him." Such a hierarchy of concerns identified here not only explains the basic logic giving rise to the strange rendering of Carmen LXXXV presented in manuscript on the front cover of the dust jacket, but it constitutes an utterly novel ordering of the aspects of a foreign text to be addressed by means of translation. Indeed, it even goes so far as to omit any mention at all of the main element guiding standard renderings, namely that of semantic or, in the more liberal cases, pragmatic sense. Among these various qualities of the original that Zukofsky cites as his primary concerns, different ones had already been emphasized by select previous translators in English, according to their own interests and daring. So, for example, Browning stressed Greek word order in his infamous rendering of Aeschylus's *Agamemnon* (1877),[29] and Pound focused on both the sound and syntax of Anglo-Saxon in "The Seafarer" (1912). But for all their respective departures from the ordinary practice of maintaining normal semantic comprehensibility, these writers operated under decidedly more conventional notions of translation as a literary mode, and so their treatments remain relatively more beholden to the grammatical limitations of idiomatic English. In this respect, the Zukofskys share a greater affinity with Continental European writers and translators such as Hölderlin and his radical versions of Sophocles; Walter Benjamin and his conception of an absolutely literal, interlinear version of the Bible as the ideal of translation; Martin Heidegger and Paul Celan in the German tradition; as well as the work of Eugene Jolas, Georges Perec, Raymond Roussel, and the OULIPO Group in the French.

Even so, the examples of markedly unconventional translations in English, as well as Modernist translation practice generally, helped to lay the conceptual and procedural foundations for the Zukofskys' explicit rejection of traditional methods and values. A formally trained classicist, Daniel Hooley has noted that "of the three components of Catullus's Latin itemized by the translators, the first (sound) seems to govern (though usually very loosely) English word choice, the second (rhythm) is seldom observed with any accuracy, and the third (syntax) is a manifest impossibility" (56). In pointing out the actual distance between the Zukofskys' stated goals and the technical reality of their achievement, these observations serve as a further indication of the couple's amateur grasp of Latin, which only emphasizes their debt to the Modernist redefinition of the practical requirements for translation. Still, by reconfiguring the very parameters under which they engage in the practice, the Zukofskys explicitly turn translation itself into a radically generative mode of literary production.

Hence, as Burton Hatlen has rightly seen, within the "Translators' Preface" "the quotation marks around 'literal' are crucial, for in effect the Zukofskys are here redefining that word" so as to stress "that the 'littera,' the letter, is an aural and visual shape, not a 'meaning.'" He goes on to characterize the work as a whole: "each translated poem has exactly the same number of lines as the original; each line of the translation contains exactly the same number of syllables as the equivalent line in the original; and as far as possible the length and the sound of the English syllables echo Catullus's Latin syllables. Thus the translation constitutes a syllable by syllable metamorphosis of Catullus's Latin into English" (348–49). Of course, the Zukofsky's incomplete understanding of Latin prosody complicates somewhat the picture that Hatlen so enthusiastically draws, but his basic argument remains instructive. Indeed, as I mentioned earlier, critics seeking to validate the Zukofsky's markedly eccentric work have done so largely by invoking its revisionary conceptual power. Thus Peter Quartermain has asserted, "The most remarkable feature of the *Catullus*, to my mind, is what it does to our sense of English as a language" (973). Most important for my purposes in this study, the Zukofskys accomplish this feat expressly under the rubric of translation. And this specific designation distinguishes their achievement from other superficially similar work such as the sound poetry of Marinetti and the Surrealists or the permutational gamesmanship of Cage's treatment of Joyce. Instead, the explicit claim to translation situates the Zukofskys' efforts within that particular tradition more than in that of other seemingly related experimental work.

Interestingly, however, Louis did not uniformly emphasize sound over sense throughout his treatment, a fact that adds a dynamic aspect to his engagement with translation as a literary mode in the *Catullus*. So in his rendering of Carmen I, Zukofsky produces a relatively conventional version that adheres strictly neither to the exact syllable count nor the syntax of the Latin, but rather reproduces, if somewhat loosely, its basic semantic content in relatively idiomatic English that does manage to capture some of the original vowel patternings. Catullus's Carmen I reads as follows:

> Cui dono lepidum libellum
> arido modo pumice expolitum?
> Cornelli, tibi; namque tu solebas
> meas esse aliquid putare nugas,
> iam tum cum ausus es unus Italorum
> omne aevum tribus explicare chartis
> doctis, Iuppiter, et laboriosis.
> quare habe tibi, quicquid hoc libelli
> qualecumque; quod, o patrona virgo,
> plus uno maneat perenne saeclo.[30]

With only minor departures from both the original semantic content and standard English syntax, Zukofsky gives a lively, easily readable treatment:

> 1
> Whom do I give my neat little volume
> slicked dry and made fashionable with pumice?
> Cornelius, to you; remindful that you
> used to dwell on my scantlings as something great,
> in that time when one solitary Italian
> you dared ransack all the ages in three—
> Jupiter!—learned and laborious papers.
> care, as you did, somewhat for this little book,
> whatever quality, patroness virgin,
> may outlast a perennial cycle.

Clearly Zukofsky emphasizes meaning over either meter or melody, except perhaps in the last lines, where he transforms the semantic content of the original, apparently, to approximate in "Care, as you did" the sequence of vowels in "quare habe tibi" from line 8, and gives "perennial cycle" for "perenne saeclo" in the last line, simply ignoring the difference in grammatical case between these words. Moreover, he fails to reproduce exactly Catullus's hendecasyllables in lines 1, 6, and 10. Comparably, in his rendering of the famous Carmen V,

> Vivamus, mea Lesbia, atque amemus,
> rumoresque senum severiorum
> omnes unius aestimemus assis,
> soles occidere et redire possunt:
> nobis cum semel occidit brevis lux,
> nox ist perpetua una dormienda.
> da mi basia mille, deinde centum,
> dein mille altera, dein secunda centum,
> deinde usque altera mille, deinde centum.
> dein, cum milia multa fecerimus,
> conturbabimus illa, ne sciamus,
> aut nequis malus invidere posit,
> cum tantum sciat esse basiorum,[31]

Zukofsky does manage to maintain the exact syllable count throughout, but again he favors semantic meaning over precise sonic similarity, except for a few individual words in lines 2, 3, 6 and 11:

> 5
> May we live, my Lesbia, love while we may,
> and as for the asseverating seniors
> estimate them as one naught we won't assess.
> Suns will hurry to set and will rise—likely:
> but for us it all means when the brief light sets,
> night is perpetual, and we are dormant.
> Dear, kiss me a thousand times, then a hundred,
> then another thousand, another hundred,
> and another thousand, another hundred
> and when we've roused that multitude of thousands,
> confounding their number we will know no sum
> of them that a malicious eye may envy
> while it keeps counting the many times we've kissed.

According to the working notebooks, Zukofsky completed his version of Carmen V in the spring of 1958, at which point he stopped working on his translations for more than two years to devote himself to other projects, most notably the volume *Bottom: On Shakespeare (1963)* and getting *A 1–12* published by Cid Corman in Japan. Picking up the *Catullus* again in May of

1960, he paid greater attention to the aural qualities of the Latin, markedly subordinating semantic meaning and idiomatic expression in English to the goal of approximating the sonic aspect of his source. So, from Carmen VI:

> Flavi, delicias tuas Catullo,
> ni sint illepidae atque inelegantes,
> velles dicere, nec tacere posses.
> verum nescio quid febriculosi
> scorti diligis: hoc pudet fateri.
> nam te non viduas iacere noctes
> nequiquam tacitum, cubile clamat
> sertis ac Syrio fragrans olivo,
> pulvinusque peraeque et hic et illic
> attritus, tremulique quassa lecti
> argutatio inambulatioque.
> iam tu ista ipse nihil vales tacere.
> cur? non tam latera ecfututa pandas,
> ni tu quid facias ineptiarum.
> quare quicquid habes boni malique,
> dic nobis. volo te ac tuos amores
> ad caelum lepido vocare versu,[32]

Zukofsky produces a syntactically challenging version in which the sound of vowels and consonants stand out as more important factors in his practice than either semantic clarity or syllabic exactitude:

> 6
>
> Flavius—that delicate lass—to Catullus
> if she isn't simply illicit inelegance,
> well, you'd talk, never pose a will to keep still.
> But the truth is I don't know what feverish
> slut scores such delights—so put out, to act fair.
> No it wouldn't be you lying bereaved nights,
> not quick to be quiet the couch is crying
> Assyrian garlands, fragrance of olive
> and pillows like pairs, in the thick of it, a
> trite rubbing and trembling shaking the litter,
> rustle of argument ambling up and down.
> Now about this *that* that *is* you'll say nothing.
> Why? it shouldn't take much to foot into the open
> the slinking backside-before that you're hiding.
> I don't care whether it's sinful or holy,
> do tell us. For I want to take you and that
> love of yours and invoke you both to the skies.

A year later, when he reached Carmen XXV:

> Cinaede Thalle, mollior cuniculi capillo
> vel anseris medullula vel imula oricilla
> vel pene languido senis situque araneoso,
> idemque Thalle, turbida rapacior procella,
> cum diva mulier aries ostendet oscitantes,
> remittte pallium mihi meum, quod involasti,
> sudariumque Saetabum catagraphosque Thynos,
> inepte, quae palam soles habere tamquam avita.
> quae nunc tuis ab unguibus reglutina et remitte,
> ne laneum latusculum manusque mollicellas
> inusta turpiter tibi flagella conscribillent,
> et insolenter aestues velut minuta magno
> deprensa navis in mari vesaniente vento,[33]

Zukofsky had come to approach Catullus's Latin even more strictly as a pattern of sounds, only bothering intermittently to adhere to the semantic meaning of his original or to concern himself with the limits of standard comprehensibility:

> 25
> Conniving Thallus, mulley, you, cony, cully, cop below—
> well, anserous medulla, well immolated auricula—
> well, pain and languid older sense, see, too extraneous—o so—
> and then qua Thallus, turbid air, rape packing off, a hell of
> come diva mull over Aries,—oscine oscitancy,
> remit my pallium to me, it's mine, vile blast who stole it—
> me Saetaban sudiarum, my Thynian tinct cartographs—
> inept—why palm them off as their sole heir whom time awaited:
> wined unctuous sopping pup, give them to us, glued tines remit
>   them,
> now let your lathy cully bottom, menacing coddled hands
> so used to turpitude be flagellated in this scribbling,
> and insolently toss a minute at my will magnified
> and soon dispensed with in a marring sea and in insane wind.

Comparably, as numerous readers have noticed, his treatment of Carmen LXIV steadily descends (or rises) into verbal chaos. And, when he finally came to render the Fragmenta in October 1965, Zukofsky's practice as a translator had reached its extremest form, whereby he treats the Latin as a sequence of sounds that generates, for all intents and purposes, a semantically independent text:

> Fragmenta
> 1. At non effugies meos iambos.

> 2. Hunc lucum tibi dedico consecroque Priape,
>   Qua domus tua Lampsacist quaque [silva], Priape,
>   Nam te praecipue in suis urbibus colit ora
>   Hellespontia ceteris ostreosior oris.
> 3. —O—O O de meo ligurrire libidost.
> 4. [O—O—et Lario imminens Comum.]
> 5. Lucida qua splende[n]t [summi] carchesia mali.[34]
>   Fragmenta
> 1. At known effigy haste my horse iambics.
> 2. Haunt, look you! I will dedicate consecrating Priapus,
>   What home is toward Lampascus, quag and silva, Priapus,
>   Name to pray *keep you ay* in cities' hubbubs of coast lit where are
>   Our Hellesponti caterers oysters where sea or oar is.
> 3. —O—O O day my own liquor airing libido's.
> 4. [O—O—yet Lari o imminence Comum.]
> 5. Look at her what splendid summit carks her mast a moll high.

If all this seems like mere cataloging, my purpose for such a broadly cursory review of Zukofsky's efforts in the *Catullus* has been neither to condemn his practice by exposing the many obvious departures from standard conceptions of translation as a literary mode, nor, clearly, to justify his accomplishment through inventive readings of individual treatments. After all, both these tasks have already been skillfully done by others with much more traditionally "solid" linguistic qualifications. Rather, I have indulged in quoting the *Catullus* at such length without extensive commentary precisely in order to show the progression that marks the volume as a whole, to illustrate the narrative aspect of Louis's and Celia's achievement. For more than merely redefining the parameters of translation as a mode of literary production, the Zukofskys' *Catullus (Gai Valeri Catulli Veronensis Liber)* effectively *enacts* that redefinition over the course of its development. Process, in other words, as well as sound, constitutes one of the crucial dimensions of signification.

As a translation in the conventional sense, of course, the Zukofskys' *Catullus* amounts to little more than a monumentally eccentric failure; for it makes tremendous demands on its readers, while returning merely the barest extent of the Latin poet's semantic content and even only intermittent humor. In this regard, the harsh dismissals of the early conservative critics remain understandable and, to an extent, even valid, since the Zukofskys so flamboyantly disregard the traditional purpose of translation as a literary mode. Yet exactly herein lies its enormous, if still largely unacknowledged, significance in the history of translation in English as a mode of literary production. A number of commentators and theorists of translation, including

Paul de Man, have observed that the word "translation" stems from the Latin word *translatio*, which breaks down into the elements *trans-*, meaning "across," and a form of the fourth principal part of the irregular verb *fero*, meaning "to bear or bring." Such observers have further noted that *translatio* itself derives etymologically from the Greek word μεταφερειν, also meaning "to bear or bring across." Thus, in English at any rate, the operation of translation stands in basic conceptual relation to the action of metaphor.

Up to now, this philological lineage has been deployed in order to emphasize the essentially poetic, rather than merely mechanical, character of translation as a mode of literary production, and insofar as it underscores the fundamental creativity of the practice, the etymology serves as a salient reminder. But I would like at this point to draw attention to the conceptual violence inscribed within the very idea of "translation" understood as the "bringing across" of semantic content from one language to another. For the copula that lies at the heart of metaphor—the evening *is* a yellow cat, God *is* Love—forcefully assimilates a pair of terms each to the other, overriding any differences through the sheer power of poetic will. Thus, as they have been traditionally conceived and produced, conventional translations implicitly stand as replacements for, rather than supplements or additions to, original works, based upon the fetishization of semantic content as the most essential aspect of a text. The "metaphorical" approach to translation as a literary mode finds no clearer expression than in the long-accepted practice of publishing renderings, even of poetry, as complete works unto themselves, without the original source-text.

In contrast to this, the Zukofskys ultimately establish a notion of translation predicated not upon a violent assertion of identity though a claim to semantic equivalence, but rather on the principle of meaningful contiguity, or, to use an expressly literary term, metonymy. In defining its contact with the original primarily along the axis of sound, their *Catullus* opens up the domain of semantic expression to radical new possibilities. Significantly, the original Cape Goliard edition prominently displays the Latin on facing pages as an integral part of the overall work.[35] Indeed, as a number of sympathetic critics have convincingly shown, Catullus's Latin fundamentally shapes the dynamics of the text as a whole. As Hooley puts it, "Through all this the Latin is there, not hovering vaguely under the play of Zukofsky's words but vividly and essentially contributing, completing the English sense. Zukofsky, always, creates in his translation, carries given meaning further than one expects, further than most approve of" (68). This explicit inclusion of the Latin text puts Zukofsky's procedures in the *Catullus* on a conceptual par with Pound's late practice as a translator of Chinese in his Confucian renderings rather than with his earlier efforts in either "The Seafarer" or *Homage to Sextus Propertius*, each of which have regularly been cited as clear precedents. For in both cases, the foreign work not only occupies a central place in the full articulation of the text, but the very marked unorthodoxies of the "translations" themselves reflect a deep engagement with and attempt to reproduce the unique expressive particularities of the respective sources in the original. Carrying forward the Modernist revolution in translation to its logical extreme, then, Zukofsky's greatest accomplishment lies in actualizing a metonymic sense of translation as a mode of literary production in which the source-text stands as at once the originary cause and contiguous fulfillment of the translation itself.

Completed in the later stages of Louis's career and arising in various ways out of the achievement of their Modernist predecessors, the Zukofskys' infamous *Catullus (Gai Valeri Catulli Veronensis Liber)* recasts the practice of translation into a uniquely generative, rather than simply imitative or mimetic, mode of literary production. In doing so, it helped to establish the conditions by which such a broad array of contemporary writers including Stephen Mitchell, W. S. Merwin, Robert Hass, Robert Pinsky, Seamus Heaney, and even Ursula LeGuin, among others, come both to translate works in languages of which they have no formal knowledge and to engage in the practice not as a form of training or apprenticeship, but rather as a major avenue of primary cultural expression in its own right and a privilege of established reputation.[36] Most important of all, perhaps, in replacing sense with sound as the major principle by which to perform translation, the volume adumbrates a process of literary creation the potential of which we as readers, critics, and, most especially, translators, have yet to come fully to terms. Even in an age of rapidly increasing globalization and worldwide cultural exchange, when languages encounter and influence and interpenetrate each other at unprecedented rates, the Zukofskys' *Catullus* awaits its proper recognition at a time when the critical establishment can recognize the principled exploration of the demands and possibilities of cross-cultural and multilingual literary production as a legitimate, and even uniquely promising, effort, instead of just a scandalous anomaly.

Conclusion

Over the course of this study, I have sought to accomplish a number of inter-related objectives: (1) to trace the changing terms for the practice of translation as a mode of literary production during the period of Anglo-American Modernism; (2) to demonstrate the ways various Modernist writers employed translation not simply as a transparent procedure for reproducing the exact semantic or even pragmatic meaning of foreign texts, but instead as a complex strategy by which to engage in different discursive arenas ranging from gender to politics to language; and (3) to show how these efforts in turn led to innovations in poetic and novelistic form associated with Modernism as a literary movement in English. In doing so, of course, I have necessarily had to constrain the enormous subject of Modernist translation, selecting relevant examples based on my own historical and aesthetic judgment, as well as according to the limits of my particular linguistic familiarities. As a result, several avenues stand open to further exploration in this expansive domain. Most obvious of these, the enormous body of Ezra Pound's work as a translator alone offers considerable opportunities for additional research and discussion. For example, it remains not just to assess yet again the "accuracy" or "fidelity" of "The Seafarer" to the original Anglo-Saxon work, but rather to consider the broader cultural meaning, within the larger sphere of Modernist culture, of its ambition to construct alternative modes of authority by extrapolating a different trajectory of poetic development within the course of English literary history. Similarly, Pound's sustained engagement with Cavalcanti, and especially his numerous renderings of the Italian poet's "Donna mi pregha" canzone, as well as the late, markedly eccentric treatments of Sophocles' *Women of Trachis* and the recently published collaborative version of *Elektra*[1] await more contextualized evaluation in light of, on the one hand, his theories of sexuality and its relationship to poetry, particularly as these ideas inform the development of *The Cantos*, and on the other, his incarceration at St. Elizabeth's for thirteen years after his treason indictment for his radio broadcasts during World War II.

On an even larger scale, the translation work of such English national writers as Richard Aldington, F. S. Flint, and Basil Bunting among the poets, and Virginia Woolf and D. H. Lawrence among the prose writers presents a different, though related, set of issues. At the very least, their generally more conservative approach to the practice of translation as a mode of literary production arguably suggests a comparatively less vexed relationship to English and it cultural legacy than either the American or Irish writers who have been the focus of this study. And this difference, in turn, indicates the capacity of translation to function under certain circumstances as a triangulated strategy for negotiating the politics of influence within Anglophone culture itself, rather than simply as the expression of a binary relationship through which a hegemonic power at once exerts and maintains its domination over a colonized Other, as a number of recent commentators on translation have recently argued.[2] Indeed, the importance of specific historical, cultural, and linguistic contexts for understanding the meaning and diverse functions of translation as a mode of literary production underscores the need to reconsider the role of translation in other phases of English literary history, as well as to explore other linguistic and cultural traditions. So, for example, even though the eighteenth century has generally been recognized as the other major period during which translation as a literary mode played a central role in the development of English literature, surely the precise nature of its importance during that time differed from the place it occupied within the domain of Anglo-American Modernism; for not only did the operative parameters of the practice itself change over the course of time, but then necessarily so too did the exact relationship between translation and other modes of literary production.

Comparably, other linguistic and cultural traditions provide opportunities for further research into the function of translation within different historical, social, and intellectual contexts. Antoine Berman's seminal study already offers just such an examination into the meaning and construction of translation in Romantic Germany. Similar studies could be usefully undertaken for French, Italian, Spanish, Russian, Arabic, and any number of other different linguistic traditions. Indeed, consideration of non-European languages, and especially ones employing non-alphabetic writing systems, presents especially fertile ground for reflection about the dynamics, as well as the limits and possibilities, of translation as a mode of literary production and cultural transaction. In this regard, Lydia Liu's important study, *Translingual Practice: Literature, National Culture and Translated Modernity—China, 1900–1937* stands out as a particularly useful example of cross-cultural work that goes beyond simple models of influence and idealized transmission of themes or conceptual notions because it demonstrates the constitutive role of translation as at once a linguistic and epistemological practice in the articulation of Modern Chinese literary culture. Additional opportunities for expressly theorized and situated comparative analyses lie in such complexly international and cross-cultural phenomena as Japanese *modanizumu* and the adoption of Anglo-European Modernist expressive strategies by Latin and South American writers. Ideally, such studies would help to renew the field of comparative literature by bringing to bear the theoretical insights and considerations of Translation Studies. And at the same time, they would give more solid historical and contextual grounding to the concerns of Translation Studies, which all too often has remained content with insisting upon the fundamental creativity, and therefore social, political, and cultural imbrication, of translation as a mode of literary production. Yet the particularities of that creativity, and therefore the specific social, political, and cultural meaning of translation, differs within various national and historical contexts, something that requires a synthesis of traditional methods of comparative literary analysis with the more explicitly theoretical reflections of Translation Studies.

If the call for such a grand methodological unification seems unnecessary or overstated in that it has largely already taken place, at least within the realm of literary studies, one need only consider the reception of Seamus Heaney's recent verse translation of *Beowulf* to realize the extent to which critics continue to view translation as a derivative mode of literary production, even as poets, operating in the wake of Anglo-American Modernism, engage in the practice as a strategy for achieving distinctly generative, rather than merely reproductive or mimetic, cultural goals. In the "Introduction" to his rendering, Heaney reveals that part of his intention in translating *Beowulf* lay in trying "to persuade myself that I was born into its language and that its language was born into me," a perhaps unavoidable situation "for somebody who grew up in the political and cultural conditions of Lord Brookborough's Northern Ireland."[3] "Sprung from an Irish nationalist background and educated at a Northern Irish Catholic school," he continues, "I had learned the Irish language and lived within a cultural and ideological frame that regarded it as the language I should by rights have been speaking but which I had been robbed of." For Heaney, then, translating *Beowulf* represented a "creative way of dealing with the whole vexed question...of the relationship between nationality, language, history, and literary tradition in Ireland." As a strategy for addressing this question, Heaney employs in certain instances a local Ulster vocabulary, using words such as "graith" ("harness"), "hoked" ("rooted about") and "bawn" ("a fort for cattle," but in Elizabethan English referring "specifically to the fortified dwellings which the English planters built in Ireland to keep the dispossessed natives at bay"). In his view, "[p]utting a bawn into *Beowulf* seems to me a way for a Irish poet to come to terms with that complex history of conquest and colony, absorption and resistance, integrity and antagonism" (xxx) that has marked Irish culture generally and its relationship to English as an instrument of political and cultural domination, as well as a medium of everyday commerce and indigenous expression. In other words, a distinct politico-cultural subtext underwrites Heaney's procedures in rendering *Beowulf*, and his translation attempts to enact both a personal and a larger socio-cultural process by which to resolve, or at least negotiate, the troubled legacy of colonization in Ireland by England.

In their various responses to Heaney's efforts, however, critics have tended to elide this aspect of his work as a translator, focusing instead on its ostensible utility by invoking some form of the entrenched binary paradigm of "fidelity" and "freedom." So, for example, comparing Heaney's *Beowulf* with another recent version by the scholar R. M. Liuzza,[4] Frank Kermode completely ignores the broader cultural ambition of the Irish writer's rendering, noting only that Heaney "grants himself a fair amount of license and relies on the poet's apprehension of 'the sound of the sense,'" whereas "Liuzza's book is in some respects more useful,"[5] apparently because of its more conventionally literal approach to the task of translation and the inclusion of different forms of scholarly apparatus. Attempting to judge between the two, Kermode ultimately waffles in his assessment, declaring "which of the two is Beowulf and which is Grendel is not easily decided" (21). Still grounded in a metaphysics of originality, Kermode implicitly reveals in this judgment the limitations of a normative, rather than functional, approach to discussing translation that takes as its standard the ideal of reproducing an original in all its uniqueness and complexity. Somewhat less impressionistically, though still fundamentally bound by a mimetic ideal, Nicholas Howe recognizes the polemical dimension to Heaney's use of Ulster vocabulary in his translation as he "turns Old English into Modern English to remake the literary and cultural history of the British Isles."[6] Even so, Howe remains uncomfortable with the extent of Heaney's departure from a conservative (and derivative) conception of translation as a mode of literary production, arguing that he "is not really a translator of the poem at all," but rather a "reinventor," as if the distinction between these two roles were readily self-evident. Indeed, Heaney's very decision to identify his expressly poetic, non-scholarly procedures under the rubric of "translation" reflects the influence of the Modernists who successfully redefined the operative parameters of the practice itself.[7] Giving voice to his own preferences for a more expressly scholarly approach to translation, Howe concludes that for a "better" (i.e., more closely mimetic) *Beowulf*, "we await a translator who has worked deeply through Old English poetic style" (37).

To be sure, some of the normatively evaluative drive of such responses as Kermode's and Howe's stems from the particular demands or conventions of book reviews for commercial publications. Yet the same conception of translation as merely a derivative practice, rather than a distinctive mode of literary production with its own unique and historically demonstrable generative possibilities, remains entrenched even in expressly scholarly discussions of different renderings. And if this situation obtains for translating works from a different phase within the history of English itself, it applies all the more fiercely to the rendering of texts from other cultures and traditions. Such conservatism reveals the tenacity of ancient ways of thinking about translation. In general, then, English-language culture has yet to fully assimilate the consequences of the Modernist revolution in translation as a mode of literary production. By and large, those of us operating primarily within English do not think deeply enough about translation simply because we do not have to. Technology and globalization have abetted the hegemony of our native language. But as the Modernists showed, renewal and discovery requires deep, transformative contact with other cultures and other systems of linguistic representation. And by liberating translation from a metaphysics of originality—that is, by considering the practice as one possible mode of generative interaction between languages—we can lay the foundation for a truly cross-cultural poetics. Rather than seeking to overcome the ostensible tragedy of linguistic difference, we can embrace the situation of Babel as a common condition of our humanity. And in doing so, we can properly recognize the significance of an approach to cultural interaction that engages and builds productively upon, rather than simply avoids or erases, cultural and linguistic differences and their implicit possibilities, not least within the realm of literary expression.

   It can't be all in one language. (LXXXVI, 563)

Appendix

Transcription of Notes for "Ballad of the Mulberry Road" from the Fenollosa Notebooks

陌	上	桑
Haku	jo	so
Highway	on	mulberry tree

日	出	東	南	隅
nichi	shutsu	to	nan	gu
Sun	rises	East	South	corner

The sun rises in the South East corner

照	我	秦	氏	樓
sho	ga	shin	shi	ro
Shines (on)	our	name of family	family clan	two storied house

And is shining on the villa of the Shin clan

秦	氏	有	好	女
Shin	shi	yu	ko	jŏ
Shin	family	has	pretty	girl

The Shin family has a pretty daughter

自	名	爲	羅	敷
ji	mei	i	ra	fu
Herself	name	make	Gauze ?	sheet Spreading

She herself made her name   gauze veil

羅	敷	善	蠶	桑
ra	fu	gen	san	sō
Rafu		excels in is skilled	silkworm	mulberries

Gauze Veil is skillful in feeding mulberries to silkworms

採	桑	城	南	隅
sai	sō	jo	nan	gu
Pluck	mulberry	castle walled in town	south	corner

She plucks mulberry leaves at the South corner of the castle

青	絲	爲	籠	系
sei	shi	i	ro	kei
Green Blue	strings	make	basket	mark (unreadable)

She makes blue strings the woof(?) of her basket.

桂	枝	爲	籠	鉤
kei	shi	i	ro	kō
Katsura	branch	makes	basket	shoulder strings strap to fasten around her shoulders

She makes the shoulder straps of her basket out of ivy branches.

頭	上	倭	墮	髻
to	jo	wa	da	kei
Head	on	to curl a snake coil	incline to one side	hair ornament (rope)
			A special ornament of geishas that falls onto left side	

On her head is coiled her one sided hair ornament

耳	中	明	月	珠
ji	chu	mei	getsu	shŭ
Ear	in	bright	moon Moon pearls	gem

In her ear shine moon gems

Transcription of Notes

緗	綺	爲	下	裙[A]
sho	ki	i	ka	kiŏ
Light green	special For some kind of two patterned cloth	makes	under	skirt

Light green "name for cloth" she makes or uses for her underskirt

紫	綺	爲	上	襦
Shi	ki	i	jo	ju
Purple	same kind of cloth	makes	upper	vest

Purple   she uses for her overcoat

行	者	見	羅	敷
ko	sha	ken	ra	fu
Go	one	who sees	Rafu	

Those who pass by seeing

下	擔	捋	髭[B]	鬚[C]
ka	tan	ratsu	shi	shū
Taking down	burden	twist (the moustache)	upper lip	moustache

Put down their load and pull the moustache on their upper lip

少	年	見	羅	敷
sho	nen	ken	ra	fu
Little	year	sees	Rafu	

The young men seeing

[A] In the manuscript notebooks, Fenollosa uses some variant or archaic characters, which I note here. Originally, 裙

[B] 頿

[C] 鬠

脱	帽	著	帩	頭
datsu	bo	chaku	sho	to
Taking off	hat	put on	gauze	head

Take off their hats and put on their head gauze (so that their fine hair can be seen)

耕[D]	者	忘	其	犁[E]
ko	sha	bo	ki	ra
To cultivate	one who	forget	his	spade or plough?

Those who work in the fields forget their ploughs

鋤	者	忘	其	鋤
jŏ	sha	bo	ki	jŏ
Uses hoe	one who	forget	his	hoe

Those who harvest the fields forget their hoes

來	歸	相	怨	怒
rai	ki	sho	en	do
Come	return	with each other	regret	angry

Those who approach and those who try to get away reproach and scold

但	坐	觀	羅	敷
tan	za	kwan	ra	fu
Only	sit	look at		Rafu

They only kneel down and stare at

使	君	從	南	來
shi	kun	ju	nan	rai
	Messenger lord	from	south	come
	Governor of province			

The lord messenger comes following from the south
And governor can have five horses in a carriage

[D] 畊

[E] 犂

Transcription of Notes

五	馬	立	踟	蹰
<u>go</u>	<u>ra</u>	<u>ritsū</u>	<u>chi</u>	<u>chu</u>
Five	horses	stand	linger	?

使	君	遣	史	往
<u>shi</u>	<u>kun</u>	<u>ken</u>	<u>ri</u>	<u>o</u>
—	—	sends	officer	go

The Lord messenger sends his officer to go or to approach

問	是	誰	家	姝
<u>mon</u>	<u>ge</u>	<u>sui</u>	<u>ka</u>	<u>shū</u>
Ask	that you	whose	house	pretty daughter

Asks her "Whose house's daughter"

秦	氏	有	好	女
<u>Shin</u>	<u>shi</u>	<u>yu</u>	<u>ko</u>	<u>jo</u>
Shin	family	has	pretty	girl

(She answers) " " (defiantly at him)

自	名	爲	羅	敷
<u>ji</u>	<u>me</u>	<u>I</u>	<u>ra</u>	<u>fu</u>

She calls her name " "

羅	敷	年	幾	何
<u>Ra</u>	<u>fu</u>	<u>nen</u>	<u>ki</u>	<u>ko</u>
Rafu		age, year	how	what, many

"Rafu, how many years (have you?)"

二	十	尚	不	足
<u>ni</u>	<u>ju</u>	<u>sho</u>	<u>fu</u>	<u>soku</u>
	twenty?	yet	not	lit.=enough= reach

" " not yet reached that

十	五	頗	有	餘
ju	go	ha	yu	yō
Fifteen?		Pretty much "rather over"	is	remains in more than

使	君	謝	羅	敷
shi	kun	sha	ra	fu
		lit.=apologize speak softly to		

The lord messenger speaks smoothly to Rafu

Lit.= if it is the same

寧	可	共	載	不
nei	ka	kio	sai	fŭ
If all right	will	together	ride	no

If you don't mind, will you ride with me? No?

羅	敷	前	致	詞
ra	fu	jen	chǐ	shǐ
	—	go into	present (offer cordial?)	speech

Rafu approaching him made speech with him

使	君	一	何	愚
shi	kun	iku	ka	gu
		only, entirely	how	foolish

Lord messenger (governor) How utterly foolish you are!

使	君	自	有	婦
shi	kun	ji	yu	fū
		yourself	has	wife= lady

Lord messenger you yourself have a (lady) (wife)

羅	敷	自	有	夫
ra	fu	ji	yu	fŭ

Rafu herself has a husband

Transcription of Notes

東	方	千	餘	騎[F]
to	ho	sen	yŏ	ki
East	direction	thousand	more than	horsemen

Over there in the East (do you?) more than a thousand horsemen

夫	婿[G]	居	上	頭
fu	sei	kiŏ	jo	to
Husband	bridegroom	takes his position	upper	head

My bridegroom husband takes his position at the head of them

何	用	識	夫	婿
ka	yo	shiki	fu	sei
What	by	recognize	husband	bridegroom

How do I recognize that he is my bridegroom husband

白	馬	從	驪	駒
haku	ba	ju	ri	kŭ
White	horse	follows	black Used only for horses	trained horse to side

By his white horse follows a palfrey?

青	絲	繫	馬	尾
sei	shi	kei	ba	ri
Blue	strips	bind	horse's	tail

Blue ribbons catch up the horse's tail

黃	金	絡	馬	頭
o	gon	raku	ba	to
Yellow	gold	put on	horses	head

Yellow metal is put on the horse's head

[F] 騎

[G] 婿

腰	中	廘	盧	劍[H]
yo	chu	roku	so	ken
Loins	across	Hepburn says its	potting wheel	sword

Across his loins is a sword

可	值	千	萬	餘
ka	chi	sen	ban	yŏ
Will	cost	thousand	ten thousand	more than

Which is worth more than 10,000,000 pieces

十	五	府	小	丈[I]
ju	go	fŭ	sho	shĭ
	Fifteen	office of county, province	secretary	
		small		

At fifteen he was a small province secretary

二	十	朝	大	夫
ni	ju	cho	tai	fŭ
	Twenty	court capital	great, upper	official

At twenty he was a grandee of the court

三	十	侍	中	郎
san	ju	ji	chu	ro
	Thirty	waiting	inside	gallant (chamberlain)

At thirty he was a gallant in waiting

四	十	專	城	居
shi	ju	sen	jo	kiŏ
	Forty	devotedly	castle	stays
			(becomes governor of	provincial home)

At forty he stays devotedly at this castle home

爲	人	潔	白	晳
i	jin	ketsu	haku	seki
Making	persons	clean	white	?

Making his person clean and white

[H] 劍

[I] 仄

Transcription of Notes

鬑	鬑	頗	有	鬚[J]
<u>ken</u>	<u>ken</u>	<u>ha</u>	<u>yu</u>	<u>shū</u>
		Pretty much has		moustache

Like growing grass his moustache is flourishing

盈	盈	公	府[K]	步
<u>yei</u>	<u>yei</u>	<u>ko</u>	<u>fŭ</u>	<u>bŏ</u>
Gracefully		public	office	walks

Gracefully, gracefully he walks to his public office

冉	冉	府	中	趨
<u>gen</u>	<u>gen</u>	<u>fŭ</u>	<u>chu</u>	<u>sū</u>
Distinguished		office	in	lit.=run

Distinguished, distinguished he moves through his office

坐	中	數	千	人
<u>za</u>	<u>chu</u>	<u>su</u>	<u>sen</u>	<u>nin</u>
Lit.=seat, room	in	several	thousand	men

In the room with several thousand men

皆	言	夫	婿	殊
<u>kuai</u>	<u>gen</u>	<u>fu</u>	<u>sei</u>	<u>shŭ</u>
All	say	husband	bridegroom	special

All are accustomed to say that my husband bridegroom is something special or fine

---

[J] 鬐
[K] 府

Notes

Introduction

1. Walter Benjamin, *Illuminations*, ed. Hannah Arendt, trans. Harry Zohn (New York: Schocken, 1968), p. 72. Hereafter cited parenthetically in the body of the text.
2. Among these include no less than Paul de Man and Jacques Derrida, who have each argued against a messianic reading of Benjamin's conception of the function of translation, and especially of his conception of "reine Sprache" or "pure language" (74). For more details of this debate, see Paul de Man, "'Conclusions': Walter Benjamin's 'The Task of the Translator'" in *The Resistance to Theory* (Minneapolis: University of Minnesota Press, 1986), pp. 73–105; and Jacques Derrida, "Des Tours de Babel," trans. Joseph F. Graham, in *Difference in Translation*, ed. Joseph Graham (Ithaca, NY and London: Cornell University Press, 1985), pp. 165–207. Both these works hereafter cited parenthetically in the body of the text. But inasmuch as Benjamin posits a "suprahistorical kinship of languages" that "is realized only by the totality of their intentions supplementing each other" (74), his conception remains *metaphysical*, if not necessarily, pace de Man and Derrida, *messianic*. See also Maurice Blanchot, "Translating" (1971), trans. Richard Sieburth, *Sulfur* 26: 82–86.
3. Ezra Pound, *Literary Essays of Ezra Pound* (New York: New Directions, 1968), p. 232. Hereafter cited as *LE* in the body of the text.
4. For an enlightening explication of this tradition, which finds its greatest flowering during the Romantic period, including such seminal figures as Herder, Goethe, Schlegel, Novalis, von Humboldt, and Schleiermacher, see Antoine Berman, *The Experience of the Foreign: Culture and Translation in Romantic Germany*, trans. S. Heyvaert (Albany: State University of New York Press, 1984).
5. Rossetti made this statement in the Preface to his volume of translations, *The Early Italian Poets*, first published in 1861. See Dante Gabriel Rossetti, *The Early Italian Poets*, ed. Sally Purcell (London: Anvil Press, 1981).
6. As cited in George Steiner, *After Babel: Aspects of Language and Translation* (Oxford: Oxford University Press, 1975), p. 256.
7. For an illuminating history of Anglo-American translation that traces the establishment of transparent rendering, or "fluency," as the dominant ideology for

translation, see Lawrence Venuti's *The Translator's Invisibility: A History of Translation* (London: Routledge, 1995), especially Chapter 2, pp. 43–98.
8. In an interview with Donald Hall, *Paris Review*, 1961. As cited in *The Marianne Moore Reader* (New York: Viking, 1961), p. 263.
9. The first set of volumes includes the following numbers: No. 1 "The Poems of Anyte of Tegea," translated by Richard Aldington; No. 2 "Poems and fragments of Sappho," translated by Edward Storer; No. 3 "Choruses from Iphigeneia in Aulis," translated by H. D.; No. 4 "Latin poems of the Renaissance," translated by Richard Aldington; No. 5 "Poems of Leonidas of Tarentum," translated by James Whitall; and No. 6 "The Mosella of Decimus Magnus Ausonius," translated by F. S. Flint. The second set featured reprints of the above volumes, together with the following additional works: No. 1 "Greek Songs in the Manner of Anacreon" by Aldington; No. 5 "Poseidippus and Asclepiades" by Edward Storer; No. 7 "Claudian's 'Carrying Off of Persephone'" by A. W. G. Randall; No. 8 "Meleager of Gadara" by Aldington; No. 9 "The Country Letters of Aelianus" by Edward Storer; and No. 10 "The Hero and Leander of Musaeus." Such a series, published by the Egoist Press, also indicates the importance of little magazines like *The Egoist* in the development of Modernism. For a thoroughly researched and historically nuanced account of this aspect of Modernism, see Mark S. Morrison, *The Public Face of Modernism: Little Magazines, Audiences, and Reception, 1905–1920* (Madison: The University of Wisconsin Press, 2001).
10. This is the same poet known through Pound's famous renderings as Li Po. In this volume, I will employ the now standard Pinyin transcription of the name 李白 (Li Bai) to refer to the historical Chinese poet, and the older Wade-Giles transcription Li Po when referring to the figure that comes about as a result of Pound's translations.
11. From the Preface to Eliot's translation, *Anabasis* (New York: Harcourt, Brace and Company, 1938), p. 10.
12. Letter from D. H. Lawrence to Kostelianksy, August 10, 1919.
13. These novels were *Mastro Don Gesualdo* in 1923, *Little Novels of Sicily* in 1925, and *Cavalleria Rusticana* in 1928.
14. This is, of course, one of Pound's several definitions of an epic, and one he repeatedly employed for *The Cantos*.
15. *The Cantos of Ezra Pound* (New York: New Directions, 1986), Canto LXXXVI, p. 563. Hereafter cited by Canto and page number in the body of the text.
16. Eliot, T. S., "Little Gidding," l. 95.
17. Hugh Kenner, *The Pound Era* (Berkeley: University of California Press, 1971), p. 149.
18. See Richard Reid, *Discontinuous Gods: Ezra Pound and the Epic of Translation*. Ph. D. Dissertation, Princeton University, 1986.
19. Williams Carlos Williams, *The Collected Poetry of William Carlos Williams*, Vol. 2, ed. Christopher MacGowan (New York: New Directions, 1986), p. 198. Hereafter cited as *WCW: CP Vol. 2*.
20. Karen Lawrence, *The Odyssey of Style in* Ulysses (Princeton, NJ: Princeton University Press, 1981).

21. Fritz Senn, *Joyce's Dislocutions: Essays on Reading as Translation*, ed. John Paul Riquelme (Baltimore: The Johns Hopkins University Press, 1984), p. 38.
22. Ezra Pound, *The ABC of Reading* (New York: New Directions, 1960), p. 58. Hereafter cited as *ABC* in the body of the text.
23. Comparably, in the essay "Dateline" originally published in 1934, he bestows upon translation a critical function, placing it as the second of five categories of criticism, the remaining of which are criticism by discussion, criticism by exercise in the style of a given period, criticism via music, and, the most intense form among the group, criticism in new composition. See *LE*, pp. 74–87.
24. W. B. Yeats, *Explorations* (London: Macmillan & Co. Ltd., 1962), p. 3.
25. *Ibid.*, pp. 75–76.
26. WCW to Calas, Dec. 4, 1940, Lilly Library, Indiana. As cited in *WCW: CP Vol. 2*, pp. 451–52.
27. A major exception to this general trend is Fitzgerald, whose version of the *Rubaiyat* exerted a profound influence over both his contemporaries and such Modernists as Pound. In the *ABC of Reading*, Pound offers the following as a critical exercise: "Try to find out why the Fitzgerald Rubaiyat has gone into so many editions after having lain unnoticed until Rossetti found a pile of remaindered copies on a second-hand bookstall," pp. 79–80.
28. Even such unorthodox translators as Abraham Cowley (1618–1667) and Francis Newman (1805–1897), brother to the famous Cardinal, both knew well the Greek from which they made their renderings of Pindar and Homer respectively. For more on Newman and his debate with Arnold, see Venuti, pp. 118–47.
29. From "The Life of Lucian," in John Dryden, *Of Dramatic Poesy and Other Critical Essays, Vol. 2*, ed. George Watson (London: J. M. Dent and Sons, 1962).
30. Matthew Arnold, "On Translating Homer," in *Poetry and Criticism of Matthew Arnold*, ed. A. Dwight Culler (Cambridge: The Riverside Press, 1961), p. 218.
31. Letter from Yeats to Joyce, 1904. As cited in Richard Ellmann, *James Joyce* (New York: Oxford University Press, 1959, revised edition 1983), p. 178.
32. Introductory Note to *The Poets' Translation Series* (London: The Egoist Press, 1915), pp. 7–8.
33. *Poetry* Vol. 26, April 1919, p. 62.
34. *Horizon.* January 1961, p. 35.
35. See J. P. Sullivan, *Ezra Pound and Sextus Propertius: A Study in Creative Translation* (Austin: The University of Texas Press, 1964). One of the classics of Poundian criticism and translational apologetics, this study begins to recognize the importance of translation for the whole of Modernism, but its singular focus prevents a more synthetic view.
36. See Wai-lim Yip, *Ezra Pound's* Cathay (Princeton, NJ: Princeton University Press, 1969). Yip examines Pound's actual practice as a translator and puts his efforts in the context of other translators of Chinese poetry during the period. In doing so, he espouses Pound's superiority, despite the grammatical errors and omissions. Both Yip and Sullivan, for all their careful exposition of Pound's methods, fail to consider the larger implications of translation itself, the meaning of *Cathay* and the *Homage* within the larger framework of Modernism.

37. André Lefévere, *Translation, Rewriting, and the Manipulation of Literary Fame* (London and New York: Routledge, 1992), pp. 96–97.
38. Antoine Berman, *op. cit.*, p. 2.
39. For a useful survey of recent theories of translation, see Edwin Gentzler, *Contemporary Translation Theories* (London and New York: Routledge, 1993). For other works that include an expressly historical view of translation, see for example Douglas Robinson, *The Translator's Turn* (Baltimore: Johns Hopkins University Press, 1991) and Willis Barnstone, *The Poetics of Translation: History, Theory, Practice* (New Haven: Yale University Press, 1993).
40. For a controversial recent attempt to define an ethics of translation, see Lawrence Venuti, *The Scandals of Translation: Towards an Ethics of Difference* (London and New York: Routledge, 1998). For an extremely charged, though ultimately problematic, discussion of translation in a colonial frame, see T. Niranjana, *Siting Translation: History, Poststructuralism and the Colonial Context* (Berkeley, Los Angeles, Oxford: University of California Press, 1992). Also see Eric Cheyfitz, *The Poetics of Imperialism: Translation and Colonization from The Tempest to Tarzan* (New York: Oxford University Press, 1991). For a discussion that combines ethical concerns with an expressly post-colonial perspective, see Gayatri Spivak, "The Politics of Translation" in *Outside in the Teaching Machine* (London and New York: Routledge, 1993), pp. 179–200.
41. See Lori Chamberlain, "Gender and the Metaphorics of Translation," in Lawrence Venuti, ed., *Rethinking Translation: Discourse, Subjectivity, Ideology* (London and New York: Routledge, 1992). For further discussion specifically concerning issues of gender and Bible translation, see E. Castelli, "Les Belles Infidèles"/ Fidelity or Feminism?," Special Section on Feminist Translation of the New Testament, *Journal of Feminist Studies in Religion*, pp. 25–39, 1990 and E. S. Fiorenza, "Charting the Field of Feminist Bible Interpretation," in *But She Said: Feminist Practices of Bible Interpretation* (Boston: Beacon Press, 1992).
42. For additional discussion of this metaphor and its relation to heteronormative conceptions of gender and sexuality, see Barbara Johnson, "Taking Fidelity Philosophically," in Joseph F. Graham, ed., *Difference in Translation* (Ithaca, NY: Cornell University Press, 1985).
43. Sherry Simon, *Gender in Translation: Cultural Identity and the Politics of Transmission* (London and New York: Routledge, 1996).
44. See Lawrence Venuti, *The Translator's Invisibility: A History of Translation* (London and New York: Routledge, 1995), especially Chapter 3, "Nation," pp. 99–147.
45. See Michael Cronin, *Translating Ireland: Translation, Languages, Cultures* (Cork, Ireland: Cork University Press, 1996).
46. For a series of essays on translation in an explicitly Derridean mode, see Joseph F. Graham, ed. *Difference in Translation* (Ithaca, NY: Cornell University Press, 1985).
47. T. E. Hulme, "A Lecture on Modern Poetry," in *Further Speculations*, ed. Samuel Hynes (Minneapolis: University of Minnesota Press, 1955), p. 69.

Chapter One

1. From "Poem by the Bridge at Ten-Shin" in *Cathay, Personae*, p. 131.
2. In its first incarnation, *Cathay* also included a reprint of Pound's translation of the Anglo-Saxon poem "The Seafarer," first published in *Ripostes* in 1912. Donald Gallup, *Ezra Pound: A Bibliography* (Charlottesville: The University Press of Virginia, 1983), p. 16.
3. For a lengthier discussion of the virtual explosion of translation of Chinese poetry during this period by such other figures as Amy Lowell and Arthur Waley, as well as of the previous generation of translators that included James Legge and Herbert Giles, see Ming Xie, *Ezra Pound and the Appropriation of Chinese Poetry: Cathay, Translation, and Imagism* (New York: Garland Publishing Inc., 1999), especially pp. 3–18 and pp. 211–28.
4. For a very fine and thorough discussion of specifically American thought on the Chinese language and Chinese poetry, as well as how that thought plays out in the development of Modernist poetry, see Robert Kern, *Orientalism, Modernism and the American Poem* (Cambridge and New York: Cambridge University Press, 1996). Hereafter cited as Kern in the body of the text.
5. Arthur Waley, Preface to *Translations from the Chinese* (New York: Alfred A. Knopf, 1941).
6. T. S. Eliot, "Introduction to *Ezra Pound: Selected Poems*" (London: Faber and Faber, 1928), p. 14. For a critical and historical survey of English translation of Chinese poetry through 1949, see Roy E. Teele, *Through A Glass Darkly: A Study of English Translations of Chinese Poetry* (Ann Arbor: UMI, 1949). Thesis, Columbia University.
7. The other two poems were "Doria" and "The Return." Thus, Pound's fascination with Chinese poetry grew side by side with his admiration for Greek.
8. Albert Gelpi, *A Coherent Splendor: The American Poetic Renaissance, 1910–1950*, (Cambridge, UK: Cambridge University Press, 1987), p. 5. The other "generative strain" of Modern poetry, according to Gelpi, is Symbolism.
9. George Steiner, *After Babel: Aspects of Language and Translation* (Oxford: Oxford University Press, 1975), p. 358.
10. It goes beyond the scope of the present study to situate Pound's achievement in *Cathay* within this context, and in any case such work has already been done. For an excellent overview of this subject that includes how both Fenollosa's and Pound's views of Chinese fit into the Western tradition of thought about the Chinese language, see Kern, especially Chapters 1, 3, and 4. For a discussion of the significance of Chinese writing in European thought, see Haun Saussy, *Great Walls of Discourse and Other Adventures in Cultural China*, (Cambridge, MA and London: Harvard University Press, 2001), especially Chapter 3, "The Prestige of Writing: Wen, Letter, Picture, Image, Ideography," pp. 35–74.
11. According to Humphrey Carpenter, Waley publicly endorsed Pound's translations, but privately ridiculed them for their lack of scholarship. Nevertheless, Waley fundamentally changed the way in which he himself translated Chinese poetry after reading Pound. So even though he derided Pound's achievement,

Waley was deeply influenced by his success. See Humphrey Carpenter, *A Serious Character: A Life of Ezra Pound* (Boston: Houghton Mifflin, 1988), p. 267. Hereafter cited as Carpenter.

12. Moreover, as Kern notes, Chinese did not even enter the curriculum at leading universities in England (Oxford) and the United States (Yale) until 1875, which testifies to its relative marginalization even within the general upsurge of interest in Orientalist subjects during the nineteenth century, much less in comparison to Latin and Greek (Kern, p. 73). For a detailed overview of European Orientalism in the seventeenth through the nineteenth centuries, see Raymond Schwab, *The Oriental Renaissance: Europe's Rediscovery of India and the East, 1680–1880*, trans. Gene Patterson-Black and Victor Reinking (New York: Columbia University Press, 1984).

13. Gary Snyder also belongs to this group of writers obviously influenced by Pound in their efforts as translators, though since he does in fact have training in Asian languages, being conversant in Japanese and able to read classical Chinese, he follows Pound in ways more directly related to an interest in Chinese and Japanese literature.

14. Wai lim Yip, *Ezra Pound's* Cathay, (Princeton, NJ: Princeton University Press, 1969). Hereafter cited as Yip in the body of the text.

15. Sandra Gilbert and Susan Gubar, *No Man's Land: The Place of the Woman Writer in Twentieth Century Literature. Vol. 1, The War of the Words* (New Haven, CT: Yale University Press, 1988), p. 148. See also chapter three in this study.

16. Marianne DeKoven, "Gender and Modernism" in Michael Levenson, ed., *The Cambridge Companion to Modernism* (Cambridge, UK: Cambridge University Press, 1999), p. 174. For a much fuller articulation of DeKoven's position, see her *Rich and Strange: Gender, History, Modernism* (Princeton, NJ: Princeton University Press, 1991).

17. Ibid., p. 176.

18. The phrase is Perry Anderson's, from his article "Modernity and Revolution," *New Left Review* 144 (March/April 1984): 96–113, as cited in DeKoven, 1999, p. 184.

19. For more information on the gendered view of translation as a literary mode, see especially Chamberlain 1992 and Simon 1996.

20. Ezra Pound, *Cathay* (London: Elkin Matthews, 1915). Title page. Hereafter cited as *Cathay 1915* in the body of the text.

21. For a more detailed discussion of the mediating influence of Japanese sinological scholarship on the movement of Chinese poetry to the West through Pound, see Yunte Huang, *Transpacific Displacement: Ethnography, Translation, and Intertextual Travel in Twentieth-Century American Literature* (Berkeley, Los Angeles, London: University of California Press, 2002), especially chapter two, "Ezra Pound: An Ideographer or Ethnographer?", pp. 60–92.

22. In his famous commentary on the requirements for translation, Dryden writes in "The Life of Lucian" (1711) that, "The qualification of a translator worth reading must be a mastery of the language he translates out of, and that he translates into; but if a deficience be to be allowed in either, it is in the original, since if he be but master enough of the tongue of his author as to be

master of his sense, it is possible for him to express that sense with eloquence in his own, if he have a thorough command of that. But without the latter he can never arrive at the useful and the delightful, without which reading is a penance and fatigue." John Dryden, *Of Dramatic Poesy and Other Critical Essays, Vol. 2*, ed. George Watson (London: J. M. Dent and Sons, 1962). Despite his flexibility on the issue of mastering the original language, Dryden clearly considered at least some knowledge of the original language necessary for translation. Following his example, theorists and practitioners of translation up to Pound, including his most influential immediate predecessors Matthew Arnold, Edward Fitzgerald, and Dante Gabriel Rossetti all accepted this without question and translated only from languages they knew.

23. Pound had submitted a version of the Noh drama *Nishikigi* to Harriet Monroe for publication in the May 1914 edition of *Poetry*. At his own request, however, this English version made no mention of his name, stating simply that it had been "translated from the Japanese of Motokiyo by Ernest Fenollosa." Thus before *Cathay* Pound had not yet laid claim to the title of translator in his dealings with the Asian texts contained in the Fenollosa manuscripts.

24. For a discussion of translation as issuing from the "afterlife" of an original work of art, see "The Task of the Translator" in Walter Benjamin, *Illuminations*, ed. Hannah Arendt, trans. Harry Zohn (New York: Schocken, 1968), especially pp. 71–72.

25. *Twenty Chinese Poems, Paraphrased by Clifford Bax* (Hampstead, England: W. Budd and Co., The Orpheus Press, 1910). In the revised and expanded version of this work, however, Bax does go further in laying claim to the mantle of "translation" by claiming the drive toward a greater semantic accuracy, saying about the poems he revised for the second edition, that the "rest I have inspected closely, and wherever I have introduced a marked alteration of meaning I have tried to bring my version yet nearer to the original." *Twenty Five Chinese Poems*: Paraphrased by Clifford Bax (London: Hendersons, 1916), p. 10.

26. See Florence Ayscough and Amy Lowell, *Fir Flower Tablets* (Boston, New York: Houghton Mifflin, 1921) as well as Witter Bynner, *The Jade Mountain: A Chinese Anthology, Being Three Hundred Poems of the T'ang Dynasty, 618–906* (Garden City, NY: Anchor Books, 1964, reprint from 1929).

27. *Cathay* 1915, p. 32.

28. Hugh Kenner, *The Pound Era* (Berkeley and Los Angeles: University of California Press, 1971), pp. 201–202. Hereafter cited as *Era* in the body of the text.

29. Sanehide Kodama, "*Cathay* and the Fenollosa Notebooks," *Paideuma: A Journal Devoted to Ezra Pound Scholarship* 11.2 (1982): 213. Hereafter cited as Kodama in the body of the text. See also Ron Bush, "Pound and Li Po: What becomes a Man" in *Ezra Pound Among the Poets*, ed. George Bornstein (Chicago: University of Chicago Press, 1985), p. 37, where he describes *Cathay*'s main concerns as "first with the recesses of poetic sensation—with the places where feelings are at once most authentic and most difficult to put into words—and then with the dedicated artist's courage as he advances into those regions." Hereafter cited as Bush in the body of the text.

30. Ann Chapple, "Ezra Pound's *Cathay*: Compilation from the Fenollosa Notebooks," *Paideuma* 17.2–3 (1988), p. 11. Hereafter cited as Chapple in the body of the text.
31. For a full account of this three-year arrangement, see James Longenbach, *Stone Cottage: Pound, Yeats, and Modernism* (New York and Oxford, UK: Oxford University Press, 1988).
32. For the fullest account of Fenollosa's rather improbable career as the foremost expert on Japanese and Chinese art in the West at the time, see Laurence Chisolm, *Fenollosa: The Far East and American Culture* (New Haven, CT: Yale University Press, 1963).
33. See Bush, Chapple, and Kodama articles cited above.
34. These six core poems were: "Lament of the Frontier Guard," "Poem by the Bridge at Ten-Shin," "The River Merchant's Wife: A Letter," "The Jewel Stairs' Grievance," "The River Song," and "The Exile's Letter."
35. In strict sinological terms, "The Beautiful Toilet" is only attributed to Mei Sheng, as it has little to do with other writings by this author. But Pound's, or Fenollosa's, "mistake" here merely indicates the extent to which we are not dealing with any sort of scholarly production, but rather primarily a poetic one with the patina of scholarship. In any event, the point is not whether they "got it right," but what they sought to do through the choices they made.
36. *Era*, p. 202.
37. The most interesting treatment of the literary consequences of World War I remains Paul Fussell, *The Great War and Modern Memory* (New York and Oxford, UK: Oxford University Press, 1975).
38. For the rules of this genre see James J. Y. Liu, *The Art of Chinese Poetry* (Chicago: The University of Chicago Press, 1962), pp. 22–28. Liu also includes a discussion of several different types of Chinese poetry. Hereafter cited as Liu in the body of the text.
39. See Yip, p. 186.
40. For a discussion of the conventions of "old-style shi" poetry, see Liu, pp. 24–26.
41. Yip's and Giles' translation from Yip, pp. 128–38; Waley's quoted in *Era*, pp. 194–95.
42. The binome 蕩子 actually connotes sexual dissipation along with alcoholic excess. Hence Yip translates the terms as "playboy." Fenollosa does not indicate this in his notes, so Pound, of course, could not have known this. It is also unlikely that he had begun to read the characters for this poem "ideogrammically." It remains unclear, then, whence Pound got the idea for "sot." Most important, however, the word choice reflects his intentions to cast the husband in a completely negative light.
43. Yip takes this approach in his translation. See Yip, p. 186.
44. Interestingly, its contemporary meaning is "concubine."
45. Bush, p. 41.
46. Kodama, p. 222.

47. Though there are footnotes to other poems in *Cathay*, most notably the one attached to "The Jewel Stairs' Grievance," those notes mainly interpret the poem as a whole and do not provide specific explanations of unique cultural details.
48. Yip's more semantically accurate rendering of this passage reads as follows:
    > At sixteen, you went on a long journey
    > By the Yen-yü rocks at Ch'ü-tang
    > The unpassable rapids in the fifth month
    > When monkeys cried against the sky. (See Yip, p. 193)
49. Kodama, p. 223.
50. For Eliot's original use of this term, see his essay "Hamlet and his Problems" in, among other places, *The Sacred Wood: Essays on Poetry and Criticism* (London: Methuen and Co., 1972), p. 100.
51. Noel Stock, *The Life of Ezra Pound 1907–1941* (New York: Pantheon, 1970), p. 155.
52. For an extended discussion of poetry by women and the effect of World War II, see Susan Schweik, *A Gulf So Deeply Cut: American Women Poets and the Second World War* (Madison: University of Wisconsin Press, 1991).
53. Ann Chapple notes that "Fenollosa only included about half of [this poem] in his notes," going on to suggest that Pound's "having found the ballad in an incomplete form gave him precedent for reducing it further, to the form it now takes in *Cathay*." She fails, however, to account for why Pound would choose to render this poem in particular, and why he included it only in later versions of the collection.
54. See transcription in Appendix 1.
55. In contemporary Mandarin, the pronunciation would be LoFu.
56. In his rough gloss on the poem, Fenollosa translates the relevant characters here as "mulberries." But this was in all likelihood merely a form of shorthand. For within the context of the poem, the character clearly means "mulberry leaves." Fenollosa obviously knew this, since in his earlier summary of the poem, he describes the woman as feeding mulberry leaves to the silkworms. See the transcribed notes in Appendix.
57. As quoted in *Era*, p. 104.

Chapter Two

1. Appearing in *Poetry* were sections I, II, III, and VI. For full citation, see Donald Gallup, *Ezra Pound: A Bibliography* (Charlottesville: University of Virginia Press, 1983), p. 255.
2. For the full review in all its amusing ill-temper, see *Poetry* Vol. 14 (1919), pp. 52–55.
3. T. S. Eliot, "Introduction: 1928" to Ezra Pound's Selected Poems (London: Faber and Faber, Ltd., 1948), pp. 19–20. In a postscript written in 1948 to this introduction, Eliot stated with slightly more openness that "Certainly, I should now write with less cautious admiration of *Homage to Sextus Propertius*" (p. 21).
4. In contrast to conventional critical opinion, Blackmur elevated the *Homage* over *Hugh Selwyn Mauberley* in the Pound canon, saying that "The 'Propertius's is a

sturdier, more sustained, and more independent poem than 'Mauberley'." For the entire review, see *Hound and Horn* Vol. 7 (1934), pp. 177–212.
5. Sullivan, p. 5. Emphasis in the original.
6. Donald Davie, *Ezra Pound: Poet as Sculptor* (New York: Oxford University Press, 1964). See also J. J. Espey, "Towards Propertius," *Paideuma: A Journal Devoted to Ezra Pound Scholarship* Vol. 1 No. 1, pp. 63–74.
7. This is the title of Thomas's chapter on Propertius in Ron Thomas, *The Latin Masks of Ezra Pound* (Ann Arbor: UMI Research Press, 1983), pp. 39–59.
8. George Steiner, ed., *Poem into Poem: World Poetry in Modern Verse Translation* (Baltimore: Penguin, 1970), as cited in Daniel M. Hooley, "Pound's Propertius Again," *Modern Language Notes* Vol. 100, No. 5, Dec. 1985, p. 1032. Reprinted in *The Classics in Paraphrase* (Selinsgrove: Susquehanna University Press; London and Toronto: Associated University Presses, 1988), pp. 28–55.
9. Hooley, *op. cit.*, p, 1042.
10. Thomas, p. 39.
11. Hooley, *op. cit.*, p. 1041.
12. Of course, the number of recent studies that have addressed the engagement of Modernist writers in the politics of their times is too great to mention all of them here. But a brief sample would include such important works as Charles Ferall, *Modernist Writing and Reactionary Politics* (Cambridge, UK: Cambridge University Press, 2001); Tyrus Miller, *Late Modernism: Politics, Fiction and the Arts Between the World Wars* (Berkeley and Los Angeles: University of California Press, 1999); Paul Peppis, *Literature, Politics and the English Avant-Garde: Nation and Empire 1901–1918* (Cambridge, UK: Cambridge University Press, 2000); Michael Tratner, *Modernism and Mass Politics: Joyce, Woolf, Eliot, Yeats* (Stanford, CA: Stanford University Press, 1995); David Weir, *Anarchy and Culture: The Aesthetic Politics of Modernism* (Amherst: University of Massachusetts Press, 1997); Rita Felski, *The Gender of Modernity* (Cambridge, MA: Harvard University Press, 1995); Michael North, *The Dialect of Modernism: Race, Language and Twentieth-Century Literature*, (New York: Oxford University Press, 1994), as well as his *Reading 1922: A Return to the Scene of the Modern* (New York: Oxford University Press, 1999); also see Sandra Gilbert's and Susan Gubar's *No Man's Land: The Place of the Woman Writer in the Twentieth Century* (New Haven, CT: Yale University Press, 1988), and especially Marianne DeKoven, *Rich and Strange: Gender, History, Modernism* (Princeton, NJ: Princeton University Press, 1991). For discussion of Pound's politics in particular, see Michael North, *The Political Aesthetic of Yeats, Eliot and Pound* (Cambridge, UK: Cambridge University Press, 1991); Peter Nicholls, *Ezra Pound, Politics, Economics and Writing: A Study of The Cantos* (Atlantic Highlands, NJ: Humanities Press, 1984), and Jean Michel Rabaté, *Language, Sexuality and Ideology in Ezra Pound's* Cantos (Albany, NY: SUNY Press, 1986).
13. Ezra Pound, *Guide to Kulchur* (New York: New Directions, 1970), p. 7. Hereafter cited as *GK* in the body of the text. Pound's word choice here becomes severely ironic in light of his subsequent incarceration at St. Elizabeth's on the basis of his insanity defense against charges of treason.

14. For entirely understandable methodological reasons, this has been the case both for criticism of Pound, as well as for that of Modernist translation as a whole. In addition to Yip's and Sullivan's work already mentioned, see for example, Ron Thomas, *The Latin Masks of Ezra Pound*, David Anderson's *Pound's Cavalcanti*, Mary Patterson Cheadle's *Pound's Confucian Translations*, Peter Makin's *Pound and Provence*, Stuart McDougal's *Ezra Pound and the Troubador Tradition*, etc.
15. For a complete discussion of this fascinating period in Pound's career, see Ron Bush, *The Genesis of Ezra Pound's Cantos* (Princeton, NJ: Princeton University Press, 1976), especially pp. 53–142.
16. Marianne Dekoven, "Gender and Modernism," in Michael Levenson, ed., *The Cambridge Companion to Modernism* (Cambridge, UK: Cambridge University Press, 1999), p. 174.
17. Ezra Pound, *Selected Letters of Ezra Pound, 1907–1941*, ed. D. D. Paige (London: Faber and Faber, 1950), pp. 90–91. Hereafter cited parenthetically as *SL* in the body of the text.
18. Other negative reviews include, in addition to the ones already mentioned, Robert Nichols, *The Observer*, Jan. 11, 1920, p. 6; Martin Gilkes, *English* 2 (1938), 77; Robert Graves, *The Crowning Privilege* (London: Cassell and Co., Ltd., 1944), pp. 212–13. For a complete review of the negative responses to the *Homage* up to 1964, see Sullivan, pp. 3–14.
19. *The New Age* Vol. 26 (1920), p. 179.
20. *Ibid.*, p. 195.
21. The "Ride to Lanuvium" refers to Propertius iv.8. For a lengthier discussion of Pound's treatment of this ode, see Sullivan, pp. 71–75.
22. Pound's knowledge of Latin has been well documented. For example, see Ron Thomas, Michael Mages, and Humphrey Carpenter.
23. For a discussion of Pound's famous "mistake" in "The River Song," see Yip, pp. 148–58. For another exception to this general tendency in *Cathay*, see my discussion of "A Ballad of the Mulberry Road" above. Also, Sullivan points out that because Pound used the Teubner 1892 text of Propertius, which organizes the elegies differently than current scholarship, much of the "patch-work" quality of the *Homage* can be attributed to his source text. For a fuller discussion of this, see Sullivan, pp. 95–104.
24. *The New Age* Vol. 26 No. 5 (Dec. 4, 1919. p. 82).
25. As K. K. Ruthven summarizes, Pound presents a figure who "expresses anti-imperialistic sentiments of a sort that would have brought exile or death to the Roman poet; he is unpatriotic where Propertius was quite the reverse (for example in IV, vi, which Pound omits from his *Homage*); he is less respectful of Virgil, less tolerant of mythological poetry, and has no interest whatsoever in Propertius's idealization of Cynthia." See K. K. Ruthven, *A Guide to Ezra Pound's* Personae *(1926)* (Berkeley and Los Angeles: University of California Press, 1969), p. 86. For a discussion of Pound's treatment of the amatory theme in Propertius, see Michael Mages, "He Do Propertius in a Modernist Voice: Pound's Summary of the Amatory Theme from the Elegies of Sextus

Propertius," *Paideuma: A Journal Devoted to Ezra Pound Scholarship* 22:3 1993 (Winter), pp. 68–89.
26. See Thomas, Ron. *The Latin Masks of Ezra Pound* (Ann Arbor: UMI Research Press, 1977), pp. 44–45. Compare also Pound's own statement in *Gaudier-Breszka* about his activity and his use of translation as a mask, where he writes: "In the 'search for oneself,' in the search for 'sincere self-expression,' one gropes, one finds some seeming verity. One says 'I am' this, that or the other, and with the words scarcely uttered one ceases to be that thing.

 I began this search for the real in a book called *Personae*, casting off, as it were, complete masks of the self in each poem. I continued in a long series of translations, which were but more elaborate masks." In Ezra Pound, *Gaudier-Brzeska: A Memoir* (New York: New Directions, 1970), p. 85.
27. For the sake of convenience, I will use the now accepted division of Propertius's *Elegiae*, as employed by G. P. Goold in the Loeb Classical Library edition, rather than the outdated Teubner edition that Pound used. Citations designate Book number in capital Roman numerals, followed by specific elegy in lower case.
28. G. P. Goold's more conventionally literal rendering of this opening passage reads as follows: "Shade of Callimachus and rites of Coan Philetas, suffer me, I pray, to come into your grove. I am the first to enter, priest from an unsullied spring, bringing Italy's mystic emblems in dances of Greece. Say, in what grotto did ye together spin the delicate thread of your song? With what foot enter? What water drink?" See G. P. Goold, trans., *Elegies of Propertius*, Loeb Classical Library (Cambridge, MA: Harvard University Press, 1990), p. 253. Hereafter cited as Goold, followed by page number.
29. For a different perspective on the presence of anxiety in the *Homage*, see Ron Thomas. The category of gender provides a way to further specify Thomas's more general claim about the anxiety underlying the *Homage*, which he sees as stemming from Pound's uncertainty over the future direction of his career.
30. In the strictest literal sense, this line reads, "Ah, let me be rid of whomever would delay Phoebus in armor/Let (my) verse proceed smoothly, polished by pumice." G. P. Goold gives these lines somewhat more colloquially as "Begone the man who detains Phoebus with themes of war! Let my verse run smoothly, perfected with fine pumice" (Goold, p. 253).
31. Goold's more conventional translation shows the extent of Pound's departures: "Else who would know the fortress battered by the firwood horse, the rivers that fought in combat with Thessaly's hero, Simois of Ida together with Jove's offspring Scamander, and the chariot that thrice befouled Hector's body on the plain? And Deiphobus and Helenus and Paris in Polydamas' armour, sorry figure though he cut, their own country would scarcely know about. Ilion, you would now be little talked of, as you too, Troy, twice taken by the power of Oeta's god. Homer also, the chronicler of your fate, has found his reputation grow with the passage of time" (Goold, p. 255).
32. Pound's abiding concern with rhythm has been well documented, and Sullivan confirms that this interest often overrides the niceties of grammar in the *Homage*. "In a recent letter to me, Pound has defended some such defiances

of the original forms on the grounds that his forms give in English a 'better sound' and that sometimes the retention of the original meaning exactly (for example, Section I—'Oetian gods' for Propertius's 'Oetian god' i.e. Hercules) 'wd...bitch the movement of the verse'." See Sullivan, p. 97 n. 13.
33. Hale, pp. 54–55.
34. Thus, Sullivan, himself a classicist, sides with Pound on the grammatical points, agreeing that tacta "suggests the opposite of *virgo intacta* (a classical phrase—see Catullus, 62, 45); thus *tactus* has a sexual meaning, frequently found in classical Latin." He thereby argues that "the translation itself cannot be called a mistake because the meaning [Pound] has used is arguably there in the context." Sullivan, pp. 96–97. On the other side, Brian Arkins casually dismisses Pound's rendering simply as "mistranslation." See Brian Arkins, "Pound's Propertius: What Kind of Homage?" *Paideuma: A Journal Devoted to Ezra Pound Scholarship* 17:1 1988: 37.
35. G. P. Goold translates this couplet, "yet the Muses are my friends, my poems are dear to the reader, and Calliope never wearies of dancing to my rhythms" (Goold, p. 257).
36. Other deviations such as "Aemilia" for "Aemilius" and the "lares fleeing the 'Roman seat'" instead of the "Lares putting Hannibal to flight" represent simply errors of a traditional sort.
37. Goold translates these lines as follows: "For you will sing of garlanded lovers at another's threshold and the tipsy tokens of midnight vigil, so that he who would artfully outwit stern husbands may learn from you how to charm forth a locked-up woman" (Goold, p. 263).
38. Sullivan, p. 100.
39. In this regard, Pound's word choice in the phrase "These are your images" hardly seems accidental.
40. This section presents Pound's rendering of elegy II, xv.
41. Pound had produced an earlier rendering of this elegy as "Prayer for His Lady's Life" (*Per.* 38) and the marked differences between this version and Section VIII of the *Homage* betoken both Pound's development as a translator and the evolving terms of his interest in Propertius as a love poet over the course of his early career.
42. This is, of course, an ancient irony that Pound takes advantage of here. For comparison, see Gorgias's defense of Helen in his "Encomium of Helen," D. M. MacDowell, trans. (Bristol: Bristol Classical Press, 1982), especially pp. 27–31. Also see Isocrates's "Helen," in *Isocrates, Vol. III*, La Rue Van Hook, trans. Loeb Classical Library (Cambridge, MA: Harvard University Press), pp. 54–97, esp. pp. 87–99.
43. Though it appears in all printed versions, "Ranaus" is apparently an unintentional "mistake" for the river "Tanaus," as indicated by Pound's willingness to have them corrected by Sullivan.
44. For a detailed comparison of this passage with the original, see Ron Thomas, pp. 54–55.

Notes

45. For a recent rendering of this work into English, see *The Argonautika* by Apollonios Rhodios, trans., Peter Green (Berkeley, Los Angeles, and London: University of California Press, 1997).
46. In line 77 of the *Theogony*, Hesiod lists the Muses in the following (presumably birth) order: Clio, Euterpe, Thalia, Melpomene, Terpsichore, Erato, Polymnia, Ourania and Calliope. See *Hesiod: Theogony, Works and Days, Shield*, trans. Apostolos N. Athanassallis (Baltimore: Johns Hopkins University Press, 1983), p. 15. For additional commentary on this line, see Hesiod, *Theogony*. M. L. West, ed. (Oxford: Oxford University Press 1966), p. 114.

Chapter Three

1. "Translator's Postscript," from Rémy de Gourmont, *The Natural Philosophy of Love*. trans. Ezra Pound. 1922. (New York: Collier, 1961), pp. 149–150. Hereafter cited as *NPL* in the body of the text.
2. For a comprehensive survey of the superstition regarding the brain/sperm connection, see Weston La Barre, *Muelos: A Stone Age Superstition About Sexuality* (New York: Columbia University Press, 1984). Thanks are due to Haun Saussy for this reference.
3. Sandra Gilbert and Susan Gubar, *No Man's Land: The Place of the Woman Writer in the Twentieth Century*, Vol. 1 *The War of the Words* (New Haven, CT: Yale University Press, 1988), p. 141.
4. Marianne DeKoven, *Rich and Strange: Gender, History, Modernism* (Princeton, NJ: Princeton University Press, 1991), p. 20. All further references cited as *Strange*. Other recent works in this vein include: Rita Felski, *The Gender of Modernity* (Cambridge, MA: Harvard University Press, 1995); Bonnie Kime Scott, ed. *The Gender of Modernism* (Bloomington: Indiana University Press, 1990); Lisa Rado, ed. *Rereading Modernism: New Directions in Feminist Criticism* (New York: Garland, 1994); and Elizabeth Jane Harrison and Shirley Peterson, eds., *Unmanning Modernism: Gendered Re-Readings* (Knoxville: University of Tennessee Press, 1997), especially. the essays "'The Sun born in a Woman': H. D.'s Transformation of a Masculinist Icon in 'The Dancer'" by Dagny Boebel, and "Gendering Modernism: H. D., Imagism, and Masculinist Aesthetics" by Michael Kaufmann.
5. Ann Douglass, *The Feminization of American Culture* (New York: Anchor-Doubleday, 1988).
6. Albert Gelpi, *A Coherent Splendor: The American Poetic Renaissance, 1910–1950* (Cambridge, UK: Cambridge University Press, 1987), p. 253.
7. Amy Lowell, *The Complete Works of Amy Lowell*, ed. Louis Untermeyer (Boston: Houghton Mifflin, 1955), p. 459.
8. Ezra Pound, "Sage Homme," *The Letters of Ezra Pound, 1907–1941*, ed. D. D. Paige (New York: Harcourt, 1950), p. 170. Hereafter cited as *Letters* in the body of the text. For an interesting discussion of the dynamics of the Pound-Eliot interaction in the composition of *The Waste Land*, see Wayne

Koestenbaum, *Double Talk: The Erotics of Male Literary Collaboration* (New York: Routledge, 1989).
9. T. E. Hulme, "A Lecture on Modern Poetry," in *Further Speculations*, ed. Samuel Hynes (Minneapolis: University of Minnesota Press, 1955), p. 69.
10. Indeed, as Lori Chamberlain and others have shown, translation as a mode of literary production has long been haunted by, or raised questions about, its gendered status as a mode of literary production in various cultural and historical contexts. See Chamberlain and Simon.
11. According to Eileen Gregory, "A study of the extant books of her library housed at Yale indicates that she apparently translated with no little effort, using standard German editions (with Latin translations, notes, and commentary), with the consistent help of dictionaries and with the mediation of French and English translations." Eileen Gregory, *H. D. and Hellenism: Classic Lines* (Cambridge, UK: Cambridge University Press, 1997), p. 55. Hereafter cited as Gregory in the body of the text.
12. For a related view, see Virginia Woolf's essay "On Not Knowing Greek."
13. This date reflects on the publication date. The novel was actually composed just before and after World War II, in 1939 and 1948.
14. For a discussion of H. D.'s novels, see Susan Stanford Friedman, *Penelope's Web: Gender, Modernity, H. D.'s Fiction* (Cambridge, UK: Cambridge University Press, 1990). For a brief selection of H. D.'s critical writings, see the H. D. section in Bonnie Kime Scott, *The Gender of Modernism* (Bloomington: Indiana University Press, 1990). For H. D.'s engagement with film, see Anne Friedberg, "Approaching Borderline" in *H. D.: Woman and Poet*. Michael King, ed. (Orono, ME: National Poetry Foundation, 1986), pp. 369–90. For her engagement with the filmic technique of montage, see Susan Edmunds, *Out of Line: History, Psychoanalysis, and Montage in H. D.'s Long Poems* (Stanford: Stanford University Press, 1994). Finally, for a discussion of H. D. in the context of modernist visionary poetry, see Helen Sword, *Engendering Inspiration: Visionary Strategies in Rilke, Lawrence, and H. D.* (Ann Arbor: University of Michigan Press, 1995).
15. Douglas Bush, *Mythology and the Romantic Tradition in English Poetry* (Cambridge, MA: Harvard University Press, 1937, 1969), p. 498. Hereafter cited as Bush.
16. Richmond Lattimore, "Euripides as Lyrist," *Poetry* Vol. LI, No. III (Dec. 1937), p. 163.
17. D. S. Carne-Ross, "Translation and Transposition," in *The Craft and Context of Translation*. eds. William Arrowsmith and Roger Shattuck (Austin: Humanities Research Center-University of Texas Press, 1961), pp. 3–31, esp. p. 7.
18. Vincent Quinn, *Hilda Doolittle (H. D.)* (New York: Twayne, 1967), p. 95. Hereafter cited as Quinn.
19. For Martz's essay, see Louis L. Martz, Introduction, *H. D.: The Collected Poems, 1912–1944* (New York: New Directions, 1983), esp. pp. xvi–xxiv. For Duplessis's, see *H. D.: The Career of that Struggle* (Brighton: The Harvester Press, 1986), esp. pp. 23–26. For Susan Gubar's article, see "Sapphistries." *Signs* 10 (Autumn 1984): 43–62. Finally, Diana Collecott has taken up these earlier strands

and woven them into a complete study of H. D.'s relationship with Sappho in *H. D. and Sapphic Modernism, 1910–1950* (Cambridge, UK: Cambridge University Press, 1999).
20. Eileen Gregory, *H. D., and Hellenism: Classic Lines* (Cambridge, UK: Cambridge University Press, 1997).
21. Quinn, p. 97.
22. I will discuss this at greater length in chapter five.
23. As cited in Glenn Hughes, *Imagism and the Imagists* (Stanford: Stanford University Press, 1931), p. 110. Hereafter cited as Hughes.
24. This was the official reason for her withdrawal, though biographers seem to agree that it was a psychological breakdown that forced her withdrawal.
25. This phenomenon is discussed in detail in Bush. Interestingly, Bush is one of the harshest of H. D.'s critics, considering her translations not only technically wanting, but also stylistically derivative of Swinburne and the Pre-Raphaelites. How he arrives at this conclusion is not entirely clear.
26. Gregory, p. 1.
27. H.D., *End To Torment: A Memoir of Ezra Pound. With Hilda's Book by Ezra Pound*, eds. Norman Holmes Pearson and Michael King (New York: New Directions, 1979) p. 18. Hereafter cited as *ETT* in the body of the text.
28. For a detailed reconstruction of H. D.'s contribution to the founding of Imagism, see Cyrena Pondrom, "H. D. and the Origins of Imagism" originally appearing in *Sagetrieb* 4 (Spring 1985): 73–100, and reprinted in *Signets: Reading H. D.*, eds., Susan Stanford Friedman and Rachel Blau Duplessis (Madison: University of Wisconsin Press, 1990), pp. 85–109.
29. Over the course of her career, however, H. D. did use a number of pseudonyms, including A. D. Hill, Delia Alton, Rhoda Peter, and John Helforth, for a variety of writing projects. Thus, she did in fact consider many of her works to be outside the purview of her Imagist persona, and in many ways, her novels can be seen as attempts to review and revise the period in her life when she was cast, seemingly irretrievably, as, in Glenn Hughes' terms, "the perfect Imagist."
30. For more information on H. D.'s engagement with *The Greek Anthology*, or *The Palatine Anthology* as it is often called, see Gregory, pp. 161–63 and 167–73, especially p. 161 n. 32.
31. Gregory also notes that H. D. used J. W. Mackail's *Select Epigrams from the Greek Anthology*, J. W. Mackail, ed. and trans. (New York: Longmans, 1911). Gregory p. 56.
32. Hughes, p. 111.
33. *Poetry* 1:4 (Jan., 1913), p. 118. Gregory posits that possibly either Harriet Monroe or Pound, not H. D., provided this caption. See Gregory, p. 55. Whoever authored it, the caption simply calls attention to the importance of the concept of translation all at once in the production, reception, and marketing of H. D.'s early poetry.
34. For more information on this collaborative episode, see Caroline Zilboorg, "Joint Venture: Richard Aldington, H. D. and the Poets' Translation Series" *Philological Quarterly* 70 (Winter 1991): 67–98.

35. *Egoist* 2 (September 1915): 139. See also Robert Babcock, "Verses, Translation, and Reflections from 'The Anthology': H. D., Ezra Pound and the Greek Anthology." *Sagetrieb* 14 (Spring-Fall 1995): 201–16.
36. For a view representative of the standard masculinist critical evaluations of H. D. and her reputation as a strictly Imagist poet, see Brendan Jackson, "'The Fulsomeness of her Prolixity': Reflections on H. D., 'Imagiste.'" *The South Atlantic Quarterly* 83:1 (Winter, 1984): 91–102. In fact, Jackson even goes so far as to dispute H. D.'s status as an Imagist, seeking more to diminish her reputation as a poet than to understand the way in which she understood her own practice as a writer.
37. H. D. *Collected Poems, 1912–1944* (New York: New Directions, 1986), pp. 37–39. Hereafter cited as *CP* in the body of the text.
38. Indeed, H. D.'s very first poetic compositions, poems modeled on those of Theocritus, were written to Frances Gregg. Much has been made of H. D.'s bisexuality, but relatively little detailed work has been done specifically on the role her lesbianism played in the development of her poetry. One notable exception is Collecott.
39. Gelpi, *op. cit.*, p. 254.
40. Duplessis defines "romantic thralldom" as "an all-encompassing, totally defining love between unequals. ... The eroticism of romantic love, born of this unequal relationship between the sexes, may depend for its satisfaction upon dominance and submission." Rachel Blau Duplessis, "Romantic Thralldom in H. D.", originally published in *Contemporary Literature* XX, Vol. 2 (Spring, 1979): 178–203, and reprinted in *Signets*, pp. 406–29.
41. Indeed, in "Epigram," the only one of the three poems published in January of 1913 to be excluded from the 1925 edition of her *Collected Poems*, H. D. pursues the poetics of feminine victimization to their funerary ends and composes an epitaph commemorating the death of an imagined Greek woman, Homonoea. As its title indicates, H. D. modeled the poem after the epigrammatic forms in *The Greek Anthology*, probably on the sepulchral epigrams of Book VII in particular. The poem reads as follows:

> The golden one is gone from the banquets;
> She, beloved of Atimetus,
> The swallow, the bright Homonoea;
> Gone the dear chatterer.

Interestingly, in the 1972 edition of her *Collected Poems 1912–1944*, in the "Uncollected Poems" section, Louis Martz has added one line to the poem as it appeared in both *Poetry* and *Des Imagistes*, citing Beinecke Library manuscripts. That final line, "Death succeeds Atimetus," adds a narrative dimension to the epigram (epitaph). It remains unclear whether the final line was one that Pound excised when he saw H. D.'s poems in the British Museum tea room, or whether H. D. added it herself at a later date. In either case, the line shows how, even from the very beginnings of Imagism, H. D. tried to expand upon the lyric confines of Imagist doctrine. If this is accurate, then Pound was not the only one to seek alternatives to the limitations of Imagism. His solutions were just the

ones that have been given critical attention and thus cultural authority. See also Gregory, p. 248.
42. Gregory identifies its source as an epigram to Priapus by Dioscoros Zonas in *The Greek Anthology*, 6.22. See Gregory, p. 248.
43. See *CP*, p. 309.
44. Interestingly, though Gregory aptly recognizes the occult dimensions of this passage, she misses the expressly gendered aspects of H. D.'s metaphor of "hatching."
45. Etymologically speaking, "coin" and "character" are related. "Character" in Greek means the "stamp" of a coin or a personality. Thanks to Haun Saussy for this useful insight. In his own work, Pound pushed this historically robust syllogism to the breaking point, demonstrating through the failure of *The Cantos* its ultimate limitations as the basis of either a poetics, or, for that matter, an economics.
46. See, for example, Yeats's statement in 1931, "I think those great scholars of the last century who translated Sophocles into an English full of Latinised constructions and Latinised habits of thought, were all wrong—and that the school-masters are wrong to make us approach Greek through Latin. Nobody ever trembled on a dark road because he was afraid of meeting the nymphs and satyrs of Latin literature, but men have trembled on dark roads in Ireland and in Greece. Latin literature was founded on documents, but Greek literature came like old Irish literature out of the beliefs of the common people." From *The Irish Weekly and Ulster Examiner*, September 12, 1931, p. 9. For Pound, see his essay "Notes on Elizabethan Classicists" in *Literary Essays of Ezra Pound*, ed. T. S. Eliot (New York: New Directions, 1954), pp. 227–48.
47. H. D., "Preface" to "Choruses from Iphigeneia in Aulis" (London: Ballantyne Press, 1916), p. 1
48. T. S. Eliot, *The Sacred Wood* (London: Methuen and Co. Ltd., 1920), p. 74.
49. H. D., "Preface" to "Choruses from Iphigeneia in Aulis," p. 1.
50. *Ibid*.
51. H. D. *Euripides Ion, Translated with Notes*, p. 32.
52. The scholarship on this issue is too massive to recapitulate in detail here, but for an introductory anthology of the works of Hélène Cixous, Luce Irigary, Monique Wittig, and Julia Kristeva, see *New French Feminisms: An Anthology*, eds. Elaine Marks and Isabelle de Courtivon (Amherst: University of Massachusetts Press, 1980).
53. For a relatively recent consideration of the relationship between gender and lyric in Modernism, see Rachel Blau Duplessis, "'The Corpses of Poesy': Some Modern Poets and Some Gender Ideologies of Lyric," in Lynn Keller and Cristanne Miller, eds., *Feminist Measures: Soundings in Poetry and Theory* (Ann Arbor: University of Michigan Press, 1994).
54. For example, in the Loeb Classical Library edition, A. T. Murray begins the epic with mention of the bard: "Tell me, Muse, of the man of many devices, driven far astray after he had sacked the sacred citadel of Troy." *The Odyssey*, trans. A. T. Murray, Loeb Classical Library (Harvard, MA: Harvard University Press, 1953), p. 13. Hereafter cited as *Loeb* in the body of the text. Similarly

Richmond Lattimore gives the opening as "Tell me, Muse, of the man of many ways, who was driven/far journeys, after he had sacked Troy's sacred citadel." Richmond Lattimore, trans., *The Odyssey of Homer* (New York: Harper and Row, 1965, 1967), p. 27. Hereafter cited as Lattimore.

55. See, for example, H. D.'s original verse drama *Hippolytus Temporizes* and also her "Helios and Athena."
56. Again, Lattimore provides a usefully literal contrast: "in her hollowed caverns, desiring that he should be her husband" (27, l. 15).
57. Gregory adds "Winter Love" from *Hermetic Definition* (1958) to this list of works with a strong Homeric subtext. But again, her interests are primarily thematic, regarding H. D.'s relationship to and view of Homer, rather than with the practice of translation as a literary mode.
58. The first of H. D.'s rewritings of Sappho, Fragment 68, first appeared in *Hymen* (1921). But as Gregory notes, she used Henry Thornton Wharton's 1896 translation as the epigraph to this poem. Thus, H. D. did not begin employing translation herself as a compositional technique until the poems of *Heliodora*.
59. Indeed, in *Heliodora* these three poems almost constitute an independent poetic unit. Only one poem, "Helen," disrupts the sequence of the three poems, appearing between "Heliodora" and "Nossis," and the interceding poem could even be seen as part of the sequence itself inasmuch as it concerns perhaps the most famous of all classical female objects of poetic depiction, Helen of Troy.
60. That H. D. can only articulate a female poetic identity in negative terms, saying merely that she is not beautiful rather that what she is instead, indicates just how completely the masculinist tradition had succeeded in defining the terms by which women would be depicted poetically. It also indicates the historical significance of H. D. as a poet.
61. In *End To Torment*, H. D. credits Norman Holmes Pearson with this description of *Helen in Egypt*. Undoubtedly there is some degree of irony in her use of the phrase, but inasmuch as she was seeking in this text to come to terms with Pound's influence on her, H. D. seems to have accepted this characterization of her own epic as not entirely invalid.

Chapter Four

1. From the first Priest's speech in Yeats's *Sophocles' King Oedipus: A Version for the Modern Stage*, in *The Collected Plays of W. B. Yeats* (New York: The Macmillan Company, 1934, 1952), p. 304.
2. For a different approach to the category of "genius" and the way in which it shapes the reading of various Modernist writers, see Bob Perelman, *The Trouble with Genius: Reading Pound, Joyce, Stein and Zukofsky* (Berkeley and Los Angeles: University of California Press, 1994).
3. Conor Cruise O'Brien, "Passion and Cunning: An Essay on the Politics of W. B. Yeats," *In Excited Reverie: A Centenary Tribute to W.B. Yeats 1865–1939*, ed. Norman Jeffares (New York: St. Martin's Press, 1965).
4. For a defense of Yeats as nationalist and liberal, see Elizabeth Cullingford, *Yeats, Ireland, and Fascism* (New York: New York University Press, 1981). For a defense

of Yeats as ardent nationalist, see Bernard Krimm, *W. B. Yeats and the Emergence of the Irish Free State 1918–1939: Living in the Explosion* (Troy, NY: Whitson Publishing, 1981). For a view that falls in between these two positions, see Grattan Freyer, *W. B. Yeats and the Anti-Democratic Tradition* (Dublin: Gill and Macmillan, 1981).

5. This is essentially the position taken by Paul Scott Stanfield in his *Yeats and Politics in the Nineteen-Thirties* (London: Macmillan, 1988).
6. Edward Said, "Yeats and Decolonization," in *Nationalism, Colonialism and Literature*, ed. Seamus Deane (Minneapolis: University of Minnesota Press, 1990), p. 84. The essay is reprinted in Said's *Culture and Imperialism* (New York: Alfred E. Knopf, 1993).
7. For Deane's views, see Seamus Deane, "Yeats and the Idea of Revolution," in *Celtic Revivals: Essays in Modern Irish Literature 1880–1980* (London: Faber and Faber, 1985), and his "Heroic Styles: The Tradition of an Idea" in *Ireland's Field Day* (Notre Dame, IN: University of Notre Dame Press, 1985). For Kearney's views, see Richard Kearney, *Transitions: Narratives in Modern Irish Culture* (Manchester, UK: Manchester University Press, 1985), and "Myth and Motherland," in *Ireland's Field Day*.
8. David Lloyd, *Anomalous States: Irish Writing and the Post-Colonial Moment* (Durham, NC: Duke University Press, 1993), p. 5. For the full essay, see pp. 59–87.
9. Majorie Howes, *Yeats's Nations: Gender Class and Irishness* (Cambridge, UK: Cambridge University Press, 1996), p. 1. Howes's work constitutes the best treatment of Yeats's politics and his evolving conception of nationality to date. For another work that takes up the subject of the politics of Yeats's writing from the perspective of psychoanalysis and reader-response, see Vicki Mahaffey, *States of Desire: Wilde, Yeats, Joyce and the Irish Experiment* (Oxford: Oxford University Press, 1998).
10. Michael Cronin, *Translating Ireland: Translation, Languages, Cultures* (Cork: Cork University Press, 1996), p. 1. Hereafter cited as Cronin in the body of the text.
11. For a textual history, see David R. Clark and James B. Maguire, *W. B. Yeats: The Writing of Sophocles' King Oedipus* (Philadelphia: The American Philosophical Society, 1989), pp. 3–22. Hereafter cited as Clark and Maguire. For a thematic analysis, see P. Th.M.G. Liebgrets. *Centaurs in the Twilight: W. B. Yeats's Use of the Classical Tradition* (Amsterdam and Atlanta: Rodopi, 1993), pp. 359–71. See also Brian Arkins, *Builders of My Soul: Greek and Roman Themes in Yeats* (Gerrards Cross: Colin Smythe, 1990).
12. The most renowned of these discussions in contemporary criticism is, of course, Homi Bhaba's edited volume *Nation and Narration* (London: Routledge, 1990). See also *Translation and Nation: Towards a Cultural Politics of Englishness*, eds., Roger Ellis and Liz Oakley-Brown (Clevedon, UK; Buffalo, NY: Multlingual Matters, 2001).
13. W. B. Yeats, *Explorations* (London, Macmillan & Co. Ltd., 1962), p. 3. Hereafter cited as *Exp.* in the body of the text.
14. For a recent critical discussion of the cultural nationalist program of Young Ireland Movement in general and of the meaning of translation as a literary mode in James Clarence Mangan's work, see David Lloyd, *Nationalism and Minor Literature: James Clarence Mangan and the Emergence of Irish Cultural Nationalism*

(Berkeley and Los Angeles: University of California Press, 1987), especially pp. 66–67 and Chapter 4, "Veils of Sais: Translation as Refraction and Parody." For a brief outline of the efforts of the contemporary Field Day Company, and the relevance of translation as a metaphor, see Seamus Deane, "Introduction" to *Nationalism, Colonialism, and Literature* (Minneapolis: University of Minnesota Press, 1990), p. 14.

15. Yeats's difficulty with learning Gaelic are well known, and his ambivalence about the situation colored his views on the entire language issue. Consider, for example, his statement that "no man can think or write with music and vigour except in his mother tongue. Gaelic is my native tongue but it is not my mother tongue." *Essays and Introductions* (London and New York: Macmillan, 1951), p. 515. Given this view, one wonders what Yeats thought of Beckett and his sustained work in French.

16. See Cronin, *Translating Ireland*, pp. 131–66. For a related study, also see Declan Kiberd, *Synge and the Irish Language,* 2nd Edition (Dublin: Gill and Macmillan, 1993), p. 197.

17. See Mikhail Bakhtin, *The Dialogic Imagination: Four Essays*. Michael Holquist, ed., Caryl Emerson and Michael Holquist, trans. (Austin: University of Texas Press, 1981), pp. 262–63 and *passim*. For a critique of Bakhtin's theories as they apply to a specifically Irish situation, see David Lloyd, *Anomalous States: Irish Writing and the Post-Colonial Moment* (Durham, NC: Duke University Press, 1993), pp. 89–115.

18. In his play *Translations* (1981), Brian Friel explores exactly this contradictory situation.

19. For a discussion of this long-standing metaphor for translation, see J. Woodsworth, "Metaphor and Theory: Describing the Translation Process," in P. N. Chaffey, A. G Rydning, and S. S. Ulriksen, eds., *Translation Theory in Scandinavia: Proceedings from the Scandinavian Symposium on Translation Theory* (Oslo: University of Oslo Press, 1988).

20. As cited in Cullingford's *Yeats, Ireland and Fascism,* p. 47.

21. For a discussion of Yeats's later engagement with the issue of compulsory Gaelic during his time as a Free State Senator, see Bernard Krimm, *W. B. Yeats and the Emergence of the Irish Free State, 1918–1939: Living in the Explosion* (Troy, NY: The Whitson Publishing Company, 1981), chapter 4, especially pp. 103–15.

22. *The Irish Weekly and Ulster Examiner*, September 12, 1931, p. 9.

23. "Plain Man's Oedipus," *New York Times*, sec. 9, p. 1.

24. Clark and Maguire, pp. 3–22.

25. As reported in Dorothy Wellesley, *Far Have I Traveled*, pp. 169–70.

26. James Flannery, *W. B. Yeats and the Idea of a Theatre: The Early Abbey Theatre in Theory and Practice* (New Haven, CT: Yale University Press, 1976), p. 65.

27. For a discussion of how "The theoretical and practical structures of Yeats's early Irish theatre embody his conflicted engagement with the idea of a national politics as mass politics and his attempts to come to terms with the (potentially) mass character of Irish nationalism in a productive way," see Howes,

chapter 3, "'When the mob becomes a people': nationalism and occult theatre," pp. 66–101.
28. The classic formulation of the importance of print capitalism, embodied in the form of the newspaper, is, of course, Benedict Anderson's *Imagined Communities: Reflections on the Origin and Spread of Nationalism* (London and New York: Verso, revised edition, 1991).
29. *Essays*, 497.
30. For a discussion of this long and complex interaction, see James Longenbach, *Stone Cottage: Pound, Yeats, and Modernism* (Oxford, UK and New York: Oxford University Press, 1988).
31. Interestingly, in the preface to his translation of *Oedipus Rex*, Jebb comments on several preceding translations of the drama, including one by Dryden. In all likelihood, Yeats read this essay and, noticing the liberties that Dryden took with the plot in adding a subplot to it, he may have felt freer to make whatever changes to the language he saw fit.
32. Yeats, *Irish Weekly, op. cit.*
33. Yeats, *New York Times, op. cit.*
34. As will become clear in later chapters, both Pound and H. D. took the word as the proper unit of translation, whereas the more traditional practice is to take the sentence as the basic unit of meaning upon which to base a translation.
35. As cited in Clark and Maguire, p. 9.
36. Murray to Yeats, November 12, 1903, *Letters to W. B. Yeats*, ed. Richard J. Finneran, George Mills Harper, and William M. Murphy (London: Macmillan; New York: Columbia University Press, 1977), p. 145–46. Only a little later, Murray would change his mind about translating the play and publish a rendering in 1911, which was used in the first English production, about which see below.
37. See especially Eliot's essay "Euripides and Professor Murray," in *Selected Essays* (New York: Harcourt Brace, 1950), p. 47.
38. As reported in Clark and Maguire, pp. 10–12.
39. *The Letters of W. B. Yeats*, ed. Allan Wade (New York: Macmillan, 1955), pp. 538–39. Hereafter cited as *Letters*.
40. See Clark and Maguire, pp. 17–19.
41. As Clark and Maguire have shown, Yeats knew of various productions, but did not "lose interest" in staging his own version in Ireland until the monetary forces of Reinahrdt and the renown of Murray made an Irish production seem like a distinct anti-climax.
42. Cullingford, *Yeats, Ireland and Fascism*, p. 182.
43. Frederic Grab, "Yeats's King Oedipus," in *The Journal of English and Germanic Philology* 71 (1972): 343.
44. Howes, p. 108. For a full discussion of this essay, see pp. 108–12.
45. Preface to *King Oedipus*, 1928, p. v.
46. Journal entry for February 11, 1927, as cited in Clark and Maguire, pp. 37–38.
47. All quotations from Jebb's translation are from *The Tragedies of Sophocles*, trans. Sir Richard C. Jebb (1904; reprinted Amsterdam: Adolf M. Hakkert, 1966), pp. 11–19.

48. All quotations from Yeats are taken from *The Collected Plays of W. B. Yeats* (New York: Macmillan, 1973), pp. 304–305.
49. Jebb, p. 29.
50. Donal McCartney, "From Parnell to Pearse" (1891–1921) in *The Course of Irish History*, eds. T. W. Moody and F. X. Martin. Revised and enlarged edition (Cork: The Mercier Press, 1984), p. 311. Of course, "the troubles" (both the term and the events) have been going on to the present, though it seems that the Anglo-Irish War marks the initial use of the term. Moreover, as it is a neutral term, both nationalists and Unionists could use it, and so it is perhaps especially apt for Yeats to use it here.
51. Yeats, *Collected Plays*, p. 306.
52. See *Explorations*, p. 127. "We can hardly do all we hope unless there are many more of these little societies to be centres of dramatic art and of the allied arts. But a very few actors went from town to town in ancient Greece, finding everywhere more or less well-trained singers among the principal townsmen to sing the chorus that had otherwise been the chief expense. In the days of the stock companies two or three well-known actors would go from town to town, finding actors for all the minor parts in the local companies. If we are to push our work into the small towns and villages, local dramatic clubs must take the place of the old stock companies. A good-sized town should be able to give us a large enough audience for our whole, or nearly our whole, company to go there; but the need for us is greater in those small towns where the poorest kinds of farce and melodrama have gone and Shakespearian drama has not gone, and it is here that we will find it hardest to get intelligent audiences. If a dramatic club existed in one of the larger towns near, they could supply us not only with actors, should we need them, in their own town, but with actors when we went to the small towns and to the villages where the novelty of any kind of drama would make success certain. These clubs would play in Gaelic far better than we can hope to, for they would have native Gaelic speakers, and should we succeed in stirring the imagination of the people enough to keep the rivalry between plays in English and Irish to a rivalry in quality, the certain development of two schools with distinct though very kindred ideals would increase the energy and compass of our art."
53. Though collected and published in *The Tower* (1928), "The Second Coming" first appeared in the magazine *The Nation* in the November 6, 1920, issue, in the midst of the "troubles" of the Anglo-Irish War.
54. See Krimm, pp. 43–47.
55. For an extended discussion of Yeats's relationship to Fascist politics, see Elizabeth Cullingford, *Yeats, Ireland and Fascism* (New York: New York University Press, 1981).
56. Grab, pp. 351–52.
57. *Letters*, p. 721.
58. ALS, Yeats to Lady Gregory; collection of Michael Yeats, SB3 (7 pp. 166–68); as cited in Clark and Maguire, p. 36

59. Most recently, Marjorie Howes has read "A Woman Young and Old" as Yeats's complex response to the Irish Free State's postcolonial version of "Irishness" and its enforcement of Catholic social teachings with their concomitant heavy emphasis on gender roles and sexuality as important indicators of and threats to national identity. See Howes, Chapter 5, "Desiring Women: feminine sexuality and Irish nationality in 'A Woman Young and Old,'" pp. 131–59.
60. "The Story of 'Oedipus the King': As Told by W. B. Yeats," *The Irish Weekly and Ulster Examiner*, 64, No. 3217 (September 12, 1931): 9.
61. R. C. Jebb, trans., *The Oedipus Coloneus* (Amsterdam: Adolf M. Hakkert, 1965), pp. 191–97.
62. See David Maguire, *Yeats at Songs and Choruses* (Amherst: The University of Massachusetts Press, 1983), pp. 202–10. Hereafter cited as Maguire.
63. As cited in Maguire, p. 202.
64. The rhythm also correlates with the tripartite division of the stages of a man's life as given by Oedipus in his answer to the riddle of the sphinx.
65. In a letter to Lady Gregory, Yeats reports that "I have begun Oedipus at Colonus—done about 10 pages—but hesitate between it & the Antigone." Obviously, Yeats chose the former. Nevertheless, he continues, "I feel that these three closely united plays put into simple speakable prose may be my contribution to the Abbey Repertory." As cited in Clark and Maguire, p. 36 n.90.
66. The edition was *Sophocle*, Tome I, *Ajax- Antigone-Oedipe Roi- Electre*, texte etabli et traduit par Paul Masqueray (Paris: L' Societe d'Edition "Les Belles Lettres", 1922).
67. The edition was the World's Classics edition of *Sophocles, The Seven Plays*, trans. Lewis Campbell (London: Oxford University Press, 1906).
68. R. C. Jebb, trans., *The Tragedies of Sophocles* (Cambridge, UK: Cambridge University Press, 1904), pp. 153–54.
69. This invention is perhaps inspired by Sappho's famous fragment, "Love... bitter sweet," from which H. D. also took inspiration in producing her poem "Fragment Forty" based on the Sapphic partial line (*H. D. Collected Poems 1912–1944*, pp. 181–84).
70. For a full accounting of Pound's suggestions and the revisions Yeats made in light of them, as well as for a wonderfully full, yet nuanced reading of this poem, see Patrick J. Keene, *Yeats's Interactions with Tradition* (Columbia: University of Missouri Press, 1987), pp. 285–310.
71. See Richard Ellmann, *The Identity of Yeats* (New York: Oxford University Press, 1954), pp. 183–84.

Chapter Five

1. According to Kenner, Pound "wrote fair copies of new Cantos on the right half of the right-hand page, the half to the left of the fold kept for second thoughts. When he chose to work at Confucius he turned the book around, so that the left-hand page became the right. So the *Pisan Cantos* run through the notebooks in one direction, and *Great Digest* and *Unwobbling Pivot* in the other" (*Era*, p. 474).
2. For a discussion of Yeats's organicism and his attraction to Italian Fascism, see Cullingford, pp. 132–33, 144–62 and *passim*.

3. From the testimony of Pound's psychiatrist at St. Elizabeth's, Dr. Wendell Muncie, as quoted in Carpenter, p. 745.
4. Also from Dr. Muncie's testimony, as quoted in Mary Patterson Cheadle, *Ezra Pound's Confucian Translations* (Ann Arbor: University of Michigan Press, 1997), p. 58.
5. Ezra Pound, *Selected Prose, 1909–1965*, ed., William Cookson (New York: New Directions, 1958), p. 90. Hereafter cited as *SP* in the body of the text.
6. Michael André Bernstein, *The Tale of the Tribe: Ezra Pound and the Modern Verse Epic* (Princeton, NJ: Princeton University Press, 1981), p. 51. Hereafter cited as Bernstein.
7. This is one of Pound's earliest descriptions of *The Cantos*, used at a time when he had yet to envision the terms of its ending.
8. All other works appearing over this span were merely collections of already published material. These include the first collected edition of *The Cantos* in 1948, the first *Selected Poems* in 1949, a reprint of *Patria Mia* in 1950, an edition of *The Letters* in 1950, *The Translations* in 1953, *Literary Essays* in 1954, and the Italian collection *Lavoro ed Usura* in 1954. For more information, see Donald Gallup, *Ezra Pound: A Bibliography* (Charlottesville: The University Press of Virginia, 1983), pp. 77–90.
9. These include William McNaughton, "Pound's Translations and Chinese Melopoeia," *Texas Quarterly* 10, no. 4 (Winter 1967): 52–56, and "Ezra Pound et la Littérature Chinoise," *L'Herme* 5 Paris, 1965; David Gordon, "'Root/Br./By Product' in Pound's Confucian Ode 166," *Paideuma: A Journal Devoted to Ezra Pound Scholarship* 3, no. 1 (Spring 1974): 13–32; Angela Jung Palandri, review of *The Classic Anthology Defined By Confucius*, *Comparative Literature* 7, no. 1 (Winter 1955): 91–93; "'The Stone is Alive in My Hands'—Ezra Pound's Chinese Translations," *Literature East and West* 10 (1966): 278–91; Eugene Eoyang, "The Confucian Odes," *Paideuma* 3 No. 1 (Spring 1974): 33–42; and Edith Sarra, "Whistling in the Bughouse: Notes on the Process of Pound's Confucian Odes," *Paideuma: A Journal Devoted to Ezra Pound Scholarship* 16, Nos. 1–2 (Spring-Fall, 1987): 7–31. The only book-length study of Pound's translation of the Confucian odes is L. S. Dembo's *The Confucian Odes of Ezra Pound* (Berkeley and Los Angeles: University of California Press, 1963).
10. Mary Patterson Cheadle, *Ezra Pound's Confucian Translations* (Ann Arbor: University of Michigan Press, 1997). Hereafter cited as Cheadle.
11. Cheadle, p. 7.
12. See Cheadle, p. 29.
13. As Cheadle notes, "Totalitarianism in Pound's Confucian sense does not mean what the word is usually understood to mean: it is not the state exerting total control over every aspect of social and individual life, but the life of the state and the life of the individual each and together having an integrity in the sense of integratedness" (Cheadle, p. 78). For further discussion of Pound's idiosyncratic use of this term, see Cheadle, pp. 98–100. Cheadle's view remains somewhat controversial, since "totalitarian" was originally a Mussolinian coinage and used as a praise word. For a more contextualized assessment of this word, see the *Oxford English Dictionary*, *Supplement* 1987, which includes an example from Pound (1937) and

talks of a "totalitarian synthesis of all the arts." This amounts more or less to the Wagnerian notion of *Gesamtkunstwerk*. Thanks to Haun Saussy for this reference.

14. The Confucian concept of Lí (禮), or Ritual or Ceremonies, as it is often translated, has been a subject of debate and examination for hundreds of years, both in China and in the West. Confucius's own discussions of this concept appear throughout *The Analects*, but see in particular, Book I: section 12; II:5; III:3–4, 17, 19; VI:25; VIII:8. For a decidedly modern interpretation of this concept in light of contemporary philosophies of language, see Herbert Fingarette, *Confucius—the Secular as Sacred* (New York: Harper and Row, 1972), pp. 6–18. Hereafter cited as Fingarette.

15. This "cult of personality" can be seen throughout Pound's prose and poetry of the late 1910s and early 1920s. His *Homage to Sextus Propertius* (1917) can be seen as an attempt to bring an Imperial Roman's ironic sensibility to bear on the follies of modern British life. In addition his little-known translation of Bernhard de Fontenelle's *Dialogues des Morts*, another work composed of a series of imaginary conversations between famous historical figures, *The Dialogues of Fontenelle* (1917), clearly demonstrates his interest in the power of individual minds to shape civilization. The sequence "Hugh Selwyn Mauberley (Life and Contacts)" (1920), organized as it is around a single, albeit frustrated, life, shows that this interest in "personality" was not just a fancy associated with bringing foreign mind-sets into English, but a crucial organizing principle in Pound's work at about this time. Perhaps the clearest demonstration and most significant poetic product to come out of these concerns are the "Malatesta Cantos" (1923), in which Pound explores the "factive personality" of Sigismundo Malatesta and the cultural achievements he sponsored, the most famous of which to Pound was the Tempio Malatestiana. For a fine contextualization of Pound's politics during his Imagist phase in relation to anarchism, socialism, and feminist political movements, see Robert Von Hallberg, "Libertarian Imagism," *Modernism/Modernity*. Vol. 2 No. 2 (April 1995): pp. 63–79. For an extensive treatment of the theme of individualism in the works of Modernist prose writers such as Conrad and Woolf, see Michael Levenson, *Modernism and the Fate of the Individual* (Cambridge, UK: Cambridge University Press, 1991).

16. The first time Pound mentions Confucius comes in a letter to Dorothy Shakespear on October 2, 1913, wherein he says with some understatement, "I'm stocked up with K'ung fu Tsze [Confucius] and Men Tsze [Mencius], etc. I suppose they'll keep me calm for a week or so" (brackets added). See, *Ezra Pound and Dorothy Shakespeare Letters: Their Letters, 1909–1914*, ed. Omar Pound and A. Walton Litz (New York: New Directions, 1984), letter 187, p. 264. The transcription of the names indicates that his source was indeed Pauthier. It is also possible that Pound had access to the various Latin versions of these books produced by Jesuit missionaries.

17. Angus Graham, *The Disputers of the Tao* (La Salle, IL: Open Court, 1989), p. 132.

18. See J. P. G. Pauthier *Confucius et Mencius: Les Quatre Livres de philosophie morale et politique de la Chine* (Paris, 1868), p. 42. Hereafter cited along with page numbers in the body of the text as Pauthier.

19. Much later, in his unorthodox treatment of the *Shi Jing*, or Book of Odes, Pound would use an astonishing range of registers in his renderings of different individual poems. For more discussion on this work, see Cheadle, pp. 151–81.
20. D. C. Lau, a contemporary translator and Confucian scholar, gives the remainder of this passage from *The Analects* (he numbers it XI, 26) as follows:

> "When the three left , Tseng Hsi stayed behind. He said, 'What do you think of what the other three said?'
> 'They were only stating what they had their hearts upon.'
> 'Why did you smile at Yo?'
> 'It is by the rites that a state is administered, but in the way he spoke Yu showed a lack of modesty. That is why I smiled at him.'
> 'In the case of Ch'iu, was he not concerned with a state?'
> 'What can justify one in saying that sixty or seventy li square or indeed fifty or sixty li square do not deserve the name of "state"?'
> 'In the case of Ch'ih, was he not concerned with a state?'
> 'What are the ceremonial occasions in the ancestral temple and diplomatic gatherings if not matters which concern rulers of feudal states? If Ch'iu plays only a minor part, who would be able to play a major role?' "

See D. C. Lau, trans, *The Analects of Confucius* (London: Penguin, 1979), p. 111. One of the casualties throughout Pound's various "Confucian" translations is the philosopher's wry sense of humor.
21. Cheadle dates the acquisition of this pirated version (Shanghai: China Book Company) at about this time. See Cheadle, p. 23.
22. The passage from the original letter reads as follows: "J'ai cité Gourmont, et je viens de donner un nouveau version de *Ta Hio* de Confucius, parce que j'y trouve des formulations d'idées qui me paraissent utile pour civilizer l'Amérique (tentatif). Je révère plutôt le bon sens que l'originalité (soit de Rémy de G., soit de Confucius)."
23. Ezra Pound, trans. *Confucius: The Great Digest, The Unwobbling Pivot, The Analects* (New York: New Directions, 1969), p. 19. Hereafter cited as *CON.* in the body of the text.
24. Even Hugh Kenner, by far Pound's staunchest and most influential critical supporter, admits that "He wrote, in fact too many pages [in this section] for the ultimate good of the poem," and that the mass of seemingly random details "poses an unsolved problem throughout the poem." See *Era*, pp. 434–36.
25. John J. Nolde, *Blossoms from the East: The China Cantos of Ezra Pound* (Orono, ME: National Poetry Foundation, 1983), p. 26.
26. See especially Bernstein, pp. 48–58 and Nicholls, pp. 112–25.
27. There are a total of fourteen appearances of the doctrine of 正名, either in character form or in transliteration. For a detailed accounting of these appearances, see *Companion*, p. 777.
28. Fingarette, *op. cit.*, pp. 14–15.
29. Indeed, from the earliest stages of Pound's career as a (social) critic, in 1913, Pound asserted the specifically ethical dimensions of writing, decrying in

"The Serious Artist," "the immorality of bad art" (*LE*, 43), and comparing the technical negligence of a lazy writer to the criminal malpractice of a physician whose carelessness endangers a patient's health. Similarly, in an essay entitled "The Teacher's Mission," Pound concludes by asserting that "False witness in the teaching of letters OUGHT to be just as dishonourable as falsification in medicine" (*LE*, 63).

30. John J. Nolde, *op cit.*, p. 26 n. 37. Also, de Mailla probably used the Manchu text because at a purely linguistic level, Manchu was easier to read and less ambiguous than literary Chinese.
31. Kenner, *Era*, p. 433.
32. Achilles Fang, "Materials for the Study of Pound's *Cantos*." Ph.D. dissertation. Harvard University, 1958.
33. Bernstein, *Tribe*, p. 40.
34. Kenner notes that the 信 character that appears "at the end of Canto 34 in the current American printing was added 20 years later," in 1960. See Kenner, *Era*, p. 432n.
35. For a detailed discussion of the "ideogrammic method" and the early Cantos, see Ronald Bush, *The Genesis of Ezra Pound's* Cantos (Princeton, NJ: Princeton University Press, 1976), pp. 10–14. Bush has provided a much needed corrective to this debate, showing that "In his collected and uncollected prose, no programmatic use of the term 'ideogram' or 'ideograph' appears until 1927." But Bush's analysis leaves unanswered many questions about the increasing presence of "ideograms" themselves as the poem progresses. In addition, people have criticized Pound's understanding of the Chinese written language since he first began discussing it in print, and a great deal of contemporary criticism remains mired in this kind of normative approach to Pound's multi-lingualism. Such criticisms are, to my mind, irrelevant, since Pound's understanding of foreign languages had a profound impact on his poetry, regardless of their accuracy.
36. These include The Reverend Robert Morrison's seven volume, three part dictionary, *A Dictionary of the Chinese Language, in Three Parts* (Macao, 1815–1823), Herbert Giles' *Chinese-English Dictionary*, and possibly Bernhard Karlgren's *Analytic Dictionary of Chinese and Sino-Japanese*. Later Pound obtained, R. H. *Mathews Chinese-English Dictionary* (Cambridge: Harvard-Yenching, 1943–44). from which he derived standard Mandarin pronunciations for the Chinese characters in the late *Cantos*. Morrison's dictionary shows the historical development of various forms of Chinese characters, which undoubtedly made Fenollosa seem to Pound to be right in his views on written Chinese. Interestingly, Karlgren is the scholar most responsible for advancing the "grapho-phonetic" interpretation of the written Chinese character, a view completely incompatible with Fenollosa's and borne out by modern linguistic analysis. Pound explicitly mentions Karlgren in the text of *The Great Digest*, p. 45; but if he did indeed possess a copy of Karlgren's dictionary, he certainly rejected his views on the nature of the "ideogram."
37. This is not to say that Pound completely discounted the importance of sound in Chinese, especially for Chinese poetry. As Cheadle astutely points out, "In

a note dated 1935 that Pound appended to Fenollosa's essay, he refers to the 'Chinese art of verbal sonority.' 'I now doubt if it was inferior to the Greek,' he continues; 'our poets being slovenly, ignorant of music, and earless, it is useless to blame professors for squalor'" (Cheadle, p. 207). For more information on this aspect of Pound's relationship to Chinese, and especially how he wanted to include sound and tone markings for his proposed "scholars edition" of the *Shi Jing*, see Cheadle, pp. 207–16.

38. Ezra Pound, *ABC of Reading* (New York: New Directions, 1951), p. 22. Hereafter cited as *ABCR* in the body of the text.
39. The "ideogram's" basis in metaphor was one of the reasons Pound found this written system so compelling as a model for poetry, and he invokes Aristotle to endorse the importance of this process: "Compare Aristotle's *Poetics*: 'Swift perception of relations, hallmark of genius'" (*CWC*, 22n).
40. For an excellent demythologization of and introduction to modern linguistic opinions on the Chinese language, see John DeFrancis. *The Chinese Language: Fact and Fantasy* (Honolulu: University of Hawaii Press, 1984). It is important to note here, however, that DeFrancis overstresses somewhat the "phonetic" aspect of Chinese, which is a fundamentally "hybrid" writing system that combines sonic and semantic indicators.
41. This is precisely the most important lesson Joyce learned from Vico, how the ancient pre-Christian men ordered their world through words, and how their conceptual frameworks could be recovered through the process of etymology. For a detailed analysis of the influence that Vico's anthropological linguistics had on Joyce, see John Bishop, *Finnegans Wake: Joyce's Book of the Dark* (Madison: University of Wisconsin Press, 1986), pp. 174–215. The similar artistic responses that both Pound and Joyce had to their respective sources constitutes one of the bases for an extended comparison of their late works. For a fine discussion of Fenollosa's view of Chinese poetry and how it fits into the tradition of American poetry as a whole, see Kern, *Orientalism, Modernism and the American Poem*, chapter 5, pp. 115–45.
42. For example, in editions of *The Chinese Written Character as a Medium for Poetry* published after 1935, in which Pound added word-by-word glosses of several Chinese poems, he connects the absence of such bilingual editions to economic sins: "There is no reason, apart from usury and the hatred of letters, for keeping at least a few hundred Chinese poems and the Ta Hio out of bilingual edition" (*CWC*, 37). And three years later, in the *Guide to Kulchur*, Pound raged again, "The stupidity of my age is nowhere more gross, blatant and futile than in the time-lag for getting Chinese texts into bilingual editions" (*GK*, 147).
43. This should not suggest that Pound believed all literary efforts should be made in Chinese. That would mean ignoring the specific characteristics of a writer's own language. Rather the Chinese "ideograms" served as models for communication, as symbols of an approach to organizing information and imagery that maintained the poetry implicit in the act of representation.
44. For more detailed explication of this passage, see Cheadle, pp. 226–28.
45. Nicholls, *op. cit.*, p. 163.

46. Elsewhere in the *Guide to Kulchur*, Pound notes that Confucius himself considered poetry an essential component to the state. Explicitly equating Italy and ancient China, Pound writes, 'The Duce and Kung fu tseu equally perceive that their people need poetry; that prose is NOT education, but the outer courts of the same. Beyond its doors are the mysteries. Eleusis. Things not to be spoken save in secret" (*GK*, 144–45).
47. Wing-tsit Chan, *A Sourcebook in Chinese Philosophy* (Princeton, NJ: Princeton University Press, 1963), p. 84.
48. For a brief overview of this controversy, one that Pound himself had access to, see James Legge's discussion, "Of the Authorship, and Distinction of the Text Into Classical Text and Commentary," in which he concludes, "Though we cannot positively assign the authorship of the Great Learning, there can be no hesitation in receiving it as a genuine monument of the Confucian school." See James Legge, trans., *Confucius: Confucian Analects, The Great Learning & The Doctrine of the Mean* (New York: Dover Publications Inc., 1971). This version is an unabridged republication of the second revised edition as published by the Clarendon Press, Oxford in 1893.
49. There is one place in the *Ta Hio* where Pound actually translates in the manner of *The Great Digest*. In translating the "Make It New" saying, which would become one of his trademark calls for aesthetic and political change, Pound actually seems to have examined the Chinese characters themselves, and he finally sounds like his old, colloquial self: "Renovate dod gast you, renovate!" Pound also appends a note explaining how he arrived at such a version.

    Or as one translator [Legge] puts it: the character appears five times during this passage (verses 1 and 2). Pauthier with greater elegance gives in French the equivalent to: "Renew thyself daily, utterly, make it new, and again, new, make it new."

    The pictures (verse 1) are: renew sun sun renew (like a tree-shoot) again renew.

    That is to say a daily organic vegetable and orderly renewal; no hangover. The "orderly" I should derive from the upper left-hand bit of the ideograph." (*TH*, 12)

    Why did Pound not undertake this kind of translation in 1928, when, as this short passage from the *Ta Hio* shows, he clearly had the capacity to do so? I would argue simply that in 1928, he had yet to develop a comprehensive idea about the intimate relationship between the Chinese character and Confucian doctrine, which came after he examined the Confucian texts in the original at some length in 1938.
50. Ezra Pound, trans., *Ta Hio: The Great Learning of Confucius* (Seattle: University of Washington Bookstore, 1928; rpt. Norfolk, CT: New Directions, 1939), p. 8.
51. Bernstein, p. 84. Within the Chinese tradition itself, the animus against Buddhism and Taoism is principally attributable to Sima Guang and Zhu Xi (authors of the *ZiZhi Tongjian* and *ZiZhiGang Mu*), and it is from here that de Mailla and Legge likely picked up and reproduced their own Confucian biases.

52. For contemporary and less idiosyncratic translations of this passage see Chan, pp. 86–87, and Graham, p. 132.
53. Pound's explication of the right-hand part of the character is imaginatively overdrawn, but basically correct. The 成 character does in fact, according to modern dictionaries, mean "completed, accomplished, to succeed, to complete." Pound's etymology, however, breaks down at this point. He saw a similarity between the 弋 radical, meaning "spear," and extrapolated from there to come up with his highly imagistic explication of the character 成. And of course, the radical on the left side of the character does not in fact contribute to the meaning of the word in any profound way. Rather it simply indicates a general semantic field to which this character belongs, and helps to distinguish it from other characters with the same pronunciations.
54. For a fuller treatment of this issue and Ford's role in the development of Imagist doctrine, see Morrison, pp. 34–35.
55. For a fine recent re-examination of the compositional history of the "Pisan Cantos" and the consequences it has for our understanding of Pound's most famous sequence, see Ron Bush, "Modernism, Fascism, and the Composition of Ezra Pound's *Pisan Cantos*," *Modernism/Modernity* Vol. 2 No. 3 (September 1995): 69–87.
56. Richard Sieburth provides a concise gloss on this passage and for the concerns of the late *Cantos* in general: "Nummulary, 'of or pertaining to money,' from the Latin *nummulus*, diminutive of nummus, coin. And prosody, a pun on two Greek words, prosodia (a song sung to music) or prosodo (income or rent)." For excellent, detailed analyses of this passage and of the general presence of economic concerns in the late *Cantos* see Nicholls, pp. 212–21, and Richard Sieburth, "In Pound We Trust: The Economy of Poetry/The Poetry of Economics" *Critical Inquiry* 14 (Autumn 1987): 142–72.
57. Pound would have likely analyzed this character as the "rain " (雨) over three "mouths" (口), over the radical for "work" (工) with people integrated in it (人), hence, a speech in complete concert with both the processes of nature (c.f. "The rain is part of the process" in Canto LXXIV) and the labor of the people. A state of complete harmony. See also Kenner, *Era*, p. 544
58. Kenner, *Era*, p. 535.
59. See note *SP*, 342.
60. In the *Guide to Kulchur*, Pound makes the consequences of money's artificiality even more clear: "The pregnant phrase is that wherein he says it is called NOMISMA because it exists not by nature but by custom *and can therefore be altered or rendered useless at will*" (*GK*, 278).

Chapter Six

1. "Our Exagmination Round his Factification for Incamination of Work in Progress." See *James Joyce/Finnegans Wake: A Symposium* (New York: New Directions, 1972).
2. The full quotation reads, "It is always worth testing out any literary theory by asking: How would it work with Joyce's *Finnegans Wake*?" Terry Eagleton,

Literary Theory: An Introduction. Second Edition (Minneapolis: University of Minnesota Press, 1996), p. 71.
3. Vicki Mahaffey, *Reauthorizing Joyce* (Cambridge, UK: Cambridge University Press, 1988) rpt. (Gainesville: University of Florida Press, 1995), p. 2 n.1
4. "I am at the end of English." In French, this phrase suggests not only the "end" historically, but also metaphorically in the sense of having used up or come to the end of the resources of English. As cited in Richard Ellmann, *James Joyce* (New York: Oxford University Press, 1959, revised edition 1983), p. 546. Hereafter cited as Ellmann.
5. For a new perspective on the political significance of the kind of reading mandated by the *Wake*, see Mahaffey, Vicki, *States of Desire: Wilde, Yeats, Joyce and the Irish Experiment* (New York: Oxford University Press, 1997).
6. Jean Michel Rabaté, *Language, Sexuality, and Ideology in Ezra Pound's Cantos.* (Albany: State University of New York Press, 1986), p. 31.
7. Senn's first volume of collected essays appear in Fritz Senn, *Joyce's Dislocutions: Essays on Reading as Translation,* ed. John Paul Riquelme (Baltimore: The Johns Hopkins University Press, 1984). Hereafter cited as *Dislocutions*. See especially the essays "Translation as Approach," "Foreign Readings," "A Reading Exercise in *Finnegans Wake*," and "Dogmad or Dobliboused?" These essays lay out the essentials of Senn's approach to Joyce. In his introduction to the volume, John Paul Riquelme mentions Senn's background as a Swiss national to help contextualize his interests in translation and in Joyce's polyglot play of language. Interestingly, another Swiss critic and thinker, George Steiner, has been the best historian and theorist of translation in this century, and he too makes an issue of his own polyglot upbringing. No doubt, Joyce himself would have made something of this confluence of circumstance, and it does suggest that having more than one language at one's disposal alters one's relationship to language in general.
8. This manuscript of this translation has been acquired by the Huntington Library, which has also published an edited version: *Joyce and Hauptmann: Before Sunrise* with Notes and Introduction by Jill Perkins (Canoga Park, CA: The Huntington Library), 1988. Hereafter cited as *Joyce and Hauptmann*.
9. *Ibid.*, p. 4.
10. Ellmann, p. 88
11. Joyce and Hauptmann, p. 19.
12. For a full accounting of these modifications as a result of Joyce's efforts as a translator, see Perkins' "Critical Commentary" in *Joyce and Hauptmann*, pp. 29–32.
13. As cited in Ellmann, p. 88.
14. Forest Read, ed. *Pound/Joyce: The Letters of Ezra Pound to James Joyce* (New York: New Directions, 1970), p. 235.
15. Ellmann, p. 75.
16. *Dislocutions*, p. xvii.
17. Ellmann, p. 196.

18. James Joyce, *A Portrait of the Artist as a Young Man*, ed. Hans Walter Gabler with Walter Hettch (New York: Garland, 1993), p. 216. Hereafter cited as *P* in the body of the text.
19. James Joyce, *"Dubliners": Text, Criticism, and Notes*, ed. Robert Scholes and A. Walton Litz (New York: Viking Press, 1969), p. 9. Hereafter cited as *D* in the body of the text.
20. "...he turns his mind to unknown [or obscure] arts."
21. For an interesting meditation on this epigraph, the only one Joyce ever employed in his work, see "The Challenge: *'ignotas animum'*" in *Dislocutions*, pp. 73–84.
22. In his study, *The Genesis of Ezra Pound's* Cantos, Ron Bush disputes that *Ulysses* influenced the architecture of *The Cantos*, arguing instead that Pound primarily gleaned from Joyce the effectiveness of compression. See Bush, pp. 193–97.
23. *Selected Letters of James Joyce*, ed. Richard Ellmann (New York: The Viking Press, and London: Faber and Faber, 1958), p. 240.
24. Virginia Woolf, *A Writer's Diary*, 50 entry for Sept. 26, 1922.
25. James Joyce, *Ulysses: The Corrected Text*, ed. Hans Walter Gabler (New York: Vintage, 1986), p. 31. Hereafter cited as *U* in the body of the text.
26. For a compilation of the numerous allusions and references in *Ulysses*, see Don Gifford, Ulysses *Annotated: Notes for James Joyce's* Ulysses. Revised and Expanded Edition (Berkeley and Los Angeles: University of California Press, 1988).
27. Early in "Telemachus," Mulligan offers to teach Stephen Greek, saying "Ah, Dedalus, the Greeks! I must teach you. You must read them in the original" (*U*, 4–5).
28. See Karen Lawrence, *The Odyssey of Style in* Ulysses (Princeton, NJ: Princeton University Press, 1981).
29. This well-known letter outlines the scheme of "Oxen of the Sun" so thoroughly that it bears reprinting in full here. Written to Frank Budgen on March 20, 1920, the letter reads as follows: "Am working hard at *Oxen of the Sun*, the idea being the crime committed against fecundity by sterilizing the act of coition. Scene, lying-in hospital. Technique: a nineparted episode without divisions introduced by a Sallustian-Tacitean prelude (the unfertilized ovum), then by way of earliest English alliterative and monosyllabic and Anglo-Saxon ('Before born the babe had bliss. Within the womb won he worship.' 'Bloom dull dreamy heard: in held hat stone staring') then by way of Mandeville ('there came forth a scholar of medicine that men clepen &c') then Malory's *Morte d'Arthur* ('but that franklin Lenehan was prompt ever to pour them so that at the least way mirth should not lack') then the Elizabethan 'chronicle style' ('about that present time young Stephen filled all cups'), then a passage solemn, as of Milton, Taylor, Hooker, followed by a choppy Latin-gossipy bit, style of Burton-Browne, then a passage Bunyanesque ('the reason was that in the way he fell in with a certain whore whose name she said is Bird in the hand') after a diarystyle bit Pepys-Evelyn ("Bloom sitting snug with a party of wags, among then Dixon jun., Ja. Lynch, Doc. Madden and Stephen D. for a languor he had before and was now better, he having

dreamed tonight a strange fancy and Mistress Purefoy there to be delivered, poor body, two days past her time and the midwives hard put to it, God send her quick issue') and so on through Defoe-Swift and Steele-Addison-Sterne and Landor-Pater-Newman until it ends in a frightful jumble of Pidgin English, nigger English, Cockney, Irish, Bowery slang and broken doggerel. This progression is also linked back at each part subtly with some foregoing episode of the day and, besides this, with the natural stages of development in the embryo and the periods of faunal evolution in general. The double-thudding Anglo-Saxon motive recurs from time to time ('Loth to move from Horne's house') to give the sense of the hoofs of oxen. Bloom is the spermatozoon, the hospital the womb, the nurse the ovum, Stephen the embryo.

"How's that for high?" (*Selected Letters*, 251)

30. Technically, of course, *Finnegans Wake* has no "first" sentence, but rather begins and ends with the same sentence, thereby forming a closed, perpetual circle.
31. James Joyce, *Finnegans Wake* (New York, Penguin, 1987), p. 3, ll. 13–15. All further references will be cited, by standard convention, according to page and line number of the *Wake* within the body of the text.
32. See Roland McHugh, *Annotations to* Finnegans Wake, revised edition (Baltimore: Johns Hopkins University Press, 1991), p. 219.
33. See John Bishop, *Joyce's Book of the Dark:* Finnegans Wake (Madison: University of Wisconsin Press, 1986), especially the chapter "Vico's Night of Darkness," pp. 174–215.
34. *Ibid.*, p. 140.
35. David Lloyd, *Nationalism and Minor Literature: James Clarence Mangan and the Emergence of Irish Cultural Nationalism* (Berkeley and Los Angeles: University of California Press, 1987), p. 117. For a complete discussion of this matter, see all of chapter four in this study, "Veils of Sais: Translation as Refraction and Parody," pp. 102–28.
36. See the essay "James Clarence Mangan" in *The Critical Writings of James Joyce*, ed. Ellsworth Mason and Richard Ellmann (New York: Viking Press, 1959), p. 76.

Chapter Seven

1. From the Zukofskys' translation of Carmen XXVIII, ln. xv. *Catullus (Gai Valeri Catulli Veronensis Liber)* (London: Cape Goliard Press, 1969). Hereafter cited by Carmen Number in the body of the text.
2. While Vladimir Nabokov certainly constitutes an important theorist of translation during the post-World War II era in America, I do not include him among this group for a number of reasons. First and foremost, his fundamentalist belief in literal semantic and syntactic adherence to the original as the only valid approach to translation represents a reactionary response to the liberties advocated and practiced by Modernist translators. Second, his version of *Eugene Onegin*, which embodies his principles of rigid literalism, does not seek to expand the boundaries or functions of translation in any way, but

rather constrains it as a literary mode to the strict, and not even necessarily felicitous, reproduction of different aspects of an original text. Thus, he returns translation to an expressly derivative, secondary status among the various modes of literary production. For his full statement, see "Problems of Translation: Onegin in English," originally published in *Partisan Review* 22, No. 4 (Fall 1955): 498–512, and reprinted in *Theories of Translation: An Anthology of Essays from Dryden to Derrida*, ed. Rainer Schulte and John Biguenet (Chicago: University of Chicago Press, 1992), pp. 127–43.

3. These include a semantically "free" rendering of Racine's *Phaedra*, as well as treatments of the Oresteia trilogy of Aeschylus. In addition, Lowell also wrote several poems in *Near the Ocean* (1967) loosely based on various Romance language poets, including Horace, Juvenal, Dante, Quevado, and Góngora. For a discussion of these treatments and how they fit into the overall thematics of *Near the Ocean*, see Stephen Yenser, *Circle to Circle: The Poetry of Robert Lowell* (Berkeley and Los Angeles: University of California Press, 1975), pp. 267–70.

4. In using this term, I follow André Lefévere's terminology in *Translating Poetry: Seven Strategies and a Blueprint* (Assen, The Netherlands: Koninklijke Van Gorcum and Comp., 1975), pp. 19–26. Though I use his terminology, as will become clear, I fundamentally disagree with Lefévere's early rejection of Zukofsky's method in Catullus. Interestingly, it seems that Lefévere himself would have had to change his mind in later years, given his own call, quoted in the Introduction of the present volume, to "analyze texts which refer to themselves as translations and other rewritings and try to ascertain the part they play in a culture."

5. Those responding positively to *Imitations* early on were no less than Edmund Wilson, who called it "the only book of its kind in literature," and A. Alvarez, who declared it a "magnificent collection of new poems by Robert Lowell, based on the work of 18 European poets." For Wilson's full review, see *New Yorker*, June 2, 1962, p. 126. For Alvarez's, see *Observer*, May 26, 1962.

6. Thom Gunn, "Imitations and Originals," *Yale Review* 51 (1962): 480–89. For Steiner's assessment, see "Two Translations," *Kenyon Review* 23 (1961): 714–21. For Louis Simpson's see "Matters of Tact," *Hudson Review* 14 (1961–62): 614–17. And for Fitts's, see "It's Fidelity to the Spirit That Counts," *New York Times Book Review*, November 12, 1961, p. 5 ff. Also see John Simon, "The Abuse of Privilege: Lowell as Translator" in Michael London and Robert Boyers, eds., *Robert Lowell: A Portrait of the Artist in His Time* (New York: David Lewis, 1970), pp. 130–51.

7. Daniel Hoffman, "Robert Lowell's *Near the Ocean*: The Greatness and Horror of Empire," *The Hollins Critic*, IV (February, 1967), pp. 4–5.

8. Ben Belitt, "*Imitations*: Translation as Personal Mode," as cited in London and Boyers. The essay was originally published in *Salmagundi* 1 (1966–67): 44–56. Hereafter cited as Belitt.

9. Stephen Yenser, *Circle to Circle: The Poetry of Robert Lowell* (Berkeley and Los Angeles: University of California Press, 1975), p. 167. For Fein's discussion, see Richard Fein, *Robert Lowell*. Twayne U. S. Authors Series (New York: Twayne, 1970), pp. 72–92.

10. "The Two Voices of Translation" in Thomas Parkinson, ed., *Robert Lowell: A Collection of Critical Essays* (Englewood Cliffs, NJ: Prentice-Hall, Inc. 1968), p. 161.
11. Interview, *Delos* I (1968), p. 165.
12. Burton Raffel, *Robert Lowell* (New York: Frederick Ungar, 1981), pp. 114 and 104–5.
13. Lowell's co-winner for the prize was Richmond Lattimore for his version of Aristophanes' *The Frogs* (University of Michigan Press, 1962). After being established in 1961, the award was not given in 1964 and then discontinued in 1965, an unmistakable sign of the declining status of translation within American literary culture.
14. Alan Brownjohn, "Caesar 'ad Some," *New Statesman* 78 (Aug. 1, 1969): 151.
15. Burton Raffel, "No Tidbit Love You Outdoors Far as a Bier," *Arion* 8 (1969): 441.
16. Robert Conquest, "The Abomination of Moab," *Encounter* 34 (May, 1970): 56.
17. Lefévere (1970, 25). For the details of his four-part critique, see pp. 19–27.
18. Guy Davenport, "Zukofsky's English Catullus," MAPS, 5 (1973), p. 72. Reprinted in *Louis Zukofsky: Man and Poet* (Orono, ME: National Poetry Foundation, 1979), p. 397.
19. Cid Corman, "Poetry as Translation," in *At Their Word* (Santa Barbara, CA: Black Sparrow Press, 1978), p. 19.
20. Burton Hatlen, "Zukofsky as Translator" in *Louis Zukofsky: Man and Poet*, pp. 347–48.
21. Peter Quartermain, "'Only is Order Othered. Nought is Nulled': *Finnegans Wake* and Middle and Late Zukofsky," *ELH* Vol. 54, No. 4 (Winter, 1987): 973. Reprinted in *Disjunctive Poetics: From Gertrude Stein and Louis Zukofsky to Susan Howe* (Cambridge, UK: Cambridge University Press, 1992), pp. 104–20.
22. Daniel Hooley, "Memory's Tropes: Zukofsky's Catullus" in *The Classics in Paraphrase*, p. 65.
23. John Dryden, "Preface" to *Ovid's Epistles*. As cited in Biguenet and Schulte, p. 17.
24. So to A. Alvarez, Lowell wrote, "Dudley Fitts in the New York Times says they should be read in a salt mine, with a grain of salt, and three hysterical Frenchmen writing in Encounter say my Rimbaud is an insane slaughter and hopeless trash. On the other hand, every decent judge from Edmund Wilson down like them or some of them. I feel misunderstood, not a bad feeling." Letter to A. Alvarez, Nov. 7, 1961. As cited in Ian Hamilton, *Robert Lowell: A Biography* (New York: Random House, 1982), p. 293. Similarly, to Randall Jarrell, he wrote, "I seem to be getting a rain of mangling reviews. Time magazine and now Dudley Fitts who says my poems should be read in a salt mine with grain of salt. I must know something about what I am doing. I'm sure I do." Letter to Jarrell, November 7, 1961. *Ibid.*
25. According to the notebooks, now housed at the Harry Hunt Ransom Humanities Research Center at the University of Texas at Austin, the Zukofskys completed Ode I on February 8, 1958 and the Fragmenta were finished on October 19, 1965. The Cape Goliard Edition of 1969 remains the definitive version of the work.

26. Personal letter to Burton Hatlen, Sept. 12, 1978. As cited in Hatlen, "Zukofsky as Translator", p. 347, n. 7.
27. Letter to Cid Corman, ALS, dated May 7, 1958. Now housed in the HRC at the University of Texas at Austin.
28. The scansion here ignores the rules of elision governing Latin poetry, which further suggests that Celia had no actual formal training in the classics.
29. Interestingly, Browning uses the word "transcribed" rather than "translated" to identify his treatment, which suggests both the extent to which he too sought to expand the boundaries of "translation" as a literary mode, but also how much more flexible the very term itself would become as a result of the Modernists. In German, Hölderlin did much the same as Browning in producing a version of Aeschylus based primarily on Greek syntax. For a discussion of Browning's approach in comparison to that of Zukofsky's, see Hooley, "Memory's Tropes," pp. 57–58.
30. F. W. Cornish's 1912 prose rendering of this ode for the Loeb Classical Library, with which Zukofsky worked in producing his own rendering, reads thus: "To whom am I to present my pretty new book, freshly smoothed off with dry pumice-stone? To you, Cornelius: for you used to think that my trifles were worth something, long ago, when you took courage, you alone of Italians, to set forth the whole history of the world in three volumes, learned volumes, by Jupiter, and laboriously wrought. So take and keep for your own this little book, such as it is, and whatever it is worth; and may it, O Virgin my patroness, live and last for more than one century" (Cornish, p. 3).
31. Again, Cornish's version reads as follows: "Let us live, my Lesbia, and love, and value at one farthing all the talk of crabbed old men. Suns may set and rise again. For us, when the short light has once set, remains to be slept the sleep of one unbroken night. Give me a thousand kisses, then a hundred, then another thousand, then a second hundred, then yet another thousand, then a hundred. Then, when we have made up many thousands, we will confuse our counting, that we may not know the reckoning, nor any malicious person blight then with evil eye, when he knows that our kisses are so many" (pp. 7–9).
32. "Flavius, if it were not that your mistress is rustic and unrefined, you would want to speak of her to your Catullus; you would not be able to help it. But (I am sure) you are in love with some unhealthy-looking wench; and you are ashamed to confess it. But though you are silent, the garlands and perfumes about the bed, and the bed itself, show that you do not sleep alone. Well, then, whatever you have to tell, good or bad, let me know it. I wish to call you and your love to the skies by the power of my merry verse."
33. "Effeminate Thallus, softer than rabbit's fur or down of goose or lap of ear, or dusty cobweb; and also, Thallus, more ravenous than a sweeping storm when... send me back my cloak which you have pounced upon, and my Saetaban napkin and Bithynian tablets, you silly fellow, which you keep by you and make a show of them, as if they were heirlooms. Unglue and let drop these at once from your claws, lest your soft downy flanks and pretty tender hands should have ugly figures branded and scrawled on them by the

whip, and lest you should toss about as you are little used to do, like a tiny boat caught in the vast sea, when the wind is madly raging" (p. 31).

34. Cornish gives the Fragmenta as follows:

   1. But you shall not escape my iambics.
   2. This inclosure I dedicate and consecrate to thee, O Priapus, at Lampsacus, where is thy house and sacred grove, O Priapus. For thee specially in its cities the Hellespontian coast worships, more abundant in oysters than all other coasts.
   3. It is my fancy to taste on my own account.
   4. And Comum built on the shore of Lake Larius.
   5. With which shines the bright top of the mast.

35. Unfortunately, in the *Complete Short Poetry: Louis Zukofsky* (Baltimore, MD: Johns Hopkins University Press, 1991), the original Latin text has been left out. While this no doubt reflects very real economic pressures and concerns, such a textual decision sacrifices the dynamic aspect the Zukofskys' achievement.

36. Inasmuch as this amounts to a largely American phenomenon, it suggests the extent to which such a rethinking of the terms of translation coincides in broad terms with the spread of a megalithic United States cultural hegemony, and the attendant dissemination of English as the dominant medium of cultural exchange. This would explain both the loosening of the "requirements" for translations, as well as its continued marginalization as a mode of literary production in our current moment. Put simply, Americans in large measure do not care about translation simply because they don't have to. But, as I hope to have shown over the course of this study, translation can do more than merely reflect the literary values and limitations of a given period. It contributes fundamentally to the articulation of culture.

Conclusion

1. Ezra Pound and Rudd Fleming, trans., *Sophokles' Elektra* (New York: New Directions, 1990).
2. For versions of this argument see Niranjana, *Siting Translation* and Cheyfitz, *The Poetics of Empire*.
3. Seamus Heaney, "Introduction" to *Beowulf: A New Verse Translation* (New York: Farrar, Straus and Giroux, 2000), p. xxiv.
4. R. M. Liuzza, *Beowulf: A New Verse Translation* (New York: Broadview, 2000).
5. Frank Kermode, "The Geat of Geats," *The New York Review of Books* Vol. 47, No. 12 (July 20, 2000): 20.
6. Nicholas Howe, "Scullionspeak," *The New Republic*. Vol. 222 No. 9 (February 29, 2000): 36.
7. In the "Introduction" to his rendering, Heaney reports that he studied Anglo-Saxon as an undergraduate at Queen's University, Belfast, though he by no means claims any sort of academic expertise in the language. In addition, he cites as aids to his rendering the work of various medievalist scholars, including J. R. R. Tolkien. In this respect, Heaney is decidedly less radical than his Modernist predecessors, who not only took a non-scholarly approach to translation, but expressly dismissed scholarship as a barrier to achieving "genuinely" poetic translation.

Index

Aldington, Richard, 4, 82, 89, 92, 96
Andreas Divus Justinopolitanus, 154, 159, 169
Anyte of Tegea, 89
Arnold, Matthew, 11, 125, 126

Bakhtin, Mikhail, 122
Benjamin, Walter, 1, 2, 17, 32, 226, 254 n.24
    "The Task of the Translator" 1923), 1, 2
Beowulf, 2, 236-7
Berman, Antoine, 1, 16, 235, 248 n.4
Bernstein, Michael Andrè, 155, 163, 171, 181
Bishop, John, 206, 276 n.41
Browning, Robert, 10, 225
    rendering of *Agamemnon* (1877), 229
Bush, Douglass, 84, 85
Bush, Ron, 33, 43, 280 n.22

Calas, Nicholas, 4, 9
Carne-Ross, D. S., 84, 85, 211
Chamberlain, Lori, 16, 30
Chan, Wing-tsit, 179
Chapman, George, 7, 10
Cheadle, Mary Patterson, 157 and *passim*
Chinese Written Character as a Medium for Poetry, The, 173-4
Clark, David R., 128, 132
Confucius and Confucianism, 155, 162
    doctrine of "the rectification of names," 166-71, 172, 174, 183

Confucian Classics, 27, 155
    Da Xue (The Great Learning), 159, 163, 174, 179-84
    Lun Yu (The Analects) 159, 167, 274 n.20,
    Zhong Yong (*The Doctrine of the Mean*), 174
Confucian political and social thought, 10, 155, 158, 160
Corman, Cid, 212-3, 221
Criterion, The, 4
Cronin, Michael, 17, 119, 122
Cullingford, Elizabeth, 133, 266 n.4

Daniel, Arnaut, 5, 31
Davenport, Guy, 212
Davie, Donald, 54
DeKoven, Marianne, 29, 30, 80
Deane, Seamus, 118, 267 n.14
de Gourmont, Rèmy, 5, 16
    The Natural Philosophy of Love (Physique de l'Amour) (1922), 5, 79
de Mailla, Pere Joseph Anne-Maria de Moyriac, 166, 169
de Man, Paul, 17, 232, 248 n.2
Derrida, Jacques, 17, 248 n.2
Doolittle, Hilda, *see* H. D.
Dryden, John, 2-3, 10, 11, 21, 129, 215, 216-17, 218, 219, 253 n. 22
Duncan, Robert, 98
Duplessis, Rachel Blau, 85, 86, 93, 100, 112
    "romantic thralldom," 264 n.40

Index

Eagleton, Terry, 191
Eliot, T. S., 4, 5, 80, 99, 132, 154, 164
   "Little Gidding," 6
   on Pound as inventor of Chinese poetry, 26, 45
   on Pound's *Homage to Sextus Propertius*, 53, 54
   on Joyce's *Ulysses*, 201
   rendering of St. John Perse's *Anabase*, 4
   The Waste Land (1922), 5, 8, 81, 202
Ellmann, Richard, 194, 195, 196, 197
Euripides, 82, 83, 84, 99, 101, 112

Fenollosa, Ernest,
   The Chinese Written Character as a Medium for Poetry (1936), 173-4
   notebooks of, 26, 28, 31, 33, 34, 35-50, 129
   theories of Chinese written language, 173-4
Fingarette, Herbert, 167, 273 n.14
Finnegans Wake (1939), 6, 8, 20, 21, 191-3, 198, 199, 200, 205-8, 213
Fitzgerald, Edward, 53, 250 n.27, 254 n.22
Flannery, James, 128-9
"fluency," ideology of in translation, 3,
Ford, Ford Maddox, 4
Friedman, Susan Stanford, 96, 112

Gaelic League, The, 120
Gelpi, Albert, 26, 80
Gilbert, Sandra and Gubar, Susan, 29, 80
Giles, Herbert, 26, 32
Golding, Arthur, 9
Grab, Frederic, 134, 144
Graham, Angus, 160
Gray, Cecil, 101
Great Digest, The (1945), 5, 153, 157, 165, 178-9, 180-4
Greek Anthology, The, 89, 92, 95, 105, 111

Gregory, Lady Augusta, 120, 121, 122, 135
   Cuchulain of Muirthemne (1902), 9, 120,
Gregory, Eileen, 85, 86, 87, 100
Gubar, Susan, 85

Hale, William Gardner, 13-14, 52-3, 54, 65, 69
Hass, Robert, 10, 21, 27, 32, 233
Hatlen, Burton, 213, 226
Hauptmann, Gerhart, 3, 10, 20, 194-5
Heaney, Seamus, 21, 233, 236
   translation of *Beowulf* (2000), 236-8
Helen in Egypt (1961), 19, 102, 105, 112-13
"Hermes of the Ways," 88, 89-93
Hölderlin, Friedrich, 2, 226
Homage to Sextus Propertius, 5, 19, 27, 30, 53-62, 77-8, 82, 114, 130, 209, 212
   early criticism of, 13-14, 52-5
   Pound's defenses of, 57-9
   see also Pound, Ezra, works by
Homer, 10, 65, 102
   The Odyssey, 7, 82, 102, 105, 154, 201
Hooley, Daniel M. 54-5, 213-14, 226, 232
Howes, Marjorie, 118, 129, 134
"How to Read" (1929), 2, 4, 6, 9, 15, 210, 216
Hughes, Glenn, 86, 163
Hulme, T.E., 81
Hyde, Dr. Douglas, 121, 123
H. D., 8, 9, 82, 130
   knowledge of Greek, 12, 83, 262 n.11
   renderings of Meleager, 8, 105, 108-09, 109-11, 112
   renderings of Nossis, 105, 109-11
   renderings of Plato, 8, 105, 106-8
   renderings of Sappho, 8, 85, 96-7
   views on translation, 19, 29, 56, 61, 83-4, 96-100, 113-14

H. D. – *Continued*
  works by
    Bid Me to Live (A Madrigal) (1960), 9, 83, 97-8
    Choruses from "Iphigeneia in Aulis," 82, 99, 101
    End to Torment (1958), 87, 88, 112
    Euripides' Ion, Translated with Notes (1938), 3, 27, 83, 84, 99, 100, 112
    "From the Hippolytus," 101-2
    Helen in Egypt (1961), 19, 102, 105, 112-13
    "Heliodora," 108-9
    Heliodora, 82, 105
    "Hermes of the Ways," 88, 89-93
    "Lais," 105-8
    "Nossis," 109-11
    "Odyssey," 102-05
    "Orchard" or "Priapus, Keeper of Orchards," 89, 93-5
    Palimpsest (1926), 83, 96-7
    Red Roses for Bronze (1931), 83, 112

"Ideograms," Chinese, 171, 172, 173-88
Imagism, 87, 88
Irish Free State, 20, 119, 133-4
Irish Literary Theatre, 123, 125, 194
Irish National Theatre, 19-20, 118, 119

Jebb, R. C. 132, 135-6, 138, 139-46, 147-8
Joyce, James
  knowledge of German, 194
  study of languages, 196-7
  works by
    Dubliners (1915), 20, 199
    Finnegans Wake (1939), 6, 8, 20, 21, 191-3, 198, 199, 200, 205-8, 213
    A Portrait of the Artist as A Young Man (1916), 197-8, 199-200
    Ulysses (1922), 6, 8, 10, 20, 168, 198, 200-1, 202-5

Kearney, Richard, 118
Kenner, Hugh, 7, 15, 33, 34, 40, 87, 170, 186, 212, 274 n.24
Kern, Robert, 25, 26, 32, 252 n.4, 276 n.41
Kodama, Sanehide, 33, 43, 45
Krimm, Bernard, 140

Lattimore, Richmond, 84, 85
Lawrence, D. H., 4, 80, 84, 97, 101
Lefèvere, Andre, 15, 210, 212, 282 n.4
Liu, James J. Y., 255 n.38, 255 n.39
Li Bai (or Li Po), 4, 10, 14, 31, 34, 35-47
Lloyd, David, 118, 207, 267 n.14, 281 n.35
Lowell, Amy, 32, 80, 81
  works by
    Fir Flower Tablets (1921), with Florence Ayscough, 32
    "The Sisters," 81
Lowell, Robert, 14, 21, 60, 209, 214-9
  wins Bollingen Prize for translation in 1962, 211
  works by
    Imitations (1961), 27, 209-19

Maguire, James B, 128, 132
Merwin, W. S., 10, 21, 27, 233
Milosz, Czeslaw, 32
Mitchell, Stephen, 10, 21, 27
Moore, Marianne, 4, 6, 80;
Morrison, Mark, 184
Murray, Gilbert, 87, 99, 131, 132, 133

Nabokov, Vladimir, 281 n.2
Nicholls, Peter, 176
Nolde, John, J., 166, 169

O'Brien, Conor Cruise, 118
Odyssey, The, see Homer

Pauthier, J. P. G.,
  translations of Confucian texts, 159, 160, 161, 178, 179
Pinsky, Robert, 21, 233
Poetry Magazine, 13, 52, 89, 92, 93
The Poets' Translation Series of The Egoist Press, 1, 12, 82
Pope, Alexander, 7, 10, 129
Pound, Ezra, 2, 3, 4-5, 6, 102, 209
  attraction to Fascism, 154
  involvement with H. D., 84, 87, 92-3,
  knowledge of Chinese, 12, 26-7, 59
  views on Chinese written language, 173-9
  views on Greek, 102
  works by
    ABC of Reading (1934), 9, 173, 276 n.38
    Analects, The (1951), 5, 20, 156, 157, 167, 171
    The Cantos, 5, 7, 8, 10, 20, 74, 77, 78, 88, 153, 155, 160, 164, 169, 172, 177, 192-3, 207; sections: "Malatesta" Cantos, 7, 159, 171, 273 n.15; Fifth Decad, 165, 170; Chinese History Cantos, 7, 155, 165-6, 168-9, 170, 171, 172, 174, 175, 176, 184; "Adams" Cantos, 165, 168, 170-1, 172, 174, 175, 176, 184; Pisan Cantos, 153, 176-7; Section Rock-Drill, 6, 156, 158, 184, 186-8; "Thrones," 158, 184, 186
    individual Cantos by number: I, 1, 153, 169, 201; VII, 29, XIII, 155, 159-62, 181; XLV, 170; LI, 170, 171, 174; LIII, 175, 185; LIV, 166; LX, 168-9; LXIII, 175, 185; LXVI, 174; LXVIII, 170; LXXV and LXXVI, 186; LXXXI, 18; LXXXVI, 6, 176-7, 207, 238; XCVII, 185
    Cathay (1915), 5, 12, 18-19, 25-35, 48, 59, 77-8, 82, 104, 129, 130, 161, 169, 220; Poems from: "A Ballad of the Mulberry Road," 35, Appendix; "The Beautiful Toilet," 34, 39-42, 161; The Jewel Stairs' Grievance," 34, 35-9; "The River Merchant's Wife: A Letter," 34, 42-7; "The River Song," 59; "Poem by the Bridge at Ten-Shin," 25
    Classic Anthology Defined by Confucius, The (1954), 5, 156, 274 n.19
    Dialogues of Fontenelle (1917), 5, 273 n.15
    The Great Digest (1945), 5, 153, 157, 165, 178-9, 180-4
    Guide to Kulchur (1938), 55, 157, 167, 177-8, 182, 276 n.42, 277 n.46
    Homage to Sextus Propertius (1919), 5, 19, 27, 30, 53-62, 77-8, 82, 114, 130, 209, 212; early criticism of, 13-14, 52-5; Pound's defenses of, 57-9; individual sections; I, 62-6; II, 67-9; III and IV, 69; V, 69-72; VI, 72-3; VII, VIII and IX, 73-4; X and XI, 74-5; XII, 75-7
    "*How to Read*" (1929), 2, 4, 6, 9, 15, 210, 216
    Hugh Selwyn Mauberley (1920), 5, 30, 55, 77, 272 n.15
    Love Poems of Ancient Egypt (1962), 5

Pound, Ezra – *Continued*
  "The Return," 6
  "The Seafarer," 2, 5, 31, 225, 234
  Sonnets and *Ballate of Guido Calvalcanti* (1912), 5, 31
  Ta Hio (The Great Learning) (1928), 5, 86, 156, 163-5, 177, 180, 181-2
  Unwobbling Pivot, The (1947), 5, 20, 153, 157
  Women of Trachis (1990), 3, 5, 234

Quartermain, Peter, 213, 226
Quinn, Vincent, 85, 86

Rabaté, Jean Michel, 193
Raffel, Burton, 211, 212
Rexroth, Kenneth, 10, 27
Rossetti, Dante Gabriel, 2, 10, 248 n.5, 254 n.22

Samhain, 9
Senn, Fritz, 8, 15, 193-4, 198
Simon, Sherry, 17, 253 n.19
Snyder, Gary, 21
Sophocles, 117, 146
Steiner, George, 17, 26, 54, 210, 248 n.6, 252 n.8, 279 n.7
Stevens, Wallace, 6, 80, 154
Sullivan, J. P., 14, 53-4, 69, 157
Swinburne, Algernon Charles, 10

Ta Hio (The Great Learning) (1928), 5, 86, 156, 163-5, 177, 180, 181-2
Taupin, Renè, 164
Thomas, Ron, 54, 55
Translation
  "creative translation," *see* Sullivan, J. P.
  as deployment of authority of the classics, 10
  etymology of, 232
  as exercise in apprenticeship, 6
  history of in English culture, 3, 10, 214-8
  history of in German culture, 2 *see also* Berman, Antoine
  ideology of "fluency," 3
  knowledge of source language required, 10-11,
  knowledge of source language obviated, 26-7
  "metonymic" form of, 232-3
  as "minor" mode of literary production, 6
  Modernist practice of, 7-13
Translation Studies, 1, 13, 16-17, 30, 119, 236

Ulysses (1922), 6, 8, 10, 20, 168, 198, 200-1, 202-5

Venuti, Lawrence, 3, 17, 18

Waley, Arthur, 25
Williams, William Carlos, 4, 10, 80
  views on translation, 9
  works by
    Al Que Quiere (1917), 6;
      Rendering of "The Cassia Tree" by Li Bai, 4;
      "Translation," 8
The Winding Stair and Other Poems (1933), 8, 20, 117
Women of Trachis (1990), 3, 5, 234
Woolf, Virginia, 4

Yeats, William Butler
  attraction to Fascism, 154
  essays in *Samhain*, 9, 123, 125, 140
  knowledge of Gaelic, 122, 123, 130, 268 n.15
  knowledge of Greek, 11, 12
  praise for Lady Gregory's *Cuchulain of Muirthemne*, 9, 120-3
  to Joyce on the latter's knowledge of German, 11
  views on Greek drama, 128-9, 134

views on translation, 9, 12, 19, 29, 61, 83, 99, 114, 117-18, 119, 120, 123, 124, 126, 134, 146, 152, 265 n.46
works by
The Celtic Twilight (1893), 122
"A Man Young and Old," 8, 117, 129, 147, 150
"From 'Oedipus at Colonus'," 147-50, 152
"From 'The Antigone'," 150-2,
King Oedipus (1928), 3, 27, 114, 117, 119, 124, 126, 134-46
Oedipus at Colonus (1934), 3, 27, 114, 117, 124, 146
"A Woman Young and Old," 8, 117, 129, 147, 150, 152

The Tower (1928), 8, 20, 117
The Winding Stair and Other Poems (1933), 8, 20, 117
Yip, Wai lim, 14, 28, 40, 255 n.39, 255 n. 41, 255 n.42

Zukofsky, Celia, contribution to *Catullus (Gai Valeri Catulli Veronensis Liber)*, 220-1
Zukofsky, Celia and Louis *Catullus (Gai Valeri Catulli Veronensis Liber)*(1969), 21, 27, 69, 210, 211, 212-13, 220-33; Carmen LXXXV, 222
Zukofsky, Louis, 10, 21, 60, 209, 210, 211, 217, 219, 220-33